TANGO IN MADEIRA

A NOVEL BY

JIM WILLIAMS

Print Edition

Licensed by Marble City Publishing

Copyright © 2013 Jim Williams

First published by Marble City Publishing in 2013

All rights reserved

ISBN 10 1908943165

ISBN 13 978-1-908943-16-3

Praise for Jim Williams' previous books

The Hitler Diaries

"...steadily builds up an impressive atmosphere of menace." *Times Literary Supplement*

"...well written and full of suspense." *Glasgow Herald*

"...the quality of the storytelling is exceptionally high." *Hampstead and Highgate Express*

Last Judgement

"...the author journalists read for their next scoop." *Sunday Telegraph*

Scherzo

"Sparkling and utterly charming. Devilishly clever plot and deceitful finale." *Frances Fyfield – Mail on Sunday*

Recherché

"A skilful exercise, bizarre and dangerous in a lineage that includes Fowles' *The Magus.*" *Guardian*

The Strange Death of a Romantic

"This is an extraordinarily witty and assured novel." *T J Binyon – Evening Standard*

"...seriously good...technically brilliant...constantly suggestive... dreamy but sinister glamour." *Times Literary Supplement*

To the management and staff of Reid's Palace Hotel,
who continue to welcome strangers with kindness,
courtesy and professionalism.

People who like quotations love meaningless generalizations.

Graham Greene

Travels With My Aunt

CHAPTER ONE

'The Emperor Karl is a descendant of Jesus Christ,' said Pennyweight with the confidence of the amiably mad. 'I expect you know that, being a Varsity chap.'

I make a point of not arguing with self-educated men. It isn't that they stick to their opinions – though they always do – but that they've studied their subject and, likely as not, are right about meaningless details, which will defeat any attempt at opposition. The founders of the world's great religions have been largely unlettered, and, whether as truth-sayers or charlatans, have turned their hard-won learning into messages of extraordinary potency. No, I don't despise Pennyweight and his kind. They have mountains of corpses to their credit.

We met on the *Kildonan Castle*, sailing to South Africa with a stop at Madeira. An outsider would have recognised a broad similarity between us: a resemblance more widespread among men of my generation – those who had served in the Great War – than any previous one. I mean that we were men in our twenties and thirties from middle class homes, who, from a passing familiarity with Latin, had become officers in His Majesty's Armed Forces, and found ourselves at the close of hostilities without skills, hopes or convictions. In its declining years, the British Empire sent gangs of such loveless vagabonds to labour as white coolies in distant possessions. It was no surprise that two of us – three when one includes Fairbrother – should fetch up on a liner bound for the Cape.

I'd noticed Pennyweight in the dining room but not spoken to him. Despite the general similarity of our type, we have no natural affinities. Some of us are clubbable and will scrape an acquaintance on the least occasion. Others, including myself, are by character or experience morose. One of my reasons for leaving England was that hostesses, seeing two of us together in the same room, would make introductions and leave us to chat over old times as if we'd been at the same jolly school.

Contrary to what one may suppose, there is no common language among veterans of war, or perhaps we wish to turn language to an unintended purpose. For we have no message to convey, merely a burden to discharge.

Pennyweight – he gave me the name like a guide naming a famous monument – had a lurking manner and wore a strange suit, part hairy and agricultural and part cut for the town, that looked as if it might have been fashionable in Yorkshire. At first I thought him middle-aged, but in fact he was only thirty-one. He was of average height, not definitely fat, but generally stout so that one would call him fat without thinking. His hair was ginger, his eyebrows invisible and his skin pale, turning to a vivid red with emotion or a touch of sun. His colourless eyes protruded in a manner that left one impaled, and I'd turned hurriedly away from him one night in the bar when he tipped his glass at me and winked.

Matters might have continued in this way if the ship hadn't hit heavy weather in the Bay of Biscay. The storms closed the decks and caused most of the passengers to retire to their cabins. A few, however – mostly men – had strong stomachs or a need for company or a belief that *mal de mer* could be overcome by exotic concoctions of alcohol and spices. They gathered in the lounge to chat about cricket or the war or play a hand at cards. I wanted none of these, but melancholy, to be enjoyed to the full, requires the presence of strangers with whose happy or sad condition one can compare one's own.

In London I'd bought a Celtic bracelet for Margaret, and now I was regretting it. I was unsure if she would welcome a present and had a vague feeling that the style had gone out of fashion. It was in front of me on a table when I heard Pennyweight speak.

He said, 'This is a turn up for the book! It isn't often one comes across a fellow Druid.'

I looked up and saw him, large and friendly and expectant. 'I'm sorry…?' I muttered.

'Say no more.' He looked around shiftily. 'Not the place to talk about these things, I understand,' he said. But, if there were a more appropriate occasion to pursue the subject, it never arose. He made only one other mention of the Druids that I recall, and that was to indicate that, while the Order possessed a portion of the Truth, he, Pennyweight, had meantime been initiated into Higher Things.

'We were wondering,' he went on, 'whether you'd like to join me, Fairbrother and Doctor Crippen in a game. Don't get the wrong idea,' he added, 'we're not a gang of those sharper fellows one hears about on these boats. Strictly small stakes. Ha'penny a point, solo whist and jokers wild. Name's Pennyweight – Captain, though I don't like to use the rank; in fact scarcely ever mention it.' He offered me a fleshy hand with close-bitten nails and I took it and agreed to join the game because the alternative was to brood over Margaret and my father.

Doctor Crispin was the ship's medical officer, a cool customer who spoke in an idle drawl. I fancy he'd passed a deal of time in the tropics, because he had the tanned, drawn look of someone who spent too long in the sun and whose blood was thinned with gin and quinine. With the passengers out of harm's way on their bunks and the more sensitive souls duly drugged, he had time on his hands. Fairbrother was another former soldier, but I suspected he had caught only the end of the affair, having spent his time in training at Camberley. I doubt he was more than twenty-five, unselfconfident, tall and on the willowy side with blond hair and a faint narrow moustache that contrasted with Pennyweight's ginger jungle.

To digress a little, I knew the name Fairbrother in the conjunction Fairbrother & Cadogan, a firm of wine importers who supplied small hotels on the south coast. Charlie Fairbrother was a gentlemanly villain and my father was such another. Between them they'd passed off some very inferior wines and no doubt contributed to the English sense of wonder at what foreigners saw in the stuff. One of the reasons for my visit to England was to persuade Charlie to take some third-rate malmsey off my hands. We had stocks of it left over from wartime when the drinking of Madeira had declined while production continued. Alas, he died while I was on the ocean and no one else was in a position to agree to such a dubious transaction despite my equally dubious offers of financial encouragement. I didn't suppose any connection between the present Fairbrother and dear dead Charlie.

We played a few rounds, which were mostly won by Crispin. Fairbrother was an over-cautious player and revealed his cards in his anxious face. Pennyweight was superstitious and relied on inspiration. He kept a metal cigarette case by his right hand and I noticed the dent from a bullet.

'My lucky charm,' he explained. 'The Hun put that dent on it. Saved a chap's life.'

It was unclear whether he was the chap in question. Whatever the truth, the charm was of no effect and, although he maintained his good humour, I saw that he couldn't afford even his small losses.

'A misfit,' was Doctor Crispin's verdict as we smoked a cigarette together that evening on deck during a lull in the storm. 'And a dreadful cheat, though too incompetent to pull it off. I took fifteen bob off the pair of them and you must be half a crown up on the night.' I remarked that his cigarette case bore the same tell-tale mark as

Pennyweight's. He turned it indifferently in his fingers. 'They make 'em in Sheffield. I've got half a dozen in my cabin. I give 'em to the ladies, when I want to make an impression.'

There had been little mention of females in our all-male company. Fairbrother revealed briefly that he had a fiancée. Pennyweight made passing references to "the womenfolk", "the mother" and "the girlfriend", but as if they were ranks in a foreign army to which he was allied but which he didn't especially like.

'I suppose you see all sorts,' I observed. I suspected that the Doctor held his passengers in contempt but made exceptions since contempt was more perfect if one could express it to persons within its general purview.

'A lot of fellows at a loose end after the war have gone out to the colonies, though I understand the bottom's been knocked out of rubber and tin. Some of 'em come back, but not many, so I suppose they do all right.' His tone was disbelieving. 'Of course, drink, disease and *les femmes* do for a lot of 'em. Fairbrother looks as if he might manage, but I can't see the life suiting Pennyweight. He's the sort who's never satisfied but always looking over the next horizon.'

As it happens neither of my fellow passengers was going to the colonies. To our surprise we were all getting off at Madeira.

'An omen,' said Pennyweight. 'We're three of a kind. Like the Musketeers. All for one and each for the others, and all that. I don't mind admitting I'll be glad to have a couple of pals. Can't say I know much about the place. I got out a pile of books, but was distracted by other stuff I was looking into. It'll be rum, living among darkies.'

'The people are Portuguese,' I said; but my point passed him as most things did that failed to fit his preconceptions.

'Much the same thing, I'll warrant. I saw quite a few Chinese digging trenches in France and learned how to handle them, which should stand me in good stead.'

'What is your business there?'

Pennyweight gave an evasive response. 'Engineering. Roads, bridges, that sort of thing.'

'The island could certainly do with them,' I said. 'Would I know your firm?'

'I'm not exactly with a firm, though I've talked to a few. I'm more in the way of a roving representative. We saw eye to eye on that – my talents lying in the freelance direction without all the red tape of being actually employed. Give me plenty of scope, that's the idea. And it makes it easier if some funny business is needed to grease the way with the locals, if you take my meaning.'

'And you?' I asked Fairbrother.

'I'm in the wine trade. My father has just died and I'm making a tour of our suppliers to familiarise myself with things.'

'Not Fairbrother & Cadogan?'

'Yes.' Fairbrother was astonished. 'Don't say you've heard of us?'

'I'm in the same line, though on the production side. House of Pinfold. I called on Charlie while I was in London – or, at least, tried to. Oh, sorry, I suppose I should express my condolences. Why is it I didn't see you?'

'I've just got back from the Médoc.' He looked at me curiously and my heart sank that he knew the rumours which had recently sprung up. 'Pinfolds? Oh, gosh! Now we're both embarrassed. I didn't think anything of your name either. The story I heard was that Pinfolds had gone bust.'

*

Once we were out of the storms, life on the *Kildonan Castle* resumed a more leisured pace, but, having got to know Pennyweight and Fairbrother, I couldn't ignore them. In particular I had hopes that, if Fairbrother were as disingenuous as he seemed, I might sell him the quantity of doubtful malmsey that was among my many problems.

Somewhere off the Portuguese coast the sun came out and we took the air. Fairbrother and I were in our semi-tropical ducks, but Pennyweight stuck to his stout woollen suit with its faint odour of *Players*. When I hinted at the unsuitability of his clothes, he said only, 'Oh, there'll be time to get kitted out later. In any case a good suit is never out of place. I had this one cut to my own design. Good for town or country, see?'

A small party was playing quoits.

Pennyweight said, 'That's the British Empire Exhibition Mission. They're off to the Cape and all points east.'

I'd heard of the planned exhibition. In the aftermath of war and depression, it was designed to make economic sense of the whole imperial venture. The result was a great affair at Wembley, though I wasn't there to see it.

'Lucky devils,' Pennyweight added.

'Why so?'

'What! Off around the world on a jaunt paid for by someone else! That'd be just the ticket for yours truly.'

'Well, I suppose they've got a job to do: finding exhibitors and so forth.'

'Don't you believe it. It's chaps like me who drum up the trade that keeps the home fires burning – and precious small thanks we get for it. That little lot know damn all about working for a living. Spongers, the lot of them. It's all a question of connections. Freemasons,' he said, then relented. 'Sorry, you don't happen to be a member of the Craft, do you?'

'No.' I recalled that Pennyweather was a Druid and wondered if there were a mortal enmity between the two secret societies.

'I tried to join,' he resumed and shook his head. 'In fact I did join briefly. I could see they'd got some notions of the Truth. I wanted to start a debate going, but they're a snobbish lot and set in their ways. They've got no time for Advanced Thinking.'

I didn't want to hear any Advanced Thinking, so I drew his attention back to the quoits players. 'Do you know any of them?' I asked.

'Not a one. I had a word with a steward – thought I might pick up a useful tip. That one – no, not the pretty one, Miss Torbitt-Bayley – the other,' he pointed out a plain woman of thirty or so, dressed in white, ' is a writer. A writer, for God's sake!'

'Is she famous?' I thought he might know. In one of those incidents that throw an unlikely light on others, I'd seen him at a table on deck with a pile of old books and yellowed pamphlets, which he guarded from closer inspection. It seemed he was pursuing a course of private study, but I didn't know what it was except that it excluded acquiring any knowledge of his present destination.

'I shouldn't think so,' he said. 'At least I've never heard of her, and I've forgotten her name. She wrote something called *The Mysterious Fairy Stiles*. A book for kiddies, I imagine.'

I didn't recognise the book either and we turned to different things. The subject of Madeira came up and I gave some description of the island.

At this point I recall an old adage that, if one spends enough time in Piccadilly, one will sooner or later meet everyone one ever knew. This was scarcely true of Madeira in those days, but, if the scope of enquiry is confined to the rich and famous, then it was approximately so. I give Churchill as an instance. He could be come across painting in odd corners of the island a few years after Hitler's war. It was in this context that the subject of

Karl von Habsburg came up. I remarked, as a piece of local colour, that the Emperor of Austria-Hungary, having been deposed for being on the losing side of the war, was in exile there. It was then that Pennyweight observed casually that the Emperor was a descendent of Jesus.

I held no strong opinion as to the divine ancestry of the Habsburgs and would have thought nothing of it. Fairbrother, however, showed an unexpected side of his character. He said, apparently seriously, 'Our own King George is a relative of the prophet Mohammed. One of his forebears married a Spanish princess, who got it from the Moors of Granada. Or so I've heard – I don't say I'm an expert on the subject.'

'It wouldn't surprise me,' Pennyweight said. He had caught a note of deference in Fairbrother's voice. 'And there's a touch of Jew blood there, too.'

'Steady on, old man. You're talking about the King.'

Pennyweight quickly retreated. 'Only a touch, old man. Only a touch. There's nothing wrong with a touch of Jew. It sharpens up the senses.'

Seeing that Fairbrother was mollified, he built on his superiority by reciting various alleged facts to which I paid no attention at the time.

However, as Fairbrother rightly summarised the matter, 'It's an awesome idea to think the Emperor Karl may carry the blood of the Son of God. It quite takes some getting used to.'

Indeed it does. But the truth is that the larger themes of life get buried in the detail, though I say this cautiously since I am not certain it was so of Pennyweight. I lost interest in the conversation and directed my gaze again at the quoits players. The sun was playing on the dress of the woman who wrote children's stories and it was dazzling. I thought of Margaret and wondered what on earth I was going to say to her.

If I'd been granted a degree of foresight, I should have wondered, too, about Robinson, who in a special sense made up the fourth our little party. It was poor Robinson who got himself murdered. One or two people thought that I killed him.

CHAPTER TWO

From the ship's rail I watched Madeira rise, green and improbable, out of the morning and a quiet sea. In much the same way, the original discoverers must have blundered into it: an island at a latitude and off a coast where islands did not exist; an error, an afterthought, a sketch for an abandoned version of creation.

'Packed already?' Doctor Crispin asked.

'Nothing much to pack. A couple of suitcases.'

'Only a short stay in England, then?'

'A business trip.' I nursed my glass of tepid gin and bitters and wondered whether to have another. 'I'm surprised to see you here,' I said. 'Don't you have any patients to unload when we dock?'

'The passengers are a healthy lot. Lucky, too. The odd sprain or fracture are not unknown when we run into heavy weather in the Bay, but this time round we seem to have escaped 'em. On the return leg we'll pick up cases of malaria or other unspeakable foreign fevers. Vastly entertaining.'

We chatted a little. He informed me that the *Kildonan Castle* would be stopping over for a few days. 'A chance for some sight-seeing,' he added sceptically. 'Speaking of which, you must know the place pretty well. Didn't you mention that your family was in the wine trade? It rather brings to mind Shakespeare – Richard the Third and all that. Wasn't his brother, the Duke of Clarence, drowned in a butt of malmsey? I don't suppose your people put him there?'

'Not that I heard of.'

From the half deck we looked down to where other passengers were gathering for their first glimpse of the island. The lady novelist was standing at the rail with a man, her husband I supposed, another military type with a certain dash that suggested he'd come better out of the war than Pennyweight and I. I remarked on the oddity of her being with the British Empire Exhibition Mission. Crispin commented that her name was Christie.

A little later Pennyweight, looking nervous and crapulous, emerged with Fairbrother. I drew back from the rail. The previous night we'd exchanged some sharp words on the subject of accommodation. He didn't ask directly if I would put him up but told a sentimental story of bunking with fellow officers in a bomb-proof near Arras.

'All pals together, sorting out the world's ills,' he said, and threw in, 'Socialism – that's the up and coming thing, mark my words.'

I answered that I couldn't understand how he had allowed himself to be in the situation of a strange land with no firm job, no knowledge of the country, no command of the language and no bed for the night.

'God will provide –' he said '- though sometimes it'd come in handy if He'd provide *until* He provides.'

I felt a little ashamed but no more inclined to put him up. In any case he said, 'I'm expecting a chum to meet me,' which seemed to close the subject.

Even so, the following morning he must have been on my mind because I said to Crispin, 'Your remark about the Duke of Clarence reminds me of the way Pennyweight talks.'

The Doctor gave me another of his cool glances and asked, 'Really? How so?'

'The knack of connecting stray facts into odd patterns. When you were a child did you ever play that parlour game, "Consequences"? I've rather forgotten how it goes, but I think the players write down sentences and then they're read out in random combinations. The results are quite funny, but, at the same time, seem to be full of obscure meaning'

'Is that how Pennyweight thinks?'

In addition to theories about the Emperor Karl, Druids and Freemasons, Pennyweight had collared me in the bar with another concerning the Templars and Cathar treasure. One of his tattered pamphlets covered the subject. He was also interested in vegetarianism, which I mention only because he'd shown himself a hearty man for steak and kidney pie and bottled stout, and I was surprised when he said he thought there was something to a diet of salads and carrot juice. 'Clears out the bowels no end,' he said. 'I imagine that in France you suffered terribly with...' He didn't finish. Nor did he elaborate on the virtues of vegetables. I was left to puzzle over his subscription to a doctrine he didn't practice. Only later did I realise that Pennyweight believed theories to be true only in a partial and special sense, in much the same way that, I suppose, Christians believe in the imperfect testament granted to the Jews. His studies were directed at a further revelation when everything would be reconciled and all secrets made known.

I hadn't worked this out when I spoke to Doctor Crispin, so I confined my answer to the Duke of Clarence.

I said, 'When you mentioned that he drowned in a butt of malmsey, it occurred to me that, when Richard was around, the Portuguese had only recently discovered Madeira. Then I thought to myself that there must have been quite a rush to get the butt of malmsey back to England in the nick of time for him to murder his brother.'

Crispin looked at me curiously, and I apologised. 'Sorry. I'm doing what Pennyweight does and wandering off the point. Obviously I'm not making myself clear.'

'No – it's not that. I think I understand.' He thought for a moment. 'You do realize that that would give Richard an alibi for the murder? Because no one would be able to work out how he laid his hands on the malmsey.'

'Now you're getting the spirit of the thing.'

Crispin grunted. 'I can see how one can have fun with it. And here's another oddity. It *was* Pennyweight who mentioned the business. I'm not much of a one for Shakespeare and had forgotten the story.'

'The likes of Pennyweight don't forget things like that. It's their strength.'

'Damned clever, though. And it rather confirms my suspicions.'

'About Pennyweight?'

'Yes. He's a sight more intelligent and cunning than you'd give him credit for.'

I was curious. I offered the Doctor a cigarette. He lit it and took the smoke in slowly. He said as if to test me, 'I had a piece of bad luck last night. Someone broke into my cabin after dinner.'

'Oh? Did you lose much?'

'A hundred pounds.'

'Good Lord. That is a lot of money to have in your cabin. Obviously you've reported it.'

'No.'

'Why not?'

'It represents my winnings from the passengers at cards. Honestly come by, I should add. But the Old Man and the Company wouldn't like it if they knew I was supplementing my income this way. They prefer to think of our games as a social activity; in fact the Captain gets an allowance so that he can lose a little and please everyone.'

'I'm sorry.'

'The thief took my stock of cigarette cases, too.'

'And you think it was Pennyweight?'

'He slipped out for half an hour – oh, I forget, you weren't there. He was complaining about something he ate and went to dose himself with one of those kaolin and morphine mixtures fellows like him are forever taking. I thought nothing of it at the time.'

'I'd rather gathered you thought he was a fool.'

'I did. But that's how sharp characters like him operate. When he was cheating at solo, he was seeing how I'd react, and he spotted two things. The first was that I knew how to play, which meant that I was probably making money out of the business. And the second was that I wasn't the type to make a fuss. Do you see?'

'Yes,' I agreed.

*

As we approached the coast, Funchal was in sunshine. The mountains, where eucalyptus and aboriginal laurel forest grew, were in mist. Below, the land fell sharply in a cascade of small terraces. The passengers, eager at the prospect of time ashore, pointed at them and debated the improbability that they could be cultivated.

Since we were both leaving the boat, I could scarcely avoid Pennyweight. In any case he was with Fairbrother – the two had struck up a friendship – and I still had designs on old Charlie's son.

'I'm staying at Reid's Palace Hotel,' Fairbrother said. 'Is it all right?'

'The best in town,' I said. When he looked doubtful, I added, 'The Emperor Karl has been staying there.'

'Watch your step, Ronnie,' Pennyweight said. 'The place is probably crawling with Hungarian assassins.'

'Do you think so?' asked Fairbrother.

I said I didn't. I told him I understood that the ex-Emperor had moved out of Reid's to a villa in the mountains where the Hungarians might murder him without causing any general inconvenience.

We moored in the roads. A flotilla of high-prowed row boats emerged like Maori war canoes from the shore bearing hotel agents, *compradores* from the trading companies, basket sellers and general nautical riffraff. Small boys stood at the bows and dived for coins thrown into the sea by the passengers, a point which didn't escape Pennyweight. He commented, 'If I were a few years younger, I'd give that a try myself. There looks as if there may be a few bob in it.' This was another allusion to his straitened circumstances, which he made without any indication of rancour: rather with a sense of wonderment that he, Pennyweight of all people, should have come to such a pass.

In the scramble, precedence was given to the pinnace despatched by Reid's, who had a private landing below a rocky bluff. As far as I could tell, this was a purely customary right, granted by the complaisant authorities against the possibility that a king or dictator might be among the visitors. I pointed the boat out.

Pennyweight disappointed me. I'd envisaged his owning some peculiar patent luggage, the kind that opened into a travelling commode for tropical climes. In reality he possessed only a plain worn suitcase and a battered steamer trunk, both perfectly respectable. Fairbrother, on the other hand, had brought more than seemed reasonable for his planned stay, but this was consistent with his lack of confidence and I imagined him paralysed by choices and deciding to bring everything.

'You look as though you're expecting to be met,' he said.

Quite unconsciously I'd looked for Margaret, though it was quite impossible that she had come. Indeed she couldn't know for a fact that I was on the *Kildonan Castle*; I hadn't written or cabled. I was hoping, I suppose, that she would know by instinct (or love, if you like) and do something wildly imprudent, but that was too much to expect and not at all a part of our arrangement.

'Are you in a hurry?' Fairbrother asked.

'I thought Teddy might be here,' I said.

'Teddy?'

'My father's … you'd probably call him a "Man Friday".' I didn't know what I'd care to call him.

Surprisingly Fairbrother remembered our business. 'You mentioned some malmsey you have in stock.'

'Yes, if you're interested,' I answered.

'There's something of a glut at the moment,' he said. 'But I'm not against taking a look at it. After all, that's why I'm here. If you really aren't in a rush, why don't you join Herbert and me for tea?'

I asked Pennyweight, 'Are you staying at Reid's?' He had been scanning the boats, presumably for sight of his chum. I saw only the usual crowd of porters, factors, and touts who would try to interest tourists in an overpriced ride into the mountains by *carro de bois*; and also Pouco Pedro, whom in general I preferred to avoid. The little man was presumably on the lookout for visiting celebrities whose names he could print in his weekly sheet and to whom he could sell dubious favours.

'I haven't decided,' Pennyweight said. His tone implied a wealth of choices from which he would make a magisterial selection. 'I was hoping my chum would be here to meet me, but it was difficult to arrange that sort of detail by the post. Ronnie's agreed to let me park my traps with him while I look around for some digs.' With dignity he added, 'Reid's isn't excluded.'

We took the pinnace and made the short distance to the landing then laboured to the top of the bluff past palms, hibiscus and a dramatic Norfolk pine. The exotic vista sparked something of the romance in Pennyweight's soul: a vision of islands in a tropical sea. Leastways he commented, 'A swarthy lot, your natives, aren't they?'

I said, 'I suppose so.'

Then, as Fairbrother was checking his reservation, he came out with another of his strange observations. 'The Emperor's wife, Zita, is a Bourbon-Parma and related to the Braganzas, who are the Portuguese royal house. One could make something out of that.'

'Could one?'

'Blood is thicker than water, eh?'

I agreed it was and waited, wondering where this would take us. Fortunately Fairbrother just then finished at the desk. He came over and asked, 'Shall we have that tea?'

We went into the lounge where high tea was being served and a string quartet was playing. Pennyweight's eyes lit up. 'Cakes!' he said.

*

I am a creature of crowds. Loneliness suits me and there is nothing lonelier. That, at least, was something Margaret and I had in common and why, instinctively, she had picked me out on an earlier occasion at Reid's when she had been with Mrs Talbot and the other British Wives. Talbot was a retired general practitioner whom my father consulted, though he no longer made any pretences about medicine. 'Laxatives, bottles of brown mixture, and aqua. If they don't set your average patient on his feet, then he'll quite likely die of whatever it is that ails him.' As to my father he diagnosed, 'Nerves, aggravated by bad digestion. I've told him he shouldn't let his man Teddy do the cooking. That spicy muck is all right for our brown-skinned brethren, but no good for the white man. It heats the blood and causes no end of trouble.'

'Mrs Talbot disapproves of me,' Margaret said as the British Wives drifted away.

I was reminded of ducks swimming in flotilla. Mrs Talbot was at the head of them, delivering verbal cuffs to those who didn't maintain formation. Although only a fortnight on the island, I knew her formidable reputation and had expected to meet a beefy, corseted woman. In fact, save for a bosom borrowed from a larger model, she was skinny and etiolated, her energy waspish and dissatisfied: a condition often affecting English women in hot climates much as scotch and bonhomie affects the men.

'Why?' I asked. I was curious as to what I'd done to invite a conversation. We were not in the lounge but on the terrace outside overlooking the gardens and the sea. Margaret had just stepped through the French window and was fanning herself. Identifying my clothes as English, she decided to speak to me, granting one of the confidences bestowed on people we do not know.

'Because I'm married to a Portuguese,' she said. 'See? Even you look shocked.'

'I don't mean to be. I'm just surprised in a general sense. I don't really disapprove. How did it happen?'

'Johnny was an attaché in London.'

'Johnny?'

'My husband. He's an Anglophile and prefers the name. Portuguese is impossible to pronounce: it sounds like speaking Spanish while eating whelks. We met at an embassy reception during my debutante year and I was swept away – much to my family's disgust, though they appreciated his money.'

She clicked her teeth to mimic the disgust, and waved a hand sharply across her forehead to catch a stray hair. Her complexion was fair, her eyes a watery blue. She was by any standards beautiful, but I thought her looks would fade early – were fading and would only get worse. Odd though it may seem, it was this imperfection that attracted my interest. A perfectly beautiful woman would have been unreal.

I asked, 'How long have you been here – in Madeira?'

She found conventional questions annoying. 'Two months. Already long enough to hate the life. And you?'

'The same. My family has estates here.'

'The House of Pinfold? I heard of you from Mrs T. She tells me your business has gone to ruin. But that may be malice on her part.'

'I'm afraid it's pretty much true.'

'I see. And you're going to salvage it?'

'I don't know. Probably not. My father still holds the reins, and, as you'll have gathered from the Talbots, he's a little … strange.'

'I like "strange",' Margaret murmured.

*

My companions were reminiscing about the war. Fairbrother had been a Cavalryman. Pennyweight was an Engineer.

'It was useful background,' he said, 'when I wangled my way into the Royal Flying Corps.'

'You were a pilot?' I asked.

'Something like that.'

I noticed his avoidance of detail.

By degrees the other passengers from the *Kildonan Castle* had made their way to Reid's. Some of them were debating whether to book into the hotel for a change during the brief stopover. Mrs Christie and her husband came in; I noticed them because I felt vaguely that I ought to recognise the names of authors. Two other groups in the lounge were the usual British Wives and those of the higher echelon of Portuguese officials and, alone and reading, was a tall, gaunt, elderly man with fair hair and a reddish beard who reminded me of George Bernard Shaw.

I asked Fairbrother the time. I was reluctant to stay longer in case I didn't make it home before the light failed. I told him I had to leave. I gave him my card, explaining, 'We're not on the telephone at the villa. I'm afraid you'll find that Madeira doesn't run to all the amenities, though Funchal is all right. You can leave messages at our shop and they'll be brought to me. If you need a guide, the hotel can arrange one, but I can help if you have any difficulties.' I held out a hand to Pennyweight, 'I hope you find some suitable digs.'

He broke off from scoffing his cake and enquired, 'Can't you stay, old man?'

I shook my head. The musicians had just begun to play Borodin's Quartet No. 2 in the palm court style. It was part of their stock repertoire, but was indelibly associated with Margaret. Without her it gave rise to a feeling of loneliness unbearable even for me.

*

My family had been in Madeira a hundred years. The senior branch continued to live in England as merchants in whatever products were profitable. The overseas estates were managed by younger sons who usually obliged by dying young or failing to marry, though there was a goodly number of fitz-Pinfolds sprung from illicit liaisons who provided clerks in various offices about Funchal, unconscious of their heritage.

My Uncle Gordon was the last in this tradition and died relatively young with no heir. My father had come out some ten years ago and drawn me to him with the bait of his own imminent demise.

I took the funicular railway up to Monte. My great-uncle, some time in the 'eighties, had bought an abandoned *quinta* as a speculation, grown fond of it and built a villa as a retreat from the summer heat of Funchal. With the vineyards sold to pay debts and everything gone except the shop and a stock of unsaleable wines, my father had taken up full-time residence there.

It had something of the heaviness of a mill owner's house in a provincial town, an expensive philistinism, save that a veranda had been added, a delicate structure with a sloping pagoda roof and fine wrought ironwork which was such an absurd contrast it achieved a whimsical style. In fine weather there was a lovely prospect, but in winter it was cold and damp and lacked modern amenities, even electricity and basic plumbing.

By the time I arrived at the Estação da Fonte the evening mist had come on and the lamps were lit with a pale white light. Across the cobbled square stood a fountain under a stone cupola. It was dedicated to the Virgin and a *carro* stood by, with the bullocks licking water from the rock face. The driver was asleep, but his boy was waiting on errands.

I gave him my bags and asked him to follow me in his own time.

The boy didn't ask where I was going. I was a Pinfold, and this, it seems, was my home.

*

I found Teddy in the kitchen. In England I'd missed his cooking. I smelled curried *espada*, and that and the lamplight, the moths and the scent of night stocks reminded me that my life wasn't without its charms.

'That smells good. Is there enough for me?' I said. 'Did you get my telegram? I'd rather hoped you'd meet me in town.'

Teddy studied me unsmiling. '*He's* in bed,' he said and stared at his fish. 'I am left always to do the needful, isn't it?'

'I'm sorry. Has he been like this since I went away? I did explain my reasons.'

I put down my suitcases. Teddy's sad brown eyes examined me with a note of scorn. 'Same-same all the time. Now *He* calls me "boxwallah's whoreson", which is not nice, very impolite.'

'No, it isn't nice,' I sympathised. 'Is he in a state to see me?'

'Maybe. I give *Him* his dinner and tell *Him* you are here, Mr Michael.'

He served the fish onto a plate, leaving enough in the pan for later. He trotted off on bare brown feet to my father's bedroom. I went to my own and washed. From the other end of the house came an angry racket.

As well as being cook and general factotum, Teddy acted as my father's secretary, which accounted for the idiosyncratic style of his correspondence during our years of separation. Back in the kitchen, he sat sullenly over his espada curry as I explained something of my business in London.

'I'm afraid I haven't had much luck,' I said. 'Charlie Fairbrother has died, and no one else has shown the slightest interest in our wine.'

At the mention of Charlie's demise, Teddy crossed himself. He cast a glance at the wall where a picture of the Blessed Virgin, draped in tinsel, hung on the bare plaster. His eyes wandered in the direction of my father's room.

'We should drown *Him* in it,' he suggested.

'Drowning people in malmsey seems to be a popular idea at the moment,' I said, but relented of the joke. 'The fact is, we can't go on much longer. Already the bank is threatening to foreclose.'

'What will happen to *Him*?'

'I suppose he'll have to come back to England with me,' I said, though God knew how we would manage.

'And me?'

'I don't know. I'm sorry.'

'Poor bloody boxwallah's whoreson,' said Teddy without emotion.

'Yes,' I agreed.

*

After dinner I took a hurricane lamp and went for a stroll. Below the house several terraces had been converted to garden, but they were being slowly invaded by eucalyptus saplings. Further down the mountain a *levada* followed a line parallel to the contour with a sharp fall to one side. I walked beside it, keeping the path by watching the reflection of the lantern on the water. The air was scented with pine resin and eucalyptus oil.

On my return, Teddy said, '*He* is ready now. All dressed and very beautiful.' He looked tired. I wondered how old he was. He was one of the small thin men who retain a hideous appearance of youth as a doll will remain a doll no matter how battered.

I said, 'You can go to bed, if you like. If my father needs anything else, I'll get it.'

He nodded. 'I shall pray that God sends us a silly fellow to buy our wine.'

I thought of the younger Fairbrother. I said, 'Yes, do that.' Later, I heard him intoning extravagant prayers to the Holy Mother to bring us an abundant supply of the world's fools. In the meantime I finished my cigarette; then, screwing up my courage, I went to face my father.

His lair was on the upper floor of the house in a room my great-uncle had decorated in the French taste to please a mistress. The walls were painted a faded rose *Pompadour* and spotted with damp. The light came from a half dozen sconces with mirrors behind them, and several paintings of the Alma Tadema school conveyed an air that was chastely erotic. My father lay in a half-tester bed in a garnish of pillows like an elaborate chocolate confection. He was wearing a floral dressing gown and eyed me balefully.

'Michael,' he said.

'Father.'

'You are late.'

'I took tea at Reid's.'

'Ah! I go there so infrequently: was it interesting?'

'I saw George Bernard Shaw – or, more accurately, someone who looks like Shaw.'

'I don't care for Shaw. His style is far too didactic.' My father closed the subject. 'You are well, I trust?'

'Tired.'

'Of course.'

'And you?'

'I am suffering from Kali's Revenge.'

'You've had a row with Teddy.'

He nodded gravely, but smiled. 'Still, you are here. You may kiss me. On the cheek, boy. On the cheek.'

I advanced to the bed and kissed him dutifully. He laid aside the pair of silver hairbrushes with which he had been toying, sighed and groaned. 'The light in here is so bad. Oh, don't sympathize – don't sympathize.' He gave me an appealing look. 'Tell me, Michael – I can't ask that idiot, Teddy – tell me how you find me.'

'You seem well,' I said, which was true in that there was no discernible change. His skin was pink and smooth. His thin hair had been recently cut and was pomaded across his scalp. His eyes had their usual feverish glitter, though I didn't blame him for this: it seemed to be an effect of heat and Atabrine.

Isolated in the house, his melancholy was relieved only by petty delights, and these were transitory. Pleased at my compliment, his joy quickly faded. He picked up his mirror, examined his face and again appealed to me. 'Michael, my boy…'

'Yes?'

'Is my lipstick smudged?'

ELIZABETH MORRIS to GEORGE BERNARD SHAW

5 Devonshire Grove

Buxton

28th September 1919

Dear Mr Shaw,

Let me state quite frankly that I wish to have your child. From your writings I believe that this proposal will not be repugnant to your feelings or beliefs. I am aged twenty-five, single, of personable appearance, and owner of an income sufficient to maintain both myself and our infant. I am employed as a teacher at an annual salary of forty-five pounds, and am beneficiary of an annuity in the sum of fifty pounds.

My outgoings are as follows:

Rent £26 0s 0d
Fuel £13 6s 8d
Dress £10 0s 0d
Food £5 0s 0d
Other £5 0s 0d
Total £59 6s 8d

You will note that I have a surplus after expenditure amounting to £39 13s 4d, which is enough for the feeding and clothing of a child. I have not made this proposal frivolously, and I trust that it will meet with your approval.

Yours sincerely

Elizabeth Morris (Miss)

G. BERNARD SHAW to SIEGFRIED TREBITSCH
(translator)

Reid's Palace Hotel

Funchal

20th March 1922

My dear Trebitsch,

What an importuning wretch you are: demanding that I write another play on the piffling excuse that it will save you from starvation. I know that I am a mere writing machine; but the ancient contraption has recently clunked out *Back to Methuselah* and a translation of your own *Frau Gittas Sühne*, and even a heartless piece of ironmongery must, from time to time, be taken apart, oiled and given a minimum of care. Hence I have been borne by boat to Madeira. It was either that or by bier to Westminster Abbey.

Even so I am spared no peace. The Theatre Guild is trying *Back to Methuselah* in New York, and *Heartbreak House* is coming off in England. From all sides rise cries that the texts must be cut because the sixpenny public won't live with them. They don't like Shaw, it seems. Can't stand the fellow. My name on the bill is like that of Carpentier's opponents in the boxing ring. The attraction is to see whether the producer (the world-famous So and So) will knock my silly head off.

Charlotte sends her best wishes. She spends her days playing cards. I swim in the sea and try to bring my correspondence up to date. The management of the hotel has provided me with a writing table for this purpose. It is in the lounge where I can watch the world go by and listen to a palm court orchestra commit vile crimes against music, which they do with the artless charm of a six year-old performing pirouettes for her parents' friends.

The situation has its interests. I satisfy at once my vanity and my need for anonymity by going around shouting: 'I am *not* George Bernard Shaw!' The hotel owner has invited me to learn the tango with his wife. A lady writer has just arrived on the boat (her name is Christie and she has written *Miss Terry Ferrat Steals*, which I take to be a novel about the modern woman). Three ex-soldiers (I know the type) have arrived with her. It is time to lock away the spoons!

Concerning the soldiers, it is evident that they are cads. The generality of private soldiers are in any case drunkards and malingerers – for which I don't blame them – but these men are former officers; and only seven or eight years ago they would have been models of honour and gallantry. One doesn't have to be an admirer of the system that produced them to feel the poignancy of their downfall. And, in a way, one respects them for it as one does Milton's Lucifer.

The truth is that theirs is a rational reaction to the war. All attitudes have undergone a revolution, and caddishness is the Bolshevism of disillusioned gentlemen who know they have been sold a false bill of goods but retain enough sense of caste to prevent their allying with the unwashed multitude. They are lone predators and we must watch them carefully, for they have a lean and hungry look.

I share fame with an emperor – Karl von Habsburg of the old family firm, presently in the hands of receivers and squabbling creditors. The Great Powers have locked him up here like a decayed relative who may go mad and run naked through the establishment. In the meantime they try to decide whether to murder him or restore him to the throne. If consulted, I shall recommend an operatic compromise: namely that they kill him but soften the event by singing over the corpse; for the present situation has notes of absurdity, most unsatisfying to a dramatist. He was living, until recently, here at Reid's; but without money, so that the bum bailiffs were called in. Now he resides in a damp villa somewhere in the mountains and remains in rude health. This is hardly tragic. It is simply the tale of a nice young man who has had a bit of bad luck.

Oh, very well – you shall have your play. It shall be As You Like It – for *I* shall not like it at all. The elements are all to hand. What could be better than soldiers, emperors and tango? I have in mind a light, one act-piece: three scenes, four actors and a single set. It should be suited to sailors in dresses and provincial solicitors who fancy themselves as leading men

One of the soldiers holds to an exotic musical theory which he explained by reference to my friend Elgar. I didn't defend him. He and I have become monuments and must expect our share of pigeons.

yours ever

G. Bernard Shaw

Editor's note: One of George Bernard Shaw's idiosyncrasies was to dispense with apostrophes unless it would result in ambiguity. Most readers find this odd and so the present text has been amended to follow the normal practice.

CHAPTER THREE

I ran across Johnny Cardozo on my way to the Praça de Constituição where we had a shop selling wine and a few souvenirs to tourists. It lost money and I would have got rid of the place except that the manager, Senhor Pereira, was my cousin or my uncle – or my brother for all I knew and anyone could prove. Johnny was lounging on the running board of a new cream-coloured motor car, smoking. Ahead the street was blocked by a *carro* and people were running about or standing and laughing like spectators at a fire. I thought I caught a glimpse of Pennyweight and was about to shout his name when Johnny called me over and shook my hand.

'I heard you were back,' he said. 'In yesterday on the *Kildonan Castle*, wasn't it? I understand you had bad weather in the Bay.'

Johnny's English was so perfect that his slight accent seemed like an affectation. He was a slick, svelte little man from his dove-grey spats to his flat straw hat, a picture of spick and span elegance.

'You're well-informed.'

'My business,' he said, and I nodded though I had only the haziest notion of his business: some form of government service about which I didn't care to speculate.

'What's going on?' I asked. The confusion had stirred the old men dozing in wicker chairs outside the Grand Café and the soldiers slouching by the Paláço. A yellow dog, which at this time of day slept under the jacarandas of the central promenade, heaved itself to its feet, contemplated movement then collapsed again in the dust. Two bullocks harnessed to a *carro* shook themselves and began to complain.

'An accident. A fellow has been knocked down.'

'By a *carro*?' If I sounded sceptical, it was because a bullock-sledge at the best of times struggles to match a man's walking pace. The same consideration didn't trouble Johnny.

'Apparently so. It occurs once or twice a year, I'm told. Foreigners don't believe it's possible – and so it happens. Don't you agree?'

I agreed. With Johnny I was always agreeable. I observed the particular courtesy of adulterers towards abused husbands if they happen to know them. When he offered a cigarette, I accepted.

Johnny pushed to the front of the crowd where a man lay on the ground. He was pale, fair-haired and wore a linen suit. There was negligible blood except a trickle from the mouth, but I knew it for a bad sign. The *carro* driver was beating his boy and it was this little drama that was attracting attention; people taking sides as to whether the boy was responsible.

'A recent arrival,' Johnny remarked.

'What makes you think so?'

'The trousers are creased at the knee from being folded in a suitcase. Take a closer look'

'I'd rather not, if you don't mind.'

'Squeamish? Not what I'd expect in an old soldier.'

I didn't answer. The Portuguese had fought in the war, but it wasn't a subject we'd spoken of. I wondered what he knew of soldiers: their delicacy in the face of death.

'He looks English. That blond hair.' Johnny's hair was black. So were his eyes. His moustache was groomed like that of a matinée idol. The first time I saw him I was struck how easy he was, how perfectly suave, possessing qualities which the English habitually despise, though I noted them only from curiosity. Johnny went on, 'It should be easy enough to establish. Do you know him? Perhaps he was on the boat. Take a closer look'

'I can see well enough. I don't recognize him. Perhaps he kept to his cabin because of the storms. For God's sake...' I said as he knelt by the body, opened the jacket and displayed the label of a Jermyn Street tailor.

'That seems to confirm it. Rather a decent suit, but hardly new. It looks as though he's come down in the world.' He examined me thoughtfully. 'Odd that you don't know him.' He closed the jacket, and the crowd, like film extras waiting on a director's cue, resumed their jabbering.

We agreed to take coffee and a brandy together as if there had been no accident and no one had died. On another occasion I'd noticed Johnny's ability to switch moods. No doubt it was a useful quality in a diplomat, if that was what Johnny had been. Apparently the body no longer interested him. Instead he enquired into my affairs in England.

'Not that it's my business,' he admitted, 'but Margaret is bound to ask. She is well, by the way.'

'Give her my regards,' I said, detecting a constriction in my throat. I suspected I wasn't alone in thinking that the capacity to lie convincingly was a talent unconsciously desired above most virtues.

'I'll let you do that,' Johnny said. 'You'll be seeing her soon, after all.'

*

Margaret had written:

Darling,

No word from you. I've had to study the steamer timetables, asking myself each day which one would bring you back to me. Oh, I know you couldn't write or cable directly, but was it really beyond you to get any message to me? Couldn't you have used your man Teddy? I don't want to reproach you. Reproaches are so ugly and so sadly revealing that love is a bad-tempered affair. Only indifference is serene. In your absence I am serene, so serene that Johnny, understanding nothing, believes I am in love with him alone.

Come to me. Do! Come to me – come to me – come to me. I want you … how? Brutally! Disgustingly! I want you as an affront to everything! I want you as tenderly as a sick child!

Come to me!

I shall be at our usual place at our usual time, before my lunch with Mrs Talbot.

Ever yours

*

My father appeared at breakfast in an indigo wrap decorated with cranes and chrysanthemums. His face was only lightly powdered. Teddy had prepared *idlis* and *sambhar*.

Seeing my father fiddling with his rice cakes I asked for the sake of civility, 'Aren't you feeling well?'

His expression became one of sweet affliction. 'Gyppy tum. That and the bloody rats making a racket all night.'

He added for Teddy's benefit, 'Excellent *sambhar*, I'm sure.'

'No rats,' Teddy said, softly and firmly. 'I find rats' nest and clear out.'

'Cockroaches, then.'

I enquired, 'Have you taken Collis Brown's Mixture?'

My father regarded me as if I were an obtuse child. 'No good for cockroaches.'

'For your stomach.'

'There's nothing wrong with my stomach that some elementary hygiene wouldn't cure. Last night I went down the garden to pay a visit to Kensington Palace and there was the most god-awful stink. Isn't that so?' He glared at Teddy before appealing to me. 'We could have plague, I shouldn't wonder. It's a damned disgrace. I'd sort it out myself but...' He didn't finish. He remembered that this morning he was clad in saintly garb. He smiled beatifically at Teddy. 'This fellow won't have anything to do with it. He thinks Sahib's thunderbox is bad karma. It causes him to lose caste, doesn't it, my boy?'

Teddy put down his spoon and glowered at his plate. 'Unfair,' he said. 'Tell *Him* unfair, Mr Michael. I am not losing caste because of horribleness of Kensington Palace. I am *Christian* bloody boxwallah's whoreson, not bloody heathen Brahmin devil-worshipper.' He dragged back his chair, rose and fled the room. My father looked at me, affecting an air of incomprehension.

This incident was typical of my father's ghastly love and I believe he regretted it. It was difficult to tell. To preserve the remains of his self-esteem, his apologies had become coded. In the same way his previously mild vanity had become exaggerated.

I went into the garden and occupied myself by cleaning the latrine. Teddy found me there a little later and excused a matter he had forgotten, namely the letter from Mrs Cardozo, which had been delivered the previous day.

Three hours later I found myself with Johnny Cardozo in the Grand Café discussing his wife and an invitation to dinner that evening, while outside a body was being cleared from the street.

*

I glimpsed Margaret at the head of the stairs, flitting like Mrs Rochester as she fixed her courage and her face. Though I was a frequent visitor to the house – Johnny's best friend, after all – the stairs led to reaches I'd never penetrated: to the confines of another man's marriage, where Margaret lied to him. Or perhaps she lied to me. It was impossible to say, for the sincerity of an adulterous mistress naturally comes with reservations. And as for Johnny, who could tell what he knew? Margaret and I had never decided on the degree of public recognition we should grant to each other. As we shook hands, would a lingering heart's beat as our fingers touched betray us? How long may a smile last and yet retain its innocence?

I was feeling uncomfortable in my evening clothes. They smelled of camphor. The trousers were folded at the knee like those of the dead Englishman. Had we really been on board the same ship?

Johnny asked, 'Will you have a Martini? I've made up a jug myself, not left it to the servants.'

Cocktails were modern: Johnny prided himself on being modern. It struck me that the same modernism, by a law of unintended effects, had led to Margaret's and my affair; for an older generation of Portuguese wouldn't have permitted a situation in which it might arise, nor tolerated it once it had arisen – though the last point was debatable: I couldn't swear to what Johnny tolerated.

It happened because Margaret wanted to learn to dance. She had taken lessons before her debutante year, but there was an instructor in Funchal, Senhor Agnello – 'Positively the most *wonderful* man,' she said – who could teach the tango. 'Not the parody they dance in Europe, but the real Argentinian thing.'

Johnny was willing, then found himself busy and offered the job of escort to an Englishman of his acquaintance, the owner of a failing wine establishment who had time on his hands. Such a gentleman.

The occasion was an earlier dinner party.

Tonight we took cocktails in the garden among the Chinese lanterns and the moths. Below us dark terraces of bananas descended towards Funchal. The *Kildonan Castle* was riding at her moorings beyond the Molhe da Pontina, and sending up the occasional festive rocket. The air was warm with a scent of mimosa.

'I thought that tonight I'd push the boat out,' Johnny said. I didn't know if his language was suggested by the sight of the liner or a desire to test out a newly acquired expression: quite possibly both. Pushing the boat out consisted of welcoming new visitors to the island. Mrs Christie was among them; there was talk that her departure might be delayed by mechanical problems affecting the ship. Also the pert Miss Torbitt-Bayley, whose liveliness had attracted Pennyweight's attention, and who was taking a holiday after an operation for appendicitis.

'You know everyone, so you can grease the wheels.'

'All right, Johnny.'

'Fairbrother says you've become chums.'

Later Fairbrother apologised. 'I didn't say "chums" exactly. It's so easy for foreigners to get the wrong end of the stick when the lingo's not their own, isn't it?' He stared into his glass. 'I say, this drink is awfully strong. What is it? Gin?'

'Martini.'

'I've heard of those. Awfully strong all the same.' With an effort at a lighter tone he confessed, 'Fact is, I don't have much of a head for alcohol. Rather a disadvantage in our trade, eh? A bit like the padre being an atheist?'

I agreed it was. I found it difficult to engage with Fairbrother's conversational style. He reminded me of boys – the phenomenon is rarer among adults – who are shunned by their school fellows for reasons that are unfathomable. The feeling towards them is not an active dislike but a visceral desire to be in other company. I was inclined to make an excuse to talk to Mrs Christie. I would have if I hadn't needed Fairbrother's goodwill.

I asked, 'Is Pennyweight here tonight? I haven't seen him.' He might have been lurking in the darkness of the garden beyond the dazzle of lanterns.

'I don't think so.'

'I thought I caught a glimpse of him in town this morning. Did he find a billet last night?'

'I can't say.'

'He's not at Reid's then? I admit I didn't think it likely.'

'No, it was a bit of bravado on his part, suggesting he might stay there. I rather think he's short of money. He talked of finding a bed with a pal – presumably the fellow who encouraged him to try his hand in Madeira.' Fairbrother's tone was sympathetic towards Pennyweight's predicament and I warmed to him a little. 'When I left him, he was ... well, a little the worse for wear. I don't like to see a chap down on his luck and I lent him a fiver – I suppose 'gave' would be more accurate. Yet – ' he hesitated '- there is something *tremendous* about him, isn't there?'

I laughed. But, on reflection, there was something tremendous about Pennyweight, and I would have pressed Fairbrother to explain it if I hadn't heard Johnny Cardozo calling dinner. And felt the grip of Margaret's hand on mine.

'Michael, it's been such an age!' she said. Her hostess smile flashed like a mirror. 'Darling, what *have* you been doing with yourself?'

I said, 'May I introduce Ronald Fairbrother? He's with Fairbrother & Cadogan. I don't recall if I've mentioned them. They're in the wine trade.'

'Mr Fairbrother!' Margaret gushed, causing him to retreat a step and give her the space to slip her arm under mine. 'You *must* see me tomorrow,' she said, still smiling.

'Are you drunk?' I asked.

'What a bounder you are. Ronald, are you going to lead me in?'

'I ... Oh, yes, if that's all right with you?'

'Michael, you haven't complimented me on my dress.' It was of grey moiré silk with a pattern of peacock eyes. 'Johnny had it made for me in Paris. I've had to have it taken in. Would you believe I've lost weight since I came to this dreary place?'

'I'm sure that's very fashionable.'

'Is that all you can say? Why don't you tell Johnny to his face that he's wasted his money?'

'I didn't mean that. And you know I didn't.'

The last remark brought the bleak little exchange to a close. Margaret granted me a smile, a 'touché', and turned her elegant back. Fairbrother whispered, 'My God, she *is* a corker, isn't she?' and followed. Though he escorted her, I noticed the slight distance between them and that she had already detected the indefinable strangeness he wore.

We were twelve at table. I was seated next to an Irish priest, Father Flaherty, who, according to Miss Torbitt-Bayley, was on his way to the Cape to become chaplain to the Catholic bishop of Natal but taking a break in his journey. 'I ought to warn you about him,' she said. But the warning never came.

A florid man of sixty or so with capacious nostrils leaned over to offer me a hand. He said, 'I hope the food and drink are good. I used to run a pretty decent pub before the Lord was vindictive enough to show me the Light. What do you want to talk about – religion or horses? I'm told the horses in South Africa are no bloody good. There's a local fly that ruins the beasts.'

'I've not been to South Africa.'

'Nor I, but I doubt you're missing much. I don't suppose there's a lot of racing here. No? I thought not. The creatures keep falling off the bloody mountains, I imagine.'

Over the consommé I heard Margaret being sparkling and silly with her neighbour, a planter taking the long route to Malaya. Fairbrother had been abandoned. Glad that he had been noticed at all, he didn't seem to mind, but I disliked the lightness that others viewed as charm. I also hated my own censoriousness. If I'd believed for a moment that this desperate frivolity was all there was to her, things would have been impossible between us.

Impossible, too, if she had credited my sour malaise.

The English, when abroad, address foreigners by speaking more loudly and slowly, exaggerating the very points that make them incomprehensible, and it seemed to me at times that something of this inflexible idiocy stood between Margaret and me: that we were divided not by lack of sympathy but of a common idiom. We were reduced, like the English tourist, to handing out coins to beggars and accepting an unintelligible blessing and impenetrable smile. Yet one should not overlook such sympathies – even the sympathy of beggars – for, so my experience tells me, their silence captures something which words disguise.

The indefatigable Johnny was pumping Mrs Christie for information about the British Empire Exhibition Mission.

'A jolly little fellow, isn't he?' Father Flaherty commented. 'But he has cruel eyes, don't you think?' He assessed mine. 'In the beer and whiskey trade, you get to judge a man by his eyes. The smiles are no guide. They all have them until that last terrible moment when the drink overcomes them and the devil pops out. But what do I know, a clerical eunuch whose taste runs to horses? Speaking of the British Empire, did I tell you I was in the Post Office on Sackville Street during the Easter uprising? No, of course I didn't. Well, it's true and every Irishman will tell you the same. Three million of us making the sandwiches for the boys with the guns, and only a jar of pickles I'd popped out to buy saved me from a hanging. Will you listen to those two!'

I could hear Mrs Christie explaining the purpose of the Mission in a low voice. She had the unemphatic manner of someone who didn't seek to persuade because the matters being spoken of were self-evident truths. Imperial trade in frozen lamb and cotton goods was the reward of victory, the cause for which millions had died: a grocer's account paid with a butcher's bill. And, for all I knew, it was so. Few soldiers who had been through the war thought any longer that it had been waged for a moral cause, and an economic banality seemed as likely an explanation as any other. The alternative was to believe, as I suspected Pennyweight believed, that it was all the working out of Occult Forces.

'They've got themselves an emperor here, or so I'm told,' Father Flaherty said.

'The Emperor Karl.'

'Now he'll be that young Habsburg fellow, the one who was booted out when Germany and Austria lost the war, am I right?'

'Yes.'

'A good Catholic family,' said the priest.

Mrs Christie's husband, who had been beyond my hearing, made an intervention for the general benefit. 'They should have hanged him, along with the Kaiser!'

In an aside Father Flaherty said, 'I understand he wasn't responsible for starting the business. Didn't he come to the Austrian throne after the old emperor died?'

'In nineteen sixteen.' I remembered the date as one remembers stray facts. I don't recall it ever had any significance.

'It's a harsh doctrine that hangs a man for the sins of his ancestors.'

'He could have brought the war to an end.'

'Do you think so, Pinfold? Do you really think so?' Father Flaherty said.

I didn't. In its beginnings, its conduct and its end, the war seemed beyond the reach of human will. Pennyweight's occult explanation was exotic, but it was not absurd.

So far I'd paid little attention to Fairbrother. It hadn't occurred to me that, lacking easy social graces, he'd been preparing a set piece and waiting for an opportunity to deliver it. Suddenly it spilled out of him.

'The Emperor Karl is a descendant of Jesus Christ!'

Like the rattle of gunfire, cutlery was laid on plates. In a panic his voice fell and he looked gloomily at the table. 'At least, that's what a chap I know told me.'

Johnny Cardozo said gallantly, 'Bravo, Mr Fairbrother! Now, what does the Church have to say about that?'

Father Flaherty had ignored Fairbrother's squib. No doubt he'd heard worse things in the priestly trade. Seeing an answer was expected, he said, 'It sounds like the old Gnostic heresy, though I don't know this particular version. Would Mister – did you say your name was Fairbrother? Would Mr Fairbrother care to enlighten us all?'

'I ... well, I don't have the full details, but I gather that Jesus didn't die on the Cross. He was admittedly pretty poorly and had to hide away and all that. But after a while he got well and ... I think I've got this right ... he married some woman or other...'

Father Flaherty nodded. 'That would be Mary Magdalen. It usually is in these tales.'

'Yes, that's it! He married Mary Magdalen and they had children – and then there's some complicated stuff about who begat whom, until we get to the Merovingian – I think that's the word – kings of France. After that there's more of the same – the begetting stuff – and ... if you follow me ... finally the bloodline descends to the Habsburgs and the Emperor Karl.'

'Then Our Lord must have lots of descendants.'

'What? Oh, I see! Put like that, I suppose He must have.'

Father Flaherty smiled. 'The Habsburgs are a very good family. I doubt they'd like the idea of being descended from a carpenter. And, after two thousand years, they'd have a lot of relatives they mightn't want to know.'

CHAPTER FOUR

Senhor Agnello was a *porteño* who danced his way from Argentina to Europe at the time of the pre-war tango craze. Ten years older and not so fleet of foot, his dancing homeward ended in Funchal where he kept a studio above a drapery in the Rua do Conselheiro Vieira. He was a small, delicate man with dyed hair and whiskers: natty in the way of a costermonger rather than a gentleman. I had a suspicion he was wanted for bigamy though I'd no grounds for thinking so except that exiles carry a whiff of undiscovered crime. I say that as an exile.

Once or twice a week Margaret and I met in a second floor room and whiled away an hour under a rattling ceiling fan to the accompaniment of a bandoneon or a record spun on an old player with a japanned horn. French windows gave on to a balcony and a soft, gold light filtered through muslin fly screens; yet, for all that it was daytime, Senhor Agnello sang *Mi Noche Triste*, crawling over the words as if they were gravel and spent cigarettes. So far as I ever understood them – and the music made me understand them well enough – they were about sad nights and a lover who consoled himself with drink.

Senhor Agnello was in the back room, but a pattern of footprints in French chalk led to a pair of white tennis shoes and an old man with a red beard who was sitting bolt upright on a wicker chair. He threw me a sparkle-eyed look and said, 'Hullo, there,' with a smooth touch of Irish in his voice. I remembered that I'd seen him at Reid's.

'Are you a fellow-customer of Senhor Agnello?' he asked. 'Perhaps you can tell me: do you have to bring your own partner?'

'If you need, he can provide a girl.'

'Provide a girl? You make it sound like a bordello.' The old fellow chuckled. 'But that's the English language for you. Like Capitalism it speaks to the heart's desires, yet leaves one thinking it doesn't fulfill one's desires at all. Will you take a seat?' I sat. He said, 'Tango, Turkey Trot, Boston – I expect you can do them all.'

I nodded.

'I once learned country dancing – but that was from Fabians on a study-retreat and probably doesn't count. Some years ago a lady taught me to dance the valse backwards. And now I'm to learn to tango. Which makes you ask: why? And the answer is that the wife of the manager of my hotel wishes to learn, and I agreed to learn with her because I'm a sociable fellow.'

'Then you have a partner.'

'Indeed I do. Oh, I see. The reason for my enquiry is that I'm damnably clumsy and likely to upset the lady. Reid's provides a most accomplished teacher but – well, the truth is I'm an old show-off and the pupil would like to impress his master.' He gave me a frank grin that began in his bright blue eyes. 'These aren't dancer's legs.' He extended them. 'Too long by half. I'm put together like a marionette with the strings tangled. In a well-ordered society it would be illegal for me to dance except to frighten children when occasion required. Now you –'

'You look like Mr George Bernard Shaw,' I said.

'So I do,' my companion agreed. 'And sound like the old fraud, too, so I'm told.'

'Remarkably like him.'

'The effect of photography, most probably. Can you swear for a fact to Mr Shaw's height or the exact colour of his beard? No, I thought not. But don't be offended. Now, as I was saying, you look like a dancing man. Unlike myself, you have the proportions: you correspond more nearly to the Golden Mean, though I doubt that Aristotle had dancing in mind.'

Not wanting to be impolite, I volunteered my name and offered a hand.

My fellow dancer said, 'I'm pleased to meet you, Mr Pinfold. My name is Sonny.'

'Pleased to meet you, Mr Sonny.'

'Sonny will do.'

'Sonny?'

'It … I suppose you'd call it a family name. But enough of that. Have you noticed the cathedral here – how it looks like a Presbyterian kirk? I'm thinking of the sparse lines. Now why do you suppose that is? An expression of the hard, puritan soul inside every fisherman, perhaps?'

'The point never crossed my mind.' An image of the Sé flickered across my inner eye: a Scottish kirk nestling among bananas and sugar cane under high mountains of eucalyptus forest and a hot sky. Sonny's observation contained a curious truth – even if not with particular reference to the cathedral – namely the exotic stamp everywhere impressed by colonists, even when their aim is a banal reproduction of home.

'If you haven't noticed, it means you must live here,' Sonny remarked. 'Don't they say that the spectator sees most of the game? When I saw you at Reid's I thought you might be a visitor like myself.'

'You saw me at Reid's?'

'I study things – can't help it, I'm afraid. You were with two friends.'

'Fairbrother and Pennyweight.'

'One of them – a plump fellow – was a touch under the weather and drew me out on a conversation about music. He had a theory – I forget what it was. He demonstrated it by playing phrases of Elgar on a pair of spoons. At least he said it was Elgar.'

'That would be Pennyweight. He has another theory that the Emperor Karl is a descendant of Jesus Christ.'

'Does he, now?' Sonny said without surprise. 'Ah well, monarchy is nothing more than the sum of its ancestry.'

'What happened to him – Pennyweight? I left early'

'He was politely escorted from the premises – I think that's how these things are described in the police reports, though no police were involved.'

The ceiling fan juddered to a halt, allowing the noise of bedsprings to be heard from the adjoining room. Sonny looked blankly at the sheet music fixed to the walls: *El Enteriano, La Vida, Alma de Bohemio*; covers in which art work from the Aesthetic Movement was blended with louche images from the Argentinian *barrios*. I'd often felt the pang of their seedy charm.

The fan resumed with a shake of French chalk. Sonny took it as a signal to talk and commented, 'You don't seem to like Mr Pennyweight.'

'He's all right,' I said.

'You were in the war together?'

'No.' I thought some elaboration necessary. 'But we both fought, and he seems to think that fact makes us chums.'

'I see. My countrymen hold the same opinion about being Irish.'

'And is it true?' I asked.

Sonny looked at me with disconcerting sympathy. 'Unfortunately it probably is.'

The door to the adjacent room opened. Senhor Agnello emerged, wearing a felt hat and a neck scarf: hallmarks of the *compadrito* and as necessary to the true tango as tails and a boiled shirt to the Viennese waltz. 'You mus' unnerstan', Meestair Pinfold,' he had once explained. 'The tango comes from the *perigundines* of my 'ome.' And, with a nudge and a wink, 'We mus' try to put it back there, eh, Meestair Pinfold?'

I agreed. I believe '*perigundines*' means brothel. At all events, Senhor Agnello's style of tango was far removed from the suavity of the dance I'd seen in London. I was interested in what Sonny would make of it.

He said, 'It seems a lady has arrived.'

Maria had followed Senhor Agnello from the other room, smiling and cheerfully scratching an armpit. She was a woman of fleshy, hairy beauty, raucous laughter and the occasional wart. My liking for her might be attributed to *nostalgie de la boue*, but I think it lay more in her generous carnality. As it happened, however, Sonny wasn't referring to Maria, but to Margaret who had just arrived, slightly out of breath.

She gave me a hasty peck on the cheek. 'I'm sorry I'm late, darling, but today is being thoroughly bloody. Johnny is in a filthy bate about one of his damned pots, and I can only stay an hour.'

I offered a cigarette, which calmed her. She smoked it elegantly, with her left arm folded below the breast to support the right and her head turning to take in the room, emphasizing the length of her neck. I was taken by the simplicity of her dress, in pink silk set off with some plain turquoise jewellery, and she still wore her hat. In a moment the stirrings I'd felt on seeing Maria – in many ways Margaret's opposite – were transferred, quickened even. And this is odd because, whatever my feelings about Margaret, I didn't like her.

I may have loved her – but that is quite another thing.

'So,' I said, 'tell me about Johnny.'

'There's not much to tell. You know how enthused he is by his bits and pieces of broken old pots. It seems that one of the guests last night has stolen a prize specimen. You wouldn't know anything about it, would you?'

'Are you sure it was a guest? Mightn't it have been a servant?'

'One would like to think so, but I know how light-fingered people of our class are. And a servant would have stolen the whisky, not some old crockery. Look, I must sit down for a moment to get my breath back.'

She took a seat. Maria had placed *Mi Noche Triste* on the gramophone and was gliding about the floor while Senhor Agnello and Sonny negotiated terms. Whatever the music claimed, my own nights were not sad. Rather, I experienced the sadness of afternoons, when the sun still blazed and people took a siesta. Today would be another, no doubt. What I saw in Margaret was a mystery, and what she saw in me even more mysterious. Our relationship reminded me of books I had read: books that engaged me but of whose purpose, if they had one, I was only dimly aware.

Margaret asked, 'What's George Bernard Shaw doing here?'

'He isn't Shaw,' I said. 'His name is Sonny.'

'Of course it's Shaw,' Margaret retorted. 'He arrived here while you were away. He's staying at Reid's.'

'He denies it. Perhaps he's a confidence trickster.'

'If you say so.' She glared at me, considering whether to quarrel. Bothered by a fly, she lost interest. 'Who cares anyway? Since the war, everyone claims to be someone else. Since the Czar was killed there are more heirs to the Russian throne than ... oh, I don't know what ... than something of which there is a great deal.'

'Do you include the Emperor up at Monte among your frauds?'

'Karl? No, he's the genuine article. He comes with a British Government Guarantee, and they should know because they brought him here. I don't want to talk of this. Kiss me.'

'What about Sonny?'

'Oh, bugger Sonny!'

I kissed her.

'Satisfied?'

'You're toying with me,' she said.

We kissed again, but this time at length: a tentative touching as if in doubt that we should kiss at all, an exploration to establish the mood, a development and letting go, a coda that might be a smile or a stroking of the cheek with the fingers. I'd kissed Margaret many times and never with certainty, for her kisses were often in contradiction to her behaviour: a wry commentary, an apology, a confession. Perhaps there is something musical in the structure and unutterable meaning of a kiss: an element of rhythm, melody and counterpoint. I can't say.

She said, 'Let's go to bed.'

'Don't you want to dance first?' I asked. Normally we danced if only as an excuse for being here, though there was more, albeit incomprehensible unless one has danced the tango and teased from its complexities the sexual challenge thrown down by the defeated.

'We don't have time.'

'Why do you have only an hour?'

'I'm to see Mrs Talbot and the other wives.'

'Can't you put them off or give them a miss?'

Margaret pushed me away. Yet again I'd said the wrong thing and I wondered if I'd receive a rebuke or forgiveness.

'I've been desperate to see you,' she said. She brushed a hair from her eyes and added, 'I do wish Agnello wouldn't play that record.'

Carlos Gardel was singing in the idiom of the slums.

*

The bed was warm. Margaret picked up a coil of black hair between finger and thumb. 'Ugh,' she said.

I said, 'We could try to find somewhere else to meet.'

'Where? Do you think Reid's or the Royal would take kindly to Senhor Pinfold flaunting his mistress? We've been into this subject before, and you know there's no alternative.'

'I'm sorry.'

'Don't be. At least this –' she indicated the bed with its scent of bodies '- is truthful.'

'I wish you wouldn't imply that everything is sordid.'

She touched my face, not unkindly, and shook her head. 'What a twister you are, Michael.'

'I love you.'

'Yes – quite possibly you do. And I love you. But it seems we don't love each other. Does that make sense?'

I removed my jacket, putting it carefully over the back of a chair. The army had made me a tidy man. Margaret's untidiness was one of the points of friction between us. She took off her hat, threw it on the floor and shook out her hair.

'Help me out of my dress. Aren't you glad I don't wear corsets? My mother says she was a martyr to them when she went to India.'

I folded the dress and placed it on the chair. I took off my trousers.

'Now my brassiere,' Margaret said and raised her arms like a girl doing calisthenics. She lowered them over my head as I fumbled the fastening and, with a chill, I felt the tip of her tongue on my forehead. I drew the brassiere off her. For a second she held it between outstretched arms as a veil over her small breasts; then smiled, let it fall and executed a turn so that I would acknowledge that she was a beautiful woman. And indeed she was. I thought again of the frail beauty of fair women in hot climes, who like flowers can pass from glory to ruin in a season. Between her shoulder blades was a faint blush of heat rash.

Sometimes we made love like strangers bumping in a crowd, with smiles and mutual apologies, incuriosity and an absence of hostility. Margaret had a self-centred energy, a thrilling intensity, which I matched as best I could with tenderness. I'm told – not just by Margaret – that I'm a remote lover, and I acknowledge it may be so:

that my tenderness is tinged with a stranger's pity and a wonderment at the point of it all.

'Cigarette,' said Margaret.

I reached for my jacket and drew out my case.

'That's new,' she said. 'Gunmetal, isn't it? And the dent?'

'I've had it since the war.'

'My poor darling,' she murmured as she did whenever I mentioned the war. 'I've heard of people being saved from a bullet by a cigarette case or a Bible. Is that what happened to you?'

'I didn't have a Bible.'

'A Bible seems more plausible than a cigarette case. One can't imagine God taking an interest in a cigarette case – unless He smokes. These days everyone smokes.' She returned the case and I gave her a light. 'Pass my clothes, darling.' She rose, poured water from the pitcher into the bowl and began to sponge herself. I held out the dress and the small flask of Coty taken from her bag. As she had often said, 'Wouldn't it be terrible to smell of sex all afternoon? Mrs Talbot would be on to me like a shot.'

'Do you really have to leave?' I asked. 'Once Sonny has gone, we could dance, if only for a few minutes. We haven't talked. You haven't asked how my business went in England.'

'Dreadfully, I imagine, or you wouldn't have come back.' She shivered. 'Forgive me, I shouldn't have said that. Then again, you haven't asked about me and Johnny.'

'You don't like to speak about Johnny.'

'He likes to make love under a mirror.'

'Under a mirror? You haven't mentioned that before. Do you mind?'

'Not especially.' She looked at her watch. 'Two minutes. We can talk about Johnny, if that'll satisfy you.' She may have believed I was jealous of him, but that wasn't true. Indeed I suspect that lovers are rarely jealous of husbands; for jealousy implies a threat to the right of possession and the lover has none. I should have been more concerned at the possibility of another lover equal to me in all moral respects and more attractive in others, but I'd never imagined Margaret as dishonest.

'I'm curious about the mirror,' I said.

'I don't know why. Mirrors are a way of convincing ourselves that we're real.'

'I didn't know there were any doubts.'

'There are always doubts. By the way, do you know a man named Robinson?'

'No. Is the name an alias? It sounds like one that lovers write in hotel registers.'

'Are you trying to be provocative?'

'I'm sorry. But what does this have to do with Johnny?'

'He thinks you know him – Robinson.'

'I don't. Who is he?'

'Somebody found dead in the street yesterday,' Margaret said.

For the moment I learned no more of Robinson: neither where the name came from, nor what Johnny Cardozo's interest might be. I remained unconvinced he'd been on board the *Kildonan Castle* unless, because of the storms, he'd remained in his cabin. In any case I was more intrigued by the notion of a mirror fixed to the bedroom ceiling, in which Johnny viewed the sexual act. It suggested a relationship between him and Margaret that was, perhaps, not dissimilar to my own and revealed qualities that were frankly puzzling: I refer to Margaret as solely an object of desire: viewed as such and possibly wishing to be so viewed.

I tried to detain her a little longer. Pointlessly, of course. Whatever was unsatisfactory between us wasn't a function of the brevity of our meetings.

She had forgiven my ill-defined crimes and was quite sweet. 'Truly, I must go, darling. Mrs T and the Imperial

Knitting Circle are waiting for me. A consignment of novels has arrived on the *Kildonan* and everything has been organised like a branch of Mudie's so that the books are circulated and we don't scratch our eyes out over who gets what.' She was re-applying her make-up. 'I have to be on my best behaviour.'

'Why?'

'Why? I should have thought that was obvious. They think I've let the side down by marrying a dago.'

I said, 'I've never thought of Johnny as a dago.'

'Nor is he,' said Margaret. 'On the contrary, he considers himself to be the perfect English gentleman. Even though he has lately taken to dressing like a White Slaver – as, indeed, have you. Now, look at me – will I do?'

'You look lovely.'

'Honestly?'

'Honestly.'

She studied me thoughtfully, then gave me a kiss which, as always, was a promise that next time we would somehow do better.

'Aren't we terrible people?' she said, her sadness not unmixed with excitement.

*

Old Sonny was gone. I told Senhor Agnello that his new client might be a famous playwright.

''E ees no dancer, that for sure, Meestair Pinfold,' he said. 'You see 'ees legs?'

We took a glass of rum together, which I finished quickly on seeing Maria casting an eye at her employer and at the door of the bedroom. Senhor Agnello never tired of emphasizing that regular exercise was necessary to every successful dancer.

I went down to the street. I debated taking a coffee and another glass of rum or returning to the shop. The afternoon was wearing on and businesses re-opening.

Beggars were setting out their patches and pi-dogs
blinking and scratching with the insouciance of
philosophers. I walked a few paces when I felt a knife in
my back, and a voice said, 'Give me your wallet, Senhor,
or I kill you dead.'

'Are you short of money again, Pouco Pedro?' I asked.

I heard the knife being folded in its clasp. I turned and
there was no one there. But since Pouco Pedro came barely
to my shoulder a lot of him wasn't there. I looked down on
a ragged straw hat, a linen jacket, cut-off twills and a pair
of espadrilles worn over bare feet. Pouco Pedro was doing
his little bounce step, like a sparring partner.

He took a jab and slapped my forearm. 'So – so, the
police didn't get you yet?' he said. 'How are you, Mikey?'

'Fine. I came in on the *Kildonan Castle*. And you?'

'Eating and sleeping. We take a drink, huh?'

We made a turn up an alleyway off the Rua da Bella
Vista and into a *cervejaria* where I ordered two shots of
rum. I smelled fish being grilled nearby and asked Pouco
Pedro if he wanted some. For some reason he never took
money from me, only a meal or a drink. Somewhere, so he
told me, he had a wife and six children and, if he was
supporting them from the mimeographed English
newssheet he produced once a week, they must have been
hungry.

He came to the point. 'This dead fellow, Robinson – he
a pal of you, Mikey?'

'No. I never met him.'

'His death make a good story, hunh? You sure he not
on the ship?'

'Not unless he stuck to his cabin.'

'You think he a soldier? A hero mebbe?'

'Most men his age were in the war.'

'But hero? Mebbe call him a hero anyway. It make a
better story.'

'Why not?'

I downed my glass of rum and thought of ordering another, but the waiter was staring at us and Pouco Pedro was nervous.

'Have you been thrown out of here?' I asked.

'Mebbe. I been throwed out of plenty places.'

'You owe them money?'

'Not money. People been telling stories about me.'

'Is that why you carry a knife?'

Pouco Pedro shrugged. He proposed we leave and I agreed. I didn't know why I drank with him in the first place except for one of those occasions, often half-forgotten, that explain the accidents of friendship.

In the light of what was to happen I may as well digress; for there was a time – not so very long ago – when a romance born of staleness and disillusion stirred me as it stirred many of us who had been cast adrift upon the tide of Empire: a romance of a particular and dangerous character because it affected men who thought they knew the world but didn't, for no-one does. So, on my arrival in Madeira, Pouco Pedro met me on the Molhe, picked up my bags, and ordered a *carro*. He gave his name as Doctor Soares, an authority on all aspects of the island, both physical and cultural, and able to effect introductions at any level of society. He didn't look like a doctor – at least not like one who had kept his licence – but that was by the way, because I didn't want a doctor. Then, in the confusion of landing, Pouco Pedro stole my wallet.

I suspected he was a police informer. Everyone suspected he was a police informer. Contrary to the popular view, this was good for business since even an informer needs to advertise. How else would his customers know where to betray their friends?

Today he wanted to know, 'You tell me if you find out more stuff about this Robinson, heh? Mebbe we sell story to papers in London, hunh?'

'Maybe,' I said. 'But if I were you, I'd write about Mr George Bernard Shaw. He's learning to tango.'

'I don't want to write about him. He's old news.'

'Aren't you curious what he'll make of the dance?' I asked, but I wasn't interested in the answer. I was hot and needed to change my shirt; and so I forgot about going to the shop and returned home.

I found that Teddy and my father had made up and were friends again. My father was wearing a silk top hat and laying out card tricks. Teddy, who wasn't without wit, beamed at me and said, 'I am promoted, Mister Michael. Today I am bloody chappatiwallah, isn't it!'

My father sniffed the air and observed good-humouredly, 'Ah! I detect the scent of rum, sex and Coty!'

GEORGE BERNARD SHAW TO ELIZABETH MORRIS

10 Adelphi Terrace WC2

19th December 1919

Dear Miss Morris,

It has probably not escaped your attention that, in this capitalist world of ours, there is an oversupply of Irishmen. We export all we can, but practically have to give the beggars away. In the circumstances, I cannot in conscience agree to dumping more product on the market, and so must sadly decline your invitation to father your child. Please accept my kind wishes.

Sincerely

G. Bernard Shaw

P.S.

May I enquire how you intended to handle the business? I am an atheist, and, for all I know, you may be a Buddhist? Or did you have a scandal in mind? I ask only out of curiosity, since there is a lady in the case – namely my wife.

SONNY to ZOË

Reid's Palace Hotel

23rd March 1922

My dear Zoë,

So that was the tango, was it? Or should I use the plural; for it seems to me that two dances were underway. One of us was dancing with a beautiful and sensuous young woman in a perfect frenzy of passion. The other was pushing a carriage containing a palsied invalid in his last extremity. We should at least agree upon this: which dance is to prevail?

In my days as a music critic, I don't recall coming across the bandoneon. It sounds like a concertina got up by Krupp to a substantial way of business. Saki once observed that a gentleman was someone who knew how to play the accordion and didn't. Ah, but the tango isn't for gentlemen, is it? Nor for ladies. Not that it matters – to me at least. I have been called a gentleman only as a prelude to an insult, rather as pugilists will shake hands before knocking each other about the head.

As to your name – Zoë – that was an inspiration of the Life Force. For my meaning you must consult an etymological dictionary (I almost wrote 'entomological': a happy mistake which makes me think of butterflies – and of you).

If you wish to teach the old duffer the true meaning of the tango, you may leave a note at my hotel.

yours ever

Sonny

CHAPTER FIVE

My father disliked Arthur Mainwaring. He called him 'a jumped up bounder' because Mainwaring & Figtree had weathered the ups and downs of the wine trade. There was, too, an element of national antipathy: the Mainwarings, despite the name, had been Portuguese for several generations since an English ancestor – no doubt a genuine bounder – had arrived in the island.

My father, of course, wasn't entirely wrong. The wine trade, like any occupation open to a gentleman, brings out the villainy natural to the species and Arthur Mainwaring was no more immune than I was. After all, didn't I intend to cheat young Fairbrother? Wasn't I sleeping with Johnny Cardozo's wife?

The day began with a call at the shop where my uncle-cousin-brother, Senhor Pereira, was dusting bottles. He was gaunt, unmarried as far as I knew, and shy. He gave me a startled look.

'I'm going to see Arthur Mainwaring,' I told him.

His expression flickered uncertainly. I caught a glimpse of my Uncle Gordon whom I'd seen in photographs and who lived on his older brother's sufferance until military glory called him to a death by enteric fever. I asked, 'Any customers this morning?'

He shook his head and returned to his bottles like a lonely deacon tending the altar candles.

Arthur's office was behind his shop in the Rua do Aljuba. He maintained the air of a country solicitor, trading on the prestige of his Englishness, no matter how spurious. It was in any case a matter of opinion, for to some extent we inhabit countries of the mind. This point had occurred to me when, on a trip to Paris a year after the war had ended, I found myself drinking with a German soldier named Helmut. By then, whatever bitterness civilians might still feel, it was no longer shared by the soldiers, if it ever had been; and former enemies found that they were citizens of the same wasteland: aliens in the countries for which they had fought. By nineteen twenty-two this notion was a commonplace. Three years before, it had been a startling discovery.

The first time I met Arthur I was surprised by a small-made man with a tawny complexion and oiled hair, and, listening to his perfectly enunciated English, I found myself keeping half an eye open for the ventriloquist. But not today.

'You'll have a drink with me, Michael, won't you?' he said, proffering a decanter of sercial. 'I appreciate the sun isn't below the yardarm but we can stretch a point. How was the Old Country, by the way? That is where you've been, isn't it?'

Arthur's language, like Johnny Cardozo's, had a flavour of borrowings from a light comedy written by someone striving to be modern.

'The Old Country is fine,' I said. 'When was the last time you were there?'

'Unfortunately I've never made it.' He shook his head. 'Some day – some day. My people are from Lincolnshire, you know?'

'Really? So you long for the mountains of Lincolnshire.'

'The … mountains … of … Lincolnshire,' he sighed. 'Ah, well, it's good to see you again. I trust your father is well. By the way, did you come over with a chap called Robinson?'

The mention of Robinson was a surprise, but I put it down to the haunting and usually meaningless coincidences that dog life. It takes the likes of Pennyweight to construct grand theories from them.

'No, I don't think so,' I said.

'I knew a Robinson once.'

'What did he do?'

'I couldn't say. If I ever knew, I've forgotten.'

I nodded sagely. Like Smith, Robinson was a reassuring name and armies of Smiths and Robinsons seemed to have no other function than to make up humanity's numbers.

'Was your Robinson the same as the Robinson we're talking of?'

'What? Oh, no. Now I recall it, my Robinson was a traveller in ladies' hosiery – or possibly sheet music. The police showed me a photograph – he's dead by the way, this Robinson, not the other one – and he wasn't the same fellow. Neither of them were the same fellow, if you follow me.'

'Why are the police interested? Why did they ask you?'

'Because we're both English,' Arthur explained, thinking the point self-evident. 'They imagined we might have business together.'

'In ladies' hosiery and sheet music?'

'That's the other Robinson. I don't know what the other one – the *other* other one – did. Neither do the police apparently. He just turned up dead.'

'Accident?'

'Murder.'

I was becoming confused in my Robinsons. Mine – assuming him to be the corpse I'd seen – had met an accidental death. Possibly Arthur was referring to the hosiery salesman. He saved me by asking, 'Did you see Charlie Fairbrother while you were over there?'

'He died shortly before I arrived.'

'Ah. I heard he was dead but wasn't sure of the date.'

'Did you ever do business with him?'

Arthur looked at me knowingly. 'A little. Charlie was none too ... *reliable*.'

'So I've heard.'

'I sold him some wine that was ... shall we say "not of the best"? Charlie didn't care. I insisted he re-label it, but he didn't, of course, and that did our reputation no good. I gather you know his son.'

'Is that why we're talking of Charlie?'

'He came in here yesterday – the son I mean,' Arthur added, giving me cause to wonder whether the Fairbrothers like the Robinsons were going to fall into confusion.

'I met him on the boat.'

'What did you make of him?'

'He seemed inoffensive.'

'*Not* like Charlie,' Arthur said.

We sipped the sercial. It was light and dry. Arthur kept a pretty good wine for his visitors.

'What does he want?' I asked, referring to the younger Fairbrother.

'He's buying up Madeira wine. Apparently there's a new drink about to take the world by storm in the present cocktail craze. The "Madeira Madman" – ever heard of it? Madeira, gin and all sorts of muck; Fairbrother mixed one for me. Absolutely filthy, in my opinion. Fairbrother intends to corner the market. What do you think? Is he a shrewd businessman or making a fool of himself?'

'I don't know.' I said. The idea was one I would have associated with Pennyweight rather than Fairbrother. The new cocktail might be perfectly sound, but to jump from that proposition to global domination of the alcohol market took grandeur of imagination. Still, I had known ordinarily unassertive men take leaps into the unknown in the belief that firm action was called for.

The drift of conversation wasn't entirely away from my business. I asked, 'How does Fairbrother intend to pay – cash or credit?'

'No one ever gave Charlie Fairbrother credit,' Arthur said with a frown of painful memory. 'At least, not after the first time. A lot of your father's problems came from that. He gave Charlie credit, and then the war came along and Charlie wouldn't pay – he probably hoped the Hun would invade Madeira. Oddly enough, he wasn't too far from the mark: did you know that we were shelled by submarines a couple of times? Of course your father wasn't to know better, being fairly new to the trade. I can't speak of young Fairbrother, but he's buying wine in a hurry to ship out on the next boat.'

'And how will he pay?'

'Bills of exchange drawn on London. You can discount them for cash here in Funchal.'

This was reassuring and brought me to my subject which was to buy a pipe of decent malmsey from Mainwaring & Figtree. Arthur regarded me with suspicion mixed with a conspiratorial gleam.

'What are you at?' he asked. 'The blending game? It won't go far in improving your stuff if what I hear about your stocks is true.'

'I can only try,' I said, and we haggled about a price which Arthur said would be high because Ronald Fairbrother had depleted his cellar. 'You're a crook,' I said.

'Absolutely, old man,' Arthur agreed. 'Supply and demand. What the market will bear, eh? And cash, old man – strictly cash'

It seemed that, in the matter of credit, the House of Pinfold was on a par with the late Charlie Fairbrother.

*

On my return there was a customer in the shop. It was Mrs Christie. She was wearing a straw hat and a cotton dress made for a village fête in a doubtful English summer. Since the war, I'd become more aware of these details of social manners, the foreignness of the everyday.

'You mustn't expect any service,' she said with a reproach directed at a ghost inhabiting the shop. 'Foreigners simply have no idea what it means.' There was no sign of Senhor Pereira, and I imagined him fleeing to the storeroom at the sight of anyone who might disturb his lonely vigil. She gave me the frank stare of a schoolmistress. 'Don't I know you? Weren't you on the *Kildonan Castle*? I suppose you're stuck here like the rest of us because of the repairs.' She looked at her watch. 'I'll give him half a minute and then I'm off. There is someone here, you know. He's lurking. Most likely he's drunk. I shouldn't wait, if I were you. There isn't much to buy.'

I was too ashamed to confess that the shop was mine. However I was mildly curious about a lady writer, though I'd no particular interest in children's stories. I pretended to be occupied with a small piece of basketware.

'I shouldn't bother with that,' she said. 'It's probably made in Birmingham – or China.'

'I believe it's made here,' I said. I named the village, where willows were coppiced and a small workshop made hampers and cane furniture.

'Really,' she said, as if to possess actual knowledge were unfair: the disreputable advantage the professional has over the noble amateur. She asked me again whether I'd been on board the *Kildonan Castle* and I admitted I had.

'Did you meet Mr Robinson?'

I was beginning to feel guilty about Robinson. I could imagine how the police secured confessions to uncommitted crimes by simply refusing to acknowledge that the accused was unconnected with events. Something of this must have shown because Mrs Christie seemed to have forgotten her time limit in waiting for an answer.

'No,' I said, 'though I've heard the name. Who is he?'

'Oh, I've no idea. *I* haven't met him. In fact I haven't met any one who has. I spoke to the purser and he told me there was no one called Robinson on the ship, which seemed to me a little unlikely since it's a very common name. I used to know a Robinson.'

'A hosiery salesman?'

'Why on earth should he be a hosiery salesman? No, he was a professional co-respondent in divorce cases. His name was always in the papers for being caught by chambermaids coming out of hotel rooms in Brighton. He worked for a firm of enquiry agents who specialised in that sort of thing and would provide a co-respondent so that respectable men could save their reputations. I can't speak to the wives: presumably they were actresses and other people with no reputation worth mentioning. I don't suppose Robinson was his real name.'

'Everyone seems to be pretending to be someone else since the war,' I commented, a phrase that had the making of a mantra. It occurred to me that Robinson's profession was an interesting one, though I was no longer clear which Robinson I meant. I said, 'He could have booked his passage under another name. It was suggested to me that he might have kept to his cabin because of the storms.'

Mrs Christie dismissed the idea. 'It wasn't stormy all the time. If he kept to his cabin, it was because he *wanted* to. And that has very sinister implications. There *were* some people who kept to their cabins.'

I was curious.

'Hungarians, I believe. I caught one of them sneaking about the corridors at night. Thieves, I imagine. One finds them on board liners. The ship's doctor had some money and a cigarette case stolen. He kept quiet about it for the sake of the Company, but a steward told me. One can't hide things like that. Servants always gossip when they're not stealing on their own account.'

Mrs Christie had nothing further to add on the subject of Robinson. She was on the point of leaving when I asked her why she had taken an interest in the dead man.

'Because of the murder mystery, of course!' she answered. I noticed an enthusiastic glitter in her eyes, which seemed quite out of place in a woman who wrote for children. The next moment she was gone, leaving a faint scent of gardenias and a memory of English gardens. Outside the sun had climbed to its zenith and shone down on banana, eucalyptus and mimosa. I needed to change my shirt.

My relative came creeping out of the storeroom. Still occupied with speculations about the dead man, I imagined Senhor Pereira briefly as an adulterer emerging shyly from a Brighton hotel bedroom. Robinson, a hearty good-natured man with a taste for whisky and tweed suits, would take his place and, conscious of his professional dignity, read a racing paper while waiting for the chambermaid to surprise him and the woman in their guilty amours. As the outcome of a potentially sordid affair, it seemed reasonably civilized and I wondered if that was how things would end between Margaret and Johnny, except that there would be no need to employ Robinson since I had no reputation worth defending. Thus distracted, I refrained from berating poor Pereira for neglecting the shop. In any case he anticipated me with a message.

'Senhor Cardozo wash ear,' he said. Pereira had never shaken off the habit of Portuguese pronunciation. ''E wash ear while you wash er-why.'

'When was this?' I asked.

'Thish mornin'.'

'Did he say what he wanted?'

''E sigh 'e want to eat lunsh. 'E infight you to eat lunsh with 'eem.'

It was twelve thirty and I'd given a thought to lunch, though Johnny's invitation was unusual. Then it occurred to me, from a recollection of something said by Margaret, that Johnny believed I knew more about the deceased

Robinson than I'd been prepared to say. Possibly I knew
something of his murder.

CHAPTER SIX

Margaret had mentioned that these days Johnny dressed like a White Slaver. He came to my shop wearing a tan tussore suit, a broad-brimmed hat of grey felt with a note of lilac in it, and spats of the same colour. On another man they might have been absurd, suggesting he was playing a role, adjusting to the demands of the heat and the island. But, like the clothes of an actor, which can seem ridiculous in the street, they looked to me exactly right in their place.

'Hop in the motor, old man,' he said. 'I know a little spot that's exactly the thing for lunch.'

'Why are we going?' I asked. 'You don't usually invite me.'

'Friendship?' He gave me his glittering smile. 'I'm at a loose end. You've been away for a month and Margaret and I have both missed you.'

'Will Margaret be joining us?'

'Not today. She's feeling under the weather. She's taken a bromide and gone to bed. Still, we can have a bite and talk of cabbages and kings, eh?'

I slipped into the motor car and we drove west in the direction of Câmara de Lobos: not an easy drive on the steep laterite road, but no drives on the island are; the precipitate slopes and deep ravines prevent it, and in most places the roads are scarcely more than tracks.

I was suspicious of Johnny's carefree mood. Adultery poisons friendship, though, like other adulterers, I found the price worth paying. It is suggested – by women, I think – that the husband is the last to know, and that may be so since men are a self-deceiving crew who expect more fidelity of their wives than of themselves. That wives are in fact more faithful may also be true, but it is by the way.

I've found that there's a comity between lover and husband, and, as I loved Margaret, so I grew to like Johnny more, not less. We shared a common pathos.

We drove to Ribeira Brava. This was further than a lunch excursion would justify and was probably the cause of my reflections on our relationship. Johnny didn't explain unless his comments about the performance of his sleek motor car were the explanation. The sea was hard by, flat and blue, with an old watchtower, some smacks at anchor and a scent of brine and fish guts. On the landward side the vertical walls of the gorge, levelled only by some terraces of banana near the base, enclosed the town.

We parked by a church that was tiled in blue and white. There was only one other car; we'd followed its dust plume from Funchal. The driver was old Sonny and a stately lady I took to be his wife. I acknowledged him.

'You know George Bernard Shaw?' Johnny asked.

'His name is Sonny,' I said.

'I know for a fact that it's Shaw,' said Johnny.

'Not in Madeira, apparently.' I wasn't being ironic. I didn't know for certain if old Sonny were Shaw or not, and either possibility raised interesting questions. For a moment I thought of Pennyweight, who could snatch deep meanings from such ambiguities. I wondered how he was getting on.

Johnny linked his arm in mine. He led me from the church into a side street to a restaurant with a garden enclosed by a wall of brown tufa. We took shelter from the sun under an awning of split canes and bougainvillea. Two tables away a party of men, half way through lunch with several empty wine bottles marking their progress, were holding a rowdy conversation in a language I didn't recognise.

Johnny smiled slyly. He whispered, 'Pay attention to those chaps. No, I don't want to talk about them now, but later perhaps. For the present…'

'Cabbages and kings?'

'And emperors, if you like.'

Johnny was known at the restaurant. The waiter brought two rum cocktails, assuming I'd drink whatever Johnny did. I wasn't fond of rum, but drank it because it was cheap. It absorbed most of the local sugar production since the entry of Brazil into the market had caused prices to collapse. Not that this was a subject of great interest, but here and there one noticed abandoned terraces that had once been given over to cane and, around Machico, were crushing mills that had fallen into ruin.

Johnny said, 'I'd have preferred a Martini, but can't get one outside Funchal.'

'Have you heard of a "Madeira Madman"?' I asked.

'I recall Fairbrother describing it to me over dinner. It sounded disgusting. A scotch would be very acceptable, but one can hardly get that at all. Ah –' he sighed '- how I miss England!'

'Were you there long?'

'Five years. Long enough for me to know that it is the home of my heart. Portugal and England have an affinity. I was very comfortable with the London set and hunted in the autumn.'

'Where?'

'Fletchitt in Lincolnshire, the Cyrils' place. Do you know it?'

'No, but Arthur Mainwaring tells me he admires the mountains.'

'I don't recall the mountains.'

We ordered food. In the meantime we talked of my trip to England. I told Johnny I'd placed the Quinta Pinfold on the market in London, hoping that some crook who'd done well in the arms trade might buy it.

'Things are so bad?' he asked.

'I'm broke.'

'How broke?'

'Desperate.'

By the time our plates of *arroz e mariscos* had arrived, the three men at the next table had reached the brandy. One was high-coloured and elderly, with mutton chop whiskers; the second was the same age, gaunt and yellow, with a waxed moustache like the Kaiser's. It was the third that I particularly noticed. He was younger than the others, raffishly handsome and stylishly dressed.

He was carrying a revolver under his jacket.

I asked Johnny, 'Why did you leave England? '

'I was invited to. Oh, nothing shameful. The English wanted someone to keep an eye on the Emperor. My country has custody of him, but he really belongs to the British. They lifted him out of Hungary after his last failed attempt to regain the throne and banished him here. Now, for our sins, we are each of us exiles. Margaret is dying of *ennui*, and the Emperor won't oblige us by dying at all.'

'Do you want him dead?'

Johnny laughed. 'Oh – let's say that it would simplify things.'

I knew very little of the Emperor Karl. For those of us who had fought the Germans, the war with Austria-Hungary had been a comic opera affair and the aftermath a pit of impenetrable politics involving countries one had never heard of ten years ago. Of course one was aware of Franz Josef, the old emperor, who had been a fixture for sixty years or more, and of Franz Ferdinand, his heir, whose assassination at Sarajevo was supposed to have caused the war. These details had once seemed important; then, in the face of the catastrophe, ceased to be important at all. Still, there was some interest in Johnny's hint at his present employment.

Meanwhile he had changed the subject. He said, 'It would quite suit me if you would take Margaret out more often. She was lively after your tango lesson. I like to see her happy. I'm sure you do, too.'

I proposed cautiously, 'Don't you think it would be better if you spared her more time?'

'Pressure of business, old man.'

'And don't you think I have any business?'

Johnny smiled: perhaps at the hypocrisy of my suggestion, perhaps at the state of my business. However, I wasn't wholly hypocritical, merely inconsistent. Part of me wanted Margaret to recognise the folly of our affair. And part of her did. A novel element was her confession that Johnny liked to make love under a mirror, but the meaning of this was beyond me.

With brandy it was my turn to change the subject. I was surprised Johnny hadn't so far raised the issue of Robinson. At the other table the three men had paid their bill and insulted the waiter, and were now leaving. The older men were drunk and unsteady. The one in the smart clothes wasn't. I thought 'soldier'. He had the look that unites us in a freemasonry which includes even Pennyweight. He nodded at me and I returned the acknowledgement.

I mentioned the subject of the dead man: said that everyone seemed to know his name.

Johnny said, 'We found a passport in his jacket. There doesn't seem to be any doubt about his identity or that he wasn't on the *Kildonan Castle*. The curious point is that the passport doesn't contain an entry stamp.'

'How is that possible?'

'It isn't – that's the curious point. By the way, he was stabbed. The weapon hasn't been found: something long and broad, so the doctors tell me. The wound was hidden by the injury inflicted by the *carro*. You don't seem surprised.'

'He was bleeding from the mouth. I was reminded of someone who caught a bayonet through the lung. The wound sounds like a bayonet.'

Johnny shrugged. He said, 'I once met a Robinson.'

'There seem to be a lot of them.'

'He was a friend of Margot Carradine, one of the Cyril girls. He said he was a climber. Perhaps he intended to scale the peaks of Lincolnshire. Shall we pay and go?'

We returned to the car. Sonny's two-seater roadster was still parked, and I spotted his wife sitting on the rocks by the sea. She noticed me, smiled and shouted gaily, 'He's swimming!'

On the journey back to Funchal, I asked, 'Do you intend to tell me about the men in the restaurant? One of them was carrying a gun.'

'I know,' said Johnny. 'He calls himself Count Bronstein, and travels on a Nansen passport. His real name is Laszló Tormassi.'

'A Hungarian?'

'Exactly. But is he a good Hungarian or a bad Hungarian – and, for that matter, which is which?'

'There's a difference?'

'So I'm told. What do you say? Shall we stop and take a stroll?'

At Quinta Grande Johnny turned off the main highway towards Cabo Girão where a high cliff drops to the sea. At the bottom lie a number of small, cultivated plots approachable only by boat. Some of my fellow passengers from the *Kildonan Castle* were already there, comparing the view and complaining of the heat, while barefoot boys hopped about them peddling souvenirs and an old woman in a red peasant costume sold flowers. Mrs Christie was taking notes, possibly for a novel. She granted me a nod.

'Hungary is a curious place,' Johnny remarked. 'A kingdom without a monarch. Are you interested in this?'

'That woman there is a Mrs Christie,' I said. 'She writes children's stories, apparently. *The Mysterious Fairy Stiles* – I don't suppose you've heard of it. Sorry, old man, do go on.'

'The King of Hungary is our friend, the Emperor Karl. The ruler, until such time as he returns, is the Regent, Admiral Horthy.'

'I see. And is Admiral Horthy a good Hungarian or a bad Hungarian?'

'That's the question. When Karl is out of the country – which in practice has meant Switzerland or here – Horthy swears undying loyalty and works for his restoration to the throne.'

'Which makes him a good Hungarian – leastways from Karl's point of view.'

'On the other hand, whenever Karl turns up in Hungary to reclaim the throne – which he has done twice already – Horthy mobilizes his troops and turfs the poor fellow out. The last time was on a British ship.'

'Ah – then that makes him a bad Hungarian. Also from Karl's point of view. Who else is interested?'

'The Yugoslavs, the Czechs, the Rumanians and the Poles. They've all taken a chunk out of what used to be the old Magyar lands. From where they stand, the Admiral is a bad Hungarian when he represents the Emperor and a good Hungarian when he sends him packing with a flea in his ear. As for the British and French governments, the Admiral is good or bad according to whether or not they want to restore the Emperor.'

'And which do they want?'

'Both. It all depends if they're currently cultivating the Yugoslavs, Czechs, Rumanians and so forth, or not: a subject which changes like the weather. Then there's Bela Kun. Everyone – except the Soviet Government – is agreed that he's bad. He's a communist. His lot seized power for a while a couple of years ago until Horthy threw them out – the Admiral was definitely a good Hungarian on that occasion. Add to the mixture democrats of various shades of opinion, some of whom are monarchists and some not, and the irridentists – that's to say the

Hungarians who now find themselves living in Rumania, Poland etcetera and would like to re-unite with Hungary but don't know how to – and you'll see that poor Emperor Karl's lot is not a happy one.'

I reflected that he seemed to have more identities than Robinson.

'In the meantime,' Johnny concluded, 'I keep an eye on the chap. One can't help feeling a touch of sympathy. He's short of cash and has had to move from Reid's to a place up at Monte – not so very far from you, as it happens. Britain and France are both agreed that he should be paid an allowance – and equally agreed that Yugoslavia, Rumania and Poland should pay it. The latter are understandably reluctant.'

'Doesn't he have his own money?' I asked.

'His lawyer ran off with it.' Johnny spared me one of his quizzical glances. 'Speaking of thieves, you don't happen to know who stole a piece of faïence from my collection the other night, do you?'

'No. Shall we go?' I was tired of the heat. I'd noticed a patch of sweat forming on the back of Mrs Christie, which she bore with the stoicism of the British Wives. My shirt was prickling my skin.

We drove back into town. Johnny asked if he might drop me at the Quinta Vigia where he had business with one of the Governor's aides. His parting shot had no obvious significance.

He said, 'Do you remember Fairbrother's mentioning a crazy theory that the Emperor Karl is a descendant of Jesus Christ?'

I said I did and that he'd got it from Pennyweight, but this, it seems, was not the point. I was grateful. The matter of emperors, messiahs and Robinsons had become an uncomfortably metaphysical subject about which one feared that monomaniacs like Pennyweight might be talking sense.

'I don't say the two things are related,' Johnny went on. 'In fact, I very much doubt it. But a few days ago an angel was seen up on the Paúl da Serra.'

'An angel?'

'So they say. It happened at night. We're not used to divine visitations and they upset the local inhabitants – not that there are very many up there. You don't happen to have an opinion, do you, Michael?'

The Paúl da Serra was an area I'd rarely been to: a stretch of bog and moorland high in the west of the island. During winter it sometimes snowed there, and, in the abstract, it wasn't difficult to imagine an angelic messenger like a figure in a Christmas card delivering his message to shepherds in a lonely landscape. Perhaps, in due course, three kings would arrive. And, if them, why not an emperor?

*

I called at the letting agent to see if, during my absence, there had been any enquiries concerning the house, then returned to the shop to wash and make some telephone calls arranging receipt of Arthur Mainwaring's malmsey at my cellars. Senhor Pereira, who often reminded me of a cross between an El Greco saint and a grotesque Dickensian clerk, cleared off to the back room. I considered again that I should fire him and get rid of the place, but he was my uncle-cousin-brother, and *noblesse oblige*.

As evening came on, I closed up and went home, taking the train up to Monte and hiring a mule for the remaining distance. I liked Monte. For half a century lotus eaters and wealthy riff raff had built villas there. Even in the best of days a good portion must have stood empty for half the year, tended only by gardeners and caretakers. Now, with war and difficulties of travel and German submarines that had shelled the island, more of them had faded into seedy gentility, their stucco crumbling behind screens of pine and eucalyptus. One was the Quinta Gordon, where the Emperor Karl was whiling away his days doing whatever exiled emperors do. Plotting his version of the Second Coming, I supposed.

The mule deposited me at home and went off into the night, led by its driver and a bobbing lantern. From the kitchen came a smell of incense, and Teddy was preparing *parathas*. My father was in his study, poring over his collection of playbills, complaining noisily of the effects of mildew and silverfish. I contemplated my evening: an hour of reading Sir Walter Scott and, at best, a game of dominoes with Teddy. If I felt adventurous I might pay some bills, or stare at them at least. On these occasions I envied Johnny Cardozo. Deceived by Margaret he might be (though this was by no means certain), but at least he had her company and a kind of loyalty; for she would never leave him – leastways not to run off with Michael Pinfold, the trickster and broken-down soldier. Quite possibly not at all. There was in her, despite everything, an integrity that I felt even if I couldn't understand it. What appeared as deceit might be only one of the compromises women make. It is chiefly men who sacrifice themselves on a point of principle: usually picking the worst out of innate stupidity. Women are self-sacrificing, but for essentially practical reasons; and this seems to me more moral. Heroism of the masculine sort is in the end merely selfishness wearing a good-conduct medal.

Teddy and I played dominoes while my father watched on and gave hints of an unhelpful character. A rat wandered in and washed itself distractedly, while keeping an eye on us like a blackmarketeer looking for a quick sale. The night was very silent so that one heard the least sound such as an orange falling in the garden.

At about ten there was a noise outside, low voices speaking Portuguese. We weren't in the habit of locking up, and the kitchen door opened and three policemen came in.

On occasion fathers – not merely my own – feel a compulsion to give advice to their sons. Since to speak of sex would be absurd, they counsel them about photography or motorcycles: metaphors for the larger issues. Pennyweight, I think, would have been very good at this. He had a metaphorical cast of mind and his theories, no matter how discredited, would remain true, if not in one sense then in another. My father's advice was to have nothing to do with the police. 'Emissaries of Satan, my boy. Emblems of his dominion over this world.' He hinted at unfortunate encounters in one of the many versions of his dark past.

Two of the policemen were spear-carriers in uniforms put together from odds and ends in the properties box. The third wore various grubby lanyards and epaulettes, but his rank escaped me. When he began to speak, I answered, *'Desculpe. Eu não falo português,'* apparently to no purpose.

My command of Portuguese was limited. Foreigners are uncomfortable with the elisions and nasalised vowels; their tongues twist around the sibilants. Teddy, however, had spoken the language since his childhood in Goa and I made it clear I wanted him to stay. My father, once satisfied that his own arrest was not presently the question, remained out of a fascination to view the forces of evil in action.

The officer lit a cigarette. I noticed he smoked *Players* and wondered how he came by them. I offered a drink. He accepted a glass of *poncha* and passed the bottle to his men.

'You are Senhor Michael Pinfold?' he asked. I admitted I was. 'You were a passenger on the *Kildonan Castle*?' I agreed to this also. The two minions chuckled as though a point had been scored in witty repartee. They helped themselves liberally to the *poncha*. The officer said, 'I wish to speak to you about one of your fellow passengers,' adding, 'an Englishman.'

For a moment I thought that Robinson in one of his many avatars had been resurrected. It occurred to me that I'd never interrogated my father on the subject. In an eventful life, he'd probably come across several Robinsons, each complete with a colourful history. Teddy and I had been drinking *poncha* over our game of dominoes and this might have accounted for my mood. I was playing with the Pennyweightian theory that there might be what German philosophers would call an *Ur*-Robinson: an archetype or racial memory of which we saw only examples. Or it might be that Robinson was an International Man of Mystery and that the many Robinsons were in fact one and the same.

'I don't know Robinson,' I said.

This puzzled my interrogator, who hadn't mentioned the name. He engaged in a sharp exchange with his men, which ended in shrugs.

'Who is Robinson?' he asked suspiciously.

I thought I might have put the same question to him.

'You know Robinson,' I said.

'I don't know Robinson,' he said.

'Yes, you do.'

'No. I don't.' He looked at me craftily. '*You* know Robinson.'

'Absolutely not,' I said. I was drunk, because suddenly I could speak Portuguese. We glared at each other.

At this point honour was even though we were at an impasse. I had a dim suspicion that we were off the true subject of the visit. My opponent, on the other hand, seemed to be coming round to the notion that there was here a new matter of greater importance that required to be investigated. Then I remembered Johnny and said, hinting at secret knowledge, 'Senhor João Cardozo has taken over the Robinson case.'

'Colonel Cardozo?'

'Yes,' I said.

It was enough to close the subject and we lit more cigarettes and Teddy tactfully opened a new bottle.

'Now I am bloody *ponchawallah*,' he whispered.

We all toasted each other, and the *poncha* must have been good because we digressed into the topic of international friendship. We concluded it was a Good Thing.

Matters being easier, I asked, 'Was there some particular reason you wanted to speak to me?'

The lieutenant (I must have picked up his rank) and I were speaking Portuguese with about the same level of proficiency. *Poncha* has that effect.

'Englishman – I have an Englishman,' he said. He gestured at me to follow.

We went outside where the night breathed jasmine and one could hear a faint ripple from the *levada*. There was starlight and a gibbous moon hung low. I'd given no thought to how the police had arrived. In the gloom, I glimpsed a covered hammock suspended from a pole. Two local men, who were in that line of business, had carried it. Sitting on a rock and smoking, their attitude, their straw hats and extravagant moustaches, gave them the appearance of members of a Gilbert and Sullivan chorus waiting to go on. The hammock was parked under a laurel and I might have missed it except that coming from it was a loud snoring.

'This is yours?' I asked in English.

'*Sim*,' answered my companion.

'There's someone inside.'

'*Sim. Um inglês.*'

'I suppose we should take a look at him?'

'*Sim*,' agreed the lieutenant.

He was wary and this may seem odd – certainly Pennyweight found it odd and slightly offensive when I told him the next day – and I can explain it only going back to a remark made by Fairbrother. There really was something *tremendous* about the ginger man, enough to shake ordinary mortals: for it was Pennyweight who was in the hammock, sprawled like a beached marine mammal, oblivious and stinking of rum. At the time, however, my reaction was of surprise and a vague horror. Pennyweight – here.

I assumed he had been unable to find his 'chum' (if he'd ever existed) and been arrested for drunkenness or vagrancy. And, no doubt to protect himself, he'd given my name as someone on the island who knew him. There was nothing wrong with this. If for no other reason than a sentimental regard for a soldier down on his luck, I'd have stood bail.

No, the horror was that, if things were as I imagined them, I might be stuck with him; and not for a day or a week but for the long stretch it would take to put him back on his feet.

It was a fine prospect: Pennyweight and Pinfold – pals forever.

'I suppose we'd better wake him,' I suggested.

The lieutenant was cautious. I wondered if Pennyweight had shown signs of violence, though that was unlikely from what I knew of his character. Also the two spear-carriers looked a pair of handy lads well capable of subduing an Englishman so obviously out of condition and worse for wear. Far more likely Pennyweight had been ebullient and talkative. He'd taken on a lot of drink: enough to speak Portuguese.

I asked, 'Has he been rattling on about Jesus and the Emperor Karl?'

The lieutenant looked at me with respect. The islanders are Catholic and inclined to superstition. I could see he might be disturbed by prophetic utterances, especially when angels were loitering in the neighbourhood of Paúl da Serra.

'There's nothing to his stories,' I said.

On practical grounds, we agreed to wake Pennyweight. I grabbed a handful of hairy suit and shook him. He mumbled and groaned a little and his face surfaced into such light as there was.

'Ish tha' you?' he enquired in a thick voice.

'That's right, old chap,' I said.

He fumbled in his pocket and took out some dentures. They were a strange set, articulated with springs, and I remembered my previous suspicions about patent luggage. After several efforts he managed to get them into his mouth.

'Can' see a bloody thing,' he muttered. Then, plaintively, 'Ish tha' really you? I thought you were...'

'Definitely,' I said. 'No one else.'

He felt for my arm and grasped it fervently. When he next spoke he had a catch in his voice and I felt a brief flush of tenderness for the poor devil. He said, 'Thank God! I've had a bugger of a day.'

'You're all right now.'

'No – no – let me say thanks. I ... I got to say thanks ... it wouldn' be right not to ... I ... You've been a brick, an absolute brick! ... I...'

I tried to calm him, but he insisted on repeating the same phrases. He was crying – drunken tears perhaps, but authentic: the tears of a million soldiers whose lives were more barren in peace than they had ever been in war, and whose twisted emotions were such that they could form attachments only to other men who had been through the same hell.

I knew then that I would be stuck with him and that there was nothing I could do about it. I told him again that he was all right and he was safe and I'd see to him. And he sobbed and clung to me, repeating his question: 'Is that really you?' and his assertion that I was a brick.

'Bless you, Robinson, old man!' he said.

TANGO IN MADEIRA – A Play in One Act

by George Bernard Shaw

SCENE ONE

A subtropical garden with a profusion of bougainvillea, bananas and a trellis hung with grapes. A table and four chairs occupy the centre. On the table is a gramophone. A view to the rear through the vegetation shows a path running left to right. To the left is a low gate. A gardener, a fit, pleasant man in his thirties, is on his knees among the plants. A stranger is at the gate. He is a youth of twenty and has the fresh-faced enthusiasm of the young. He carries a rucksack and wears a Jaeger suit with breeches and sandals and could be mistaken for a vegetarian on a walking holiday in Wales. He calls out to the gardener.

STRANGER: Hullo there! I say, you do speak English, don't you? My Portuguese isn't up to much. Excuse me. *[He fumbles in his pocket, produces a slender book, studies it and continues – very badly.]* 'O Senhor fala inglês?' Have I got that right?

GARDENER: *[pleasantly]* I don't know. It depends on what you intended to say.

STRANGER: I said, 'O Senhor…' *[frustrated]* Here, you'd better take a look. *[He shows the book to the Gardener and points.]*

GARDENER: This phrase?

STRANGER: Yes. Now, have I got it right? 'O Senhor…'

GARDENER: Forgive me. Those two letters – N and H – you pronounce them as N and Y? 'O Sen-*yor*'?

STRANGER: Yes. The fellow who wrote this phrase book is very clear about that.

GARDENER: Why not spell the sound with an N and a Y?

STRANGER: *[puzzled]* I see what you mean. It would make more sense, wouldn't it?

GARDENER: Do go on.

STRANGER: 'O Sen-*yor* fala inglês?'

GARDENER: *[taking the book]* May I look again? That final S in 'inglês' – you pronounced it with a shushing sound.

STRANGER: I did.

GARDENER: I suppose the same fellow was clear about that, too?

STRANGER: *[decidedly]* Yes, he was.

GARDENER: But the first S in 'Senhor': you pronounced it softly – like an S, in fact. Was that a mistake?

STRANGER: No.

GARDENER: But you are pronouncing the same letter in two different ways?

STRANGER: Well that's not my fault, is it? I didn't invent the beastly language. I don't know why Portuguese spelling isn't as straightforward as English. In any case, you have no grounds for complaint. It's your lingo, after all.

GARDENER: Mine? No, you are wrong. I can't speak Portuguese.

STRANGER: Oh! Well, that's going to make communication difficult if neither of us speaks Portuguese, isn't it?

GARDENER: We could try English.

STRANGER: What? *[enlightened]* Oh! Right! Well, it would have been easier if you'd come out with it and answered my question. I asked, 'O Senhor fala inglês?' which means, 'Do you speak English?' And you were supposed to answer, 'Sim', which means 'Yes'.

GARDENER: How do you spell that?

STRANGER: S – I – M.

GARDENER: There's an M at the end, is there? I didn't hear it. I thought I caught a nasalized vowel.

STRANGER: *[cross once more]* Let's not get into all that again.

GARDENER: No, as you say. Well? Can I help you?

STRANGER: *[recollecting his purpose]* I was wondering if you could give me some directions, and perhaps a glass of water. Madeira is a lovely island, isn't it? And it seems to have been entirely unaffected by the war. I was walking in these mountains and seem to have got myself slightly lost. Where am I?

GARDENER: *[opening the gate]* Do come in. This is the Quinta Gordon. As for water, I think we can do better than that. Tea perhaps?

STRANGER: Rather, that's awfully decent of you. You're very civil for a gardener. I suppose the master is out, eh? *[He looks about him.]* This is a very nice place. Who lives here?

GARDENER: *[indicating a chair]* Please take a seat. At present the house is being borrowed by the King of Transleithania.

STRANGER: The King! Gosh! I've heard of him. He was overthrown when the war ended, wasn't he? There was a revolution and all sorts of stuff. Hasn't he been exiled here? *[slyly]* I imagine he's a bit of a tyrant, isn't he? A beggar to work for? Go on, you can tell me.

GARDENER: *[offended]* He isn't in the least bit a tyrant.

STRANGER: *[disappointed]* Isn't he? I suppose you mean that he's kind to his servants. Tyrants are often kind to their servants. Politeness serves them in place of morality.

GARDENER: He is a very moral man – or so I believe.

STRANGER: Ha! If he's so moral, why didn't he bring the war to an end sooner?

GARDENER: *[thoughtfully]* Perhaps he tried and failed.

STRANGER: *[more heated]* Failed? How could he fail? He was Supreme Ruler and Commander-in-Chief of the army. He could have ordered a surrender.

GARDENER: You think he should have surrendered?

STRANGER: Certainly. He would have spared a lot of bloodshed.

GARDENER: I see. Let me ask: if it was so easy, then why did your King George not surrender?

STRANGER: *[astonished]* King George? Surrender? Why on earth would he do that? We were in the right, after all.

GARDENER: Most people in Transleithania thought that you were in the wrong.

STRANGER: You were wrong.

GARDNER: We were right.

STRANGER: Wrong!

GARDENER: Right!

STRANGER: *[outraged]* GREAT BRITAIN IS ALWAYS IN THE RIGHT!

GARDENER: *[mildly]* I beg to differ.

The STRANGER *puts up his fists and assumes a boxing posture.*

GARDENER: Why are you doing that? *[He moves evasively to the other side of the table.]*

STRANGER: You've insulted my country. I insist you withdraw your remarks.

GARDENER: You want me to surrender?

STRANGER: Yes.

GARDENER: No. You surrender.

STRANGER: Don't be absurd. I'm in the right. Come on, put up your fists.

GARDENER: Are Englishmen always so aggressive?

STRANGER: I am not being aggressive. You are the aggressor. I am merely defending my country's reputation.

GARDENER: *[as curious as foreigners always are when confronted with English notions of morality – which is to say that the explanation is as comprehensible as Portuguese]* Hypocrite.

STRANGER: Warmonger! Come on, fight like a gentleman. *[He makes a lunge across the table, which the GARDENER avoids with no effort to strike back. They circle the table, freely repeating 'Hypocrite' and 'Warmonger'. Finally the STRANGER ceases and lowers his fists. He addresses the GARDENER with offended dignity.]* You, sir, are a cad.

GARDENER: Am I? And what do you consider makes a gentleman?

STRANGER: Gentlemen, sir, will stand their ground in an argument and allow their brains to be beaten until one or other of them sees reason.

GARDENER: I... *[overwhelmingly perplexed]* No, you are right: I am obviously not a gentleman. I apologize.

STRANGER: Are you apologizing for not fighting or for insulting my country?

GARDENER: That too, if you wish.

STRANGER: *[mollified]* That's very decent of you.

A woman appears on the path at the rear of the garden. She has fair hair, is young and very beautiful. However she has had children, and her manner must suggest a wife, not a girl. She notices the two men.

WOMAN: *[cheerfully and affectionately]* Hullo, Charlie, I see you have a friend with you. I was making tea. Would you both like some?

CHARLIE: That would be most welcome, my love.

WOMAN: What is your friend's name?

STRANGER: Robinson.

CHARLIE: Mr Robinson and I were just discussing politics. He believes that *our master*, the King, is a tyrant and a warmonger. By the way, did you know that in Portuguese the letter S is sometimes pronounced S and sometimes isn't?

WOMAN: How odd.

CHARLIE: *[to ROBINSON]* For the sake of completeness, you ought to say that the King is a tyrant, warmonger and spelling reformer.

ROBINSON: I understand our own King George collects postage stamps.

CHARLIE: Really? What a strange lot these warmongers are.

WOMAN: I'll bring the tea. [*She blows a kiss at CHARLIE, who returns it. She exits along the path. CHARLIE'S gaze follows her until she is lost to view then returns to ROBINSON. The two men sit down.*]

CHARLIE: Do you not think my wife is beautiful?

ROBINSON: [*stiffly*] I couldn't possibly say.

CHARLIE: Why not?

ROBINSON: It isn't the done thing. One must never suggest to a fellow that one finds his wife beautiful.

CHARLIE: Could one mention the fact that she was ugly? Forgive my curiosity.

ROBINSON: No. One should pretend not to notice other men's wives at all.

CHARLIE: But what if she were in the same room? Serving tea for example?

ROBINSON: Well, one would acknowledge her presence, of course.

CHARLIE: So you would treat her like a servant?

ROBINSON: [*indignant at the thought*] No!

CHARLIE: Don't get angry. I don't want you attempting to hit me in self-defence again.

ROBINSON: There are subtle differences between how one would treat a wife and a servant. As a foreigner you mightn't detect them; but they're very important and make English home life what it is.

CHARLIE: I imagine they do. Are you married?

ROBINSON: No. Actually, I'm rather opposed to the thing in principle – marriage.

CHARLIE: Goodness! Do you mean you favour celibacy?

ROBINSON: Not that. I mean that I support free love. *[loftily]* I'm something of a radical.

CHARLIE: How fascinating! Do you practise it?

ROBINSON: *[embarrassed]* No. It's a point on which my fiancée and I disagree.

CHARLIE: I understand. She wants to get married.

ROBINSON: No, no – it's not that at all. She's also in favour of free love. She'd be willing to set up home with me tomorrow. However, although I'm all for the principle of the thing, I think the practice has to wait until the social conditions are right. *[dismayed]* Unfortunately the social conditions in Sevenoaks don't look like coming right – at least not in the foreseeable future.

CHARLIE: *[sympathetically]* I think I'm beginning to follow you. May I hazard a guess that you're a pacifist? – I'm speaking of the principle, of course.

ROBINSON: You do understand! Pacifism! It's the only sensible policy.

CHARLIE: Once the social conditions are right, eh? You know, I suspect I'm becoming a bit of a radical myself.

ROBINSON: *[energetically removing his rucksack]* If you're serious, I have some pamphlets. *[He takes several out of the bag, dropping them in his anxiety to make a new convert. He picks one up.]* This one you'll like: 'Public Sanitation and Social Revolution'. It's a corker! *[He passes it to CHARLIE who handles it as though it were a wet fish. He picks up another.]* This one is pretty good, too: 'Applying Socialism to the Wholesale Distribution Trade' – I don't like to blow my own trumpet, but some of my own work on the Blue Books went into that. This one…

CHARLIE: You don't happen to have one on spelling reform, do you?

ROBINSON: Isn't that what the King is interested in?

CHARLIE: Yes. I thought I would start him on radicalism, at first, in a small way. Begin with spelling reform, then gradually move to sanitation and wholesale distribution. I would leave free love and pacifism as a sort of grand finale.

ROBINSON: Isn't he a bit too set in his ways?

CHARLIE: Oh, I don't say it'll be easy. He is a tyrant and a warmonger after all. But once we've set the villain by the ears with schemes for municipally-owned gas works and a system of electric street lighting, I fancy he'll capitulate. There's no stopping progress. I'm getting quite enthusiastic at the project. By the way, would you repeat that phrase of Portuguese for me?

ROBINSON: *[examining CHARLIE cautiously before deciding there is no harm in the request]* 'O Senhor…'

CHARLIE: You can stop there. That first O – you pronounced it OO.

ROBINSON: *[suspiciously]* That's right. It's what's in the book. Look, are you challenging what the author has to say on the subject? Let me tell you, he's an expert on Portuguese.

CHARLIE: Is he Portuguese?

ROBINSON: His name is Pinfold, but I don't see what that has to do with anything.

CHARLIE: I was merely pointing out that he isn't consistent on the subject. The second O, the one in 'Senhor', you pronounced in the regular way – not like OO at all.

ROBINSON: *[becoming irate]* Are you going on about spelling reform again? You seem to have a bee in your bonnet about the subject.

CHARLIE: I'm sorry? 'Bee'? 'Bonnet'? I don't always understand your English idioms.

ROBINSON: Dash it all! Now you're challenging the way I speak my own language! You foreigners understand English well enough when you want something from us.

CHARLIE: Please, please, don't get excited. We don't want another outbreak of pacifism.

ROBINSON: You started it.

CHARLIE: No I didn't.

ROBINSON: Yes you did!

CHARLIE: No, I... *[he pauses]*. Forgive me. You're probably right. I keep forgetting that I'm supposed to surrender at the first opportunity.

ROBINSON: *[only partly satisfied]* You should stop going on about spelling reform. The subject is ridiculous. I'm beginning to think you're being satirical.

CHARLIE: I didn't intend to be. I thought I was being practical. How can we carry out a social revolution, if we can't effect even a simple reform like spelling? It'll help if you bear in mind your ultimate goal.

ROBINSON: Communism?

CHARLIE: I was thinking of free love in the streets of Sevenoaks.

CHARLIE's wife appears on the path bearing a tray with the usual accompaniments for tea. She maintains the same appearance of radiant happiness. CHARLIE stands up, takes the tray and places it on the table. He embraces his wife.

CHARLIE: Zoë, my darling!

ZOË: *[playfully]* Now, now, Charlie. You'll embarrass Mr Robinson.

CHARLIE: *[in a good humour]* Not at all. Mr Robinson is a radical. He wants to make love in public places. We've been discussing spelling reform and municipal gas works and vegetarianism.

ROBINSON: We didn't talk about vegetarianism.

CHARLIE: Didn't we? Oh, but you are a vegetarian, aren't you?

ROBINSON: *[impressed]* As it happens, I am. How on earth did you know?

CHARLIE: A lucky guess, I expect.

ZOË: *[passing ROBINSON a plate]* Well, you needn't worry about these sandwiches. They contain only cucumber.

ROBINSON accepts a sandwich. ZOË pours the tea. A soldier in a pale grey officer's uniform passes along the path. Seeing the little group, he gives a brief nod and continues his walk. ROBINSON appears disturbed.

ROBINSON: *[nervously]* Is that ... the King?

CHARLIE: The tyrant and warmonger – are you anxious to meet him?

ROBINSON: *[distracted]* And spelling reformer – you said he was a spelling reformer.

CHARLIE: So I did. That's probably where the tyranny and warmongering started. A man bold enough for spelling reform will clearly stop at nothing. Well, do you want to meet the King or not?

ZOË: Charlie, you shouldn't tease Mr Robinson.

ROBINSON: Yes, I should like to meet him.

The officer reappears, returning along the path. CHARLIE put two fingers to his lips and gives a costermonger's whistle.

CHARLIE: Oy! Come here!

The officer stands frozen, as if uncertain that he has been summoned.

ZOË: Charlie! Sometimes you have the most vulgar manners.

CHARLIE: Sorry, darling. I can't help it. I had an Irish nurse. I don't wish to disparage the Irish, but being brought up among them gives one an eccentric command of English. Mr Robinson, I'm sure, is very fond of the Irish. He hasn't said so, but I can tell he's an internationalist.

ROBINSON: Well…

CHARLIE: When social conditions are right, naturally.

ROBINSON: Oh yes! Yes, I think I'd consider myself an internationalist with that proviso.

The officer quits the path and approaches the table, where he stands stiffly though not at attention.

OFFICER: Zu Befehl.

ROBINSON: *[to CHARLIE]* What did he say?

CHARLIE: 'Zu Befehl'. It's German.

ROBINSON: How do you spell it?

CHARLIE: Z – U – B… *[enthusiastically]* Don't say you're acquiring an interest in spelling!

ZOË: *[sensibly]* You're becoming silly, Charlie. We have to satisfy Mr Robinson's curiosity about meeting the King.

CHARLIE: *[a little ashamed]* Absolutely right. I was forgetting myself. *[to the officer]* Hermann, our guest wishes to meet His Royal Highness, the King of Transleithania. Can you tell him where he'll find the tyrant and warmonger?

OFFICER: *[profoundly puzzled]* I don't understand, Sire? You are the King.

ROBINSON: *[leaping to his feet]* You! *[He begins searching furiously in his rucksack.]*

CHARLIE: *[a trifle smug, but also curious at ROBINSON's frantic rummaging]* So it seems.

ZOË: You ought to apologize to Mr Robinson.

ROBINSON: Apology be damned! *[He pulls a revolver from his rucksack, turns to face the others and assumes a heroic stance. He fires a shot into the air.]* Don't anybody move!

END OF SCENE ONE

CHAPTER SEVEN

The following morning I found Pennyweight taking the air by the *levada*. He was still wearing his hairy suit, shapeless at the best of times and today covered with nameless stains. Yet, despite that and his excesses of the previous day, he carried himself with a certain swagger which stemmed, I suppose, from an inner certainty. He was, whatever the world might think, Pennyweight *Triumphans*: sage, saint, hero; no word captures him entirely. I knew only that I found him on my hands and had no idea what I was going to do.

It was a curious aspect of my life that I wasn't a good man, but had somehow collected a crowd of dependants living on my meagre charity. My father was sunk in a depression lit only by flashes of old malice, Teddy was an innocent who knew nothing except to be my father's friend, my uncle-cousin-brother Senhor Pereira was a shop keeper too frightened to receive any customers, and now I had Pennyweight who trusted that an old chum, a perfect brick, wouldn't let him down.

'How are you feeling this morning?' I asked.

'Pretty chipper,' he answered.

'You were decidedly under the weather yesterday.'

'I'm not used to the food, old man. Must have eaten something that disagreed with me.' He was perfectly serious. His blue eyes were free of guile or embarrassment.

'Have you breakfasted?'

'A darky gave me some soup and cold rice pudding.'

'That would be *sambhar* and *idlis*. It's what Teddy normally cooks for breakfast. By the way, he wouldn't appreciate being called a darky. He considers himself a European. His names are Ignatius Francis Xavier Maria.'

'Then why do you call him Teddy?'

'I've absolutely no idea.'

'Maria's a woman's name,' Pennyweight said suspiciously.

'After the Blessed Virgin.'

'Ah.' A pause. 'Say no more. A left-footer, eh?'

We took a stroll along the *levada*. To our right the mountain fell away and, beyond Funchal, the sea was white in the morning sun. The dew had brought out the scent of mimosa. Drifts of agapanthus would soon be in flower. Pennyweight breathed deeply and paused to stretch his arms to the side, raise them above his head, then touch his toes. He didn't look like a man who took regular exercise and I assumed this little show was for my benefit. Although he was Pennyweight the Great, he had to be conscious of a degree of humiliation.

'This is a nice place you've got here,' he said. He looked about him as though comparing our *quinta* with his own vast ancestral estates. 'But it could do with taking in hand.'

I was annoyed at his tone of superiority. 'I'm trying to do that. Unfortunately we don't have any money.'

'Money – there's the rub, eh?' he said.

We stopped where any further progress along the *levada* would become dangerous, though Pennyweight suggested gamely that he would be prepared to go on. On the return walk, he remarked, 'I don't like to mention it, but, as I was pottering about earlier, I ran into a ghastly old poof in a nightie. He was flouncing around like a tart with a hangover. I cast no aspersions, but a fellow could get himself a name if he hangs around with Catholics and queers.'

'That was my father,' I said. 'And he's not queer.'

Not queer, I thought – but definitely odd.

*

Like Karl von Habsburg I inherited an Empire – in fact several Empires, one or two Alhambras, and the occasional Palace Theatre of Varieties.

My father was a third son. Uncle Percy was the heir, Uncle Gordon was granted the apanage of the properties in Madeira, and my father was offered a choice of the Army, the Church or the Indian Civil Service.

Accordingly he chose the Music Hall.

As a young man – this would be in the eighteen eighties – he had a pleasing light tenor voice and a slim, elegant carriage. He sang sentimental ballads with copious references to mothers and violets, and rousing celebrations of the Royal Navy. My birth probably owed a great deal to his ability to call forth tears from susceptible young women, and to the aristocratic manner that naturally goes with wearing a starched dickey and a tailcoat.

He gave up the singing profession before I was born. I don't know if it was the result of an amorous entanglement or a mellowing of his voice under the influence of cigars and whisky, the common downfall of juvenile singers. He became one half of Izzy & Mo ('The Jewish Jesters'), the other half being 'Uncle Harry', a dour man named Johnson, who haled from Birmingham. Neither, so far as I am aware, was Jewish. My father wore an orange bowler hat and a check suit in maroon and yellow and Uncle Harry sported something similar in pink and green. Their jokes, as I recall them, were directed at the Irish and the Scots. Why they were called Izzy & Mo remains in the realm of those mysteries so characteristic of my father's life.

The comic phase continued until he went on his Grand Tour. He was never the same man afterwards, and it's a pity the details are vague, but he brought back no photographs or souvenirs. I was ten years old and the decision to travel was taken suddenly. I remember only our landlady (we were in Newcastle) informing me in tears that he'd gone away and the rent was overdue.

My father was abroad for twelve months. He was in Peking during the Boxer Rebellion and on the North West Frontier entertaining the troops during an uprising. He also appeared in Moscow before the Czar, and amused the Kaiser in Berlin. My father always insisted that Uncle Harry had accompanied him. He denied my claim to have seen his partner on the boards in Glasgow under the name 'Jock Sporran' and to have received a shilling and a pat on the head. Harry, he said, had a twin. Certainly I never saw him after the Grand Tour. My father said he was captured by the Boxers and horribly murdered. Whatever the case, the Tour wasn't a financial success despite the appearances before the crowned heads of Europe and, at its conclusion, my father had neither money nor work. Only later at school did I suspect that his account wasn't wholly accurate. It was Lappin Senior (killed at Ypres) who pointed out that it was unlikely the Czar would take to Irish jokes told in English by a faux-Jew in a maroon and yellow suit.

Though there can be justifiable questions raised about my father's history, there can be none about his commitment to the Music Hall. This was proven by the aftermath of his brother's downfall.

My Uncle Gordon shared the family tendency to melancholia (inherited by Senhor Pereira perhaps, though the case isn't proven), and created a vacancy in Madeira by running away to join Kitchener in the Sudan, where he died of a fever. This was before the Grand Tour, which might have been avoided if my father had been willing to take up the post. Instead the business was put under a manager, whose thefts were partly the source of our problems.

The Great Alberto was a magician aged sixty or thereabouts. I used to meet him from time to time as we toured the country. He had severe tremors and a grey, careworn face which he disguised with vivid makeup, a habit my father acquired from him. I'm inclined to think he had Parkinson's disease, but his fellow-theatricals had a morbid fear of contagion and charitably attributed his frailty to excessive drink.

At this juncture – my father's impoverished return from his travels – the Great Alberto decided to give up the magic business. He wanted to join his sister in Sparkbrook and manage a public house, where his shaking and trembling wouldn't excite comment. He hadn't any children but he wished the act to continue under the same billing and was willing to train his successor. My father's given name was Albert.

There was, of course, a financial side to the transaction: a value to be placed on the training and the goodwill. My father approached Uncle Percy. It was apparently an acrimonious meeting, concluded only when my father informed my uncle that, unless the money were provided, he would have to go on another Grand Tour. Presumably the fate of Harry weighed on my uncle's mind. At all events my father became a magician.

He made a modest living at it for several years. For me, as an adolescent, there was even a certain cachet in having a relative who was a theatrical. But his outgoings were always greater than his income and he had to cover the difference with various expedients.

In my father's world it's a wise child that knows its own mother. I believe mine died in childbirth. I haven't the slightest recollection of her.

My father had a malicious sense of humour, but he wasn't a cruel man. Despite everything, his relations with Teddy were tender even when one of his insults had reduced the poor fellow to screaming at him in Malayalam and Portuguese. If he had led a regular life or been one of those widowers who are morosely contented with one

attempt at marriage, then I might have expected to be
brought up with pictures and mementos of my mother and
told stories about her. Unfortunately the itinerant life of
the music hall meant that we were forever moving and our
possessions were limited to the contents of a couple of
trunks. Everything that was not strictly practical was
abandoned.

My father never remarried (assuming he ever had been
married), but he was attractive to women and equally fond
of them. They came mostly from the theatre; those in
ordinary life leading settled existences incompatible with
his roving temperament.

Only theatricals understood him. I recall a dozen or so
who lived with us for a period and scores who appeared as
fleeting faces on the stairs – as common as Robinsons.

It wasn't that my father was a bad man – I have few
memories of quarrels – but his women had careers of their
own. At the end of a tour or a season their work would
take them to other theatres in other towns and there would
be a friendly parting. This meant tears perhaps, and a
promise to meet on another tour. But it was a promise that
could never be kept, for by then each party would have
another lover.

In this nomad life the memory of my mother became
lost. I suspect my father lost it, too. We lived in lodgings,
usually boarding in terraced houses at the cheaper end of
industrial towns. I recall damp patches on the ceilings, fog
leaking through draughty windows, the hiss of gas lights,
the pop made by the hob when it was lit to boil a kettle.
And scents: the inevitable cooking smells, the beds and
unwashed clothes, the evanescent perfume of whatever
woman had stayed the night, the stink of urine in the
chamber pot. The memories aren't unpleasurable. After a
late house at his most recent Empire, my father would
often come home with a whiff of whisky and cigars and

we would eat cockles from a paper bag while his damp overcoat steamed gently in front of the fire.

For economy's sake my father preferred to share lodgings with his various women. This allowed him to take two rooms so that I could have my own. I wasn't troubled by the presence of strangers, but, though I didn't realise it, it had an effect on my ability to capture the memory of my mother. For what other woman would wish to be reminded by a photograph that another had once been far dearer to the man she was with; or to overhear stories told to a child, which necessarily must emphasize the perfections of that dead parent?

These were not negligible women. Neither their feelings nor my father's were false for being finite. Often they maintained the illusion that this time was in some way different and that by luck and planning it would be possible to stay together forever. I knew because I could hear them. I could hear them even though they huddled and whispered over a table. They talked of sharing their lives, while in front of them were their only shared possessions: a large pork pie and a bottle of India Pale Ale.

From the age of seven I was sent away to a succession of schools, though I spent the vacations with my father. I believe he, rather than the family, met the cost. I say this because my schools were changed frequently, there was always a hint of unpaid bills, and sometimes I would start part way through term, coinciding with my father's receiving cash after a benefit performance.

My tenth year was spent out of school. My father had disappeared abruptly on his Grand Tour and forgotten to make any provision for my education.

Though that year was unusual in that my father was absent, some of its aspects are revealing. We were living with a fellow artiste at lodgings in Newcastle when the call came with a night time knock on the door and my father answered. Beryl was an assistant to an act involving large numbers of pigeons and dogs. At the time she seemed as surprised as I was and her reaction was to look at me and say, 'Now, what am I to do with you?' And the answer was that I followed her round the country for a year, shared her bed, fed the animals and made myself as useful as I could. She had a weakness for gin and Chinese sailors.

Beryl wasn't the most personable of my surrogate mothers. My presence was an obstacle to her nautical interests and our relations at times were frosty: she blaming my father for clearing off and leaving his brat. But the fact is that she took care of me and I never feared that she wouldn't. Of all the women, she was the one he came closest to marrying – for her loyalty as much as anything else. However, on his return, the demands of their respective lives asserted themselves. We went to Glasgow and she went to Rotherham. We pursued Imperial glory. She became a Mrs Chang and acquired an interest in a laundry.

I had no mother, nor any experience of men in a settled relationship with women. At the time it never occurred to me that things might be otherwise. Children assume that the patterns they perceive reflect universal patterns. Neither did school disabuse me. My fellow boarders were occasionally orphans; more commonly the sons of soldiers, planters and colonial civil servants who saw their parents infrequently and spoke of them distantly. Indeed by comparison, the peculiar characteristic of my relationship with my father was its intensity.

In nineteen eleven, my father made another approach asking for money to clear some pressing debts under threat yet again of a Grand Tour. By then my Uncle Percy had finally succumbed to the family weakness and gone melancholy-mad, leaving his affairs in the hands of trustees who were unwilling to relieve my father's difficulties except at a price and didn't care if he went on an impromptu Grand Tour. He was exiled to manage the family wine business. I went to Oxford and at last to Hell and Madeira.

At some point I became an inveterate thief, and I don't doubt that the causes both of this and the difficulties of my relations with Margaret lie somewhere in the present account, open to the theorizing of those who have theories about these things.

For my part I think I might have behaved better if I'd been able to translate self-knowledge into action. But of all dark arts, learning from experience is the most esoteric.

*

As we walked back to the house, I interrogated Pennyweight in more detail about his circumstances and how he'd come to be arrested.

'I didn't have a bed,' he admitted. 'The pal who was supposed to meet me off the boat didn't turn up. I went to Reid's with you and Fairbrother, rather hoping that one or other of you would lend a hand. Fairbrother gave me five bob.'

'He said it was five pounds.'

'No, no, five bob,' Pennyweight insisted. 'A little mean, I thought. Even a pound would have found me a room. Anyway, I hung around Reid's on the off-chance. I remember getting into a row with an idiot of an Irishman who had some very strange views about Elgar. The next thing was, I was shown the door. I've spent the last couple of nights under a palm tree in some park or other.'

'I thought I saw you in the Praça de Constituição the day before yesterday.'

'I wish you'd stopped me. I don't mind admitting I'd have appreciated a hand.'

'Go on.' I was curious whether he would, of his own volition, come to the matter of Robinson. Curious, too, about a point of resemblance between him and my father: a spirit of hopefulness that made even their sins forgivable.

Pennyweight had lost his defensive swagger. I was sad for his sense of shame.

'Look, old man,' he apologized. 'I know it looks bad, turning up like this in a strange country, without the lingo or a penny to my name, but the fact is I was relying on a definite promise from a pal. I mean a promise from a *pal* – you ought to be able to take that sort of thing to a bank, don't you think? I've been awfully let down.'

'I imagine you've had a rough time since the war,' I suggested.

Pennyweight nodded. 'I'm an engineer – did I tell you that? The trouble is I seem to have lost my concentration since I came home from the army. There're lots of fellows in the same boat – I mean I'm not complaining. And don't get me wrong: I'd do it all again, oh yes. Plucky Little Belgium – King and Country – let your scoffers say what they like, the words do mean something. A chap has to expect to be knocked about in life, and at least these are things worth being knocked about for.'

On this side of the house was a paved area with some orange bushes in tubs and a pair of rattan chairs and a table, all shabby like everything else. I invited Pennyweight to take a seat and said I'd ask Teddy to drum up some tea. When I returned from the kitchen, he was quietly taking a hydrangea flower apart.

'I tried the disabled dodge for a while,' he said.

'What's that?'

'Didn't you play that game? Lots of chaps did. I strapped my left arm up behind my back and sold pins and razor blades from a tray.' He grinned forlornly. 'I damn' near lost my arm for real – constriction to the blood flow, you know? Gas or blindness would have been better. I did that until I got thirty days for vagrancy – which between you and me was a blessing since it was December and perishing cold. I've a suspicion the magistrates are always ready to give His Majesty's soldiers a bed for Christmas.

The bobbies, too, can sometimes be relied on for a decent cell on a cold night. And the Salvation Army: they're all right except that there're a lot of mad people in their places.'

Pennyweight fell silent. I said nothing. I was moved by pity but also by surprise at his admission of petty dishonesty. Later I realised that Pennyweight was one of those who imagine others to be essentially as themselves: the difference being only that they are more or less successful. If I hadn't tried 'the disabled dodge', it was only because a stroke of luck had come my way which made it unnecessary. Of people who were conspicuously successful or honest, he commented that 'they probably have something going for them on the side'. As far as the present revelation was concerned, he would have been content, I think, with the usual facile expressions of sympathy; it was I who couldn't cope with their inadequacy. I don't know what his war record was like – he was a dodger and shirker, I suspect – but he possessed his share of bravery. Although he sometimes expressed resentment at 'the toffs' and 'the higher ups', this came from his half-baked social theories not from his experience in the war. The latter was for him always a matter of shining principle, an event in which pals like angels had granted him a revelation about the possibility of human selflessness. Was it any wonder that I wanted nothing to do with him?

My father had risen and come onto the terrace followed by a barefoot Teddy, bringing the tea. He was carrying a volume of Palgrave; it was his habit to prime his melancholia by reading the metaphysical poets. He saw the chairs were occupied, sighed and brought himself another.

I asked Pennyweight what else he had done when his friend had failed to meet him.

'I went to see the British Consul. If you ever find yourself in the same boat, I wouldn't recommend it. The fellow said he'd never heard of Robinson. Never heard of Robinson!'

'I used to know a Robinson,' said my father with a flicker of interest. 'He was a contortionist. If it's the same chap, he isn't beyond passing a dud cheque. Exactly the sort of fellow who wouldn't admit to his own name.'

'I told him I was a captain, even though I don't like to mention my rank,' Pennyweight continued indignantly. 'Apparently mere captains cut no ice in Madeira. They're too used to dealing with the nobs to take any notice of lowly folk.'

I asked how he'd come to know Robinson, and the response contained the unsettling implication which had troubled me ever since I first heard of him: namely that the dead man had been a stupendous giant who bestrode the world. It was simple perversity on the part of the Consul not to acknowledge him. Or possibly the machinations of Dark Forces. The details were somewhat lost in Pennyweight's enthusiasm. He told me he and Captain Robinson had been 'great chums'. Robinson was a parfait Christian knight, a hero in the vein of Rupert Brooke.

'And it was he who invited you here,' I asked.

'Yes. I got a letter from him.'

'From Funchal?'

'Casablanca.'

'Casablanca? That's in Morocco.'

'I know,' said Pennyweight, affronted at the suggestion that he mightn't. 'I looked it up. Interesting place. I shouldn't mind going there.'

'Never mind that. What did he want?'

'He offered me a job. Said he needed a stout heart to lend him a hand. Sent me a boat ticket and twenty-five pounds – knew he could count on me not just to run off with the money.'

'Did he tell you what the job was?'

'Not exactly,' Pennyweight said. 'He simply told me that it was up my street and he'd make it worth my while … five hundred pounds, to be precise.'

'Good Lord!'

'Just what I thought. So you'll understand, Pinfold, how it is that I turned up here with nothing but a few bob and the clothes I stood up in. I'm not a complete chump, you know.'

'Except that Robinson wasn't here to meet you.'

'I admit that was a bit of a blow,' Pennyweight said. He was sad and puzzled: shaken at the thought that his faith might have been misplaced, though I suspected his doubts wouldn't last. Given his *idée fixe* about the captain's character, as with the other exotic notions that comprised his mental furniture, the facts would be reinterpreted until they confirmed his prior beliefs.

I said, 'I wouldn't mention that you know Robinson to anyone else, if I were you.'

GEORGE BERNARD SHAW to THOMAS DEMETRIUS O'BOLGER (American biographer)

Reid's Palace Hotel

Funchal

24th March 1922

My dear O'Bolger,

You are the most persistent and impertinent fellow of my acquaintance, and I regret having anything to do with you. Your only excuse is that you get it from that old Peeler, your father – and that is feeble enough since I got precious little from mine. However, since fathers lie at the bottom of your concerns, I had better give you the history of Shaw *père*.

Your error is in the basis of your question. Like the paternal policeman you ask: 'When did you last beat your wife,' without first establishing that the lady in question was beaten at all. In the present case you assume that my father's life was ruined by my mother's association with Vandaleur Lee, and that, in consequence, he took to drink. Why do you insist on this point despite my attempts at correction? Do you have aspirations to writing tragedies? Melodramas? Am I to assume the role of Hamlet and avenge my father's ghost (a difficult proposition since Lee is under the sod)?

Let me be clear. My father was a committed teetotaller who was an inveterate drunkard. This was so before he married and was known to everyone except my mother, who was left to make the best of it. It was so before Vandaleur Lee ever came on the scene.

My mother was interested in music and a passionate singer. Lee was a conductor and singing teacher, who perfected the Method which allowed my mother to take up the same profession of teacher in due course and maintain her voice perfectly until an advanced age. That there was a sympathy between them must be admitted.

The *ménage à trois* was set up in Dublin on economic grounds. My father's business was declining. Lee's required premises which would allow him to make an impression on his customers. The sharing of a house that neither could individually afford answered the case.

In due course Lee went to London and set himself up in grand style in Park Lane where he enjoyed a period of success. Later he abandoned the Method and became a charlatan by persuading the daughters of the ignorant rich that he could make them sing like Patti after a few lessons at a guinea a time. My mother and sister also went to London, but they maintained a separate establishment and were financially independent of him. Once my mother discovered that Lee was an apostate to the Method, she cut him and had not seen him in a considerable time when he died of a brain disease. The circumstances of their estrangement should convince you that it was the musical connection that was the key to their relations.

Whether my father approved of Lee is by the by. His character and financial circumstances were not calculated to keep a wife by him, Lee or no Lee. You must not imagine any blazing hatred between them. In due course my father conquered his habit of drinking – at least, if he took a drop in his final years, it wasn't to the embarrassment of his family and friends.

Those in brief are the facts of the case. I shall write to you at greater length to explain them more circumstantially. I turn now to a more general point.

Your question stems from your particular prejudices concerning the nature of marriage. I do not care to argue the merits of the entire institution, but point out that a deviation from the conventional does not imply that one or other of the parties is exercising the rights of Sultan over a harem. Indeed, if the Sultan of Turkey were to live in Dublin, I suspect his harem would be a very quiet and respectable affair – the police and the neighbours wouldn't allow otherwise.

There is nothing inherently evil or destructive in a *ménage à trois* of a sentimental kind. Coleridge lived with the Gillmans; Herbert Spencer with the Potters. I don't say the condition is ideal or better than any other, but it seems possible within it to jog along in the usual way. A marriage is like an omnibus: once it is set on its route, the number of passengers scarcely matters provided that they do not attempt to drive. I have had sentimental relations with several married women and no one has been the worse for it.

Now you must decide how to proceed. Your publishers are exercising understandable caution in seeking my endorsement of your work, or my *imprimatur* at least. You do not have it and, without it, any lawyer will tell you that you will face difficulties in citing either my works or any of my correspondence. As to the latter, I don't begrudge you in the slightest. By all means sell my letters. They belong to you and will likely fetch more than your book. Remember, however, that the copyright belongs to me and they may not be published.

There! I have put the matter fairly. You must give up your wrong-headed approach or accept the consequences. I'm not concerned as to the interpretation you place upon my life. You may disparage my works and call me a blackguard for all I care. But you must get the facts right. I won't have them misrepresented for the sake of a splash in the Hearst press.

This letter has gone on too long. I must finish it and go to a tango lesson with a delightful young woman. I recommend the same to you.

faithfully

G. Bernard Shaw

CHAPTER EIGHT

I went to Reid's looking for Fairbrother. He was out on a tour of wineries and I left a message for him, phrasing it that he might want to cast an eye over my stocks but without indicating that I was in any hurry to sell.

Pennyweight accompanied me, playing the role of stout supporter, delivering a weighty nod every now and again. I'd suggested he stay up at the *quinta*, but, since we were chums, he felt he'd be letting me down if he didn't dog my footsteps. How I was to explain my grisly companion to Margaret was beyond me.

Outside the hotel I ran into old Sonny, looking very spry. He was packing a hamper into the roadster I'd seen the previous day. I asked how he was enjoying his stay on the island.

He said, 'It's a beautiful place,' and looked at me expectantly as if I were about to offer to sell him a souvenir. The Quinta Pinfold for example. The thought did cross my mind.

'We're off to Porto Moniz,' he explained. 'I thought we'd go by the Paúl da Serra. Would you recommend that?'

'There isn't a road,' I said. 'You might try to cross Encumeada over to the north coast, but I'd be careful to check the spare wheel and the battery. And take a fan belt just in case. It isn't easy.'

'But beautiful?'

'Certainly that. Angels seem to like it,' I added.

'Do they now?'

'There's been an apparition.'

'Has there? Ah – why do I doubt that? I suppose because visions are usually of the Virgin Mary. People in that way of thinking can't be doing with lesser minions. We're all socialists when it comes to dealing with the Divine and feel we're perfectly entitled to hobnob with the toffs.'

'You've had a small accident,' I said. I pointed out the damage to one mudguard.

'He's always smashing cars,' Sonny's jolly spouse answered.

'I'm afraid that's so,' said Sonny. 'The Spirit is modern and bang up to date, but the Flesh is a shaky old relic of the last century. By the way, Mr Pinfold, you haven't happened to find a wallet, have you?'

'No.'

'Only I lost one at Senhor Agnello's dancing studio. You don't think he's a thief, do you?'

'Hardly likely. Are you still dancing?'

'Oh, yes. I now have a perfectly formed notion of the tango. However, as with other theories, the putting into practice demands a Fabian approach. Fortunately I have a most attractive partner.'

'Maria?'

'No.'

'Then who?'

'Mrs Cardozo,' he said. 'I hope you won't take offence. I'm told her husband doesn't.'

*

As we walked away, Pennyweight enquired, 'Is it true they've seen an angel at … whatever the place is called?'

'Paúl da Serra. No, it isn't true. There are no angels, only peasants who drink too much *poncha*.'

'What's that?'

'A sort of rum cocktail.' It crossed my mind to ask him, 'Have you heard of a "Madeira Madman"?'

'A drink, isn't it? Fairbrother mentioned some such thing: Madeira, gin and other stuff.'

'He thinks it's about to take the world by storm.'

'Can't say. Cocktails aren't in my line, though there was a tipple we used to make up in the trenches: brandy and red wine, when we could get them. Ditto surgical spirit, the more the merrier. "Painful Death" we called it.'

'I can see you might.'

We reached the Rua da Imperatriz Dona Amelia. Pennyweight's hairy suit was a magnet for urchins, and several yellow pi-dogs, attracted by the savoury smell of *Players* were following us. I was thinking of a tactful way to raise the subject when he asked, 'This angel business – do you think it might have anything to do with the Emperor?'

I should have realized the danger of making observations of an unusual kind in Pennyweight's presence: his capacity for treating speculation as certainty; his ability to combine pieces of mental flotsam into ingenious synthesis. I repeated that there was no angel.

'The Watchtower crowd said that Christ was going to return in nineteen fourteen,' he said, as if this were a crucial consideration.

I pointed out that the Second Coming hadn't happened. Or, if it had, no one had noticed.

'That's true, but the war broke out, don't you see?'

'So?'

'God moves in mysterious ways,' he said. 'Perhaps the war was a Warning. Perhaps we've been granted a Last Chance. It doesn't do to pooh-pooh these things, old man. Those Bible fellows may not have got it absolutely right, but it's a pretty impressive effort.'

Mrs Christie was in the shop again. She said, 'You misled me, Mr Pinfold. You didn't tell me you were the owner.'

I asked how she had found out.

'I recalled your name. And this *is* the House of Pinfold. It was a simple matter of deduction. By the way, you should fire your man. He's skulking in the back room again.'

'Can I help you? I remember that last time you were looking at a small piece of basketware.'

'I checked what you said. There is a village – Camacha – where they make that sort of thing. My husband and I have decided to go there before coming to any decision.'

I was disappointed, but more on principle than at the loss of profit on one basket.

'I came to ask if you'd discovered any more about Mr Robinson,' said Mrs Christie.

'What makes you think I have – or that I'd be interested?'

'Because you live here.' It seemed this was a sufficient reason. 'His death is the talk of Funchal. And he was British. Unless he was masquerading, of course.' There was something engaging in her last words, and she added, 'I do love a good murder mystery, don't you?'

I asked if she had a theory.

'Oh, of course,' she said. 'It's as plain as a pikestaff. Robinson came here to kill the Emperor Karl. He was probably put up to it by the Jews.'

*

My own theory about Robinson was that he was a smuggler, most likely arranging consignments of hashish from Morocco. I wasn't certain what Pennyweight thought. I could see that Mrs Christie's notions that he might be an imposter or on a mission of world-shattering import would appeal to him.

When, on the morning of his arrival at the house, I told him that Robinson was dead, his reaction was stoical. He said, 'Poor Captain. Still, it comes to us all.' Then he remarked that he was still feeling peckish after breakfast.

I thought him heartless, but quickly realized that it wasn't that at all. In my random world, murder was a rare event: unexpected and shocking. Pennyweight's world, however, was far from random. Events were actuated by deep currents of meaning: patterns, plots and manifestations of the Occult. A man was as likely to be murdered as to pop off with a case of flu.

Pennyweight's eyes followed Mrs Christie to the door. 'An impressive woman, that one,' he said as though commenting on a lion with an uncertain temper. He rummaged in the pockets of his suit for an elusive packet of *Players*. Among a miscellany of garbage he turned out a grubby piece of paper. 'Oh ho!' he cried. 'I thought I'd lost this.'

I asked what it was.

'Personal matter,' he said, shifting to a cautious tone. When I pressed him, he admitted, 'It's Robinson's address. A bit of an embarrassment, losing it like that'

'You have Robinson's address?'

'Didn't I just say so?'

'Here in Madeira?'

'His address in London wouldn't be much good, would it, old man?'

'Why didn't you mention it before?'

'I'd lost it, hadn't I?' said Pennyweight. He unfolded the paper. 'Mind you, it wasn't much use when I did have it. I couldn't make myself clear to the locals.' It seems this had surprised him and he suspected trickery. He confided, 'They don't speak Portuguese, you know. They speak patois. The French speak patois, too. I'm surprised nobody teaches it.'

'May I see?'

Pennyweight handed me the paper reluctantly. Someone had written the name of a *pensão* in laundry marker. No street or number was given, but I surmised it was likely to be in the old town, somewhere beyond the Capela do Corpo Santo. It shouldn't be especially difficult to find, I said, and suggested we go there.

'I don't know about that, old man.'

'Why on earth not?'

Pennyweight looked at me uncomfortably. 'Sleeping dogs and all, eh? It crosses my mind that the Captain's business may not have been strictly in accordance with King's Regulations, if you take my meaning.'

I understood then that, having found what he no doubt considered 'a comfortable berth' with me, Pennyweight wasn't minded to risk it. He had probably taken to heart the old soldier's maxim 'Never volunteer for anything'. Despite his bias towards the esoteric, another level of his mind was severely practical. Robinson was dead, after all. I appealed to his sentimental side. 'Don't you think the family would like to know more?'

'Oh, well,' he conceded, 'I suppose we ought to do the decent thing by the Captain's people. There may be a photo for his old mother or something.'

I waited until evening and we had closed the shop. It was impossible to leave earlier because Senhor Pereira had encountered two strangers in the course of his day and was having a panic attack in the back room.

Meanwhile the rain, which had been hanging over the mountains, came on and I thought of Sonny's expedition to Paúl da Serra or Encumeada. My warning had been serious. Despite the smallness of the island, the mountains were remote and dangerous. The narrow roads had acute bends and startling precipices.

Rain brought down the temperature and sent the beggars and pi-dogs scurrying for shelter. In the slack hour the café proprietors lounged in their doorways, eying the street as if contemplating the taking of hostages. A carpenter was working in an alleyway by the light of a hurricane lamp.

'*Faz favor...*' I uttered the standard formula of my hesitant Portuguese. The carpenter gave me his slow attention. Piled around him were newly planed planks and the air smelled of wood chips and fish glue. The tableau reminded me of a Nativity scene: kings and angels, and now this.

'*Faz favor...*' Did he know the location of a certain *pensão*? I offered the piece of paper, knowing he couldn't read, and he accepted it as testament of my sincerity. Yes he did know the place. '*O Senhor...*' This is what you do, Mister – the 'Mister' a formula for which English has no equivalent. The carpenter's right arm, more muscled than his left, extended in vague indication. '*Obrigado*,' I said. Pennyweight tipped his hat.

'You seem to have a handle on this patois business,' he said.

The *pensão* was over a cheap restaurant in a ramshackle three storey house set among the fisherman's cottages near the old fortress of São Tiago. A girl was singing *fado* to an accompaniment of mandolin and guitar; a pi-dog was licking its hind quarters; a beggar was shaking a coin in a wooden cup.

Pennyweight sniffed. 'I can't see this place suiting Captain Robinson. He was always very particular.'

'Perhaps Robinson was down on his luck,' I suggested.

'Something smells good.'

'*Espetada* – grilled meat. You find it everywhere.'

'Your darky ought to cook it; it fairly gives a fellow an appetite. I suppose the Captain could have been down on his luck. We all have been lately haven't we, Pinfold?'

'What do you think he was doing in Morocco?'

'Search me. What does a chap do in a place like Morocco? They grow dates there, don't they?'

'Robinson was interested in dates?'

'I shouldn't think so. But he was there and I'm here, and nothing turns out quite as one expects, does it?'

This was another piece of Pennyweightian philosophy and as valueless as the rest. My father was a music hall magician and became a wine producer. Old Sonny was learning to tango. Life is unpredictable and most truths are trite.

Pennyweight put on another show of reluctance to see Robinson's lodgings, but I cajoled him. A table and a fat woman barred the stairs at a landing. The woman sucking on a fish bone and somewhere a child was bawling.

I went into my Portuguese routine. She growled a response in which I caught '*cinco*'. I asked for the key, but the key was out, or the room had no key, or she wouldn't give me the key: I can't say which; only that she allowed us to pass.

Pennyweight tipped his hat again and wiped his brow. 'Hot,' he said. The *pensão* was sandwiched between the heat of the sun and the restaurant: a layer of fat, still air.

Below, the girl was weeping over the *fado*. The child was still bawling and the pi-dog had stirred itself. It sneaked in hopefully, its feet tapping behind us along the boarded corridor. When we halted, it sniffed at Pennyweight's crotch and licked his hairy suit. The door of room five was unlocked.

What happened next is a little uncertain because it happened quickly. Someone was already in the room and he put me on the floor with a solid punch to the jaw. Pennyweight was at my heels and received the same. We went crashing down, but because of the suddenness there was no fear or panic. I heard a voice pray, 'I trust, Lord, that You're taking notice of the things I do for Your sake,' and then, 'Will you two boys get up off your arses and stop looking like a pair of blithering fools?'

A candle shone in my face.

'Why, it's Mr Pinfold,' said Father Flaherty. He offered me a hand.

'You hit me,' I said.

'I did,' agreed the priest.

'And Pennyweight, too.'

'So that's Mr Pennyweight? Good day to you, sir. Your friend Mr Fairbrother mentioned your name.'

'You're a rotten blackguard,' Pennyweight muttered.

'So I am,' Father Flaherty admitted. 'It's a handy thing to be in the priestly game. I owe you boys an apology. There you were, a couple of lads who'd spent four years battling the Germans, and me who'd been clearing the pubs of Dublin for half a lifetime. It was hardly a fair fight. Will you forgive me?'

I got to my feet, Father Flaherty showing no disposition to knock me down again. He shone the candle round the room, revealing bare plaster walls, an old bed, a curtained alcove for clothes and a battered dresser with a pitcher and basin for washing. A cut-throat razor and a set of brushes lay on the dresser; a woollen suit hung in the alcove; a pair of polished shoes was arranged neatly with the toes pointing under the bed.

Father Flaherty said, 'This is poor Robinson's room. I take it this is what you came to see? I was just going through his things to make up a parcel to send home to his mammy. I'm sure you had the same in mind; may the Lord bless you for it. Will you take a look, now that you're here?'

'Have you found much?'

'No. He wasn't a sentimental man and there's little of a personal nature. He had a sister named Lavinia.' He passed me a book, a volume of Byron. 'Her name is inscribed in the cover. No doubt she'd like it back. There's a Bible, too, one of those the army handed out. It seems well used, which must have been a comfort to him.'

'Any letters?'

'None. Then again, a man doesn't collect much correspondence when he's travelling.'

'You're making very free with the Captain's stuff,' Pennyweight interjected.

'Do you not think that someone has to?' the priest answered. 'Or had you in mind that the wee folk would do it? Sure it's a sad business, Mr Pennyweight, especially if you were a friend of his, which I take to be the case.'

The exercise now seemed pointless, but I performed it all the same: opened drawers, went through pockets; a matter of moments only. I found little, certainly nothing to explain Robinson's presence on the island or how he'd arrived, merely indications that like the rest of us he had found himself in straitened circumstances. The cuffs on his shirts had been trimmed with scissors; the heels of his socks had been darned. I asked Pennyweight, 'Was he a Catholic?'

'Not Robinson!' said Pennyweight as though I'd suggested he was a Hottentot.

'A man doesn't quibble about these things when he's about to meet his Maker,' said Father Flaherty. 'A dying sinner is a very broad-minded fellow when it comes to matters of religion.'

'You were with him?'

'Not at the very moment of the stabbing, but I gave him the last rites. He made a beautiful end.'

'I didn't see you.'

'Why should you have noticed? We hadn't met. I saw you, though. You were with Mr Cardozo.'

'You didn't mention the incident when we had dinner with Johnny.'

'As I recall, you didn't raise the subject yourself. Now, if you're satisfied, do you not think a drink would be in order?'

We left Robinson's room. The child still bawled. The hopeful dog still followed. The fat woman stood up and bowed her head and Flaherty gave her a blessing. The *fado* music still played and it was hot until we reached the street where the rain had stopped and a boot black had set out his box again.

Across the way a jumble of shadow marked a collapsed building. Perhaps it was a relic of the famous shelling by the German submarine; more likely the result of a kitchen fire or the shoddy work of a crooked builder. I'd seen whole villages smashed to pieces by war, but only the faintest memory stirred and it didn't trouble me. It was my indifference that disturbed. I felt that the absence of nightmares was, if not unhealthy, indecent at least; for the horror experienced by the survivors was a collective lament for the dead, and I had somehow broken ranks and deserted. Only a fool would pray for a portion of the miseries I'd seen in my fellow-soldiers. But a wise man would wonder at the price paid for his exemption.

We went into the restaurant. Two fishermen were hunched over a scrubbed table. The *fado* singing came from a gramophone. At the sight of a priest in his soutane, the fishermen half-rose then went back to their food.

'What'll you have, boys?' said Father Flaherty. We asked for beers and he muttered something to the waiter.

'You speak Portuguese?' I said.

'No, but a little Latin and a lot of bloody cheek will get you a long way. Now, how do you come to know poor Robinson?'

'I didn't know him.'

'But you did, Mr Pennyweight.'

'We were in the war together,' Pennyweight admitted. He added, 'I was a captain, though I make a point of not mentioning it.'

'There's a coincidence, then: both you and Robinson turning up here in the back of beyond.'

I wondered if Pennyweight would rise to this. On some issues he was evasive: on others, such as his peculiar views of the Emperor Karl, he was embarrassingly frank. Now that Robinson had died under mysterious circumstances, I could imagine his building that fact into the fabric of his theories. His reply was merely a knowing look.

The beer came, bottles of Coral, and the waiter pulled the cork. In the doorway two tarts paused to weigh their prospects and our friend the hopeful dog poked his nose in. For a moment a distant ship's horn overlaid the *fado*.

Father Flaherty took a sip of his beer and changed the subject. 'Your Mr Fairbrother proposed me an unusual drink.'

'A "Madeira Madman"?' I enquired.

'So it was. He set great store by it. This time next year we'll be drinking nothing else, it seems.'

'Did he make you one?'

'He did. It was … interesting: is that the term? Mr Fairbrother tells me he was also in the war – as indeed who wasn't? Did he know Captain Robinson?

'You seem remarkably interested in Robinson and his friends.'

Father Flaherty laughed. 'Is no one to take an interest in the poor man? Would that not be a terrible thing? You forget that I have a pastoral duty, Mr Pinfold. Now, your reasons, if I may say so, are much less clear.'

I said, 'The police didn't know where Robinson was staying.' I was guessing, but Johnny hadn't indicated otherwise.

'No? Possibly not, if you say so. But people will tell things to a priest that they wouldn't care to tell a policeman. I admit that I'm not so fond of them myself.'

'The police in Funchal aren't so bad,' I said, thinking of those who had brought Pennyweight home.

'Is that so?' Father Flaherty answered. 'Well, you should know. But my own thought on the subject is that somewhere in the heart of every police force there is a dark cellar, a little ante-chamber of Hell, where we shall meet the whips, the manacles and the rubber truncheons. The only difference between a civilised and an uncivilised country is the depth at which the cellar is buried.' He smiled sadly. 'Poor things, the police can't help it. It's in the nature of the beast, like Original Sin. But this is not a topic for a pleasant evening among friends.'

He glanced at the door, where the tarts, the bootblack, the beggar and the pi-dog were waiting for us. 'Do you suppose those girls have need of a priest?' He raised his glass. 'Drink up, boys, and let's pray for old soldiers. May the Lord grant them a revelation to lead them out of their darkness.'

GEORGE BERNARD SHAW to T. E. LAWRENCE
(author of Seven Pillars of Wisdom)

Reid's Palace Hotel

Funchal

26th March 1922

My dear Lawrence,

Are you a charlatan or a great man? That's the question I've been asking myself ever since Sydney Cockerell introduced us. Don't be offended. I'm not suggesting you are one of the petty confidence tricksters who prey on the elderly ladies of Brighton. No, the higher charlatan operates at the adventurous end of prophecy: supplying bogus evidence to support an authentic insight. Joseph Smith, the Mormon Messiah, humbugged everyone. But, for all that, I suspect he was a truly religious man.

What are we to do with you? Obviously you must publish your book, or the material to estimate your character will be incomplete. Without it, you are Lawrence: the pensioned-off soldier and nuisance to the authorities (notwithstanding the honours they try to give you). With it, you are 'Luruns Bey': the ... well, what exactly? That's the point, isn't it? Until the book is out, your experiences in Arabia will remain incoherent and frustrate you. Once it is done, you will be reborn; and I suspect it will be into something fearsome.

Now I'm an old hand at the prophecy game. I've been right about everything on all possible occasions, and much good it's done me. I could weigh in with hints as to how the thing is managed; but I doubt they would be of use to you. The essence is to find your own voice. The prophet cries in the wilderness. It would be a fine wilderness if he found himself in a crowd of know-alls with nothing to do but comment on his style like drama critics.

I suggest only that you stay away from newspaper work. You will simply gain a reputation as a pamphleteer. It is forgivable if you need the money: for the rest, the twopenny prophecies of the newspapers are forgotten by the next day. As a result of journalism, I have spent half my life penning explanations of what I wrote in the other half.

Now there are times when prophecy is in the air: when every chiliast foretells the end of the world. We are living in such a time. Empires lie smashed about us and we pick over the ruins. The tired old mythologies and the tired old nostrums are trotted out to explain and effect a cure. One finds them even here.

In the middle of this island lies a high moor, the Paúl da Serra. Only yesterday Charlotte and I went there in a hired de Dietrich (the going rate is several million escudos – or four pounds a day to you and me). Imagine a place five thousand feet up in the clouds, and roads as reliable as a policeman's testimony in a Fenian case, and there you have it.

Near a village called Serra de Agua we found ourselves halted. In front of us was a bullock cart, and on the cart a statue of the Virgin Mary, and round the cart a parcel of pious cutthroats being harangued by a priest.

Now I don't speak Portuguese, and the priest didn't speak English; and it took some negotiation before we agreed to misunderstand each other in French, which was a fine thing to attempt with the wind whistling round us, the mist about and a light rain falling.

'These,' says the priest, 'are humble shepherds,' introducing two of the cutthroats who have been scrubbed and polished for the nonce. 'They have seen an angel,' he tells us. The angel appeared in the sky at night; and, sure enough, there was a star. Beyond that he doesn't go. He recalls Joan of Arc and that visions of angels aren't always for the good in his line of work. The statue of the Virgin is removed from the bullock cart, and priest and cutthroats disappear singing into the mist. Somewhere out there, they hope to find their Heavenly King. And, like the rest of us, they are doomed to be for ever disappointed.

Wilde once said: 'Everyone is born a king, and most people die in exile.' I suspect this is true only of those who dare to claim the kingship. You may wish to consider it before you stake your own claim.

yours ever

G. Bernard Shaw

CHAPTER NINE

I didn't believe life had a plan, merely surprising outcomes like a series of card tricks. Pennyweight held the opposite opinion, and I wouldn't care to say which of us was right.

In the closed society of the island it was inevitable that I should have met Margaret, but to treat inevitability and purpose as the same thing seems to me a mistake. As for Pennyweight, I'm not convinced that ordinary cause and effect had much place in his universe. He set more store by serendipity: the fact that three old soldiers should find themselves on a boat bound for Madeira. To me it was a meaningless coincidence and events might have turned out otherwise. But, in Pennyweight's eyes, a Higher Power had ordained the binding together of our fortunes.

If, as was always more likely, I'd first run into Margaret at one of the affairs organised by the British Wives at the Quinta Magnólia, I doubt much would have come of it. My face would have been one of those whose memory we sacrifice for the sake of simplicity. Instead, we met at Reid's and it fell out that for a few minutes we were alone, and that I stole her powder compact.

A week or so later there was a gathering at the British Club. It was December and showers confined us to the building where Arthur Mainwaring, dressed as Santa Claus, handed out presents to children while their red-faced fathers swigged whisky and their mothers sipped cocktails and there was a little dancing to a gramophone.

'Do you think Mr Mainwaring is drunk?' Mrs Talbot asked me.

'I believe he's trying to be jolly. It's rather expected.'

'He doesn't look jolly in the least. He's far too thin for the part, too short, and he has dark skin. Father Christmas doesn't have dark skin. I wanted Harold to take the part. My husband is awfully jolly unless he's talking about medicine. But Arthur Mainwaring is pushy when it comes to mingling with the genuine English. Have you seen his wife?'

Margaret found me by a window looking onto the drenched gardens.

She remarked, 'You stole my powder compact,' and laughed. 'I can't believe you had the cheek.'

'I'll give it back to you,' I said.

'Poof! As if it mattered. It's a cheap thing, a piece of faux Fabergé Johnny picked up in Paris. He tries very hard, the darling, but he doesn't have a very good eye except for his pots. You, I imagine, have a very good eye, if you're in the thieving business. So why did you do it?'

'I steal things. It's a habit.'

'Have you seen an alienist about it?'

'No.'

'You should. Since you evidently didn't take it for money, there must have been another reason.' She smiled. 'Were you trying to make a pass at me?'

'I don't think so.'

'Are you sure? You were fairly bound to be caught. If I'd merely lost the thing, the staff at Reid's would have certainly handed it in. The only other people who might have stolen it were the British Wives. And I know that none of them did – not because they're especially honest, but because, if that sort of thing were going on, it'd be talked about. That left only you.' She put her hand to her face and peeked through the fingers. 'Oh, don't say you're one of those stupid criminals who clutter up the police courts. That would be so disappointing.'

'Even more disappointing for me.'

We exchanged cigarettes. Hers were a Turkish blend. She continued a conversation begun that first afternoon at Reid's: about the life she and Johnny Cardozo had led as diplomatic spouses in London: the unwelcome posting to Madeira. At that date, I hadn't met the husband but gained an impression of him as one does in certain clever novels in which characters are talked about but never encountered: that is to say that he was particularly vivid without the ambiguities that cloud observation. I don't mean I understood everything. For example it wasn't clear to me that Margaret loved him. But that isn't so surprising: most women tolerate their husbands and are only occasionally put on their mettle to decide if they love them.

'He's here today,' Margaret said.

She pointed out a svelte Portuguese, who was talking to Rutherford, the manager of the shipping line. He was like his wife in one respect: the air of metropolitan chic, which contrasted rather unfortunately with the faintly seedy colonial manner of the other guests. I could imagine their being admired, but never liked. Mrs Talbot had hinted as much. 'Her dress is Poiret,' she said. The point was so subtle I might have missed it.

'Johnny, may I introduce Michael Pinfold?'

A firm handshake. A glittering smile. 'Michael –' emphasized warmly '– I'm so glad to meet you at last. House of Pinfold, isn't it?' A hand was laid affectionately on Margaret's. 'Darling, I have to go. The Governor expects me at the Quinta Vigia. Michael, why don't you come for dinner with us? I'll send you an invitation.'

'*Até breve.*'

'You speak Portuguese? Wonderful!'

He left, and Margaret's eyes followed him. I counted the beats to see if they parted casually. After a long glance, she returned to me with a smile and we continued our discussion of London society, a subject about which I knew nothing; but this is immaterial to a thief and magician.

Outside the rain dripped from the orange beaks of the strelizias and the scarlet poinsettias. Inside a round of carols had ceased and the gramophone resumed.

'Do you dance?' Margaret asked.

'After a fashion.'

'You mean you dance very well. Men who don't are always very emphatic on the point. They say they have two left feet. Always the same expression "two left feet" – now, why do you think that is?'

'I've no idea.'

We took a turn about the floor.

Mrs Cardozo said, 'We've talked about me. That was very forbearing of you. Most men assume that women can't wait to hear about them. But you aren't like them – Michael, isn't it? For one thing, you don't have two left feet. Do you suppose that it's always the same pair of feet – that they pass them around? That would be just the sort of thing men would do.'

'Yes,' I said. 'It's the same pair of feet.'

'Oh? Then why don't you have them?'

'I can't afford the club subscription.'

She laughed at the only joke I ever made to her then asked, 'Well, what about you? I suppose you're an ex-soldier: everyone is.'

I agreed I was.

'What a beastly business. England should have followed the Madeiran system.'

'What's that?'

'Haven't you heard of their famous Submarine Fleet of Terrestrial Navigation?'

'No.'

'It was quite the most splendid affair, beautifully dressed and drilled and awfully chic. When the King, Don Carlos, visited the island and saw his submariners parading in front of him, he pronounced that they were quite the smartest sailors in the Portuguese Navy.'

'That must have been very pleasant for them.'

'Oh, it was. Except for two embarrassing details. Firstly, they didn't have any submarines: in fact absolutely no ships – they were, after all, a *terrestrial* fleet. And, secondly, they weren't actually a part of the Navy: just a troop of jolly young men who liked to dress up and march about.'

'I see. And what happened?'

'The King thought they were making fun of him and ordered the unit to be disbanded. There was also a Torpedo Fleet of Terrestrial Navigation,' she added. 'Naturally they had no torpedoes.'

'Does this story have a point?' I asked.

'None at all. I'm merely making polite noises. Civilised people do.'

We reached one of those moments when conversation ceases not because it is exhausted but because words have stripped the subject like a fleshing knife to reveal its emptiness. Margaret said of the singing infants, 'Aren't children abominable?'

I hadn't asked if she had any. When I did, she answered, 'Good God, no!' and as an afterthought asked, 'Do you?'

'Not that I know of. I'm not married.'

'*Not that I know of*,' she repeated. 'What a telling remark. Like the vulgar humour of a travelling salesman.'

'I'm sorry.'

'It doesn't matter. I never expected anything better,' she said. Then, 'I can't stand these children. I must get out of here or be sick. Has Freddie Rutherford ever given you the tour of the Club?'

'No. Is there anything to see?'

'Not really. Some famous signatures in the visitors' book and a framed menu celebrating the Relief of Mafeking. I'm feeling faint; will you take me out of here? No one will notice, or care if you do.'

We slipped out of the door into a corridor past servants bearing trays of canapés. Margaret led me by the hand to an airy upper floor bathed in low daylight and another corridor of framed sepia photographs.

'What's up here?' I asked.

'Bedrooms for visiting members and fainting ladies. What did you expect?' She knocked on a door, got no response and tried the handle. 'Do you have your pick locks handy?'

'I'm a thief, not a burglar.'

Despite appearances, I wasn't certain where this exchange was leading. She had lost her animation. My first thought was that she'd been drinking and this was a mood swing which would lead to regrets. My second, which I reviewed with the detachment granted by a stiff whisky, was that such situations led to false accusations of indecent advances.

I thought her face looked a little heat-worn even in this season and that the island wasn't kind to her. I imagined vague causes of distress, more from curiosity than sympathy. She removed a Kirby grip from her blond hair and gave it to me. I allowed her a moment to reflect, then opened the door. I asked, 'Are you sure about this?'

'You're the one who made a pass at me,' she said, which was scarcely an answer, but she went into the room and stood dim in the shuttered shadows, facing me, her arms straight by her sides. I mention this last point because I hold the picture very clearly: its peculiar innocence: its veiled accusation. And I would have stopped except that she said, 'You are a cad, aren't you?'

And, of course, I am.

*

Four months later we lay in the bed in Signor Agnello's back room, picking hairs out of the sheets.

'This one is grey,' Margaret remarked. 'I always said Maria was older than you supposed. Another woman can tell.'

'I think my exile is coming to an end soon,' I told her. 'In the next few days I hope to sell my wine stocks to Ronnie Fairbrother.'

'What about the rest of your property?'

'We had to get rid of the vineyards and the winery. The shop is leased; I can let it lapse. The *quinta* and everything else can go to ruin: it really doesn't matter since only the land is valuable. I'm trying to find a tenant until I can sell it. My aim is simply to get in whatever cash there is to be had, and to stop useless expenditure. An agent can handle the rest.'

And my father, Teddy and Senhor Pereira? In the face of insoluble problems, one arms oneself with indifference. The poor are always with us; yet we still sleep quietly. If we feel the occasional moral panic or fit of benevolence, they merely keep our consciences in trim.

'Will you come back to England with me?' I asked.

'And leave Johnny?'

Her question supplied the answer. Never once had she criticised Johnny or said directly that she didn't love him. I didn't seek to argue the point; no more than the thief can argue he owns the goods, however intense his desire. There was nothing to say that was new: that Margaret didn't understand for herself. *With me, darling, everything will be different.* I might put that case, maintaining it with every shabby pretence and piece of self-deception and even win her agreement for a day. But I doubt I should have accomplished anything more than a piece of moral bullying.

Margaret sat on the edge of her bed, putting on her stockings. The shutters were closed but sunlight filtered through a broken louvre. I noticed her skin was the colour of rain clouds, the blues and pinks of a failing day; and I was reminded of a Dégas sketch I acquired in Paris at the end of the war. Acquired in the usual manner, and lost in the same old way.

'Will you light me a cigarette?' she asked. Love-making made her tender. I took a cigarette from my case, the one with the bullet mark. 'I suppose you stole that, too?' she said.

'From a doctor called Crispin. He's a card sharper.'

'Is it wrong to steal from a thief?' she asked with a small flash of anguish.

'Probably not. Are you stealing from me?'

Apparently my question amused her. Women have a wry view of men (no more exact term springs to mind). 'Oh, you must answer that for yourself,' she said.

We dressed and went into the studio. Senhor Agnello was taking a nervous girl through some basic steps. She had come with an older woman – mother or aunt, no doubt – and was very pretty. I could see that her tango would be as respectable as folk dancing; as physically intimate as pushing a perambulator. I felt a little sad for her.

Margaret asked, 'Shall we? But try to keep it decent – *pour les enfants.*' She nodded in the direction of the girl who, dressed in white, glowed as a gold apparition in the light breaking through the fly screen. 'By the way, thank you for offering to make an honest woman of me, if being a *divorcée* can be called honest. You were intending to marry me, weren't you?'

'Yes.'

'And endow me with all your worldly debts? What a lovely, old-fashioned man you are sometimes.'

Maintaining the proprieties, we did a circuit of the floor. I said, 'I understand you've become old Sonny's partner. What's he like?'

'He can't dance for toffee, and he's an outrageous flirt.'

'Anything else?'

'He talks a great deal. That's what makes him so attractive.'

'Sonny?'

'You wouldn't understand. You're not a talker. You have no notion of the seductive power of words.'

'Where does that leave me? You make me sound like a prostitute.'

'I understand prostitutes talk a great deal. It's so much more pleasant than – the other thing.'

The music stopped. Margaret gave a polite clap, a reflexive memory of debutante balls. Girl and aunt looked at each other puzzled, then clapped as well, supposing it was part of the ritual of the tango.

'I must go,' Margaret said.

'Fine. I've got an appointment to see Ronnie Fairbrother.'

'What a poor, scared rabbit he is. Give him my love all the same.'

'I'll do that,' I said. I watched her gather her bag from one of the wicker chairs. She took out a powder compact and examined her face in the mirror. 'You have a new one,' I said. I took the piece of faux Fabergé from my pocket and offered it. 'I've been meaning to give this back to you.'

Margaret looked at it, then at me. 'Sometimes you can be perplexingly honourable,' she said.

She took the compact and placed it in her bag. She kissed me on the cheek. I felt her lips linger on the lobe of my ear.

'Do you love me –' I asked '- or hate me?' It's strange how these fundamental questions raise themselves at odd moments, and how dull they sound once spoken.

'Yes, I probably do,' Margaret answered.

She raised a hand and stroked me gently across the temple.

She said, 'Do you think you could be like Sonny? He's so amusing.'

SONNY to ZOË

Reid's Palace Hotel

25th March 1922

My dear Zoë,

There is no risk in telling a man you love him. 'Love' is a commonplace word, popularly understood in these situations as a mild affection. What you must never say is that you find him 'interesting'; for, having a high estimation of himself, he will believe you and fall hook, line and sinker. What is worse: he will assume his 'interesting condition' to be a permanent state of affairs, seek to engage you in his lightest remark, and end by boring you stiff.

I, of course, am immune from the latter vice, having been declared 'interesting' by common acclaim, so that one more endorsement – even by a fascinating female – adds but a mite to the general heap. On the other hand, if you tell me you love me, I shall believe you implicitly and be as happy as a puppy dog. The truth is that your Sonny is a poor, timid thing. It is only on paper and in imagination that I do anything brave.

And in the tango. You have made a hero of me. Admittedly you are aided by the conventions of dance which allow me to stomp and trumpet my adoration without being obliged to come to the point. Then again, if your parfait gentil knight were to try his hand in the lists at his age, he would only come off his horse.

That's enough for a short note. In any case, I don't think I've got to the bottom of this tango business: the light and shade: the come hither and go thither. Oh, there's love there all right: and of a teasing kind, too: enough to unsettle a staid old fellow and fool him into thinking he's a thing of glory. But the sly venom of it! The oxymoron in motion!

Good night! My head is stuck in a bucket of cold water. I am baying to the moon.

yours ever

Sonny

GEORGE BERNARD SHAW to MRS PATRICK CAMPBELL (Actress)

Reid's Palace Hotel

Funchal

Madeira

25th March 1922

Stella, Stella

I have advised you, pleaded with you and ranted at you. If nothing else serves my turn, what am I to do? Poison you, I suppose. You will – yes, absolutely *will* insist on carrying on like a shopgirl: announcing our amours for the benefit of travellers on every passing omnibus: exposing my declarations of love (now as pathetically dead as one of Dickens' orphans) to those who will say no more than, 'Oh my! Don't the old geezer go on so? And 'er no better than she should be, as should 'ave knowed.'

Belovedest, we are becoming ridiculous.

Those damned letters! Why did I ever write them? Why am I writing this one? I can excuse myself that I had no notion I was corresponding with a low character who would sell them to earn a few shillings for the gas meter (stick your head in the oven – do!); but that still doesn't explain why I committed my feelings to paper. Yet lovers do, don't they? Especially the timid sort who would be overwhelmed by fleshly endearments. Oh, how beautifully innocent we were, for all our wordy passions!

Evidently I misread your side of our exchanges. I'm a sly old dog and have got by for years, deceiving the public by writing with such entire sincerity that no one has believed me. But pish! I am a mere novice compared with my darlingest Stellissima whose words spun such threads that they yanked the heart out of me, while I didn't for a moment suspect the falsity of it all.

Clearly I don't understand English. I shall give up the theatre and write advertising copy for patent medicines or book jackets for publishers.

Stella, Stella! Don't you see how bitter your folly makes me? How angry I become with her who was my beloved above all beloveds? How the past becomes spoiled? For you did love me (and you only make me doubt you by assuring me that you still love me even though you want to print my letters)! And I loved – do love – you as far as this bloodless writing-machine can be said to love anything save its own conceits.

I still offer you a compromise. By all means write your book. Let the public read our letters. Only first let me see them and advise you in the selection and editing. There is enough of wit, amusement and gossip in them that we do not have to spill our hearts' blood. You may do as you wish with your husband, but I have Charlotte to consider who was distressed enough when the business between us came out all those years ago. Is it not callous on your part to put her through the mill a second time?

Ah, but there is money to consider! My Stella has to eat, and must satisfy the needs of her friends, and has always ignored the advice of the sage political-economist who told her most sternly that she must put some loot aside in a sock under the bed. It comes down to it, does it not, that I wrote my letters not for my heart's delight but for the benefit of the bailiffs? Well so be it.

I am working on a play – the saddest, littlest thing of one act, three scenes, four characters, no costumes or sets to speak of, but with enough of meretricious Shavian wit to pack them into the cheap seats. And you shall have it; for it has a part designed for Stella: a woman – I call her Zoë in homage to my beloved's Life Force – of a certain age and with all the beguiling maturity that entails, and who shines against the men (perfect idiots, the lot of them!). And she dances – just as my Stella dances! – just has she has led me a dance! You shall do the tango. You shall do it in an agony and frenzy such as have never been seen before. The Argentinian ambassador will fall into a swoon. The Lord Chamberlain will eat his pencil.

Say that you will do it, and forget this damnable affair of my letters. Oh, Stella, Stella, Stella!

GBS

GEORGE BERNARD SHAW to G. K. CHESTERTON (Author)

Ayot St Lawrence. Welwyn

21st May 1922

My dear G.K.C.

Well, that's it! The cat is out of the bag (it is a measure of my distress that I can't think of a better cliché). Mrs Patrick Campbell has published our correspondence and, as I foretold, we are both damned for it. I had time to prepare myself when extracts appeared in the *New York Herald* before turning up in *The Queen*. Still I have been made to look a complete fool and Max Beerbohm's cartoons are deft in giving me the appearance of the front end of a pantomime horse and Mrs Pat the air of Widow Twanky. Let this be a warning to those who have relations with married women – even of a technically innocent character. Be sure to get your solicitors early on the case. Let your first letter be a contract.

Not, of course, that there was ever a question of setting the law on Mrs Pat. The French, I understand, have a statute to cover the situation, but we do not – they, being more inclined to illicit liaisons, have the foresight to protect themselves against indelicate revelations. There was of course a matter of copyright: I might have prevented publication of my side of the exchange. But to what end? Mrs Pat could still have disclosed her own letters, and my silence would only have led people to suppose that I had something shameful to hide. And, in any case, she was so sorely in need of the money. Whenever she has had any, she has been generous and imprudent and if it weren't for the income from this episode, she would have been reduced to working a beat in Jermyn Street (or so she tells it).

I did offer to help. During my recent sojourn in Madeira I knocked together from bits and bobs in the dusty attic of Shavianism, a slight piece that would have brought in the sixpences and which had a perfect role for her. In the end, however, it came to nothing. The subject was the Emperor Karl, late of Austria-Hungary, and, when the poor young fellow died, the heart rather went out of me. I don't know why, because in the ordinary way you may hang emperors and I shan't care fiddlesticks. I can only explain my dismay by thinking that his was a special case of the destruction and disillusionment accomplished by the war; and, since the convention is that the fate of kings is the stuff of tragedy, so Karl became the exemplar of all those ragged-trousered old soldiers who have been exiled from what is pleased to call itself the civilized world. I have met enough of them. Indeed I came across several cases in Funchal.

To return to *l'affaire Mme Patrick Campbell*, I cannot in truth regret my letters. If people are to be trapped in marriage beyond its useful life, one must expect that emotions will seek an outlet in relations of a sentimental character. My mother had such relations with Vandaleur Lee, her singing master, though there was never any question of sexual impropriety between them. It is true that my father did not like this alienation of his wife's affections, but that is by the by. Assuming for the moment that Vandaleur Lee had never existed, my father's distress would have differed only in matters of detail, since he and my mother were long out of sympathy. I try to explain this to Demetrius O'Bolger, my American biographer, but he will have none of it. He wants to turn my family history into a melodrama and make out that my emotional life has been damaged by Vandaleur Lee's example. I deny this.

If, as I say is quite natural, one finds that marriage will not serve one's emotional needs over the long haul; and if, living in the world as it stands, one does not wish to cause a scandal, then a decorous connection with a married woman has advantages over one with a spinster. The very fact of marriage sets bounds. Man and woman, from their respective dugouts, may bombard the opposing lines with posies of words and cause little harm.

Before Mrs Pat, I had a most affectionate friendship with Ellen Terry, which injured neither of us. During my recent excursion to Funchal, I formed a tender regard for a young married lady, who, with Mrs Pat, became the model for Zoë (the heroine of my late but scarcely lamented play). She perfectly understood the conventions of our relationship. Indeed she was otherwise experimenting in the same vein. She was married to a villain and in love with a bounder. Unfortunately she had that optimism, common to women, that she could take this pair and make something worthwhile of them. Instead she found herself in possession of two dilapidated properties and, despite her aspiration to be an urban improver, became merely a slum landlord.

Before I finish, may I ask if you know anything of the tango? It came to my attention in Madeira and impressed upon me its almost sacramental character. The notion may strike you as blasphemous (though only out of Catholic habit), but if Jesus had danced the tango rather than breaking bread, the act would have been more truly expressive of his passion. In such a case your priests would now execute the *corte* in front of the altar and Bach would have composed for the bandoneon. Only hallowed custom makes this alternative seem absurd. Didn't the Apostle John sanctify foot washing rather than the Mass?

I have gone on too long and must catch the post. I excuse myself by saying that I do not understand and then write:

rather I write in order to understand. I imagine you find much the same thing.

ever

G.B.S.

CHAPTER TEN

I found Fairbrother in the garden at Reid's. A crowd of tennis players and sunbathers was engaged in horseplay; and, sitting under a palm tree with a book in front of him, he looked lost and lonely so that I felt again that sense of discomfort: the desire to be elsewhere.

I don't know why Fairbrother evoked this response in everyone. When one ignored some small nervous tics, he was a perfectly presentable man, even good-looking. His manner was always friendly, though a little uncertain.

'Hullo, Pinfold,' he said. He stood up and we shook hands formally. He called a waiter over and indicated his drink. '*Para o meu amigo.*'

'Are you learning Portuguese?' I asked.

'I have a phrase book.'

'All the same, I'm impressed.'

He was pleased but embarrassed at the compliment. I imagine it was something he wasn't used to. I saw him at school: his modest successes greeted with the gruff acknowledgement granted to a plodder while more attractive scoundrels were praised for achieving anything at all. His hesitations and ineptness made his conversation sometimes seem shyly flirtatious.

'I've ordered the same as I'm drinking,' he said. 'It's a bit of a surprise.'

'A Madeira Madman?'

'Oh ... you've heard of it.'

'Pennyweight mentioned something.' I could see he was a little crestfallen and added with a show of enthusiasm, 'I've been looking forward to having one. But no-one seems to know the recipe.'

'It's a secret.'

'I'm sure it'll be worth it.'

That subject disposed of, we looked around the garden for another. Beyond the hibiscus and a stand of bamboo the view gave on to the sea and the Ilhas Desertas lying in the milk of a faint horizon. The tennis players and sunbathers were having a boisterous time. When a ball came in our direction, Fairbrother stared at it as if it were a threat. I kicked it back and got a smile from Miss Torbitt-Bayley, a smile which Fairbrother might have earned if he'd had the wit and confidence.

'Speaking of Pennyweight,' he said, 'I haven't seen him since our first night. I do hope he's all right.'

'He's at my place,' I answered. 'I've given him a spare room. It seems that the pal he was always talking about didn't show up.'

Contrary to my expectation, Pennyweight wasn't haunting me. After his initial confusion over my father's sexual tastes, he'd struck up a rapport with the old man. It began on the second night when my father laid out some card tricks and pocket illusions, and began to discourse about dead magicians and their art. There is a common, albeit unconscious suspicion about conjurors: that their petty tricks disguise an authentic knowledge; and that, behind the exoteric kiddie-magic, they can do the real thing if they so choose. My father was himself not beyond hinting that the Great Alberto had initiated him into the mysteries of necromancy, and I'd always had half an inclination to believe him, even though I knew that the Magus had ended his days as a publican in Sparkbrook. I can only imagine how it was for Pennyweight, for whom a faith in the reality of Ascended Masters was as natural as a belief in Lloyd George. At all events, this morning I'd left him rummaging delightedly among my father's books where he expected to find God knew what tome of ancient lore.

I decided to introduce the subject of Robinson, and asked Fairbrother if he knew him. I didn't mention that Pennyweight did.

'You're the second person to ask me that,' he said.

'Oh? Who was the first?'

'The husband of that very pretty Mrs Cardozo, who gave us dinner. At first I thought he was just a nice enough little dago, but now I'm not so sure. There's something a touch sinister about him that one can't put one's finger on. He claimed his interest in a foreigner was a diplomatic one, but I think that's eyewash. Anyway, he told me about the murder and said the fellow was called Robinson; and asked did I know him and all that.'

'And did you?'

'I couldn't honestly say. But I don't think so. There used to be a Robinson at my school.' Fairbrother's voice fell. 'A beast and a bully, if you must know. If it was him and he's dead, then "serve him right" is what I say. But I've no reason to suppose it was him. The photograph was no use at all. *My* Robinson was a spotty tick with one of those horrible haircuts they gave us, and couldn't have been more than seventeen when I last saw him. There's every chance he was killed in the war – so many fellows were.'

'Did he have a sister called Lavinia?'

'Why should he have a sister called Lavinia?'

'Did he?'

'I've no idea. Chaps at school didn't talk about their sisters, except to wish they were dead. It wasn't the done thing. Why are you asking me? Did *you* know Robinson? Mr Cardozo seemed to think you did. You wouldn't lie about that sort of thing, would you?'

Johnny was wrong. I didn't know Robinson. I wasn't even sure why he interested me. Not for the fact of his murder: people are murdered every day and our interest goes no further than a mild prurience satisfied by the newspapers. Nor was I unduly troubled by the atmosphere of vague suspicion that I was implicated in the death, though a solution to the mystery would have suited me. If anything, the explanation lay simply in his name: that he was Robinson, son of Robinson, of a race of unknown Robinsons. I had a feeling – not so much a philosophical insight as one of the facile notions by which we interpret experience: like a sneaking belief in horoscopes – that there was something profound in that fact. I suppose it had to do with the war. The death of comrades – the snuffing out of those whom one knew in the particular – had been greeted with a muted response by those of us who stayed sane. My friend Bennett was killed: shot through the head at Ypres. Poor Bennett – thank God it wasn't me. I survived him; wrote to his mother; sent her mementos; divided the rest of his kit with his fellow officers; and had a drink to his memory.

Bennett wasn't the cause of my horror, because his fate was in some way comprehensible. The true horror lay in contemplation of the great democracy of the dead: in the fate of those I had not known, not the fate of those whom I knew. The strategies devised to cope with personal grief failed at the level of the general. I'd unconsciously despatched Bennett with a private liturgy. The glass of army rum and the distribution of Queen Mary's chocolate ration were the blood and body of my covenant with him. The curse for sticking his head above the parapet was my collect for the day. The drunken song about the whores of Piccadilly was my psalm. Bennett – God bless him – got the send-off all soldiers expected; and valued more than a padre's piffle. But how could one lament the unhallowed dead – the Robinsons?

If this or something like it hadn't been going through my mind, I'd have lost my temper with Pennyweight when I found him searching my room that morning.

I'd left him having breakfast with Teddy and gone for a walk along the *levada*. My father was in bed, playing the *grande dame*; probably testing how Pennyweight would react; wondering if he could induce his guest to bring him a cup of tea and a lightly boiled egg. If so, he failed. The ginger man cast an eye on Teddy and said, 'Chop chop! Bwana's calling!' and Teddy, to his credit (perhaps recognising another 'original' like my father), took it in good part.

'What the hell do you think you're doing?' I asked.

Pennyweight's lumbering form was hunched over the chest by my bedside, going through a drawer.

'Oh – hullo, old man,' he said. In one hand he held the volume of Byron's poetry given to Robinson by his sister. I'd pocketed it without Father Flaherty's noticing. 'I didn't realise you'd kept this. I thought the vicar had it. Going to return it, were you?'

There was no reproach in his voice, but his question drew the sting from my own. I hadn't thought of what to do with the book: I'd stolen it simply from force of habit. I took it from Pennyweight and repeated in a more normal voice, 'What the hell do you think you're doing?'

'I...?' He was genuinely puzzled: distracted to another time and place. He examined himself as if to take in the fact of his actions. Then he stood up and muttered, 'Sorry, old man. I never thought about how things would appear. I was just trying to get the hang of this rambling old place and sort of wandered in here out of curiosity.'

'You were going through my things.'

'Yes ... yes, I was. Shouldn't have done that. Very bad form. No excuse really, except that during the war one got used to going through other fellows' stuff. We had to, didn't we? It wouldn't have done to send packets of dirty postcards and French letters to the widow, would it?'

'I'm not dead.'

'No – no, of course not. A slip on my part. You'll forgive me, won't you?'

I put the book back in the drawer. 'All right, you're forgiven,' I said. 'Just don't let me catch you at it again.'

'Scout's honour. It was just an oversight.'

Surprisingly, this incident put me in a good temper with Pennyweight. I believed him implicitly, and the poor devil was so pathetic that he put out of my mind the feelings of self-pity that haunted me. It seemed like a good occasion on which to raise again the subject of what he knew about Robinson.

'Just how well did you know him? I asked.

Pennyweight threw me a cagey look. 'I've told you already. We were bosom pals.'

'Where was he born?'

'Oh, somewhere in the shires,' Pennyweight said airily.

'What school did he go to?'

'Does it matter? I don't see how it helps in discovering who killed him.'

'Humour me.'

'It was a good school. One of the Finest In The Land. I don't recall it exactly.'

'Was he married?'

'No,' said Pennyweight more definitely. 'He had a fiancée. I forget the name, but he used to write to her regularly ... well, fairly regularly ... except towards the end.'

The last hesitation wasn't a part of his habitual vagueness. I asked, 'The end? What do you mean by that? Robinson survived the war.'

He shrugged. 'In a manner of speaking.'

'He was wounded?'

'Not exactly.'

'What then?'

Pennyweight tapped his right temple.

'Shell shock?'

'I believe that's what they call it,' he said. 'He was off his head for a while – barking mad, if the truth be told. He got religion. Of course a lot of chaps did, but the Captain wasn't that sort at all. In fact quite the contrary. He was what they call a Bolshie nowadays: reckoned Keir Hardie and Shaw and Wells had got it right and the world would go to the devil unless it pulled its socks up. He had an awful down on Mr Lloyd George and Sir Douglas. If he hadn't been a gentleman, he'd have been up on a charge.'

'But he got religion?'

'Started quoting Blake – he's a poet, you know? Had visions. Saw angels.'

'Angels?'

'Hordes of the blighters. There was no reasoning with him. In the end they took him away – someplace in Scotland, I believe. We rather lost touch after that until he wrote to me.'

'From Casablanca.'

'Yes. He knew old Pennyweight was a man who'd stand with him. And so I would have, if ... if...' He breathed in deeply and I could see he was crying. He took a grubby handkerchief from his pocket and dabbed his eyes. He went on, 'Anyway, this is all between you and me – right, Pinfold? *De mortuis* ... and all that?'

'Of course, old man,' I told him.

'Good,' he mumbled. 'I knew you were a brick.' He opened his hand. 'I found this medal of yours.' He passed it to me and I slipped it into my jacket. He said, 'Military Cross, isn't it? You don't see many of them. Captain Robinson had one. Picked it up at Loos. Wouldn't say anything about it. I don't suppose you talk about yours either?'

'No,' I said.

I preferred not to think about that day. I collected the medal for a lucky piece of funk and confusion. And poor Bennett got his bullet in the head.

*

The waiter brought a tall glass. Chunks of ice and sundry pieces of vegetation floated in it.

I asked Fairbrother, 'Is this a Madeira Madman?'

'Yes,' he said, adding cautiously, 'I'm still in the process of adjusting the mix, so it may not be absolutely bang on.'

I took a sip with his eyes fastened eagerly on my lips.

'You don't have to say you like it,' he said. 'Not right away. It isn't that sort of drink. It's for the more sophisticated palate.'

I put the glass down. 'Where did the idea come from?'

'My pa. He felt we had to give a fillip to the market for Madeira: meet the modern taste for cocktails head-on. What do you think?'

'Very sophisticated.'

'Not too much, I hope. You'll get the hang of it after a second. And a third one will definitely give you –' he made a noise like a train coming out of a tunnel '- a *whoosh*!'

'I imagine it would.'

Remembering my brutal intention to cheat Fairbrother, I was about to propose that we visit my cellars, when we were distracted by the arrival of Doctor Crispin in the company of Mrs Christie and her husband. The Doctor spotted us, came over and shook hands.

He drawled in his usual even tone, 'We're still stuck in port, as you see. The engineers are working like coolies, but they're waiting on some part or other. I'm neither use nor ornament at a time like this, so I thought I'd take the tour. Do you fancy a hand at cards later? Bring some friends?'

I thought I'd try the subject of Robinson on him and asked, 'Have the police been to see you about the Englishman who was killed here the other day? There was an idea that he may have been on the boat.'

'The Old Man scotched that one,' Crispin said, rather firmly.

'I wonder how you can be so certain? I understand there were one or two passengers who didn't put in an appearance.'

'That always happens. Some people never find their sea legs, and stick to their cabins.'

'I heard mention of a party of Hungarians.'

'Possibly,' Crispin answered.

I hadn't considered that Fairbrother was one or two drinks ahead of me, but he now said, 'Robinson was probably travelling on false papers. It wouldn't be too difficult to stay out of the way. One can always bribe a steward. One can bribe anyone in these shipping companies.'

Crispin froze, only for a moment and with reason enough. Then he smiled and said, 'I'd best be getting back to Mrs Christie. I'll say so long. Perhaps I'll see you again?'

'Yes, let's meet and have that game of cards,' I agreed and gave him a handshake and a frank, manly gaze. I'd spared the Doctor during our game on the *Kildonan Castle*, but now I had a mind to take him to the cleaners.

In the meantime I had Fairbrother to deal with. He was evidently drunk, though not incapable. Alcohol took him as it does habitually shy men: without the truculence or bonhomie of the habitual toper, but as if light-heartedly inspired by his own fascinating qualities. Soon he would fancy himself a comedian and start telling silly stories. I decided to get him outside the hotel, where the fresh air would probably clear his head. Unfortunately Mrs Talbot was in the lounge, waving a collecting can.

'For Mr Robinson,' she said, dangling the can under my nose.

'He's dead,' I answered.

'I know that,' she retorted. 'But he has to be buried, doesn't he?'

'You're collecting for his funeral?'

'It's tomorrow, and, since he appears to have no family here, it's time for the British Community to rally round.' Mrs Talbot examined me disapprovingly. 'To be frank, I'd have expected you to take a lead. You were his friend, weren't you? Still, these things get left to the wives, as usual. Then again, you don't have a wife. I ought to introduce you to Ursula Lambourne. She's a very attractive young woman despite her squint.'

'I don't mind chipping in five bob,' Fairbrother interrupted, giving Mrs Talbot a killing smile. He took out his wallet, oblivious to the fact that the lady thought five shillings a poor show. 'There you are, my dear,' he said.

I found some escudos in my pocket, thought better of it and contributed a sovereign. Robinson was my friend, after all.

Then I pointed Mrs Talbot at a man I'd noticed standing by the entrance to the cocktail bar, apparently watching us, and suggested she touch him for a donation.

The man was Count Bronstein, alias Laszló Tormassi – the good or bad Hungarian, depending on one's point of view.

CHAPTER ELEVEN

A man is known by his friends. At Robinson's funeral mine were Fairbrother and Pennyweight.

The British contingent turned out in force. Mrs Talbot, her ample bosoms jutting from her skinny frame, harried shifty husbands into a semblance of decency, so that we might make the usual show of pompousness and hypocrisy. Still I was pleased. I would have something to tell Lavinia.

I'd decided to write to Robinson's sister. God alone knew why. I had no introduction except a stolen book of poetry, and no consolation to offer beyond pieties in which I no longer believed. To force myself upon her under such a ragged excuse was not the action of an honourable man, but that was scarcely a consideration. In the end, Lavinia was a cipher as Robinson was a cipher, their names a matter of happenstance; and there, perhaps, lies something of an explanation.

For I was tired of anonymous death.

More than its horror, which merely dulled the senses like a shabby raree-show, I hated its indifference. Bennett died and I lived; and neither outcome was to any noticeable purpose. Admittedly this was one of the commonplace insights granted to everyone. Yet, for all that, the agonies of the commonplace are true agonies and not to be despised for being met on every street corner.

We gathered at the British cemetery at the corner where the Travessa de São Paolo meets one of the streams that cross the town below a high bluff and another of the old Portuguese forts, a place where decent English sentiments are expressed and angels with Pre-Raphaelite faces erected among palms and bougainvillea.

Pennyweight tapped my chest. 'You should have worn your Military Cross, old man.'

'You won the Military Cross?' asked Fairbrother.

'Our boy is a bit of a hero,' Pennyweight said.

'I'm not a hero,' I said.

I didn't like to think of my medal, though it was one of the few valuable possessions I hadn't stolen. I don't know why. Probably it had something to do with Bennett and the bullet in his head.

It was eleven o'clock, the sun was beating down, and we were overdressed and sweating except for Margaret who stood a way off, talking to the lean figure of Sonny under the shade of a parasol.

Fairbrother was complaining he felt a little seedy. In the course of our business the previous day, he'd sampled a fair number of wines on top of his foul cocktails.

From Reid's we'd gone to the old convent of São Francisco, where I'd rented a part of the cellars shortly before a fire gutted my own. It had occurred about two weeks after my arrival on the island, when the dire state of the business had become apparent. The cause of the conflagration was still a matter of debate between myself and the insurance investigators.

Fairbrother was enchanted by the charm of the ancient *adegas*, the cross-beam wine presses, the scent of oak barrels, the vats of satinwood and honeyed notes of wine.

He admitted he was still learning the business, his training being as an accountant, and I imagined that, in a fatherly way, old Charlie had wanted to set him up as an embezzler, though I couldn't see Ronnie taking to the life. It seemed a shame to cheat him, but I put my qualms aside as the shallow sentiment a trickster necessarily feels if he is to appear sincere.

'What exactly do you have?' Fairbrother asked.

Frankly I didn't know except that the wine varied from indifferent to bad. Slapdash management in earlier years, petty dishonesty and the furtive movement of stocks on the night of the fire had played havoc with the records.

Fairbrother had provided himself with a list of the good years, but that was all right since I knew the list and had labelled the bins accordingly: all excepting the superb malmsey I'd bought from Arthur Mainwaring, which was modestly ascribed to a year of no particular merit.

'Truthfully, I shouldn't let you try that one,' I warned. 'It isn't up to much. It'll give you the wrong idea of the rest.'

Fairbrother gave me a sly-dog look and said, 'Well, we have to start somewhere, don't we.'

'Don't say I haven't warned you,' I told him truthfully enough.

I drew off a sample and passed it to him with more apologies. He held it to a candle to judge the colour, sniffed it and went through the general rigmarole. Then he sipped it and smacked his lips.

'Not bad. No, in fact it's very tasty,' he said.

'Good enough for a Madeira Madman?'

'Oh, I should think so. It's only a cocktail after all, and the taste'll be masked by a wallop of gin, not to mention the other stuff. And, let's face it, the people who drink these things are riffraff.'

'Do you think so?'

'Don't you?'

I didn't answer. I put the remark down to an effect of alcohol like the cynicism he'd displayed when mentioning bribery in Crispin's hearing. It wasn't that I disagreed with either comment; but I disliked them in Fairbrother's mouth because it suited me to consider him an innocent. I didn't want him to be like me.

I gave Fairbrother the rest of the tour: told him a tale about the process of producing Madeira, most of which was inaccurate since I knew little of the subject, and for historical colour showed him a goatskin *borracho*, in which wine was formerly carried down on foot from the mountains. Then I poured him another shot of Arthur's splendid stuff and took him back to my shop where we could haggle over the price.

I agreed to take payment in bills of exchange drawn on London. Fairbrother told me he would take delivery in a few days, when a boat for England would be loaded at the Molhe.

*

'I'm sorry your father hasn't been able to come,' said Mrs Talbot as we stood in the cemetery dust. Glancing at Margaret and Sonny, she remarked, 'Mrs Cardozo really shouldn't associate with Bernard Shaw. Decent people don't approve of him, even though the critics cry up his plays. He should be ashamed to be here after the things he wrote about the war.'

'Are you sure he's Bernard Shaw?'

'Who else should he be? The Russian Czarevitch no one believes was shot? I suppose your father is ill with his nerves,' she added with unexpected sympathy.

'You're very understanding,' I said. This morning my father had appeared in a tight suit of tails and spent an hour singing at the piano, recalling his Victorian youth as a light tenor.

'One has to be,' said Mrs T. 'I got to know him rather better while you were away in England. Someone had to take him his medicines and bits and pieces, and he couldn't rely on that darky of his. Harold wouldn't do it, but he was happy to lend me the runabout. You know, your father took me by surprise. He has the most beautiful voice.'

The service was conducted by the Anglican chaplain, but he had agreed to let Father Flaherty say a few words. Without guidance from Pennyweight, there was doubt over the deceased's religion.

Mrs Talbot asked, 'Was Mr Robinson a Roman? I think it's presumptuous of Father Flaherty to suppose he was. Robinson doesn't sound like an Old Catholic name, and it certainly isn't Irish. It may not matter, since it isn't the poor man's fault if a priest gets a hold of him. Still, his family may be offended. I used to know some Robinsons from Colchester. They were very strict Baptists, though the daughter was interested in Spiritualism. I don't suppose they're relations. It's such a common name. Does anyone yet know why he was murdered?' She paused for a reaction. Perhaps she had heard rumours and expected a confession. Disappointed, she said, 'It was robbery, I imagine. And such a shame. Think of it. To go through the horrors of the war, only to be killed by some Portuguese rascal with a knife.'

I left Mrs Talbot to Pennyweight and Fairbrother. Pennyweight explained that he'd been a captain, though he didn't like to mention it. I'd advised him again that he shouldn't refer to his connection with the dead man. Fairbrother, pale and crapulous, stood by: always the man no one wanted to talk to.

I approached Margaret and old Sonny. It struck me how comfortable they were with each other: that they had an indefinable air of intimacy; not that of lovers; at least not of those who are lovers in the usual way.

The burial service was taking time to get started. The gravediggers had pushed off to a remote corner for a smoke and showed signs of being drunk. The flower-sellers in their striped dresses, the boys and the dogs were creating the usual nuisance, calling from beyond the high wall.

Sonny and I shook hands. I asked, 'Did you get to the Paúl da Serra?'

'I did. I drove up to Encumeada as you suggested and took an energetic stroll. And very interesting, too. We didn't get as far as Porto Moniz, which was the original plan.'

'Any problem with the roads?'

'A flat tyre on the return, but nothing else.'

'Did you see the angel?'

He grinned and wagged a finger at me. 'Now, for all your cynicism, Mr Pinfold, isn't it the truth that you want the angel to exist? Wouldn't it simplify things wonderfully if God would give us a sign?'

'Perhaps. My question was whether He has.'

'Let's put it that some people seem to think so. While we were near one of the villages – Serra de Agua I think it's called – we came across a procession led by the village priest. He told me – if I've got him right – that one of local girls has been miraculously healed of measles. At least, he said measles though he may have meant smallpox – or perhaps he said smallpox and I understood measles. We were speaking French, did I mention that?'

'He thinks the angel healed her?'

'I got the impression he was suspending judgment. A priest can get into trouble with his bishop in the matter of miracles and angelic visions. Joan of Arc was burned for some such, and becoming a saint is a poor consolation unless one has a very firm belief in the hereafter. Let us say that his congregation is very enthusiastic at the idea. The shepherds have been scouring the mountains in the hope of discovering a relic. No doubt, if they find one, they'll erect a shrine for the sixpenny public and both priest and bishop will be very happy.'

I'd noticed Mrs Christie among the mourners. I wasn't especially surprised. She had struck me as a woman with a strong sense of the proprieties. Sonny, thinking Margaret and I might have things to say to each other, proposed to have a word with her. They'd met briefly at the hotel.

'Have you danced with him again?' I asked Margaret.

She threw me an amused glance, which drew her eyes away from following Sonny. 'Not since I saw you yesterday. I've hardly had time, have I? But, as it happens, he's invited me to join him this afternoon, and I think I shall.'

'Where's the pleasure? I thought he couldn't dance.'

'He can't. He takes steps as though he's on a hike. It's screamingly funny, and I think he puts it on for effect. He's a bit of an old ham.'

'He makes you laugh?' I asked, knowing that I didn't make her laugh.

'All the time. I can't tell you how marvellous it is to be admired and amused at the same time.' Margaret looked at me seriously, raised a hand as though to touch my face, then thought better of it in the circumstances. 'The fact is, Michael, that I'm tired of feeling like Our Lady of Sorrows. Whether I love you or don't love you is rather beside the point. Being with you doesn't lift the gloom. Oh, you give me all sorts of other things – wonderful things – but not that.'

'Why are you unhappy? I've never understood.'

'I don't know that one ever understands one's own unhappiness. One simply blames other people. Though I don't blame you – nor Johnny for that matter. But things are as they are. You have all sorts of qualities. Not the least is that you're kind and like to think the best of others. I think you could be happy, if the bloody war hadn't spoiled you.' She brightened. 'You're not jealous of Sonny, are you? He doesn't dance the tango half so well as you do. You are absolutely thrilling to dance with. It's all that passion and unrequited longing, I suppose. Tango is wonderful for that. Much better than sex. I think I'll risk a kiss on the cheek,' she added and her elegant neck stretched forward as her lips delivered it lightly. 'There. Old Ma Talbot can go hang herself. All we're doing is dancing. That's what we do, isn't it? Put all of ourselves into the dance without ever coming to the point?'

*

Father Flaherty began the Latin burial service. One or two of the mourners crossed themselves. The rest looked uncomfortable as if in the presence of something vaguely improper. I put my hands together and closed my eyes and found myself thinking of Robinson and his sister Lavinia: imagining them as an unmarried brother and sister living quietly somewhere in the country, attending church on Sundays, inviting friends to tea with seedcake and behaving as respectable minor characters do in English novels.

As images go, it was a religious one: for it was sexually immaculate and paid homage to the icons at which people worship, who aspire to peace, kindliness and a quiet life. And, despite its banality and the falsity of detail (after all, what did I know of Robinson?), I was moved by a sense of loss: both his and mine.

When I opened my eyes, Johnny Cardozo had come to reclaim his wife. Johnny the honorary Englishman, in a smart woollen suit and homburg hat, with his flashing dago eyes and dago teeth.

'Hullo, Michael, how are you?'

'Fine. And you?'

'Busy.'

'Have you solved our murder mystery? Am I a suspect?'

Johnny grinned as if to say what a kidder you are, Michael. 'I make progress.'

Margaret slipped her arm through his and rested her head against his shoulder. I looked for a suggestion of irony, but there wasn't any. Johnny cast a fond eye over her, and at that moment the conventional part of my soul wondered why they hadn't had children. Margaret had suggested that they disgusted her, or perhaps she meant merely that they would be an inconvenience to the life of glamour she and Johnny imagined in London. Whatever the case, Johnny had his wife and I never would have her; and, despite the matter of my affair with Margaret, I wished them happiness and thought that children were a part of it. My thefts have never been motivated by malice.

'Don't you think Margaret is looking well and beautiful?' Johnny said. 'It's the dancing. I like a woman who dances, don't you? She comes alive. Even ugly women come alive when they dance. I'm glad she's learning the tango with you. But I think you have a rival in Mr Sonny.'

'I thought his name was Bernard Shaw?'

'Is it my business what he calls himself?'

We stood a while in silence. Father Flaherty was still going through the service while the grog-faced British males fidgeted and their wives grew faint in the heat. A canary had taken station in one of the trees and was singing. On the side of the cemetery facing the *ribeira* I noticed, through the gate, a motor car and, beside it, a man fanning himself with his hat and another watching us intently while smoking a cigarette.

I asked Johnny, 'Why do I have a feeling that Count Bronstein is haunting me?'

'Is he?'

'I saw him yesterday at Reid's, and he's here now.' I pointed out the men beyond the wall. Johnny looked at them indifferently.

'Old soldiers shouldn't spy,' he said. 'They don't have the skill.'

'Is that what Bronstein does?'

'I would have him deported, but my masters in Lisbon and London are concerned with the politics of the case.'

'Good Hungarian or bad Hungarian?'

'Precisely.'

'I can see why he's spying on the Emperor. But why on me?'

'Perhaps he is spying on me?' said Johnny. 'I am making a joke, Michael. Spying is one of the most pointless activities known to man. One would be better off reading the newspapers.' He indicated Father Flaherty. 'I must go. The priest intends to make a speech about the dead man, and I don't want to listen because there is nothing to say. By the way, Michael, will you be coming to our place tomorrow evening?'

'I wasn't expecting to. Is there a reason?'

'Rutherford thinks the British community should put on a show for poor Robinson. A "wake" – is that the expression? Normally one would expect to talk about the deceased on such occasions, but since no one knew him, it promises to be a dull affair. He suggested the Quinta Magnólia, but the Club has such a stuffy atmosphere; so I offered to act as host.'

'I'll be there.'

'Good man,' said Johnny. 'Margaret, my dear...' He took her hand and drew her away. '*Adeus*, Michael.'

'*Adeus*, Johnny.'

*

I felt a brushing against my leg like an importunate dog. I looked around then down, and saw Pouco Pedro bouncing at my side.

'Hi, Senhor Mikey,' he said.

'You're wearing new clothes,' I said. The battered straw hat, cut-off trousers and espadrilles were gone, replaced by a brown felt, a white seersucker suit and tan shoes. 'Have you come into money? Murdered your wife for the insurance?'

'You forget sometimes that I am a doctor,' Pouco Pedro said with dignity. Then, 'Don't talk about murder. It's a very serious subject. Also insurance. You have problems there with your fire, mebbe, eh?''

'Why are you here?'

'Because it's a story, mebbe. And I am the owner of the best English newspaper in Madeira, hunh.'

'It's a one-page rag.'

'So I own the best one-page rag in Madeira. Same difference. You know this man Robinson, hunh? Some people whisper that you are killer because you Mr Robinson's friend and mebbe sleep with his wife – if he got a wife, which nobody knows.'

'I don't know him: no more than he does,' I said, pointing out Father Flaherty.

The priest had begun his eulogy. He seemed tired. His voice, which had chanted through the Latin service, had dropped to a normal tone and many of the mourners, mistaking the moment, began to talk among themselves, check their watches and leave. I had to strain to catch what he said; and, when it came, it was scarcely a speech but a brief meditation.

He said, 'Eight years ago the world sent its boys to fight in a great war. They were heroes, and nothing can detract from that. But we sent them out foolishly, and like fools they died; and it is because we are guilty in this knowledge that we are here today for the funeral of Captain Reginald George Robinson whom nobody knew.

'Was he personally a hero? The truth is I can't tell you for certain, but I think the answer is "yes" for the simple reason that, in this war unlike other wars, the heroism lay not in great deeds but in surviving the grinding days of death. And we know that Captain Robinson survived after a fashion. He was an officer in the Royal Engineers and latterly in the Royal Flying Corps. He had a sister called Lavinia who wrote her name in a book of Byron's poems; and he had parents, because that is in the nature of things. Doubtless he had other loved ones, too: a wife or fiancée perhaps; and friends, old comrades, the only people who would understand what he went through. These details do not amount to a biography, but they are enough to act as his grave marker. By them we know that Robinson was a human being; but, for the rest, they tell us no more than that he was like ourselves. This is fitting. We have been granted a new breed of heroes: a legion of petty men of no particular pretensions, who have been surprised into courage. Let us pay them honour.'

At that Father Flaherty finished, as if too disheartened to say more. And what he had said was too much for those without ears to hear. Someone murmured, 'I do believe that fellow is drunk,' and someone else added, 'You can't expect patriotism from an Irishman.' But, since a disturbance would have been bad manners, the incident of the eulogy was allowed to pass into the realm of gossip at the British Club. The mourners filed out of the cemetery, tipping beggars as they went. I proposed to Pouco Pedro that I buy him a drink.

We found a *cervejaria*. I ordered two shots of *poncha*.

Pouco Pedro said, 'You let me know if you find out more about this Robinson, hunh? I got a newspaper to write.'

'I thought you made up the news,' I said.

'You are not fair to me, Senhor Mikey. Also, mebbe you should be a detective: find this man's killer so people don't talk bad about you.'

'I wouldn't have a clue how to go about it.'

'That bit is easy. You talk to people and go looking places.'

'In that case, I'll do a deal. The *Kildonan Castle* is still stuck in the port. I'd like to know why.'

'That's no problem. She broken down.'

'Maybe. But why hasn't she been repaired?'

Pouco Pedro shrugged. He was used to things that broke and were never repaired.

'You pay me?' he asked.

'Ten pounds.' I still had some of the money I'd taken from Crispin's cabin.

Pouco Pedro whistled. 'This got something to do with Robinson?'

'I don't know. I shouldn't think so. You tell me. Where else do I start?'

'With the police? You working for the police, hunh?'

'Why should you think that?'

'I see you speaking with Colonel Cardozo.'

'What about him?'

'He's a dirty swine, that one.'

'So? I thought you did business with the police?'

'Not that one,' the little man said, and I waited while he finished his glass, licked his lips, removed his hat and smoothed the glistening hairs across his scalp. I wondered if I was going to find out something about Johnny: something to explain the unease he seemed to cause in everyone except me, though I ought to have been the first to feel uneasy since I was making love to his wife and he suspected I was a murderer.

'Colonel Cardozo kills people,' said Pouco Pedro. Then, 'This is just a story, you understand?'

'Like the stories in your newspaper?'

Annoyed, Pouco Pedro retorted. 'You not be so funny when you dead, Senhor Mikey.'

Then he threw in a laugh, meaning that men like us don't worry about that sort of thing.

MICHAEL PINFOLD TO LAVINIA PALISER

Quinta Pinfold

Monte

Madeira

21st August 1922

My dear Mrs Paliser,

Your address has been given to me by the War Office, who also tell me that you have been informed of the death of your brother. Those of us who commanded men during the war often had to write letters of condolence and know that they cannot take away the pain, and that the most heartfelt sentiments sound like commonplaces in comparison with the agonies felt by the next of kin. If my condolences seem brief and dry, it is out of respect and a sense of inadequacy. My feelings are sincere for all that.

I have come by a volume of Byron's verse with an inscription from you to your brother. There is nothing else among his effects that seems to be of a personal nature, but such as there is has been collected and will be sent to you, if you wish. Concerning the book, it was evidently very much valued, to judge from the signs of use. It is in my possession and, if you are willing to receive me, I should very much like to deliver it in person. I shall be returning to England very shortly and it would be no trouble to visit you.

Your brother's death has greatly affected me. For those of us who survived, the peace has been as trying a time as the war, and many of us have been driven to strange expedients comprehensible only to others who have found themselves in a similar situation. It has been difficult to maintain courage and honour in a world that seems to treasure neither, but I believe that Captain Robinson's intentions were always to act in a way that would bring credit to his family.

Forgive me if I express myself obscurely. It is only by explaining matters to others that one explains them to oneself. If we meet then, perhaps, everything will become clear.

Yours sincerely

Cptn. Michael Pinfold (rtd.)

CHAPTER TWELVE

I found the kitchen filthy and the household rat dining on the remains of some *dosas*. I decided to have it out with Teddy. He was on the terrace, paring the soles of his feet with a clasp knife.

I said, 'We need to have a word. The kitchen is in a disgusting state. The dishes haven't been washed for two days, and the floor isn't swept. The bloody rat acts like he owns the place.'

Teddy folded the knife slowly. He turned his painful eyes on me.

'Ha!'

'What does that mean?'

'Ha! Leave everything to me, isn't it? Teddy is to make everything beautiful and fragrant, while you are *so so* busy, and *He* is in his room thinking of throat cutting.'

I hadn't seen my father since breakfast the previous day. In the evening he'd been sobbing in his room, but I'd got use to the symptoms of his depression. Pennyweight, too, had paid no attention after a casual remark that he'd heard someone crying and thought it a bit rum.

When I explained, he answered, 'Ah. In that case, say no more. We got used to that sort of thing, didn't we? I wasn't beyond doing some blubbing myself. Never could take to being shelled. It got on the nerves rather. Machine guns, on the other hand, used to put a spring into a fellow's step.'

My father owned a cut-throat razor with a mother of pearl handle. I asked Teddy where it was.

'*He* has it, oh yes! *He* will cut his lovely throat and make Teddy an orphan!'

He often referred to himself as my father's son. I wasn't certain if this was a metaphor or a truthful relic of the famous Grand Tour. At times the actual or putative by-blows of my father and uncles made me think that Pinfolds grew like weeds in the earth's unregarded corners.

'*He* is mummy and daddy to me!' Teddy cried, 'And *you* are going home to England and Buckingham Palace – which is not like smelly horrible Kensington Palace – and Tower of London and mountains of Lincolnshire. What about *me*?'

'You should marry,' I suggested lamely.

'Ha! Who will marry poor bloody boxwallah's whoreson? You want me to go back to Goa and marry low-caste bloody heathen darky, isn't it!'

'I didn't say that.'

'It is easy not to say, Mr Michael! You are so high and mighty, even though you don't love *Him* at all!'

He burst into tears and I had nothing to add of any comfort. Perhaps I'd take care of him when I closed our affairs in Madeira. Perhaps I wouldn't. I noticed that his clasp knife and the shavings from his feet were spotted with blood.

On our way into town, Pennyweight remarked, 'I probably shouldn't say this, but your house is in a bit of a state. I don't think Teddy is earning his keep. Place reminds me of a dug-out I shared with a pair of Glaswegians.'

*

That evening I returned the piece of faïence I'd stolen from Johnny Cardozo. Margaret caught me slipping it into the cabinet where the collection was kept.

'You're getting slack. The coppers are going to catch you one of these days. Don't you care any more? Oh, God, you're not turning honest, are you? First you give Johnny his pot back. Next you'll be returning his wife. Honesty like crime begins with small things.'

We exchanged cigarettes, my Virginia for her Turkish blend, a romantic cliché that went with our mannered way of making love. Margaret glanced into the garden where the mourners were clustered under the Chinese lanterns, drinking heartily.

'They're talking about Robinson,' she remarked. 'Would you believe it? Of course they don't know anything of him; so they're telling stories about all the Robinsons they ever knew and speculating whether they're the same man. That and war stories – those who are young enough to have served in the last war. Those who aren't talk about South Africa and the Sudan. Is it Robinson who's turning you into an honest man?'

'I've just cheated Ronnie Fairbrother out of several thousand pounds.'

'Have you? I shouldn't be so sure. In any case, I wasn't suggesting you'd had a conversion on the road to Damascus. You're far too calculating for that sort of nonsense. By the way, would you like to spend the weekend with me? Don't act so surprised.'

I shouldn't have been surprised. It was Margaret's way to throw a mark of affection into our exchanges, relieving them of utter bleakness while making no commitment. Her emotional reticence perfectly mirrored mine.

'Johnny?'

'It was partly his idea.'

'Why?'

'He'll be tied up with the Governor at the Quinta Vigia. The island is crawling with Hungarians and they're worried about the Emperor.'

'Where do you propose we go?'

'São Vicente, the Wentworth place – far enough so that no one will know us. Johnny is perfectly happy that I should go off there – walking, communing with nature, that sort of thing. He considers it very English.'

'Will he know I'm going?'

'Don't be silly. Even Johnny isn't that tolerant. Say "yes", then we'll join the others so that no one will talk.'

In the garden Rutherford was taking messages of sympathy as though he were Robinson's relative. I overheard him say, 'I'd have preferred to hold this "do" at the Club, but Johnny Cardozo offered. Frankly I don't like his oiling his way into the British Community, but funds are low and one can't afford to look a gift-horse in the mouth. Also it wouldn't do to get on Cardozo's wrong side.'

I didn't hear any more of Johnny's wrong side. Father Flaherty was at my elbow with two large glasses of scotch.

'Take this, it's for you. I noticed you at the funeral and thought you took the business rather to heart.'

'I thought you did, too.'

'You mean the speech? It was as close as I could come to putting the complacent English bastards' noses out of joint without causing a riot. I'm glad it was appreciated.'

One of the younger women had brought her children. Pale and distressed, she watched as they crept on their knees hunting sleepy lizards among the rocks. I imagined her as the wife of one of Rutherford's clerks, someone who lived in the nethermost reaches of British society. Only inexperience could have accounted for her *faux pas*. I fancied her husband was the young thin man who had no head for gin and was trying to tell jokes to Arthur Mainwaring. Mrs Talbot had indirectly but pointedly enquired if the children were not up too late. I caught a bright reply, 'Oh no, they often stay up late. And I'm sure somebody would say if they were any trouble.' Then Margaret's voice was snapping, 'Never mind the bloody children! Let them stay. Oh, God, I need a drink!'

'Makes you glad you don't have any, doesn't it?' Crispin drawled as he slid from the shadow of a poinsettia. I hadn't noticed him at the funeral, but the ship's officers were here tonight. He asked, 'Are we on for that game of cards?'

'Tomorrow night suit you? Bring a friend.'

'Are you proposing to invite anybody? I reckon my chances against Mainwaring, Talbot or that fat idiot…'

'Rutherford.'

'Anyone except Pennyweight. He's got no money and I can't stand any more of his stories. Not Fairbrother either. He's far too wet to be fun.'

'I think my father would like to play. He's rather under the weather and could do with cheering. But he doesn't travel. We'll have to play at our place, Quinta Pinfold. Anyone in Monte will tell you where it is.'

'Righty ho,' Crispin said, flicking his cigarette into the flowers, and he returned to his friends.

Father Flaherty re-filled our glasses.

'I was at your shop a couple of days ago.'

'I must have been at the *adegas*. Fairbrother has bought some of my wine. I had to see to the packing.'

'Your man pulled a vanishing act as though he was on the run from the police.'

'That would be Senhor Pereira. He's shy.'

'From a glimpse I thought I detected a family resemblance.'

'He's an uncle or a cousin. Or possibly my brother.'

'That seems to be the way among colonists and islanders,' Father Flaherty said. 'We used to think that sending missionaries was the cure. But after five years they have more children than Old Mother Hubbard. This is not a society in which to raise them. Does Mrs Cardozo have a problem in that direction? I couldn't tell if she was sympathizing with that poor young woman or angry with her. The latter, I thought. Why do you suppose she doesn't have any of her own? I've known women do the most desperate things in that situation. By the way, have you seen this?' He took out a copy of the news sheet produced by Pouco Pedro. 'It says that Captain Robinson was in the Navy.'

'It also says I was his friend. You shouldn't believe anything Pouco Pedro writes. Have you really been commissioned by the Bishop to investigate our angel?'

'I went to pay my respects to His Grace, and we talked the matter over but that's as far it went. Contrary to what you may suppose, the Church doesn't care for miracles over much. They act as a focus for fanatics and in nine cases out of ten are fraudulent or deluded. The last thing His Grace wants is to lend the present visitation credibility by an official investigation. I think he'll wait and see if the fuss dies of its own accord.'

'And what do you think personally?'

'Ah, now isn't that a question? I try to exercise caution in these matters. Have you not noticed that there's no notion so foolish that two people won't believe in it and a third take their money?'

'Are you thinking of Pennyweight and his ideas about the Emperor?'

'Each to his own. In Ireland we worship shamrocks and orange sashes. The besetting sin of humanity is idolatry, and most of the time we don't know it. We bow down to the idols of history and our own fancy and give no reason for them than tradition and the genius of our minds, as if those were sufficient excuses for anything.'

'You could condemn Catholicism on the same grounds.'

'You most certainly could. Lord knows we've worshipped enough idols in our time – and I don't mean those pretty plaster saints one sees in churches. You should become a Catholic, Mr Pinfold. A priest even. Something tells me you have the temperament for it.'

Before I could answer, Rutherford was tapping his glass as a sign for silence.

'Ladies and gentlemen…'

We assembled around him: men, women, and a giggling child holding a lizard by the tail. The warm night wrapped us in scents of whisky, gin and mimosa.

'Fellow countrymen –' no mention of honourable dagoes such as Johnny '- we come to ... er ... celebrate ... yes, *celebrate* the memory of Captain Reginald George Robinson...'

'And to give one in the eye to Paddy the Priest,' murmured Father Flaherty.

'Plucky Little Belgium,' I said. 'King and Country.' I noticed Pennyweight standing at attention. 'Shall we slip away for another drink?'

We went through the French window into the large saloon where Johnny Cardozo kept his best scotch. It was in a cabinet on which stood a gramophone. I glanced at the records and saw *Mi Noche Triste* to which Margaret and I had danced so often.

I poured two drinks and passed a glass to the priest.

'Why did you call at my shop?'

'To ask for a favour – bless you for the drink – yes, to ask you for a favour, which, as it happens, touches on this business of the angel.'

'I thought you weren't involved?'

'Involved – no. Interested – yes. Call me a superstitious old Jesuit, but the fact is I have time on my hands and would like, for my own sake, to get to the bottom of the thing.'

'I don't see how I can help.'

'Do you drive?'

'Yes. But I don't have a car.'

'I have a car. The monastery arranged one for me, but the monks are poor creatures in the way of driving. Could you take me to Serra de Agua tomorrow? Or would I be taking you away from your work?'

He wouldn't be taking me away from my work. Still, I had no interest in the angel; or thought I had none. I said

I'd take him, but it was one of those decisions that might easily have gone the other way. I stipulated only that we had to be back by evening because of my card game with Crispin.

We took our drinks to the window. Rutherford was still expatiating. He knew nothing about Robinson, but was telling how the world had gone to the dogs and the Bolshies and the Yellow Peril were taking over. This wouldn't have happened if Robinson had been alive. Nothing would have happened if Robinson were alive. His decency would have put a stop to it.

Father Flaherty asked, 'Did anything strike you about Dr. Soares' account of the funeral?'

'Apart from the fact that Pouco Pedro got his facts wrong?'

'I was thinking of an omission.'

'I don't follow?'

'He doesn't mention that Robinson was murdered.'

I lit a cigarette at one of the girandoles.

'He wouldn't want to annoy the authorities by drawing attention to crime. He has a...' I forgot the term which described Pouco Pedro's delicate relations with the police.

'But everyone knows the facts.'

'The facts can be ignored if no one refers to them.'

This appealed to Flaherty. 'Now you remind me of the tale of the Emperor's new clothes. No one must speak of his nakedness.'

'Exactly.' The remark reminded me of Margaret's story of the Submarine Fleet of Terrestrial Navigation, which was wholly real until someone observed that it had no ships.

'Except that it isn't like that, is it? In the real world, if the boy were to reveal the truth, the crowd would rather stone him for his pains than face its own foolishness. Naked Emperors have little to fear. By the way, Dr. Soares was there when Robinson died. I didn't know him but he isn't a person one could miss – not with his looking like one of the wee folk.'

I hadn't seen him, nor had Pouco Pedro mentioned his presence at the murder scene. Then again, Robinson had been killed just before I ran into Johnny Cardozo, and Pouco Pedro might have cleared off, which would be unsurprising.

I also remembered that he carried a knife.

'And, of course, you were there, too,' said the priest.

'You think I may have killed him?'

'No, of course not. Still, it would help to know who did the deed, don't you think?'

In the garden a band had struck up. Johnny had had a dance floor laid on one of the terraces. It was one of his errors of taste, like his clothes and the faux Fabergé powder compact he'd given to Margaret. However this mistake like the others, if that is what they were, was oddly successful. After a stir of disquiet among the mourners, several of them began to dance. The women were still wearing black and made a vivid effect against the red of hibiscus picked out by lantern light.

My companion groaned and stretched his limbs until the joints cracked. For all his vigour, he was an elderly man and a little drunk. He stared into his empty whisky glass, spinning it in his fingers.

'Did I ever tell you I was a bottle a day man until I was Shanghaied into the service of the Lord? No, I'm not inviting myself to another one, Mr Pinfold. Now, concerning this murder, have you considered what it tells us of the character of the murderer?'

'I don't know it tells us anything.'

'Come now, you can do better than that. Captain Robinson was cut down in broad daylight in a crowded street where anyone might have seen the crime. Think on it: the risk that the murderous devil took – the self assurance – the flamboyance – the vanity! Didn't the fellow fool everyone?'

'Like a conjuror,' I suggested. 'But, equally, mightn't it have been done in a moment of impulse by someone who had cause to hate Robinson – someone who had no thought for the consequences?'

Flaherty sighed. 'Now isn't that the trouble with drink – that it makes you think you're wiser than you are? You're quite right, Michael: one shouldn't jump to conclusions.'

*

I wasn't surprised when Pennyweight didn't propose to come home.

'I thought I'd take a stroll around the town,' he said.

'Do you have any money?'

'Now that you raise the subject, old man…'

I gave him what I had, keeping only the carriage fare. I didn't ask what he would do, because I knew the answer. He would get drunk and sleep under the palms of the Jardim de Santa Catarina, or the police would fetch him, or I should have to go to the station to post bail.

Whatever happened, the outcome in Pennyweight's eyes would be Providential: another instance of the coded messages delivered by God to the *Illuminati*.

I left him to touch Fairbrother for more funds, and went in search of my driver, it being too late for the last train to Monte. One or two motor cars jostled for space with the *carros* in the narrow lane that ran alongside the villa and the beggars had gathered. I saw a woman going from vehicle to vehicle, mouthing her little litany of apologies: '*Se faz favor … desculpe … com licença.*'

In the lane it was dark. The moon hid behind a cloud and one by one the lanterns in Johnny's garden were burning out and I could hear servants calling to each other like night birds.

The thin man with the wretched wife and two children was debating whether to walk or waste a fare and deciding on the latter because he would lose caste if they walked. 'I thought Mrs Cardozo was damn' rude to you about the children,' he said.

'I don't think she meant to be rude. I thought she was just upset,' said his wife.

'Rude? Upset? You make the most stupid distinctions. And the dancing! For God's sake, what were you doing agreeing to dance!'

'Mrs Rutherford was dancing.'

'Don't be stupid! Her husband doesn't have his way to make. He can do anything he pleases.'

'I'm sorry, darling. Don't let's quarrel.'

But they would quarrel. She knew it.

He said, 'The trouble started when you let the children play with the lizard – filthy, disgusting things. I tell you but you don't listen. You never listen. You don't know how dashed hard it is to make an impression among these snobs.'

In a moment of insight I understood that he beat her. I saw the bruise beneath the face powder; heard the tremble of a voice that didn't know if even an apology was enough. The woman's self-abasement only served to make her husband more angry and he snatched her off into the shadows.

I went looking for my *carro*. The beggars were flitting like moths in an avenue of lit cigarettes and someone was beating a pi-dog until it howled. I found myself following the local woman I'd noticed. One by one she approached the drivers, asking, '*Você conhece o Senhor Pinfold?*'

'*Estou aqui*,' I said.

In the darkness I nearly bumped into her. The press of people forced us almost face to face, and I saw that hers was heavily pock-marked, though she might otherwise have been a pretty woman. '*A Senhora fala inglês?*'

'Little … very little.'

'Do I know you? *O seu nome?*'

I gathered her by the arm and led her between a pair of bullocks to the shelter of the garden wall. Two of the drivers had placed a lantern on the ground and were playing backgammon. The woman looked panicky; I felt something of the same, but put it down to the crowded lane with its blind crush of people, bullocks and dogs: one of those situations that fall easily into chaos and injury.

I repeated my question. Would she tell me her name?

'Soares – I am Mrs Doctor Soares.'

'Pouco Pedro's wife?'

'*Sim.*' She was proud. It was bizarre that anyone could be proud of that fact.

'Is he here?'

She shook her head. 'He hide.' I got her to say that again. 'He hide. He frightened!'

I made no sense of this. I'd fitted Pouco Pedro for a comic part, not this one. An unfamiliar noise made Mrs Soares bury her face in my shoulder. It was Father Flaherty; I couldn't see him but he was calling one of the hammock bearers. '*Ave Domine!*'

'Foreigner,' she whispered into my jacket

'A priest. He's speaking Latin.'

I held the woman close to me as though we were lovers or partners in a dance. She was very slender. It was difficult to think of her as the mother of six children. (Had Pouco Pedro said six – since when had I listened or cared?) 'Has your husband had some sort of problem with foreigners?'

'*Sim.*'

'What kind? Nationality? *Compreende?*'

She couldn't say. She'd never seen them. Pouco Pedro hadn't told her. Only that he was making enquiries for his friend, the most respectable Senhor Pinfold, and had

stirred up ... something. He had gone into hiding because
...

'You help?'

I didn't answer. The mean thought had come to me that
this was none of my affair. I told myself Pouco Pedro
probably knew something of every piece of dirty business
on the island and I'd be a fool to suppose a connection
with mine. Then again, it was possible he knew something
of Robinson's death: he had been there after all. As Father
Flaherty had said, it would help to know.

'You help?'

Senhora Soares forced a piece of paper into my hand. I
had to stoop to read it by the lantern of the backgammon
players and she stooped too, so that we made a foursome
around the light like figures in a Caravaggio painting

One word was written on the paper, but it meant
nothing to me.

Sabotage.

CHAPTER THIRTEEN

Her name was Angélica because her parents thought she would be as beautiful as an angel. But she caught smallpox and never became beautiful at all.

I woke with the head of Pouco Pedro's wife beside me on the pillow and the children fretting in the next room. There were two of them. He had lied about having more.

I rose and washed. She lay on the bed with her eyes pointed at the ceiling and her ravaged face expressionless. Today I could speak Portuguese. Some days I can. I made small talk until she got up abruptly and went to take care of the children, leaving me in a silence so profound that I could hear the sound of shame like rats in the wainscot.

I walked to the shop where I kept a razor and a change of clothes for those occasions when I couldn't make it home. My relative, Senhor Pereira, was sleeping on a pallet under the counter. Seeing me, he vanished into the store room. It seemed I'd fallen into the class of strangers to be feared.

Wine on top of whisky made me thirsty. Senhora Soares had offered it in the neat room with its patched fly screen, the bed, her husband's old Remington typewriter and the dictionary he used to craft his English: the room, in fact, where he was Doctor Soares, the gentleman scholar.

I don't give this as my excuse for sleeping with her, and she needs no excuse. Perhaps she was lonely; certainly she was frightened. Also she had to buy the aid of the honourable Senhor Pinfold and bind him to the dishonourable cause of Pouco Pedro. I downed a flask of water then remembered I'd agreed to join Father Flaherty at the Savoy for breakfast.

'Have you given any more thought to becoming a priest?' he asked. 'If I may say so, you look this morning as though the job may have its attractions. In my experience, a man needs a good ballast of sin before he undertakes the perilous voyage of virtue.'

'I never said I wanted to be a priest.'

'No sensible man would, but the Almighty has a terrible way of turning a deaf ear to our desires. Take my own case. I was a sinner and very good at it; but the Lord comes indirectly and leads us a merry dance before He gets to His point. Sometimes He is as seductive as a woman.'

'Were you ever married?'

'No. But I have more than my share of children – mostly in the bar-keeping trade as it happens. Now, will you have some breakfast?'

*

The priest had hired an old Lanchester. I checked the oil, the fuel and the spares and agreed we could go angel-hunting. I put aside any thoughts of Pouco Pedro or his wife. He was safely in hiding, so she told me, and would make his way to the *quinta* come nightfall.

We drove to Ribeira Brava by the same winding road I'd taken with Johnny Cardozo, threading between terraces of banana and yams, green and dusty, the sun out and the air hot and still. At Quinta Grande we were held by a funeral: not Robinson's but a local notable who merited policemen and a gang of rented mutes.

Ribeira Brava takes its name from a river flowing through a steep ravine. Ahead the road tracks the coast in a meandering fashion. To the right it cuts into the interior along the line of the ravine, rising to Encumeada, after which it falls to the north coast. On a map the distance is nothing. On the ground one goes from vines and sugar cane to high moorland in the space of eight miles. Cars break down or get pitched into the ravine because the road is narrow and unsurfaced, or rocks have fallen, or an ox cart is in the way or…

Sometimes cars just disappear: small mysteries that are unsettling rather than sinister.

My companion amused himself reading his breviary. I kept my eye on the road. This early in the morning the ravine was filled with shadow. Only on the western flank did the mountain tops break out in a glittering stripe of green-gold, below which the blocks of terraces sagged like collapsing brickwork. Pouco Pedro had written about this land.

I can't speak for all adulterers, but I doubt I'm alone in finding that the deceived spouse becomes sanctified: becomes not a person but a cult object brooding over the sexual ritual; more interesting in his absence (or hers – since I've no reason to suppose a difference) than in the flesh; more the subject of awe and enquiry, even by a partner who thinks he or she knows everything. Pouco Pedro wrote books: had always written books. They lay in unpublished piles about the room where we made love. Travelogues, histories, romances: Pouco Pedro was a polymath. His petty existence as a journalist and occasional police spy was a cover for an adventurer of the mind.

'What are you looking at?' Angélica asked as she poured the wine.

'I didn't know Doctor Soares wrote books.'

(Note the respectful 'Doctor Soares'. The magician and the successful seducer proceed always by distraction.)

'*Sim*. He is very clever. He knows many things.' Angélica gave me the glass and passed her hand over the manuscripts as I imagine she often did: not reading them but absorbing their essence by a sacramental touch. 'That is why you are friends – because you are *muito intelligente, também*.' And she smiled at me, her beautiful teeth sparkling in her ugly face.

From which the rest followed.

'A penny for your thoughts,' said Father Flaherty.

'I didn't want to disturb your reading.'

'Can you pull over for a moment? Nature and age both call.'

I halted and Father Flaherty went off into the eucalyptus to relieve himself. When he returned I asked, 'Why did you become a priest?'

'Ah. So the job is catching your interest, is it? Well, let me tell you: it wasn't out of conviction. It was just that the Almighty kept making a bloody nuisance of Himself, so that I joined up simply to keep the fellow quiet.'

'And does He keep quiet?'

'For the most part. When you have a congregation to think about, you don't have much time for God. I sometimes think the Church is a Satanic conspiracy to put sinners off religion. Is it that you have Sin on your mind this morning? You can tell me, and we'll have a good chuckle together. That's all most sins are worth.'

This exchange made me think of Pennyweight and that there are strange doctrines followed by lonely priests. Pouco Pedro, it seems, was one: otherwise it was impossible to understand Angélica's reverent affection for his heaps of unpublished learning. Pennyweight was another. His fervour relieved him of complete absurdity; made one bizarrely respectful. The Russians have a tradition of holy fools, and Pennyweight shared something of it.

I wondered where he was this morning. Probably nursing a hangover after collaring some poor unfortunate in a bar like the Ancient Mariner and the Wedding Guest, which reminded me that he had read the poem and identified with the narrator in his own mad way, since, for him, the old sailor was a model of arcane sanity.

'Coleridge was a Higher Adept,' he had explained. 'It stands out a mile if you know how to read these things. Probably a Freemason too.'

*

At Serra da Agua we called on the priest at a lime-washed house with boxes of wallflowers at the windows. He was in his garden, tending yams and gourds.

'You can leave him to me,' said Father Flaherty. 'I have the gift of tongues – Latin and blarney.'

I went to kick my heels in the dusty road that passed by the village before winding the steep climb to Encumeada. To the west the ravine reared to the misty height of Lombo do Mouro, about which Pouco Pedro had no doubt written. Among his manuscripts was *Legends of Madeira*, produced with an eye for the tourist market. Village by village it plotted saints, demons and undiscovered murder, wrapping its tales in lush descriptions apparently borrowed from the country-life columns of the English newspapers. I had sat and leafed through it while Angélica removed her clothes.

Joining me, Father Flaherty said, 'He's gone to fetch the shepherds who witnessed the miracle.'

'Does he believe it's genuine?'

'I wouldn't go so far as to say that. But the poor beggar doesn't own a pot to piss in, and a blessing from the Lord would be a fine thing, seeing that He's been sparing of them lately. Do you think we could get anything for our thirst?'

'Why aren't the shepherds with their flocks?'

'I fancy "shepherd" is an honorary title for a pair of rascals, which is why the priest has his doubts. For my part I think it's typical of the shifty way the Almighty carries on: forever slumming among rogues such as myself.'

We found a bar run by a widow in black, ordered a couple of Coral beers and took them outside among dust and pots of geraniums. The widow sat in the shadow of the door working a piece of lace. I looked toward Lombo do Mouro and low drifts of white cotton cloud, and didn't care to think of searching the Paúl da Serra for signs of angels.

The priest came to us with two stocky, skulking *morenos* in woollen bonnets and tyre-shod shoes. Father Flaherty smiled at them genially and ordered more beers.

'Will you help me now, Michael? I don't think these fellows will be susceptible to my Irish charm and winning ways. It may be they'll expect a more tangible reward, but I'm a poor man and wouldn't wish to be robbed.'

'Have you ever been robbed?'

'It's been tried – I shouldn't like to be tempted to violence. *Bom dia*, gentlemen.'

'*Bom dia*,' they grunted, and I knew at once that I wouldn't be able to understand the rustic accents.

The priest smiled. Behind the soiled cassock he seemed a cultivated man: at least he had as much culture as one attributes to a pair of steel-rimmed spectacles with a cracked lens. He asked me in Portuguese, 'Do you want me to translate the local dialect? My name is Father Ruiz.' He extended a hand. 'It will be a pleasure to speak my own language.' He meant that he was a Lisboner, an educated man who could read and probably wrote a little too: another emperor in exile. His hands were calloused and he was ashamed of them.

'Do you believe these men?' I made an impromptu suggestion: 'Don't visions happen only to virgins?'

'They are the most unreliable sort. Virgins are...' he didn't complete the sentence. Perhaps he feared slipping into heresy by way of a generalisation.

'Are they honest men?'

One of them was grinning. The other was calculating the value of my clothes.

'No. They are liars and thieves, the worst men in the village.'

'Then why should we believe them?'

'What is the value of a miracle to such? They are not cunning enough to steal something which is not hard and present in front of them. Also everyone knows them, and they could not expect to be believed.'

'But apparently they were believed.'

'For that same reason. Am I expressing myself well?'

'We're to believe them because they're liars?'

'It is subtle, yes?'

I explained this to Father Flaherty. 'Do you understand?'

'Oh, yes. They think in much the same way at home.' He tipped his glass in a silent toast to Father Ruiz. A dog, sensing a hopeful movement, came over across the dusty street. It sniffed then urinated into the geraniums. 'Will you ask them what it was they saw? *Exactly*, mind you.'

'Lights,' said the First Ruffian. I had no names and mentally labelled them like minor characters in Shakespeare.

'How many?'

'One,' said the Second Ruffian.

'Your friend said 'lights' – more than one.'

'He exaggerates. He drinks.'

'Was he drunk that night?'

I didn't get an answer.

'Were you drunk too?'

'They were both drunk,' Father Ruiz commented. 'They keep a still and make rum, but no one knows where it is. Probably out there.' He waved a hand towards the mountains.

'Maybe all they saw was a shooting star.'

'Not a shooting star!' the First Ruffian interrupted. 'Do you think shepherds are fools, Englishman?'

'They were drunk and they saw a shooting star.'

'Not a shooting star!' The man was furious, but even a liar becomes angry at being doubted – the matter is one of honour, not honesty. 'Shooting stars make no noise! Angels make a noise!'

'A noise? What noise? Voices? Bells? Heavenly choirs?'

He roared. 'Like this!'

He roared again, full-throated. The dog scuttled off, children fled, the widow stopped her lace making. He began laughing and his friend laughed with him because they'd frightened the Englishman and the priest. He finished his beer and turned the glass upside down. 'You like that, eh?' he asked Father Flaherty with Ruiz stammering to keep up with him.

'I know a good tale when I hear one,' Father Flaherty answered.

'Not a tale,' said the First Ruffian.

'What then?'

'The wrath of God!'

*

'Do you believe them?' I asked.

'Certainly,' said Father Flaherty. 'When a man sets about faking revelations he usually throws in the Blessed Virgin and an Apostle or two – after all, there's no extra charge. Our boys' story invites disbelief, and so I'm inclined to credit it.' He jabbed a finger toward the hot sky. 'On the other hand, whether You-Know-Who has had a hand in the matter is a debatable point.'

Father Ruiz led us towards the poorer end of the village where dogs and children gathered as if by gravity. I noticed his shoes needed mending: the soles flapped so that he proceeded by small steps in a coolie trot.

We reached a dilapidated cottage on an arid terrace overlooking the *ribeira*. Below us water flowed thinly in a bed of dry stones among willows and browsing goats. The cottage had been repaired with odds and ends of stone, tile and tar paper. Yet flowers grew by it as they did everywhere on the island: another profusion of geraniums.

A cheap crucifix had been nailed to the door and a garland hung under it. Father Ruiz crossed himself and muttered a blessing.

'It is expected,' he said. He looked to Flaherty, one professional to another, then rubbed his spectacles like a cat washing its face.

I wanted to ask him how it felt to be reduced to a village ju-ju man.

The priest called out, then opened the unlocked door and went inside. There was a single room with a single shuttered window and a swept earth floor. The furniture was sparse and broken, but everywhere were heaps of gimcrack religious stuff: pictures of the Virgin from church magazines, plaster figures, rosaries; more than any family would need, assuming it needed any at all. Father Ruiz had intimated that the villagers were treating the cottage as a shrine. The junk was a votive offering left furtively by night in gratitude for the miraculous cure. But the offerings were placed only at the door and no one came inside.

After all, and despite the miracle, smallpox is infectious, and the God of villages is a capricious deity whose character is not love but an ineffable slyness.

'*A rapariga está cá.*'

The girl was lying on a palliasse. She looked about nine, but poverty retards and she was likely older. She wore a red striped dress and a blue bodice and had been powdered so that she smelled of – I think it was frangipani, but whatever it was amounted only to a flowery note behind a stink of waste and sour straw. Her face reminded me of one of those Victorian dolls with a wax head and false hair and a smile of mad sentimentality.

'*Como se chama?*' My mind engaged the language again.

'Her name is Graça,' said Father Ruiz. 'A good name. It speaks to the mercy of God.'

In His mercy God had given her a face that would be scarred for life. His miracle had stopped short of the cosmetic; but, as Father Flaherty never tired of reminding me, in His misdirections the Almighty was as artful as the Great Alberto, slipping wonders from out of His sleeve while no one was looking. Thus Angélica was cursed with a pock-marked face so that the unlovable Pouco Pedro could be awarded the wonder of a woman who loved him.

'She began to recover on the night of the Visitation.' Father Ruiz used the language of a believer. The miracle of the shepherds was one thing and this was another.

'People often recover from smallpox,' I said.

'In this village they die. Half of the children die young from smallpox or other things.'

'He didn't fix her face.'

'Perhaps He intends to devote her to the Church.'

'A nun?'

'It is possible. Then the face will not matter. She has always been a good child.'

I didn't answer. I was angry – not in disbelief but that the priest should attach merit to such a filthy exercise of Divine pity. I asked Father Flaherty whether he had seen enough. He said that he had.

As we returned to the car I asked him, 'Well? How do you like your two shepherds and a virgin?'

He looked at me benignly. 'Peace now, Michael.'

'Don't tell me you believe in this supposed miracle!'

'How shall I put it? I see nothing of the supernatural in it, but neither did I expect to. God is too subtle for our ways. Didn't I tell you that He comes at you like a woman with His veils and His come-hither eyes? He fairly makes your head spin trying to decide if He loves you or hates you, and a fine merry dance you have. Don't be angry now. It's only because you have a good heart.'

He halted to gaze towards the mountains. 'Where exactly do you think the lads were when they saw the angel?' He looked at Ruiz. 'Did you ask them that?' I translated to the priest.

I doubted they knew. The high moor could be a fearsome place, the night had been filled with mist and rain and they had been out of their heads on bootleg rum.

'They call it Paúl dos Embriagados.'

'Will that be on a map?'

'It's a joke,' I said. 'They mean the place where they get drunk. They won't take you there because it's most likely where they keep their still.'

I imagined it as a bothy thrown together out of willow wands and the two men huddled together with a bottle while outside it rained. Except that it didn't just rain. An angel had passed over in a bright light and a voice had announced the wrath to come.

'Is Senhor Pinfold right about that?' asked Father Flaherty.

Father Ruiz nodded.

'Do you think you could find it, Michael?'

'No. There's no road beyond Lombo do Mouro, and miles of wasteland. In any case, what would I be looking for? What traces does an angel leave?'

'You could find their still. At least you would know you were in the right place.'

'They probably dismantle and hide it. There are small caves you'd hardly notice. You're not listening to me. The Paúl da Serra isn't a place where you go blundering about. You can die out there.'

We had reached the church. Father Flaherty said, 'Michael, can you lend me some money? You get out of the habit of carrying it when you wear a dress for a living.'

I gave him what I had and he passed it to his fellow priest.

'For the Glory of God, Father. I suggest you get yourself another pair of shoes.'

The two men embraced and in their eyes I glimpsed the mystical Third who led them through the paces of His lonely dance.

'Now isn't that a poor sad beggar?' said my friend as I opened the door of the car for him.

I agreed, but I was thinking of a parting observation made by Father Ruiz, which I hadn't translated. For my own peace of mind, and expecting nothing, I asked him if an Englishman by the name of Robinson had ever made any enquiries concerning the angel. He hadn't. Father Ruiz didn't know the name. But he did have something to tell.

He said, 'You are more generous than the other foreigners who came.'

'There were others?'

'Yes. Four men.'

'Where did they come from?'

The priest shrugged. 'To me they are all the same. One of them, perhaps two, was English – I can recognise the language even though I do not speak it.'

'Can you describe them?'

'Two elderly men and one younger, who was very smart. The fourth was the Englishman. He was fat and had a red moustache. Do you know him, Senhor Pinfold?'

I shook my head in disbelief not denial. God was in His Heaven and scattering His angels to fox the believer and the unbeliever alike.

What on earth had Pennyweight been doing here? Was there a connection with the Hungarians? With the Emperor?

GEORGE BERNARD SHAW to WILLIAM
ARCHER (journalist and playwright)

Reid's Palace Hotel

Funchal

28th March 1922

My dear W.A.

So it is four years since your dear boy, Tomarcher, was killed. Damn! Damn! Damn! If I thought it would help, I should tell Reason to boil its head and give a rousing three cheers for table-rapping. Instead, the black dog has got us both by the throat and we slouch through the world: old men, too tough, chewy and useless to be worth Death's time of day.

Don't look to me for consolation. Expect nothing of monuments and Remembrance Days and Angels of Mercy bringing balm like Father Christmas hauling presents. Away with them all! Tomarcher's monument and true remembrance are that we labour on, bleakly unconsoled, to make the best of a misbegotten peace and castigate the fools who would throw away whatever it is that was won.

Quand j'aurai fait le brave, et qu'un fer pour ma peine,
M'aura d'un vilain coup transpercée la bedaine,
Que par la ville ira le bruit de mon trépas
Dites moi, mon honneur, en serez-vous plus gras?

At least your dear boy escaped the ruination of the victors. Pity them. They are here in the hotel: a gang of old soldiers on the cadge. I call them The Three Cads because they remind me of a third rate music hall act: the show going on because it must go on. Pity, too, the defeated. My old friend, Siegfried Trebitsch, has sold his wife into slavery and eaten his boots. Though I feel broken into pieces, I have promised him a play, which he can put on or turn into soup: whatever serves.

In a house above the town, one of the villains survives: the former Austrian Emperor, Karl – except that he won't play the villain. He is, by all accounts, amiable, liberal and possessed of all the virtues, domestic and otherwise. In short he is that most ridiculous specimen: a thoroughly decent man, fit for nothing but building public libraries while the world goes to pot. For my part, I have been accused of many things, but never of decency. Do you recall Wilde's aphorism? 'Shaw has not an enemy in the world, and none of his friends like him.' Bless the poor devil, but he was often right.

The tragedy of life and the tragedy of drama are quite different things. My father was an adamant teetotaller. But he was a teetotaller who drank. I defy anyone not to laugh. Now you may think that Karl's situation contains the stuff of tragedy. Isn't the downfall of kings what it's all about? Ah, but the tragic hero has always a whiff of the monster about him, and what sort of tragedy is it where the fellow absolutely refuses to die? No – it won't do. You can't make one out of a decent man: not if he's the genuine article. If we look to Karl to fulfill that role, we must wait until he goes mad and takes up writing.

The upshot is that I am old and the war has made me tired, cynical and avaricious. A cheap, tawdry success would suit my book. Give 'em what they want, I say.

Hurrah for Vincent Crummles! Yah boo to Ibsen!

ever

G.B.S.

TANGO IN MADEIRA

SCENE TWO

The garden as before. Ten minutes later. CHARLIE, ZOË, and HERMANN are sitting at the table drinking tea. ROBINSON is stalking up and down, brandishing the gun and occasionally pointing it at the others. CHARLIE and ZOË are relaxed. HERMANN has the impassive manners of the military.

CHARLIE: I must say, it's very decent of you – very British of you to let me finish my tea before you murder me.

ROBINSON: I'm not a murderer. *[He assumes some dignity.]* I am an assassin.

CHARLIE: Isn't that the same thing?

ROBINSON: *[stiffly]* Not at all. If it were, then there wouldn't be two separate words. And, if I were you, I should be careful in making any disparaging remarks about Britain.

CHARLIE: I forgot. They tend to bring out the pacifist in you. Well? I've almost finished my tea. What happens next? Do you intend to slaughter … *assassinate* me on the spot?

ROBINSON: No. First of all, I want you to listen to my reasons.

CHARLIE: I'd rather not. It's bad enough being killed without being persuaded that you are right to do it. Even worse, you might kill me for a thoroughly idiotic reason, and where would be the glory in that? I don't think anyone would be considered a martyr who was executed for the sake of free trade or bi-metallism. *[to ZOË]* You don't suppose he's been hired by the publishers of dictionaries, do you? I've always said that spelling reform was a dangerous undertaking, but you wouldn't believe me.

ZOË: Hush, dear. I think you ought to listen to Mr Robinson.

ROBINSON: *[gratefully]* Thank you, ma'am. *[He grants ZOË a bow, which she receives very prettily, thus causing him some emotional confusion. He takes a piece of paper from his pocket and reads from it grandly.]* The Indictment. First count. That you, Karl August Christian Lewis von Hohenhuffundpuff, King of Transleithania, Archduke of Hungonia, Duke of Boguslavia, Voivoda of the Banat of Timishar, Count of Sklavonia…

CHARLIE: Stop there. I am *Cardinal-Archbishop* of Sklavonia. *[to ZOË]* I am right about that, aren't I? Wasn't it Uncle Freddie who was Count?

ZOË: Yes, dear, though there's a vacancy since he was blown up. You could be Count if you wanted.

CHARLIE: I might do that. I've always been uncomfortable with being Cardinal-Archbishop.

HERMANN: Sire, you did receive a dispensation from His Holiness.

CHARLIE: Even so, a Cardinal with seven children: I sound like one of the Borgias, not a happily-married man with a loving wife. *[He exchanges affectionate smiles with ZOË.]*

ROBINSON: May I go on? *[He coughs and reassumes his dignity.]* First count. That you, Karl Augustus…

CHARLIE: Et cetera, et cetera … Cardinal-Archbishop of Sklavonia – and Count as soon as I can get round to it. You must remind me about that, Hermann.

HERMANN: If Your Royal Highness is still alive.

CHARLIE: Always subject to that, of course.

ROBINSON: …did unlawfully, wilfully and maliciously cause war to be declared by the United Kingdom of Great Britain, the Republic of France and the Kingdom of Italy.

CHARLIE: Very good. Did you have a lawyer help you to draft that? Or perhaps you are a lawyer?

ROBINSON: No, I'm a librarian.

CHARLIE: Ah, that probably explains your hostility to spelling reform. *[to ZOË in a whisper]* What did I tell you! Now were getting to it!

ROBINSON: How do you plead?

CHARLIE: Not guilty. I'll pass over who exactly declared war on whom, but simply point out that the war had been going on for two and a half years before I came to the throne. As it happens, I had nothing to do with starting it and thought it a thoroughly bad thing, which I tried to stop.

ZOË: So you did, Charlie.

ROBINSON: *[indignantly]* Hah! *[He reads from his paper]* Second count. That you permitted said war to continue and did nothing to bring it to a conclusion.

ZOË: Absolutely untrue! I won't have you accusing Charlie of such a terrible thing!

ROBINSON: You can't deny that the war continued for another eighteen months after your accession.

CHARLIE: *[reluctantly]* He's right about that.

ZOË: Shut up, Charlie. You did your best to stop it. You know you did. *[to ROBINSON]* He sent out peace feelers to King George and also the French. The reaction was abominable. They wanted him to betray the Kaiser and hand over a large amount of territory to the Italians – the *Italians*!

CHARLIE: *[sorrowfully]* Don't get excited, dear. Mr Robinson thinks that I ought to have simply surrendered – and perhaps he's right. Millions of those poor soldiers' lives might have been saved.

ZOË: Oh, Charlie! *[She breaks into tears.]*

HERMANN: *[snorting]* Surrender! Unthinkable! We were in the right!

CHARLIE: I wouldn't say that if I were you. Mr Robinson has a gun and gets very bad-tempered when he's in a pacifist mood. *[to ROBINSON]* In the end, I was quite prepared to betray the Kaiser in the interest of peace – the worst that could happen was that people would consider me a cad. I was even willing to give some territory to the Italians – all those places where they were in a majority. But they wanted large areas of Sklavonia, where the people weren't Italian at all, though they may have been five hundred years ago (my history of the subject is a little vague). I couldn't agree to that. I was the Cardinal-Archbishop, after all. *[despairingly]* And what did it matter in the end? I couldn't hold the Kingdom together. Everything fell apart. The Kaiser fled. The Italians took what they wanted. *[CHARLIE takes ZOË in his arms and holds her lovingly]* Perhaps I could have stopped the war if I'd been wiser and stronger. Perhaps I am guilty as charged. *[with quiet courage]* You've convinced me. You'd better go ahead and shoot me after all.

A pause. ROBINSON is silent and a little uncertain. HERMANN is uncomfortable.

HERMANN: *[to CHARLIE]* Were you really prepared to abandon the Kaiser and give away parts of the Kingdom? I knew nothing of that.

CHARLIE: It was my responsibility. I knew the army and the nobility would never agree. I assumed that once I'd signed the peace treaty I'd find myself decorating the trees in Hohenhuffundpuff Street, just like poor Uncle Freddie. It didn't seem fair to drag anyone else into the business.

ROBINSON: *[moved]* That was very decent of you.

CHARLIE: Thank you. *[He releases ZOË who in turn looks admiringly at him and venomously at ROBINSON. CHARLIE pats ZOË's hand and gives her a comforting kiss. He addresses ROBINSON again.]* May a condemned man have a last wish?

ROBINSON: What? Oh, yes – that is usual, isn't it?

CHARLIE: I should like to dance.

ROBINSON: *[embarrassed]* I don't dance.

CHARLIE: I meant with my wife.

ZOË: *[radiant]* Darling!

ROBINSON does nothing as CHARLIE places a record on the gramophone. It is a tango and is sung in Spanish. He bows to ZOË who rises with an expression of joy on her face.

CHARLIE: The song is about a poor fellow who has lost his mistress and expects to die in the morning. The last part is quite appropriate, don't you think, Mr Robinson? Do you speak Spanish? You should learn. The spelling is fairly rational as these things go. Little scope for reform there.

CHARLIE takes ZOË in his arms. They dance beautifully and sensuously. The movement takes them around the garden, deftly avoiding the furniture with dramatic pauses and turns. ZOË's posture is boneless: her expression intermittently pained, joyful, angry. CHARLIE dances fearsomely, displaying the dominance and self-doubt of sheer will. That they love each other is evident. That their love will succeed is not. They move in a succession of alternate passages of possession and loss: of finding and abandonment. ROBINSON watches with fascination and horror until the sight becomes unbearable and he turns his gaze away. Even so he cannot avoid hearing CHARLIE who intersperses comments in the dancing. These are delivered bitterly or philosophically.

CHARLIE: What do you think, Robinson? Tango is like making love in the afternoon, eh? ... Is this a dance of love or a dance of death? ... Do you think social conditions will permit it to be danced in Sevenoaks? ... Wouldn't you rather hold a woman than a gun?

At last the music ends and CHARLIE and ZOË subside in each other's arms.

ZOE: *[elated and exhausted]* Charlie, Charlie! You've never danced like that before!

CHARLIE: *[slowly and tenderly]* I never realized how much I loved you. Whatever I've felt before has been in comparison mere tepid sentiment. I want to speak like a hero in cheap romantic fiction and shout out my love from the sixpenny seats in a cinema. I want ... to make love in the streets of Sevenoaks until the dogs bark and the babies cry! *[to ROBINSON]* Go on – kill me and be damned!

HERMANN: Sire!

CHARLIE: Oh, do be quiet! Can't a man die when he's ready for it? I've been a King, a Cardinal-Archbishop *and* danced the tango with my wife. How many husbands can say the same? Well, Robinson? What are you waiting for?

ROBINSON: *[uncertainly]* There are additional charges. I can't execute you until you've had a fair trial.

CHARLIE: *[bored]* Oh, God! How absolutely English! And, pray, how exactly do you propose to give me a fair trial? Are we to expect twelve good ratepayers to join us? Do you suppose that, somewhere, there are a dozen grocers who have experience of trying to end a war or rule a country of a score of squabbling nationalities? I've confessed that I've failed. Look around you. Here I am, exiled in Madeira without even Napoleon's excuse that he was for a time a successful conqueror.

ROBINSON: *[earnestly]* But you might be innocent.

HERMANN: Be careful, Sire. It's a trap. The English will make any respectable excuse to salve their consciences. They invented Methodism and still acquired an empire.

ZOË: But Charlie is innocent!

CHARLIE: There, there, dear. I'm not certain any more. *[to ROBINSON]* You'd better read out the next charge.

ROBINSON: You seem remarkably eager to die.

CHARLIE: Well? Isn't that what you want?

ROBINSON: I don't know. *[dismayed]* It seems a little unsporting if you simply confess to everything.

CHARLIE: I haven't exactly confessed. I just don't care any more. I come from an unlucky family.

ROBINSON: Don't say that. Chin up! How are you unlucky? Hasn't your family ruled Transleithania for centuries? Been Dukes of this and Cardinal-Archbishops of the other, and … that thing I can't remember?

CHARLIE: Voivoda?

ROBINSON: That, too. You have palaces and hunting lodges, paintings, china and all sorts of treasure. *[He looks at ZOË and cannot avoid an expression of longing]* And a beautiful wife.

CHARLIE: I thought you never told another man that his wife was beautiful?

ZOË: *[pleased]* Don't complain, Charlie. It's rude.

ROBINSON: I can't help it. *[passionately]* It's true! You're the luckiest man in the world!

CHARLIE: Apart from the fact that I'm about to be executed.

ROBINSON: Well … yes … apart from that.

CHARLIE: I still say I'm unlucky. I shouldn't be King at all – in which case you'd have no cause for killing me. The original heir to the throne shot himself over an unhappy love affair. His successor, my Uncle Freddie, was blown to pieces in Hohenhuffundpuff Street. The late Queen was assassinated by a madman on Lake Geneva. My father died after a visit to the Holy Land. And I am to be executed by a vegetarian pacifist from Sevenoaks – now if *that* isn't unlucky, I don't know what is. So, if you don't mind, I'd be glad if we could get this business over. The next charge, please.

ROBINSON fumbles with his paper. His dignity now seems a little worn.

ROBINSON: Third count. That you are a tyrant and an oppressor of the will of the people.

CHARLIE: *[more lively]* No – I definitely deny that. I tried to revive Parliament and extended the franchise. Admittedly democracy didn't get very far, but I only had eighteen months to make my mark and there was a war on. The problem was that I couldn't get the politicians to agree about anything. The Hungonians vetoed anything the Boguslavians wanted, and the Boguslavians vetoed anything the Hungonians wanted, and they both vetoed anything that anyone else wanted. The only thing that the politicians agreed upon was a desire for jobs and pensions. I was the only democrat among the lot of them – and I was King!

HERMANN: *[sternly]* You should have used the army to crush the Boguslavians.

ZOË: *[to ROBINSON]* Please forgive Hermann. He's a Hungonian. *[She smiles winningly at ROBINSON and slyly taps her head with reference to HERMANN]*

HERMANN: I saw that! *[to CHARLIE]* The fact remains, Sire, that, at your coronation, you swore to uphold inviolate the historical territories of the Crown of Hungonia.

CHARLIE laughs delightedly. He seizes ROBINSON's arm, neither noticing that it is the one with the gun.

CHARLIE: Ha, ha! Here, Robinson, you've got to listen to this one – the story of my coronation oaths! By the way, must I keep calling you Robinson? Don't you have another name?

ROBINSON: *[very reluctantly]* It's Reginald.

CHARLIE: Reginald – excellent. Lets be democratic about it. You can call me Charlie. This is Zoë. And this is Hermann – but I suggest you call him General. Where were we? Oh, yes, my coronation oaths. I swore to maintain inviolate the historical territories of the Crown of Hungonia. Unfortunately, these happen to include the whole of Boguslavia, which was conquered by Saint Stephen the Boguslav Slayer in the ninth century. Isn't that so, Hermann?

HERMANN: Yes, Your Majesty.

CHARLIE: *[confidingly]* Very good. However, what Hermann doesn't like mentioning is that I also took the coronation oath to maintain inviolate the historical territories of the Crown of Boguslavia, and – wouldn't you know it! – these comprise the entirety of Hungonia which was conquered in the eighth century by Saint Lewis the Hungonian Impaler!

HERMANN: *[testily]* We have priority by right of later conquest.

CHARLIE: I know. And the Boguslavians claim *they* have priority by right of the earlier title. As it happens, Reginald, *both* Hungonia and Boguslavia were conquered by the Ottomans in the fourteenth century, but, for some inexplicable reason, no one suggests that the Turks are entitled to any say on the subject.

ROBINSON: *[fascinated]* How on earth did you manage to take two contradictory oaths?

CHARLIE: *[jolly]* Go-od question! You see, it's like this. My birth language is German. My natural language is the English I learned from my Irish nurse. The Hungonians speak Magyar. The Boguslavians speak Macedonian. And the coronation oaths are written in Church Slavonic, which hasn't changed since the twelfth century – or, more correctly, the pronunciation has changed but the spelling hasn't: in fact they don't resemble each other in the slightest. In consequence, I didn't have the faintest idea what the blasted coronation oaths meant!

ROBINSON: I see why you're interested in spelling reform.

CHARLIE: At last!

ROBINSON: *[thoughtfully]* I'm prepared to give you the benefit of the doubt on the last charge.

CHARLIE: You mean I'm acquitted?

ROBINSON: Yes – but I'm afraid I'll still have to execute you on the first two charges.

CHARLIE: Even so. *[to ZOË excitedly]* See, darling, your old hubbie isn't such a bad 'un after all! *[to ROBINSON]* Well, I suppose we'd better get on with it while we're all in the mood.

HERMANN: *[solemnly]* I propose that we sing the Hungonian National Anthem.

CHARLIE: Must we? *[embarrassed]* I'm sorry to admit this, Hermann old chap, but I don't know the words.

HERMANN: You don't?

CHARLIE: I don't speak Magyar. I used to get through the business by mouthing silently. I don't even know what the title means.

HERMANN: 'Dearest land, Hungonia, from sea to shining sea…'

CHARLIE: Stop there. Hungonia doesn't have a sea coast, shining or otherwise.

HERMANN: We *used* to, Sire. At the time of Saint Bogumil and the Massacre of the Sklavonians.

CHARLIE: *[firmly]* No anthem. Wait – we'll sing 'God save the King'. The king in question isn't specified and, in the circumstances, I could do with a bit of saving. You don't mind, do you, Reginald? Everyone take their timing from me.

CHARLIE begins to sing loudly. Everyone stands with arms by their sides. ROBINSON sings fervently. Only HERMANN does not fall in with the others. As the first verse reaches its end, he strikes at ROBINSON knocking the revolver from his hand. There follows the usual stage business, as comical as possible, in which the various parties struggle for the gun in an atmosphere of pass the parcel with the weapon being picked up and thrown one to another between CHARLIE, ROBINSON and ZOË until HERMANN gets a firm grip on it and fires a shot into the air which brings action to a dead stop.

HERMANN: Nobody move! Now I have the gun!

END OF SCENE TWO

CHAPTER FOURTEEN

Footsteps sounded on the path and a rap came at the door. For a moment I thought it was Pennyweight and half expected to hear his voice booming cheerily, 'Hullo, old man! I've just been having a noggin with Jesus' – or it might be with the Emperor or an angel. Or perhaps I would find Pouco Pedro, sidling out of the shadows to say, 'Hi, Senhor Mikey. I have information for you. What's it worth?'

In the realm of my dependents, no possibility was too exotic.

In fact it was Crispin and a companion, both slightly the worse for wear. He said, 'I have got the right time, haven't I? You look as though you weren't expecting us.'

I said I was sorry; that I was thinking of something else; and I invited him in. He winked at his companion. 'May I introduce Van?'

'Hullo, Van.'

'Mike.'

Van was the engineering officer of the *Kildonan Castle*. He was a South African called Van der Moewe, but if he had a first name I never heard it or have forgotten. They followed me silently into the house, reminding me of the legend that a vampire may not cross the threshold unless invited: not inappropriately since they were both tall, spare men. Crispin was dark; I could imagine his tanned, manly face having a certain attraction for women. Van der Moewe was fair with abraded red skin and a sullen air as though he liked solitary drinking or fighting in bars.

We went into the billiard room.

'An interesting place you've got,' the engineer said for form's sake.

I'd sold the table to the British Club to clear some pressing debts but I was fond of the room. It had been fitted out by my Great Uncle Walter in the gothic revival style with a throne made of stag antlers and vivid scarlet and gold wallpaper. The paintings were of girls in smocks picking flowers, thatched cottages screened by lupins and hollyhocks, and a large canvas of a Scottish glen where Highland cattle grazed morosely in a water meadow. My Uncle Gordon had added them before he went off his head and ran away to join Kitchener in the Sudan. The family tendency to melancholia often expressed itself in sentimentality.

Now everything was softened and faded and there was a noticeable smell of damp; but sometimes I'd come across pockets of ancient cigar smoke trapped in drapes and stuffed chairs; and, with these relics of my equally gothic family around me, I'd wonder what form my own melancholia would take and whether my collection of trinkets, strays and stolen wives was an early sign.

I always supposed it would end in blowing my brains out.

'May I introduce my father?'

'Mr Pinfold,' said Crispin.

'Sir,' said Van der Moewe.

'Charmed,' said my father with a sweet smile.

For the occasion he had wiped off his makeup except for traces behind the ears and his pale cheeks were dimpled like a baby's. He was wearing slippers and old trousers and had swathed himself in a long tartan shawl. The impression was of a mildly eccentric invalid, perhaps Jane Austen's Mr Woodhouse, which was quite likely what he had in mind.

I said, 'I'm sorry, I'm forgetting myself. Can I offer you a drink?'

'Brandy and soda,' said Crispin.

'Whisky,' said Van der Moewe.

I pulled the bell cord and a miserable Teddy trotted in sporting an old red mess jacket, my father's idea. He bowed and made a *namasti* – an intentional touch of irony which had also caused him to go barefoot. My father had forgotten to prescribe shoes.

Crispin asked, 'Do you know how to play draw poker, Mr Pinfold?'

'I think I played it once, long ago,' said my father, hinting at a church social and children merrily playing poker in sunshine, innocence and rose gardens.

'We can take it easy until you feel comfortable with the rules.'

'You are most obliging.'

Teddy poured the drinks.

I asked Crispin, 'Do you know yet when you'll be leaving?'

'Van can tell you better.'

'Are you an engineer, Mike?' Van der Moewe asked.

'No.'

'Right. Well, it's a problem with gears to the propeller shaft. We ought to have spares to fix it but we found them broken or missing.'

'Can't the yard in Funchal help you?'

'Not out of their stock, but they're trying to machine replacements.'

'My, my,' said my father.

Crispin drained his glass. 'At any rate it isn't a crisis yet. We were scheduled to make a stop, so the delay is less than it appears. And the passengers – God bless 'em – seem happy enough. Well? Shall we play? I've brought cards, still in their wrapper – is that all right?' He showed me the pack; they were printed with red lozenges, white margins and the name of the shipping line, the last a precaution against the marked decks available in magicians' supply shops. I indicated I was content and we sat down at the table.

In the first hour, with intervals of conversation, we played a dozen hands of no particular consequence. The stakes were small as we felt each other's playing style, betting half-crowns. I was up two pounds and my father was down a pound to Crispin. Teddy refilled the glasses from time to time and brought in some snacks. Van der Moewe's eyes followed him. His gaze was intense but lacklustre: the eyes of a man examining a whore: with interest but without hope.

'Your kaffir doesn't wear shoes,' he observed. 'I always make my kaffirs wear shoes. You get no work out of the lazy beggars if they've got bad feet. Have to watch out for ticks and jiggers. They play hell with you.'

I marked him as a man impressed by nothing: who assumes everyone agrees with him so that his pronouncements were like oracles: incontrovertible. He probably interpreted his charmlessness as forthright honesty.

He said, 'Women should wear shoes. I don't like women with hard skin on their soles.'

'What do you make of this angel business?' Crispin asked as if expecting a quarrel. 'It's all anyone seems to talk about since the fuss over Robinson died down. I think it's all tommyrot.'

'More things in heaven and earth, eh?' said my father.

'Have you heard any more about Robinson?' I asked

'Why do you care?' said Crispin.

I shrugged. What was I supposed to tell him: that some people thought I was the killer? That I was playing at being a detective? I had no idea how to go about the business.

Van der Moewe persisted in his own train of thought: 'I knew a woman who didn't wear shoes. Picked up a parasite. Wrecked her liver.' He signalled Teddy to pour him another whisky before ending obscurely, 'It's one of my rules in life.'

I won two modest pots then went down ten pounds to four kings held by the South African in a hand dealt by Crispin. My father asked to go to the toilet.

'Does anyone mind?' I asked. 'I'm afraid we don't run much to plumbing and use an old latrine in the garden. If you boys want to … well, there's a pot in the corner.'

'Unsavoury places sometimes, these old houses, aren't they?' said Crispin. His friend spared a suspicious look but didn't object.

I ushered my father outside into the darkness upwind of Kensington Palace. A breeze was stirring the eucalyptus and raising a plangent sound from the *levada*.

'Do you really want to go?' I asked.

'Of course not,' my father said. 'Fine friends you've got. Bloody cheats, the pair of them.' His outrage was at their clumsiness. He despised lack of skill in the matter of card manipulation.

I knew Crispin cheated: he'd robbed Fairbrother and Pennyweight during our games onboard the ship. His technique was to mark the high cards with his thumbnail during play, and deal seconds whenever necessary. I hadn't minded since he'd had the discretion to let me win a little as cover for his depredations, though it motivated me to break into his cabin. Tonight I'd noticed only that he and Van der Moewe were working as a pair. They exchanged hand signals and decided which of them would take the pot. Their system was one used by the common run of sharpers and my father and I read it easily while using a code of our own.

'You'd better use the latrine; they may be watching,' I suggested. 'What are they doing, other than the hand business? The cards looked all right to me.'

'They've switched the deck.'

'Switched? How do you know?'

'I marked the faces of the threes – no one ever marks the faces, still less the threes; so they didn't notice. Last time I looked, my mark wasn't there. The switch was done when Teddy brought the snacks, but they covered it by letting you take a couple of small pots before they hit you for that tenner. Are you laughing, Michael?'

'Well, one has to, don't you think? After all, we were planning to cheat them. What have they done to the deck? Can you read it?'

'They're playing with "trims",' said my father, who ought to know, for he was the heir of the Great Alberto. Crispin had shaved one edge of the court cards, which caused the pattern on the reverse side to be off-centre and easily readable. Combined with hand signals to a partner and a little second-dealing, it was enough in the ordinary run to guarantee success. In a way I admired him for his effrontery. A matter of professional respect, I suppose.

I caught a whiff of cigar smoke. Crispin had stepped outside to smoke a cheroot; I glimpsed his white suit as an aqueous shimmer among the laurels.

'You'd better use the latrine,' I told my father. He tested the handle.

'There's someone inside.'

'Is there?' I tried the handle too. I encountered resistance, then heard a voice.

'*Boa noite*, Senhor Mikey,' said Pouco Pedro.

'Good God! What are you doing here?'

'I didn't want to come into the house. Not with your friends. You glad to see me, Mikey?'

'No, I'm bloody well not. For God's sake shut the door.'

The three of us squeezed into the latrine. I placed the hurricane lamp on the floor where it provided a ghastly light, and grabbed Pouco Pedro by the lapels.

'What do you mean by scaring me half to death?'

'Why are you so cross? You were expecting me.'

'Not in the bloody toilet in the dead of night.'

'That's not my fault.' The tone was injured. 'You ask me to go sneaking round the *Kildonan Castle*, and I been sneaking. Where is my ten pounds you promise, hunh?'

'Later. We'll have to deal with this later. I've got two officers from the ship here at the house.'

'Here!'

'Keep the noise down. Yes, *here*. I'll get rid of them as soon as I can.'

'But...' Pouco Pedro didn't finish. I felt his hands scrabbling against mine. Then he asked, 'You will please stop strangling me, Senhor Mikey?'

I let go. 'Sorry ... I'm sorry. I'll get Teddy to bring you a drink. Whisky all right?'

'I don't like strangling. Beer, please. Not whisky. Makes my stomach burn.'

'I think we're out of beer. Will brandy do?'

'Brandy is not so bad, thank you. And food?'

'I'll see what I can arrange.'

Pouco Pedro grunted appreciatively. 'Sandwiches, hunh? Tuna fish?'

I took my father by the arm and led him back towards the house. 'Interesting friends you have,' he said. He seemed pleased.

Van had joined Crispin and both men were now blocking the path. I wondered how much they'd heard. Crispin extinguished his cheroot and looked at me appraisingly. I thought, for a moment, that he was preparing for a fight, but the drink he had taken seemed to switch his mood and he asked only, 'Are you all right?'

'We're fine.'

'Good. That's a splendid old thunder box you've got there, but they can be dangerous places – you get gas if they're not properly ventilated. I used one once, lit a cigar and damn' near blew my backside off.'

He didn't move. I hoped they'd been too concerned about the game to think of anything else. Most likely they were wondering whether in some way we, too, were going to rig the cards, though we'd left them on the table and they'd had opportunity to search the room in case we'd hidden another pack. A car passed slowly up the lane beyond our boundary, the thrum of its engine noticeable in the silence. Crispin paid no attention, but for me it was a rarity; more so when it stopped.

I asked, 'Shall we get back to cards?'

Crispin became amenable. 'Of course, old man. Van and I were thinking you'd lost the taste for the game after the last hand.'

'Luck of the draw.'

He chuckled. 'That's the old soldier speaking. If the bullet has your number on it … eh?'

'Something like that.'

Before we sat down I caught Teddy and whispered to him in Portuguese that he should pop into Kensington Palace and not be surprised at what he found. Then I took my place and we resumed the game. I glanced at the cards. My father was right: the pack had been trimmed; but for the next three hands it made no difference because the run was with my father and he won a few shillings.

In any case the cards are neutral if both sides know how to read them.

My father took fifteen pounds on the next hand. Crispin smiled philosophically. 'Do you want to raise the minimum bet? I'm getting tired. By the way, doesn't the Emperor live around here?'

'In the village. I don't mind raising the stakes. Ten shillings?'

'What do you say to a pound? Do you ever see him – the Emperor?'

'No. A pound is fine. On reflection, I may have seen him a couple of days ago. He was in the garden.'

'I think it's your deal, Mr Pinfold. In the garden? What does he look like?'

'Youngish, scarcely more than thirty. Has a moustache. He reminded me of a railway clerk – always assuming it was him, of course. During the war I saw his photograph in the paper.'

'Newspaper photographs!' Crispin laughed as if at a well known joke. 'Still, it must be odd, what do you think? To be an emperor and in exile? I'll open for a pound. To be an emperor and in exile, eh? A rum way for life to turn out.'

The last remark reminded me of Pennyweight, who was fond of observing, 'It's a rum old world,' with a suggestion that he and the Ascended Masters had a trick worth two of that. A rum old world – I was never certain if that was the fundamental question which philosophers tried to address, or the fundamental answer of which nothing more could usefully be said. The whisky was going to my head and I was worried for Pouco Pedro, stuck in the latrine, and for Pennyweight, conversing with angels and fellow drunks. It had occurred to me that the mysterious motor car that had passed up the lane might have been bringing him home, but half an hour had gone by and there was no sign.

The deal passed to Crispin, who won five pounds on a full house – kings and queens – not so difficult with a trimmed pack and control of the cards. He put a good face on his disappointment at the size of the pot. 'You're not so heroic since we raised the stakes.' As a response, we bid the next hand to fifty pounds with a show of nerves. I took it with four aces to Van der Moewe's full house, jacks and sevens. The South African turned on the ship's doctor.

'Damn this, man! What kind of a game have you got me into?'

'It's the way the cards fall,' Crispin answered, and perhaps he thought it was – at least for a while. He or his partner continued to win on his deal; and my father or I won on my father's. Only Van der Moewe and I dealt honestly from lack of skill; and even here the Pinfold Boys had the advantage since we could read the trims and the others' signals. We took them for a hundred pounds. A rum old world.

'I've had enough,' Van der Moewe said. He was furious and drunk. I rang the bell for Teddy. He came in carrying a heavy blackthorn stick.

'I think we should finish, don't you?' I said to Crispin, who considered the position, then nodded. When he spoke he was calm, even friendly.

'It's been an interesting evening, Mike – Mr Pinfold. I've learned a lot, and one always has to pay for one's lessons. I'm sorry we've been had, Van, but that's the way it happens.'

'Is that it? You're going to let them rob us?'

'I wouldn't call it robbery, old man. Not exactly. Mike, do you have a cigarette?'

I offered my case. Crispin held my wrist and examined it.

'Nice cigarette case. I used to have one like it.'

'Keep it if you like.'

'As a souvenir? Ha ha! This is perfect! No, you keep it, old man. Mr Pinfold, I think it's time Van and I said goodbye.'

So they took their coats and there were more farewells. Perhaps things might have been different but for Teddy's courage and the South African's incapacity. I lit a hurricane lamp and walked them down the path where I noticed Pouco Pedro lying under the laurels.

Crispin lit another cheroot and offered a hand. 'You talked about quitting this place.'

'We're selling up.'

'With your luck I'm surprised you have to. What are your plans?'

'To go back to England. After that I don't know.'

'Perhaps you'll be taking the old *Kildonan* on our return trip from the Cape.'

'That's possible.'

Crispin nodded. 'Wasn't Napoleon exiled here?'

'I think you'll find it was Saint Helena.'

'Right – well, I suppose you'd know. Still, they're strange places, these islands. What with emperors and angels and … do you follow me? I heard a story that you were sleeping with the wife of the chief of police: Mrs Cardozo, a very smart piece.'

'Johnny Cardozo isn't chief of police. He's a diplomat – concerned with the Emperor Karl, as it happens.'

'And his wife?'

'We're dancing partners. We take tango lessons together. Johnny knows about it.'

'The tango.' Crispin was amused. 'They call that "the dance of life and death", don't they? At least someone does. Probably Dr. Johnson or Oscar Wilde – they seem to have said everything that anyone quotes. "Good night, sweet prince" – that's Shakespeare, isn't it, the fellow who drowns his victims in malmsey? Say goodnight to the Emperor for me. Lord, I'm drunk and Van is going to feel bloody terrible in the morning.' He turned and took his sleepy companion by the arm. They swayed down the path together and began to sing.

I turned back to the house and halted by Pouco Pedro. I'd hoped that he, too, might be drunk, but someone had cut his throat. I'd have to bury him or tell his wife, or possibly both, but it was late and, for now, I would ask Teddy to give me a hand bringing him into the house.

My father hadn't moved from his chair. He seemed serenely cheerful. 'I haven't had so much fun in years,' he said. He was tired but had a glow that said thoughts of razors were far from his mind. I kissed his cheek as I used to when a boy. 'Children – ' he shook his head ' – the boxwallah's whoreson came up trumps, didn't he?'

'Yes. He was an absolute brick. Are you all right? Do you need help to get to bed?'

I began snuffing the candles until the light faded from the girls in smocks, the cottages and the Highland cattle.

'Yes, I should like a hand,' my father said. With difficulty he rose to his feet, and playing cards fluttered from the folds of his shawl where he had secreted them.

LAVINIA PALISER TO MICHAEL PINFOLD

The Laurels

Cavendish Road

Buxton

Derbyshire

14th. September 1922

Dear Captain Pinfold,

Please accept my thanks for your letter. Your simple condolences and the delicacy with which you touched on other matters concerning my brother affected me very greatly. The truth is that you are the only person who has bothered to correspond since Reginald's death, and I put that down to the fact that you served with him in the war. You are right, of course. Only another soldier can understand the mental pain he went through and the difficulties of adjustment to a world that no longer seemed to make much sense to him. Everyone else was embarrassed by the nature of his illness, which some chose to call 'malingering' and others treated as outright madness; and his imprisonment was the final straw which caused all his former friends to desert him. You will therefore understand my gratitude at hearing from someone who seeks to judge him only by the higher, better light to which he aspired.

I should appreciate the return of the book of poetry. I gave it to Reginald as a parting gift before he first went to France. For the rest, you may give his clothes and any other possessions to any worthy cause, though, if he had a

Bible (which I am sure must be the case), I should also like to keep it – could you bring it to me? After his illness he gained a great consolation from Holy Scripture and found there signs of a larger purpose, though he was never able to explain it to me. You are no doubt aware of the 'crime' which resulted in his being sent to prison, and I suppose it was a crime to steal from a charity. However, you should understand that he did not act selfishly. Every penny that he took was given to poor unfortunates who found themselves down and out at the end of the war. The charity in question was for the relief of animals, and he felt that there were nobler objects; and I believe that he was right – in his intentions, if not in his methods.

I should very much like to meet you. When Reginald was released from gaol he was in a condition of some distress and I was afraid of a relapse into his illness. My husband and I were unable to do anything for him because he left the country almost immediately and we received no news except a single postcard from Casablanca. We did not even know that he was in Madeira: still less the reasons for his being there. Perhaps you are able to enlighten us?

I have taken the liberty of informing Reginald's fiancée that you have written. Before the war, they were planning to marry. After his breakdown he would have nothing to do with her. His desertion of her was, of all things that he did, the most cruel. And yet I feel that there must have been a reason – one that was not entirely unworthy. I do not expect that I shall ever understand it: but it may be that you can persuade me that Reginald did not intend to act dishonourably. I should like both of you to meet. I feel sure that you could lessen her pain. In case I should forget later, I would caution you that, at Reginald's request, she was informed that he was killed in action during the war. She does not have all the true facts, which are too sad to speak of.

Please write to me again upon your return to England. Although Buxton is a small, quiet town, it is not so very difficult to reach by the railway.

Yours sincerely

Lavinia Paliser

CHAPTER FIFTEEN

Teddy gave me a hand to steer my father to bed. The old fellow was cheerful. Tonight he was safe from the razor. He said, 'We fair saw that pair off, didn't we, sonny boy? Yon Crispin is a sinister cove. Teddy, will you pass me my haemorrhoid cream? I thought the South African – Van, what sort of a name is Van? – had bone instead of brain.'

Once my father was settled, I took Teddy aside and explained that there was a corpse in the garden – or, at least, I thought so. As with other things that disconcert the mind, I was beginning to have doubts: as if the body of Pouco Pedro lay only in the realm of bare possibility, where it would stay unless I recognised its existence. Pennyweight would have understood this. For him reality was a malleable notion that one could cudgel into shape with magical manipulations.

We went into the garden. With night a mist had crept down the mountain and Pouco Pedro's face was covered in fine droplets, which sparkled in the light of the hurricane lamp. In life his image had been one of bobbing and ducking mobility. Now, in repose, his features were gravely composed, appropriate, at last, to his claim to be a doctor of something or other: probably some form of quackery but possibly not. I wondered if he had been a friend when I knew so little of him. Perhaps he was. I'd taken his wife, which seemed to be the hallmark of my friendship.

'So now you are murdering people, isn't it?' Teddy said.

'I didn't kill him,' I said. 'Why aren't you surprised?'

Teddy gave me a puzzled look as though he were disqualified from holding an opinion. 'Are you calling the sleuths to nab the bad fellow who did this, Mr Michael?'

'No.' I'd thought about it but was defeated at the prospect of explaining the event. I had no idea who killed Pouco Pedro and only the vaguest theory as to the reason. His last message had mentioned sabotage, and presumably came from his investigations into the breakdown of the *Kildonan Castle*. But the 'why' and the 'who' remained mysteries.

Regardless of motive, it crossed my mind that Crispin might have been involved. As engineering officer, Van der Moewe was certainly able to cause havoc. Yet neither had killed Pouco Pedro. They had been under my eyes during the entire period between the encounter at the latrine and his death. Magic apart.

I asked Teddy if he'd help me move the body into the house.

'It is very disgusting,' he said, but agreed all the same.

We carried it through to the boot room and placed it on one of the low wooden racks. I stopped the rat holes with rags and old shoes, then bade Teddy goodnight.

'I shall pray for the poor chappie,' he said.

*

In the morning I buried Pouco Pedro in a spot downwind of Kensington Palace where the smells would mask the decomposition of the body. Teddy stood by me, displaying good-natured sadness for a stranger.

It was an unsentimental affair, but I'd been through many similar occasions during the war. I wasn't without feeling but I suppressed it; for it wasn't grief but, rather shame that I felt, which, being selfish, is more agonising than regret at the loss suffered by others. So I put grief aside, locked away with my other unconsidered sins. When it came – as most likely it would – it would strike as night terrors or a fit of tears on an occasion when I'd drunk too much. Such feelings for others as I had were for Angélica Soares. At some point she would have to be told; but to present her husband's death as a mystery would be to do her no favours. Death is acceptable. Meaninglessness is not. Glancing at Teddy as he muttered a prayer, I wondered if he were in fact my brother. I should have liked it if he were.

Pennyweight still hadn't appeared. I went to his room in case he'd turned up while I was asleep. The bed was neatly made up, army fashion. In tidy ranks on the table were his shaving kit and a tin of denture adhesive: evidently he hadn't planned on being away. Next to these was a bayonet in its sheath. Like me he'd kept one as a souvenir.

I took some time to study the reading matter he'd brought. It comprised several journals from the Theosophical Society and a book about the Templars. He also had a collection of pamphlets, the kind that are privately printed on yellow paper and use capital letters and italics profusely. The texts were scattered with Latin phrases and there were various maps overlaid with cabalistic symbols proving God knew what. I was looking for a clue to the connection with Robinson. Why, above all people, had he chosen Pennyweight to join him in Madeira?

Lounging in the doorway, smoking a cigarette, Margaret said, 'You're not ready, are you? Don't tell me you've forgotten about our weekend.'

I had forgotten until she appeared, beautiful and fresh, wearing a straw hat pulled over one eye so that the other seemed sly and witty.

She looked about her. 'Do you know, this is the first time I've been here? I've still to meet your father.'

'How do you wish to be introduced? As my mistress?'

'Tsk tsk, Michael,' she said.

I took her into the main saloon and offered a drink while I packed a small case. The decayed grandeur impressed her; she said, 'It reminds me of home. My family lost its money, too. Nowadays we potter about trying to make ends meet without working, and marry-off our daughters to rich dagoes.' She marked the last comment with a weak smile mixed with an affection that wasn't for me. 'Johnny doesn't really understand, poor darling. He buys lots of stuff to please me, but it's all such a fraud. You can't really buy the charm of utter failure, can you? You have to be born with it like a feeling for religion.'

I asked, 'Are you like this when you're with Sonny? I mean wistful.'

She turned on me brightly. 'No. With him I'm young, womanly and fascinating. He calls me Zoë.'

'Why?'

'I don't know. It's something to do with the Life Force, whatever that is.'

On an impulse I kissed her. The kiss was long and tender and afterwards we remained holding each other with her head on my shoulders and I ran my fingers through the hair at the nape of her neck. Despite our difficulties we never quarrelled, and this, now I think about it, was odd and not necessarily hopeful, for there are exhausted marriages where peace is merely a bitter truce. Arguments were in any case contrary to my character. And, again, this was not necessarily a hopeful sign insofar as issues have to be resolved: if not by conflict, then by deception. There was no avoiding the fact that I was a trickster.

She said, 'I wish I could be for you as I am for Sonny.'

'Can't you?'

'No – with you it wouldn't be genuine. And yet it is with Sonny. Truthfully, the woman he sees *is* me.'

'And the woman I see?'

'The same – even if she looks completely different. Oh, damn it, I'm crying, Michael.'

'Why don't you leave Johnny?'

'Would you believe I love him? Isn't it terrible that one can love several people at once?'

'I believe you. Now dab your eyes.'

I offered my handkerchief and she took it. 'Also,' she said, 'I think he kills people. But one can never be sure, can one?'

*

Now I recalled: above the cabinet holding Johnny Cardozo's collection of faïence was a photograph: a portrait of a man in military uniform against a background of drapes and classical impedimenta. The last time I examined it, I tried to recall if Portugal had a king or a dictator but rather thought that for the moment it was exotically democratic. Now, contemplating my friend's *alter ego* as a secret policeman (assuming he was one – which wasn't clear), I reverted to my first idea that the picture was a shrine to an autocrat, though the autocrat in question might be Johnny's parent. Father Flaherty had made a remark about the sin of idolatry. It was so insidious that the sinner could not recognise the altars at which he worshipped.

'The house at São Vicente belongs to Vera Wentworth,' Margaret said. 'You may not know her since she doesn't keep up with the British Wives. Her husband was killed in the war and now she has a lover, one of the Governor's people. A place in the country isn't much use to her. It gives her a thrill to let it for assignations, and she's very discreet.'

However, after a hard drive over Encumeada, we didn't go immediately to the house. Margaret wanted lunch at a restaurant in the village and afterwards, while the world continued its siesta, she proposed we walk along the shore. Atlantic breakers were rolling onto the pebble beach bringing drifts of sugar cane. Piles of it had been gathered and set alight, and the sun shone violet through a smoke plume. It reminded her, she said, of childhood holidays in Suffolk: there was such a beach near Aldeburgh – though no mountains, of course, and the driftwood wasn't sugar cane, and ... well, it wasn't really like Suffolk at all but had brought the memory back so that she wanted to run barefoot. And did. Barefoot along the shore and barefoot back to the village, spinning her shoes by their straps and beckoning me on.

It was for such a sight, such a moment of exaltation that I might die. Or so I was to understand: slaughtered in a display of jealous *machismo*. I wasn't sure that I cared. Margaret had pointed out her different behaviour towards me and towards Sonny, and there was no reason to suppose Johnny was more consistent. An affront, which out of justice and honour he would punish in a stranger, he might forgive in me from generosity – who could say? I didn't particularly believe either in his murderous instincts or my privileged position: only that Margaret was so human, so intensely and tenderly desirable that, if to possess her was a risk, it was no matter.

The Quinta Wentworth was a small villa on the side of the ravine. The village lay below, a huddle of houses built of tufa and a church with a chequerboard spire. Our route to São Vicente had taken us through Serra da Agua where I called at the church and enquired of Father Ruiz whether the foreigners had returned. They hadn't, but I was forced to explain to Margaret about Father Flaherty and the search for an angel.

'I don't like this angel,' she said. 'Johnny is very interested in it.'

'Is he religious?'

'Johnny?' She gave a high laugh.

Now, as evening drew in, we sat outside and watched the lamps come on by ones, the sea turn from turquoise to indigo, and a boy gather the goats foraging among the willows. The air was mild and scented with the tang of burning cane; with mimosa and Coty.

We sat side by side in wicker chairs. I told her of my father, my various mothers, the Empires of my childhood, the emperors met on my father's Grand Tour. She told me of her family, her schools, her dogs and her horses. We found the gramophone and played *Lagrimas* and danced a tango with slow, delicate steps around a palm tree. And we laughed: there in the garden, for the fleeting joy of it, with the last notes of the tango finding us in each other's arms, gay and a little absurd. Margaret was more tangible, more sensuous than I'd ever known her; and if, in my smiles, there was a note of irony, it was only because I despised cheap romantic fiction, though life occasionally presents us with its vulgar, sentimental effects.

Margaret told me that she was pregnant.

*

My father used to be a gunfighter. During the course of his Grand Tour he made an appearance in Dodge City where his feats of legerdemain were much appreciated by cow pokes and gamblers. Subsequently he joined the Harry Haze Gang and robbed several trains. After the age of twelve, I didn't have to believe any of this.

What is certain is that my Uncle Gordon fled Madeira to join Kitchener's war against the Mahdists, and, if enteric fever hadn't killed him, he would have done his best to be a *beau sabreur*.

'You belong to a family of thieves and fantasists,' Margaret said. 'What a hopelessly Byronic hero you are!'

I was fantasist enough to hope she might leave Johnny. Thief enough not to feel guilty at the thought. As for heroism, I knew from the war that it was largely a matter of recklessness and bad judgment, which was why those of us who survived turned out to be such poor specimens. Unlike Pennyweight I had no all-explaining vision, merely a rag bag of insights, most of them false, and a few petty principles, all of them compromised. After a fashion I tried to act decently, and I felt a warm sympathy towards others; but these qualities seemed no more than habit and shallow sentiment: not the mark of a moral human being.

I was half glad when Margaret told me she would stick by Johnny.

And the child that she assured me was mine?

My breath caught when she told me, and I said that was wonderful, or something to the same effect. I pressed her again to marry me. To her enquiry how I felt about becoming a father, I said lightly that I thought I would rise to the occasion. The words are not especially important; for Margaret detected the lack of conviction which may have had something to do with my faint moral scruples. At the time I believed I was sincere. Sincerity has always been the mark of my deceptions, as if they are representations in code of some other state: perhaps a truth too frightening to confront.

In the silence after this sterile exchange, we heard the clip clop of hooves and the whinny of a horse.

'Someone's coming here,' Margaret said.

I slipped out of bed and into the next room and peered out of the shuttered window. I saw two bulls-eye lanterns swinging and the faint outline of horses.

'Who is it, do you think?'

'I don't know,' I said. 'The police?' I imagined a pair of merry rural gendarmes casting a quick eye over the normally empty property.

'That's probably it. Johnny most likely asked the local bobbies to look in for my safety. You'd better get some clothes on and hide. I'll get rid of them.'

She got out of bed and put on a silk robe. I heard her naked feet tread softly on the stairs and, as I waited for her to dispose of our visitors, I lit a cigarette from the night light. With the mood dissipated, the interruption gave me a feeling of relief so that I shouldn't have cared if Johnny had walked in. Like every lover who seeks more than a casual affair, I had often mentally dramatised such a confrontation.

What I didn't expect was Count Bronstein.

*

'You will please put your clothes on, Mr Pinfold,' Bronstein said. In one hand he gripped a Webley service revolver. With the other he reached to a chair, picked up a shirt and threw it to me. Behind him stood a second figure masked by the glare of the bulls-eye lantern.

I forget my exact reply. It was something conventional: puzzlement, outrage and false dignity. Scenes like this occur so infrequently in life that they take on a theatrical character from lack of any other knowledge of how to behave. This was equally true of Bronstein who had the manner of a stage villain in the suave tradition.

'What have you done with Margaret?'

'She is perfectly safe. Please hurry, Mr Pinfold.'

'Is it me that you want? I have to ask, because this business doesn't make much sense.'

'Do you have some boots? We have travelling to do and it will be easier if you wear boots.'

'Yes, of course I've got some bloody boots. What's all this about?'

'Later. Come now, finish dressing.'

We went downstairs. Several candles had been lit in the room below and Margaret was curled like a cat in a chair with a cigarette and a glass of gin beside her. The third intruder – there were three in all – was holding a gun on her but her fear was distorted by sheer annoyance.

She asked, 'Do you know who these dreadful people are, Michael? What do they want?'

I shook my head.

Bronstein asked her, 'Will you now please get dressed, Mrs Cardozo? I will allow you to be alone since we have

Mr Pinfold. And do you have boots? Please wear boots if you have them. The night is warm, but you may wish to take a coat.'

I said, 'You're being very considerate.' Bronstein shrugged. One of his companions laughed and I noticed the man was slightly drunk. Since most crimes seem to be committed under the influence, I could think of no reason why kidnapping should be an exception.

We waited for Margaret. Bronstein's companions sat down. One of them moved stiffly as though he had arthritis, and both were elderly. It would be easy to be amused at these geriatric bandits, but there was something impressive about them: a mildness that was more dangerous because it went with fixity of purpose.

This, it seemed, was what fanaticism looked like. Vaguely comic.

Margaret came back into the room. Bronstein smiled and said, 'You look most attractive.' He gave a little bow, very *mitteleuropäisch* and old-fashioned as if the war had never happened. There was a quaintness, too, in the gang's clothes: tweed suits of Norfolk jackets and breeches, and felt hats with badger brushes in the bands. The effect was civilized, frightening and a little mad.

Bronstein spoke to the others; I suppose it was in Magyar because I didn't understand a word. To Margaret and me he said, 'Shall we go? I assume you can both ride? We shall have to tie your hands, but the route is not so difficult and the night is clear.'

Outside the house was a string of five ponies, small animals in poor condition. Bronstein apologised for them.

'Mrs Cardozo?' He helped Margaret into the saddle and checked the bindings on her hands. The pony was held on a loose tether to the one in front. 'Mr Pinfold?' I mounted. My long legs hung almost to the ground, adding to the air of the ridiculous, the terrifying nonsense. One of the elderly men, carrying a lantern, climbed on the lead animal. Bronstein, with the second lantern, took the rear. The night was clear, and we rode our train of ponies with the lanterns bobbing and the silence and the starlight.

We went through the village at a trot, disturbing the dogs; then turned eastwards along the coast until the noise faded and we were left with nothing but the sound of hooves, the hush of a quiet sea and, to our right, the hemming wall of cliffs from which poured threads of waterfall. Making little above walking pace, we were at this for two hours until I saw the faint silhouette of Ponta Delgada ahead, a clutch of houses and a church by the sea, growing closer until they appeared as a shimmer of whitewash blued by the moon.

At the entrance to the village Bronstein called a halt.

'We will dismount here, I think. The streets are cobbled and we must be silent.' He asked Margaret with apparent seriousness, 'Do you promise not to make a noise – not to shout or scream?'

'I ought to yell my head off.'

'But you won't, I think. And Mr Pinfold – what shall we do with you? You are a soldier and a hero.'

'I'm not a hero.'

'So modest.'

I shrugged. 'Gag me if you like.'

'You don't mind?'

'You'll do it whether I mind or not.'

Bronstein grinned. 'As you see, I am a polite man. Andreas, help Mr Pinfold from his horse and gag him.' I was taken down and gagged.

We blundered through the village with the cobbles snagging our feet in the blackness until we reached the small quay. A steam launch, its funnel poking through a sun awning, was moored there and I was hustled on board. I looked for Margaret.

'Don't worry,' said Bronstein. 'We don't make war on women. We shall leave Mrs Cardozo behind. She will have to be tied and, unfortunately, gagged, but the villagers will find her in the morning and restore her to her husband. He is your friend, isn't he?' Bronstein hesitated and looked at me curiously. 'I confess I do not understand how you can be the friend of such a man.' He unfastened my gag. 'Well, do you not have an answer?'

I shook my head. I had a friend called Johnny Cardozo, but who he was and what he did were mysteries. I liked him, whatever his crimes might be. And he chilled me less than Bronstein, who was thoughtful and considerate.

We put to sea and I was given some food. Afterwards I was left below, seeing nothing of the journey: sensing only the calm ocean and the rhythm of pistons. It seems probable the food was drugged, because I drifted into a deep sleep and have no recollection of being landed. I dreamed of Margaret, though not of Johnny: of Margaret and old Sonny, who charmed her in ways that I could not. I dreamed of Pouco Pedro and that I was a good man who would make amends and marry his widow. In my dream Angélica Soares was beautiful, as women always are when we love them.

I came to in a small room. It was day and slats of light were coming through a shuttered window and a friendly though worried voice was speaking.

'Here's a queer how-d'you-do, old man. It's a rum world we're living in, isn't it?' said Pennyweight.

ELIZABETH MORRIS to GEORGE BERNARD SHAW

5 Devonshire Grove

Buxton

28th December 1919

Dear Mr Shaw,

Perhaps I expressed myself too bluntly, but your own writings are to the point. I appreciate that you are a busy man and do not know me, and I should therefore have expected that your reply to my request would be short and droll.

I will not disguise myself behind false modesty. I am an intelligent, independent woman, perfectly capable of analysing my situation rationally to come to a considered decision. Surely I am exactly the type of woman whom you idealise in your works? Am I not entitled to an equally considered reply?

My request is unusual only because I express what other women feel. The war has left many in my situation, bereft of any reasonable hope of marrying and of raising a family in the conventional manner. Others, for the sake of paltry notions of decency, are willing to accept their fate. I am not.

What then am I to do? There are men aplenty who would be prepared to 'oblige' me. I say nothing of their morals, but, speaking *rationally*, why should I accept the biological hazards of mating with an ordinary man? If I were in love, it would be a different matter, but I am not; and therefore reason is the only criterion I can use to guide my choice. You trumpet your superiority. I merely take you at your word.

I assume that your postscript was intended facetiously. I am not a Buddhist – nor any other sort of '-ist'. I am a free thinker. The point is in any case immaterial since I am not asking that you should marry me.

Please reconsider my last letter and your reply.

Yours sincerely

Elizabeth Morris (Miss)

GEORGE BERNARD SHAW to ELIZABETH MORRIS

10 Adelphi Terrace WC2

19th January 1920

My dear Miss Morris,

You offer your services as the mother of my child with fewer qualifications and less experience than I should require of a cook. You say that in your case matters might be different if you were in love; and I say that matters might be different if *I* were in love. But, since neither of us is in that happy state, the subject does indeed fall to be considered rationally.

Now reason suggests to me certain problems with your proposal. The first is your situation. As I understand these things, it is the practice and, for all I know, the law, that a woman should resign her employment upon her marriage. Clearly you must maintain the pretence of a marriage in order to avoid a scandal that would be at least equally fatal to you. Or do you have in mind to pose as a widow? If so, I still foresee difficulties of a practical nature; for a woman cannot make a plausible pretence of widowhood unless she has first provided plausible evidence of a husband, which will scarcely be possible in a town and among persons who already know you. Once you announce your nuptials, your friends will desire to see the fellow, and unless you intend to claim that he died on the wedding night from an excess of passion, I do not see how you can refuse them.

Marriage is the very devil, isn't it? For many years I believed that I was not the marrying kind. I was able to have relationships of a tender character without taking a step that was contrary to my principles. Then it happened that my wife and I found ourselves in circumstances of quite decorous propriety, but which could not continue except subject to a misconstruction curable only by tying the knot. And so we hied ourselves to the Registry Office and the deed was done; though the Registrar showed an inclination to marry the bride to the best man on grounds of good taste. Thus principles are sacrificed.

You are evidently a young woman of courage enough to fight for any cause. I, however, am a downy old bird. I fight my battles only on a field of which I am the master. It is one thing to rail at mischievousness and folly. It is another to act as if they do not exist. I believe in equality of income, but a rich man's silver spoons are as safe with me as with anyone. And, in the same spirit, I do not advise others to act upon a principle that will bring them to disaster.

Let us come down to cases. If you have a child, you will lose an annual income of forty-five pounds and the pair of you will starve.

Now consider how we are to manage the delicate side of the business. What do you propose? I see nothing for it but that we must book into an hotel somewhere as Mr & Mrs Robinson: the former a spindly old gent of 65 and the latter an attractive young woman of 25. I can tell you with confidence what will happen. The jolly innkeeper will telephone the police or the nearest circus.

sincerely

G. Bernard Shaw

SONNY to ZOË

Reid's Palace Hotel

29th March 1922

Zoë, Zoë

Dancing the tango with you is driving me stark mad! Why did I ever take you as a partner? Why did you let me? Not the least of the curses you have called upon my head is a liking for bad lyrics – in Spanish! Posterity will damn you for bringing the acknowledged master of English letters to this pretty pass. And what of music? Hurrah for Eduardo Arolas and to hell with Wagner? Love has made me so ridiculous that I bark at dogs and beggars give me money.

The mountains are full of angels and emperors: the town of toy soldiers, all broken and patched up. Do you not see that we are living in a fairy story peopled by characters from Andersen? Forget Rider Haggard and John Buchan: there are tales more dangerous than theirs: ordinary life goes out of the window and we are magically transformed – bewitched!

Beware! says the Sage (the Ides of March are gone, but Life never did imitate Art exactly). I am not at risk. I am a cunning old cove, and cowardice and a glib tongue are the best forms of armour. But what of my Zoë? Reckless of the consequences she attracts the love of every blackguard who casts his eyes on her – she *will* do so – she can't help it. She has nothing to fear from me: I am shambling toward the grave and there's no more harm in me than in a toothless dog basking before the fire: you may love me in the same fashion – indeed you say you do love me. Pinfold – there lies your peril!

Life is not the tango: you cannot draw him on only to push him away. I know him. He is a decent man with just enough knavery in him to make him dangerous. He has courage, too, and a curious sense of honour. At the last, he will let you go with his love and his blessings heaped upon you; and they will be as foul as a stepmother's curses because they will leave you with a lifetime of regret. Get rid of him now! I don't know what you want of him, but it will not be worth the price. Whatever you do, grant him no cause to forgive you. His forgiveness will blight any chance of happiness.

Oh, dearest Zoë, I fear for you. The tango is such a perilous dance and stirs up the emotions beyond any power of reason. Sometimes I hate you – it makes me hate you – but you know that already. When the music starts and we embark upon it, taking the first hazardous step onto the floor, we gamble that in the wild spinning of love and hatred it is love that will win out. But there is no certainty, my darling child. Only Art can predetermine the outcome in favour of love. Life is not so obliging. In the end it kills all of us.

I am rattling on like a fond fool. If I give more vent to my feelings and express them to their fullest banality, I shall have to abandon the theatrical game and write short stories for ladies' magazines.

This letter should be in purple ink on scented notepaper, but I don't have any to hand.

ever

Sonny

CHAPTER SIXTEEN

'I don't suppose you understand a word I'm saying? Damned embarrassing,' complained Pennyweight. 'I don't have the stuff with me – you know? – the stuff that holds the false teeth in? Cheap bloody things … never fit properly … make me look like a horse unless I use the stuff … buggered if I can remember its name … you know … the stuff?'

I rolled on my cot. My mouth was filled with bile and a taste like bad spirits.

Pennyweight said, 'I feel like one of those fellows who wear a hairpiece. D'you know what I mean? People staring all the time and sniggering as if your flies are undone. I used to know a chap. Wore an awful ginger job. What was his name?'

'Robinson.'

'No, not Robinson. He was a blond and his hair was all his own. I don't know who's been putting the story around … I say –' his voice became indignant '- you're not drunk, are you?'

I smiled, feeling a flush of affection and remembering Fairbrother's description of the fat man. That he was tremendous.

He eyed me edgily. 'You should get some water down you, if you've got a hangover.'

'What about you?'

'I don't know what you mean. *I've* not been drunk, and you shouldn't go around saying a fellow's been drunk when he hasn't.'

'What happened to you the other night? Why didn't you come home?'

'I was … researching,' he said as though plucking the word from a doubtful corner of his pockets. 'Travel broadens the mind, you know. It was getting a bit stuffy at your place – no offence. I thought I'd take in some of the sights. Yes – well – I admit I had a few drinks, but that wasn't the problem: I've got the measure of the local tipple. No, it wasn't that. It's the food. Something in it disagrees with me. Same thing happens to chaps in India – Egypt, too. It's no reason to go casting aspersions. Anyway, you've got no room to talk,' he finished conclusively.

I opened my eyes again. A yellow glare was shining through the jalousies. Pennyweight was lowering over me.

'You've got a black eye,' I said.

He lumbered back to his cot and sat down heavily. 'Glad to see you're all right – hangover apart.'

'You're limping.'

'I hope you're not going to go on about my being drunk.'

'How did you get hurt?'

'They roughed me up a little – oh, not too badly.' He squinted at me, looking for sympathy. 'Their heart doesn't seem to be in it. It was a bit like being beaten up by the Salvation Army. Damned odd.'

I sat up. My head swam a little before settling. I took in the small room, three or four paces square with whitewashed walls and an earth floor. The furniture comprised the two cots and a chamber pot. 'Do you mind if I use this?'

'Feel free, old man. It's rather more savoury than that old thunderbox you've got at home, if you don't mind my saying so.' While I urinated, he went on, 'I've tried the window. There's a bloody great metal bar on the outside. They keep the door padlocked.'

'And who are "they"?'

'Germans as far as I can make out – foreigners at any rate. Between you and me, they're a bit potty. D'you know they dragged me off into the mountains looking for angels? I ask you!'

'Did you find any?'

'You'll be asking next if I believe in elves and pixies,' Pennyweight said.

By degrees I got his story out of him. Restless for new company, he'd wandered through Funchal accosting strangers in bars. This was what he called 'research' – and, in a way, it was. He had a deep belief in meaningful coincidence and hidden patterns, and from his miscellaneous reading and stray acquaintances he constructed his Higher Wisdom: not a reasoned philosophy but an inexpressible insight into the secret forces behind Creation. For all his ridiculousness, Pennyweight was a prophet torn by lonely agonies.

Somewhere in his ramblings he'd run into three 'Germans' – 'nice chaps with whom one could talk about the war, no hard feelings and all that' – and pushed on to a brothel: 'just to chat with the girls, you understand.' And then he passed out, or was sandbagged. The latter, he suggested.

'They broke the spring that holds my choppers together. Dashed difficult to get 'em repaired. D'you know where we are?' he asked.

'Porto Santo, I think. I was brought here by boat.'

The only other nearby islands of any size were the Ilhas Desertas, which were uninhabited. It was possible we were still on Madeira – that we'd simply abandoned the ponies in order to throw pursuers off the scent and the boat had put into a fishing village further along the coast, but I thought this unlikely. My answer apparently meant nothing. Pennyweight looked at me strangely.

'Any idea why we're here?'

'I thought you might tell me,' I answered: which was the wrong thing to say, for Pennyweight assumed again his slightly offended air.

'That's rich,' he said. 'After all, you're the one who was Robinson's pal.'

*

Through the jalousies I could see blue sky and a windmill. It had triangular sails on a spidery rig: the kind against which Don Quixote tilted.

'We're on Porto Santo,' I repeated. 'What makes you think I was Robinson's pal? I never met the man – unless you count seeing his body.'

'That's not what it said in the paper.'

I tried to grasp what he was getting at.

He quoted, ' *"The service was attended by his oldest friend, Captain Michael Pinfold"*. You could have knocked me down with a feather when I read that. I think it's damned unsporting of you not to have told me.'

'The newspaper got it wrong. Believe me, I didn't know Robinson.' I saw no point in trying to explain Pouco Pedro's famously high standard of journalism. 'In any case, what does that have to do with our situation?'

'They kept going on about him – those German chaps.'

'About Robinson?'

'They wanted to know why he'd brought me to Madeira – not the only ones who'd like to know, I may tell you. Well, yours truly wasn't going to enlighten 'em. Didn't you tell me that I shouldn't let on about the Captain? Also I got the idea that they didn't exactly know *who* it was that Robinson brought out, if you follow me. We seemed to be talking in circles. They knew damned well what Robinson was up to, but they weren't about to tell me in case they'd grabbed the wrong fellow.'

'So you gave them my name.'

'Not straight away,' Pennyweight said shiftily. 'They gave me a bit of a going over.'

'But you must have realised I couldn't have known Robinson. You were serving with him.'

'Not after he left to join the Navy.'

This explanation stumped me for a second as I grappled with the vagaries of Pennyweight's thought. Then I protested, 'He was never *in* the Navy. He was suffering from shell shock in a bloody madhouse in Scotland. You told me so yourself.'

Pennyweight blinked. 'Don't lose your rag old man. How was I to know? The newspaper said he was in the Navy. The madhouse story could have been something put about by the Secret Service wallahs – if that's what you two were up to.'

'We weren't "up to" anything.'

'If you say so.'

'It's the truth, damn it.'

'If you say so.'

There was no point in repetition. In any case Pennyweight didn't seem to mind if, as he saw it, Robinson and I had dragged him into some nefarious business. Secrets and conspiracies were the ordinary stuff of life and couldn't shock an initiate into the Higher Mysteries.

He asked, 'D'you have any smokes? I'm out of *Players*.'

I offered my case.

He examined it, noting the dent. 'I've got one like this,' he said. 'It saved a fellow's life.' He looked at me guilelessly. 'It's odd how many fellows had their lives saved by a cigarette case that caught the bullet. It makes you think, doesn't it?'

He lit the cigarette and lay down on his cot.

'About Robinson…'

'Say no more. I can understand if it's all hush hush.'

'That's not what I meant. I want you to think, man. *Why* did Robinson bring you out here?'

'I don't know. He never said. I always thought it was because he knew I was a steady chap.' He paused for a moment. 'Of course, if he was mixing himself up in this angel business, he might have wanted a second opinion – someone to tell him if it was all on the square. I pride myself on knowing a lot more about that sort of thing than your so-called experts. And you've got to be careful, mind you. The Occult attracts a lot of people who are, quite frankly, barmy.'

I was about to say that the angel had nothing to do with the affair, when it came to me that it did: that, in some way, it went to the heart. Hadn't Bronstein and his friends taken Pennyweight to Serra da Agua? That I could make no sense of it was beside the point. Magic and madness, angels and emperors were in the air, and Pennyweight was a true philosopher.

'Bronstein is a Hungarian,' I said.

'Bronstein?'

'Our host. His real name is Laszló Tormassi.'

'There was me, thinking he was a German.'

'Doesn't it mean anything to you?'

'Not a thing, old man.'

I tried to recall what Johnny Cardozo had explained about good and bad Hungarians, and the difficulty in distinguishing between the two. As best I could, I repeated it.

'So it's all to do with the Emperor,' Pennyweight said smugly as if he knew already. 'Can't say I'm surprised. Did I ever tell you that Karl is a descendant of Jesus Christ?'

'Yes, you did.'

'It gives you food for thought, doesn't it? I mean: there could be something to this story about the angel. One can imagine Jesus's descendants hobnobbing with 'em. D'you have another cigarette? Funny about the Captain, though. I wouldn't have said that angels were his sort of thing at all

– not before he went mad and started talking to 'em. When he wasn't a radical, he was a staunch Protestant – "Onward Christian Soldiers" and all that. I'm not sure Protestants believe in angels – leastways not this side of heaven. Perhaps he was still bonkers? What d'you say? I wonder how he came to know the Emperor?'

I had no idea.

*

In the quiet of the day I heard the flap of windmill sails and sighs and clicking as Pennyweight cleaned his false teeth with a finger nail and tried to repair the spring. The room heated as the sun got up and I dozed on my cot, dreaming of Margaret and our child.

Oh yes, it was our child, she said. Women know these things, she said, though I understand this isn't true. It was our child because she wanted it to be so, albeit she wanted nothing else of me except to make love and dance the tango. And this, I thought, was reasonable. Even in love there is an element of calculation, and I felt no resentment that Margaret should think I was a bad bet. I imagined her with the child: the bloom of satisfaction filling in the colours that sunshine and the island had bleached from her. And if Johnny was in the picture, then good luck to him. I thought he would make a fond father notwithstanding that he might be guilty of sundry murders, assuming the dark rumours to be true.

A voice at the door instructed us to get up and stand at the opposite wall beneath the window. We obeyed and the door opened. The elderly man named Andreas was bearing a tray. Behind him a friend held a gun. The tray was placed on the ground in front of Pennyweight. 'Don't I get breakfast?' I asked.

'You will come with me, please,' said Andreas.

I followed into a second room – it was a small house with probably no more than two rooms on the ground floor: too small for more than a fleeting thought of escape.

Then I was faced with Bronstein, who was sitting behind a deal table which was bare except for a plate of biscuits and a pot of tea.

He treated me to his level gaze: a good-looking man, not above thirty, with a self-control I instinctively distrusted. He glanced at the teapot, the plate and at me and said, 'I'm sorry I can't offer you breakfast, Mr Pinfold, but our catering arrangements are somewhat improvised. Would you like tea? A biscuit? These are bourbons, these custard creams, and these ... ah, ginger nuts. Are my descriptions accurate? I have to practise my English.'

The tea was sweet with condensed milk; the biscuits soft and damp. Bronstein fussed over them. A lizard, frozen yet alert, was fixed in the middle of the wall. The absurd Alpine hat with its badger brush and a loden coat were hung behind the door.

'What do you make of Mr Pennyweight?' Bronstein asked.

'You shouldn't have beaten him up.'

'That was nothing. You know it was nothing. Are you his friend?'

'After a fashion.'

'Is he also a friend of Colonel Cardozo?'

'They may have met – I can't recall. No, they're not friends.'

'Does he share the affections of Mrs Cardozo with you?'

'Don't be bloody impertinent.'

Bronstein smiled – genuinely, I think. 'You seem to have a very limited capacity for anger. I've seen it in soldiers before: those who haven't become twisted by frustration. Mr Pennyweight tells me you have a medal. I can believe it and I imagine you don't care in the slightest about that or anything much. What does Mrs Cardozo see in you? Is it a case of mutual sexual fascination?'

'I don't know why we're talking of her.'

'Very well, shall we speak of Mr Pennyweight instead? A buffoon, yes? It seems so ... *implausible* that Mr Robinson should ask him for help.'

'I can't say.'

'No? But you knew Mr Robinson well. You were in the Navy together. In..."the Senior Service", yes?'

'No. I was never in the Navy. I didn't know Robinson.'

'The newspaper...'

'Don't believe what you read in the newspapers.'

'It was written by your friend Dr. Soares. He was surely in a position to know the truth?'

'Pouco Pedro...' I didn't finish. I found myself reluctant to say he wasn't my friend. It is a curious effect of interrogation: that it leads to introspection and an unwillingness to lie. The result is an equivocation which may appear as dishonesty, though it is no more than the answering of questions one never puts to oneself. Pouco Pedro's relationship to me was such a question. Johnny Cardozo's might be another. As for Margaret I felt I had an answer, but it was like one of those given in dreams that can never be formulated in the waking day, which is perhaps why we danced. I had been no friend to Pouco Pedro and I preferred not to think of him at all.

Bronstein offered the biscuits again. 'If you are frank with me, Mr Pinfold, you may persuade me that we are on the same side – try the custard creams – you may find me an ally. What do you know of the angel of the Paúl da Serra?'

'A superstition.'

'It doesn't interest you?'

'No.'

'Yet you went to Serra da Agua to ask questions about it.'

'I was invited by a priest – Father Flaherty.'

'And his interest?'

'Angels – miracles – priests.'

Bronstein sighed. 'Did you betray Mr Robinson?' he asked.

'No,' I said.

'Not for the sake of Mrs Cardozo? For your friend Colonel Cardozo? Do you know who killed him? My friends and I have wondered if Robinson wasn't working secretly for the Colonel.'

'As far as I know, Johnny's interest in Robinson started when he was murdered.'

Bronstein nodded. I felt he was a man soured by a vague despair, wearying rather than fatal, like someone burdened by a wife he can neither love nor divorce. He had gentle brown eyes, though these things are matters of interpretation.

He reached across the table and punched me in the face.

*

Pennyweight asked, 'Did Bronstein clock you one? He's got a good straight right, hasn't he? I ought to have mentioned it. Looks as if his two friends gave you a good kicking as well. What did he want to know?'

'About Robinson.'

'And angels?'

'Them, too.'

'I thought as much. It seems to be a fixation. I told you this gang are a little potty.'

I tried the old question: 'What *did* Robinson want you here for?'

'Search me, old man. I'm only a humble engineer. Here, let me bathe that eye. What a shiner!' Pennyweight used a grubby handkerchief and a bowl of water, then cadged another cigarette. 'I'm coming round to the view that it must be to do with that damned angel after all. I told you, didn't I, that the Captain got a dose of religion at about the time he went off his trolley? If there were tales of angels and miracles going about, he may have wanted a level head to advise him.'

'Five hundred pounds is a lot of money to pay.'

'Not for a "pearl of great price" as it says in the Good Book.'

'Bronstein implied that he and Robinson were mixed up in something together. He said that Robinson was betrayed – or, possibly, that Robinson betrayed him. Does that make sense to you?'

'Clear as mud.'

'That's why he won't come clean about their business. He doesn't know whom to trust.'

Pennyweight had no more answer than I did. But he had blitheness of spirit: assurance that all was for the best. He admired his handiwork on my face then proposed, 'I'm going to get a bit of shut eye. Grab it while you can – isn't that what the army taught us?' In a minute he had dozed off, his lips curled back and his false teeth locked together in a corpse's grin.

Before I drifted off he woke for a moment and asked, 'If I shaved my moustache off, d'you think I'd be a bigger hit with the ladies?'

*

I slept the restless sleep of boredom I'd known in the trenches. When I woke the room was dim; a few slanting rays broke through the jalousies and a plate of cold food lay by the door. Pennyweight was lying on his cot, making free with my cigarettes.

'You awake, Pinfold?' he asked.

'Yes.'

'You missed lunch.'

'It doesn't matter.'

He rolled over and fixed me with his soft, drinker's eyes. 'I was thinking,' he said. 'It was a bit of mistake for us both to deny knowing Robinson. '

'Why?'

'Because that chap Bronstein wants to keep one of us in order to do whatever it was that Robinson was supposed to do. At the moment he's scratching his head wondering which of us it should be.'

'I see.' For once Pennyweight's point seemed reasonable. Despite my black eye and aching bones, I was puzzling over the Hungarian's restraint; but it made sense if he didn't want to antagonize Robinson's accomplice unduly. 'What do you think will happen to the other one – the one he doesn't choose?'

'Ah – well, there's the rub. I think he's for the chop.' The set of Pennyweight's mouth hardened. 'Bronstein has the bloody-mindedness I saw in the brass hats during the war. He doesn't *want* to kill one of us, but, when push comes to it, he will – and he won't lose any sleep over it, I can tell you.'

'In that case, I hope he chooses you to survive.'

'That's very decent of you, Pinfold.'

'Don't mention it.'

'I can see why you won that medal.'

Pennyweight got off his cot and began the token exercises I'd seen once before: a physical equivalent of his undisciplined mental efforts. He caught me watching him and smiled. 'Funny,' he said, 'to think of old Pennyweight being useful for once.'

'Don't run yourself down.'

'I'm not, old man. I mean – I always knew I was preparing myself for something: something important. All that time I put into studying the Higher Knowledge – there had to be a purpose. Of course,' he added, 'many are called but few are chosen. It might be that the Masters wouldn't think I was up to it. Then again, there are Dark Forces at work – you should never underestimate them, Pinfold.' He examined me nervously. 'Look here, old man. You and I both know I'm the chap Bronstein wants – but it occurs to me that he might make a mistake – go for the wrong 'un. If that looks like happening, you'll put in a good word for me, won't you?'

'And sign my own death warrant? All right, if you like.'

'You will? My God but you're a brick, Pinfold – a top drawer first class brick!'

Throughout my sleep I'd been vaguely aware of conversation in the other room: voices rising and falling; sometimes heatedly. They were discussing who should live or die, I supposed. My agreement to Pennyweight's request wasn't a matter of heroism – nor was it despair: merely the passing indifference to life that comes when one's mood is flat. Now that I'd made a decision, it gave me a spark of interest: not enough for me to say to Pennyweight that I'd rather he died than me, if that was all the same with him; but a lively curiosity as to what would happen next and whether I'd have the nerve to go through with my promise. It was in much the same vein that I'd won my medal. If I hadn't been thoroughly indifferent to my own fate, I should have gone mad on the spot when Bennett took his bullet and spread his brains all over me. An hour either way and I'd have been cowering below the parapet, clinging to life like a dear friend.

A knock came at the door and a call from Andreas to stand by the wall.

'Looks like this is it,' I said. 'Good luck.'

Pennyweight was standing like a soldier on parade, nervously contemplating his glorious future. 'You'll remember, won't you?' he said

The door opened. This time Andreas was carrying a gun and his colleague was also armed. Old and absurd in his mutton chop whiskers, he seemed quite determined and I fancied it would be a mistake to despise him. I had a suspicion that he was moved by dark currents akin to those that moved Pennyweight: strange idols and incomprehensible certainties that could be quite deadly to the infidel.

He pointed at Pennyweight. 'You,' he said. 'Come.' Whether to life or death wasn't specified. Pennyweight hesitated, then marched forward briskly but with a lingering look in my direction. 'You won't forget, will you, old man?' he repeated.

'I won't forget,' I assured him.

The door closed and no one returned to ask my confirmation of anything.

A little later I heard a shot.

I admit it had occurred to me that if Bronstein thought that Robinson had betrayed him, he might want to get rid of Robinson's accomplice. I mention this point because, although I believe my motives in letting Pennyweight go forward were selfless, one can never be certain.

CHAPTER SEVENTEEN

After the shot came sounds of voices, horses and the purring of a motor car engine. The sun had gone down, and an afterglow struck the windmill sails pink against a royal blue sky. I dragged the cots to block the door.

Shortly, two more shots rang out from a way off. The shooter was using a rifle. A feel for the rhythm of the firing action told me it was an Enfield, though this information was of no consequence except as a disquieting reminder of the war. A further shot was returned from the house, which caused some consternation so far as I could judge from faint jabberings of Portuguese carried on the still air. After that we all settled down to the quiet business of killing each other.

During the war I'd been called on once or twice to lead trench raids. There was a standing order to harass the enemy even in the inactive sectors, and the troops hated it because the raids stirred up reprisals to no purpose.

That was how Bennett caught his bullet and I won my medal: fighting off a party of Germans armed with rifles and stick grenades on a night of which I have no visual memory, only the feel of Bennett's brains on my face and the taste of blood because in my frenzy I bit a German and tore off his ear.

Somehow in the scramble I did something heroic, or so they tell me. I'm inclined to think the incident didn't happen at all or not in the way they said, or, if it did happen and there was a hero, then it was someone else – quite possibly Bennett. There wasn't a battle, just a brutal scuffle like a brawl in a pub alleyway, and the Germans were drunk: no doubt because they, too, were frightened as we used to be when we fired ourselves on rum before our own raids. In the morning we counted the bodies and reconstructed the event for the report; and in the process we created a bit of glory because we had wanted to be brave but knew that we weren't.

Tonight around the house the fools with guns did much the same thing. There was no racket: only furtiveness. The shots, when they came, were isolated like those of poachers in a distant wood. Yet for me they were terrifying, the silences as well as the sounds, and I found myself shaking and vomited into the stinking chamber pot. I muttered words of encouragement to myself as if I were the captain of the school team faced with a boy who wouldn't play the game because of the rowdy toughs.

Oh yes, in my time I've been a capital fellow, quite capable of killing or being killed, with nothing much in the difference. But I'm prouder of my cowardice than of my heroism. I stand on it as proof that at heart I'm an honest man.

By degrees the shooting died away to be replaced by voices. They were puzzled and I doubt the speakers understood exactly what was happening any more than I did. Then a door somewhere in the house banged open and I heard men in the next room and a sliver of light slipped under the door to mine. One of the voices was Johnny Cardozo's. He was calling my name.

'I'm here, Johnny,' I said.

'Thank God.'

The door rattled as I dragged the cots away. Then it opened and Johnny was standing in the space, looking dapper in boots and riding breeches and beaming his head off.

'Michael!'

'Johnny.'

We embraced then stood back to admire each other. He smiled and said, 'Our friends scared the devil out of me. I thought they might have killed you.'

'No – I'm all right. But I think they may have done for Pennyweight.'

'The fat, ginger-haired fellow? We haven't found any bodies, but it's damned dark out there.'

'Can you ask your men to search?'

'Of course.' He took a report from one of his men and gave some orders; then began to laugh. 'Would you believe that we've been blazing away for half an hour and no one on our side has been hurt?'

'It sometimes happens that way.'

'Are you sure you're all right? You look as though you've been knocked about a bit.'

'I'm fine,' I said.

'Good! That's excellent! This is wonderful sport, don't you think?'

'Oh yes. Wonderful.'

We went outside where the sky was clear and starlit and the air in my nostrils was warm and scented with powder residue and cigarettes. A car and half a dozen horses stood in the paler shadows and Johnny's men, in the excitement of successful mayhem, flitted to and fro like gypsies making camp.

'Where are we?' I asked.

Johnny waved toward a sprinkle of lights in the middle distance. 'Near Pedras Pretas.'

I'd been right about Porto Santo. In a moment of relief I found myself marvelling how pretty it was, and on this night more than any other, like a place seen for the first time or experienced with that acuity of senses which comes from being in love.

'Why do you think Bronstein made his base here?' I asked.

'Because it's remote?'

I remembered something. 'He has a steam launch. I was brought here from Ponta Delgada. He may have a place there, too.'

'I know. We found it this morning.'

Johnny left me a while to have a smoke under a palm tree. When he returned he said, 'There's no sign of your friend Pennyweight. We'll look again in the morning.'

'Do you have all of Bronstein's men? There were three of them.'

'So far we have only one.'

He pointed out Andreas. His men were roughing the old fellow up, tugging at his mutton-chop whiskers as if to satisfy themselves that he was real and terrifying enough to account for their fright. Johnny watched them indulgently; intervening only to stop any real injury.

'I've got a boat near Vila Baleira,' he went on. 'If you feel well, I suggest we return tonight to Funchal.'

'I don't think I can make it home.'

'I'll give you a bed for the night.'

'And Margaret?'

'She's very well after her little escapade,' Johnny said. 'She's been worried about you.'

*

Johnny had caused the ferry for Funchal to be held back. We steamed away from Porto Santo leaving a plume of sparks to join the stars, and sat in deck chairs and drank scotch: two old friends, in mood with the gentle night, sharing the tender memory of violence as if it were a romance that had occurred in our youth.

Johnny asked, 'Do you think you can tell me what has been going on, Michael?'

The question sounded vaguely philosophical, so that I hesitated before answering, 'Robinson was supposed to be working for Bronstein.'

'He told you so?'

'Pretty much.'

'For what purpose?'

'I don't know. He didn't say.' I offered, 'It seems to have something to do with the Emperor – and the angel, the one on the Paúl da Serra.'

I laughed. Johnny laughed. 'But seriously, Michael – why did Bronstein kidnap you?'

'He thought I knew Robinson.'

'Did you?'

'You know I didn't. I would have told you.'

'And Mr Pennyweight?'

'The same thing.'

'He knew Robinson?'

'You'll have to ask him – assuming he's still alive.'

I was feeling dehydrated and switched to beer. The steward brought me a Coral. Madeira was ahead of us, outlined against the western sky with the lights of Machico beaded along the shoreline and the mountains piled behind.

Johnny asked, 'What is he like, Mr Pennyweight?'

'An idiot – an old soldier who was hit hard by the war.' The description struck me as cruel, though accurate as far as it went. I omitted any reference to Pennyweight's 'tremendousness': it was too absurd, and Johnny was unlikely to understand since to see the fat man in that aspect took an act of faith like a convert's belief in the holiness of his prophet. Johnny ran with what I gave him.

'Like Robinson in fact. Oh, of course, you don't know. We've had some information through the British consulate. Before the war Robinson was quite a promising chap – his family is in banking apparently. But he got a bad case of shell shock. Afterwards he couldn't take to civilian life. He deserted his fiancée and did a spell in gaol.'

'What for?'

'Fraud. He stole money from a church charity. It surprised everyone since he was thought to be very religious. What branch of the army was Pennyweight in?'

'The Engineers – he built roads, bridges, field fortifications. He told me he came to Madeira in the hope of finding work in that line.'

'Field fortifications?'

'Roads and bridges. I can't see any connection with Bronstein except that both of them seem to be interested in the Occult. Pennyweight draws mystical lines on maps.' I added in a momentary inspiration that at the time seemed weirdly plausible, 'Probably he expects to find buried treasure or the Holy Grail.'

Johnny looked at his glass then at mine. 'Do you think, perhaps, that you've had too much to drink? Ha ha, the Holy Grail!'

'The Emperor is a descendant of Jesus Christ – so Pennyweight tells me.'

'That idiot Fairbrother said the same when he made a fool of himself at dinner. Do you think he is?'

'Does it matter? The question is what Robinson thought and what Bronstein still thinks. Their motives don't have to make sense. Am *I* making sense?' I examined the dregs of my beer and the steward waiting for further orders. 'I suspect you're right and I have had too much to drink. By the way, Bronstein seemed to have an idea that Robinson might have turned traitor and have been working for you.'

'No, that isn't true,' Johnny said.

*

We arrived at Funchal in the small hours. Johnny's car was parked on the Molhe with a police guard sleeping on the rear seat. The *Kildonan Castle* was still at her moorings, brightly lit but silent as a house might be after a party when the servants are clearing away and the signs of brief joy are swept into the bin.

'Home!' said Johnny. His manner was merry, as it can be in the aftermath of a good gunfight. 'I don't expect Margaret will still be awake, but you'll be able to see her in the morning. She was dreadfully upset at what happened; and of course she didn't get any sleep last night.'

That was pretty much all he said about her. He didn't ask me to explain my presence with his wife at the Quinta Wentworth, which was frankly inexplicable except by telling the truth. It did occur to me that Johnny, too, might have kept a mistress and therefore have complaisant views on the subject, but he'd never mentioned one. This was one of the occasions when my father's peculiar history left me without a compass to navigate the strange oceans of other people's marriages.

At the villa the servants were asleep except an old man who served as major domo and appeared in a dressing gown over which he wore a uniform jacket. Johnny confirmed that Margaret had taken a bromide and was asleep. He ordered a small decanter of whisky to be brought to the saloon then dispatched the old fellow to bed.

Once we were buried in a pair of club chairs and the girandoles were lit, Johnny said, 'Did I tell you that my stolen pot has been returned? I missed it terribly – a very fine piece.'

'Perhaps it was never stolen.'

'No, it was stolen right enough. But it just reappeared in its usual place and the servants deny all knowledge. If one of them had taken it, the simplest thing would have been to "find" it, so to speak.'

'Very odd.'

'Yes: odd to think that one of one's friends – or a guest at least – is a thief. I'm not especially annoyed. How does the English expression go: "It takes all sorts to make a world"? And thieves can have their uses,' he concluded. Margaret had made a similar gnomic remark, asking whether it was possible to steal from a thief. By a process of association it brought Crispin to mind.

I asked, 'Do you know about the problems with the *Kildonan Castle*?'

'I believe they've had a breakdown.'

'I heard a suggestion of sabotage.'

'Really?' Johnny was intrigued. 'Are you making a point?'

'I assume Bronstein and his friends arrived here on the *Kildonan* – leastways there's talk of a party of Hungarians who kept to their cabins. They may have intended to leave in the same way.'

'And the sabotage?'

'Robinson's death has thrown their plans and they need more time. I think Bronstein has bribed some of the ship's officers to arrange a short delay.'

'The operative word would be "short". One can't delay a ship indefinitely.'

'That's my point. Whatever it is that Bronstein is up to, he has to act quickly.'

*

Margaret brought breakfast. She wore a wrap of peach-coloured silk and sat on the edge of the bed as though she were my mother and I were an invalid child. She had opened the shutters and the morning light was clean and optimistic.

'Did you sleep well, darling?' she asked as she arranged the tray and fitted a napkin around my neck. 'Does the good boy want some eggy-weg?'

'You're in a cheerful mood this morning.'

'Relieved,' she answered without looking at me. She stared at one of the plates. 'See, I've cut the toast into soldiers so that you can dip them.' She took one of the pieces between her fingers and offered it to my lips. She murmured, 'I was frightened. I thought that man – Bronstein – might kill you.'

'Were you hurt?'

'No. I passed an uncomfortable few hours until dawn when I was found by a fisherman. Now, do eat something. You smell of whisky and cigarettes. I'll have a servant run a bath.'

'How did you explain my presence at São Vicente to Johnny?'

'I told him you volunteered to drive me there. He knows I hate the dreadful roads – I scarcely ever drive. I said we lost track of the time.'

'It sounds a pretty feeble excuse.'

'That depends on what you want to believe. Oh my God, you've got a black eye.'

'I was beaten up a little – nothing too bad.'

'My hero,' Margaret said. 'And to think that I went dancing.'

*

The maid drew a bath. I shaved with a borrowed razor. Margaret returned with some clothes. 'Yours are fit only for a jumble sale. These are Johnny's – they may be a little tight.' I put them on. The shirt wouldn't fasten at the collar and the trousers came only to the ankle. Margaret admired me. 'You look very louche: a little piratical or like Senhor Agnello when he dresses as a *compadrito*. But, then, you are louche, aren't you? That's part of your charm. It's no wonder you dance the tango so well.'

'Did you really go dancing yesterday?'

She looked sad. 'Is that really so appalling? I was desperately worried. I couldn't sleep or simply sit around doing nothing except wait for news of you.'

'I understand.'

'Do you?'

'Yes. Was Sonny there?'

Margaret giggled quite girlishly. For a moment her face was filled with the freshness that the heat of the island was slowly wearing down. She said, 'I've told you what an outrageous flirt he is. This time he was full of stories about his relations with Mrs Patrick Campbell. Have you heard of her? The actress? She must be fifty if she's a day and her reputation is all behind her, but, to hear Sonny tell it, she's still love's young dream.' She stopped laughing. 'Don't you think it would be lovely – to be an old man and an old woman and still in love with each other? I don't suppose that will happen to us. We'll do something miserable to spoil it.'

'That's exactly what we intend to do,' I reminded her. I meant that I was going home and she was remaining with Johnny.

And if we didn't – if we stayed together, would we still spoil things?

Probably. Margaret would have an affair with someone who offered more than I could, and I would continue to steal other men's wives until I understood why or made an end of myself.

It came to me then with sudden clarity that we would never progress beyond the tango. Where all other courses foundered in contradiction, its heightened moments held everything in a balance that was quite perfect: exquisite in its tawdry sincerity so that one could believe that love, hatred, life and death were abstractions requiring no resolution and that, if the moment were frozen, one could be completely happy.

On the way into town, to collect a change of clothes from the shop, Johnny asked with a grin, 'Are you going to congratulate me?'

I said, 'What for?'

'I'm to be a father.'

'Congratulations.'

'Didn't Margaret tell you?'

'No. She probably thought it best coming from you.'

We were at the spot where Robinson had been killed, though there was nothing to show for it. 'I'm going to catch his killer, you know?' Johnny said.

I nodded, though I was half-inclined to think that
Johnny had arranged the death. Wasn't that what Pouco
Pedro had hinted – and hadn't he perhaps killed the little
fellow too? He looked wistful but that meant nothing.
Even if he'd murdered Robinson he might feel sorry; for I
doubt that he hated the man.

'Yes, I'm to be a papa,' he said. 'I rather thought of
asking you to stand godfather to the child.'

'That's kind of you.'

'But it won't be for months.'

'I suppose not.'

'And you'll have gone home,' he said. 'Truly, Michael,
I'm going to miss you.'

THE DAILY MAIL

14th February 1920

Disturbance at home of Bernard Shaw

Young Woman Arrested

The police were called yesterday evening to the home of Mr Bernard Shaw at Adelphi Terrace WC2. Miss Elizabeth Morris, of Buxton Derbyshire, was found in an hysterical state, making accusations of an indelicate nature against the playwright. At Mr Bernard Shaw's suggestion a doctor was called and the young woman removed from the premises.

CHAPTER EIGHTEEN

I changed clothes from my stock at the shop. Senhor Pereira, ordinarily placid, displayed a nervous energy, reminding me of Pouco Pedro.

'What's wrong with you?' I asked.

He was trembling, as though I were going to punish him. He answered, 'Where you going, Senhor Michael?'

'To find Mr Fairbrother. Has he been here?'

Senhor Pereira nodded, then cried out, 'Ee shay you going to shell the wine!'

'That's right.'

His reaction was that of a stunned father receiving news of a bereavement. He stammered, 'If you shell wine, then you not need shop.'

It was true. I'd need neither the shop nor the shopkeeper.

'Don't worry,' I told him. 'I'll take care of you.'

But I didn't think I would. The death of Pouco Pedro had shaken my belief in my capacity to help those who trusted me. Goodwill wasn't enough, and I suspected that at times it reached only so far as to get me out of the momentary embarrassment of telling others that they should go to hell. Senhor Pereira gave me the bleak smile that the poor reserve for their benefactors.

The previous night, returning with Johnny from Porto Santo, I'd noticed a freighter moored on the shoreward side of the *Kildonan Castle*. This day or the next, my supply of third rate malmsey would be on board and that part of my problems with it. I needed to get the bill of exchange from Fairbrother and take it to the bank. Going over the various matters troubling me, I made a mental note to visit the letting agent again to press him to find me a tenant. I wondered, too, where Pennyweight was and whether the War Office would give me the address of Robinson's sister Lavinia, and whether she would reply to my letter and what I was going to do about my father and Teddy. As for Pouco Pedro's widow, I knew I would do nothing for Angélica Soares.

I found I wanted to dance as another man might want a stiff drink. If I went to Senhor Agnello's place, I might find Margaret there with Sonny. I hadn't asked her plans for the day.

At Reid's I enquired after Fairbrother and was told he'd checked out and paid his bill. His bags had been sent to the *João Zarco*, which was the name of the freighter lying in the bay. I wasn't alone in looking for him – so the clerk told me – Arthur Mainwaring had called and left a message.

I wandered into the gardens to get a drink and think things over. Sonny was at a table writing letters in the shade of a tulip tree. He gave me a friendly wave and offered a seat beside him.

'You're alone,' he said. 'Take a seat, man. My wife is sight-seeing.'

'I was looking for Mr Fairbrother,' I told him.

'Not for Mrs Cardozo?'

'I thought she might be with you.'

'Practising that damnable dance?'

'You seem to like it well enough.'

'It defeats me, Mr Pinfold. So much was obvious after the first lesson, but I keep at it like the tongue prying at a cavity in one's teeth. Mrs Cardozo tells me that you, on the other hand, are an excellent dancer.'

'I can't say.'

'I shouldn't be surprised if you were. You put into your legs that which you can't put in your mouth. One can't reasonably expect to be expressive in every medium. I have words and a little music, which in all honesty ought to be enough.'

The waiter came and I ordered a beer; Sonny asked for a fruit juice. He turned his genial gaze in my direction, reminding me of Father Flaherty, though the beefy priest was his physical opposite. The resemblance lay in the philosophical tenor of his remarks, though these days everyone, including Johnny Cardozo and Margaret, seemed to be speaking in aphorisms.

I wondered if I were catching Pennyweight's eye for the esoteric buried in the everyday: for the world as a palimpsest to be inscribed with our own meaning.

'You don't seem to be a happy man, if I may say so,' Sonny observed. 'Is that a good beer? I understand they make it locally, but I'm no judge. No – not a happy man, despite being blessed with the love of Mrs Cardozo.'

'Has she told you that?'

'We've talked a great deal. Words – didn't I just mention that they were my forte? We've talked a great deal, and laughed, too. She has a very ready laugh: has a talent for it, which most people don't: they laugh like they sing, poor devils.'

The remark called up an image of Margaret spinning in laughter around the floor of Senhor Agnello's seedy studio: a version of the tango we hadn't yet danced. I felt a sudden yearning to see it: a borrowed joy such as one gets when a woman one loves tells of something that has made her happy. I wanted so much that Margaret should be happy. But sometimes a desire for another's welfare can be a source of shame, because it underlines the fact that one has done nothing to bring that happiness about.

Perhaps that thought made me peevish. I remarked, 'Laughing doesn't sound like the Margaret I know.'

'I suspected as much. She said something to the same effect. She told me that, with you, she feels dark and very complex; but that with me she doesn't. It occurs to me that she may be reflecting the demands we put upon her. Mine are so very light – the amusement of a whimsical old fellow – that she may not notice them at all. It's a pity though, that you don't see her the way that I do. She isn't half so hard or sophisticated as she pretends.'

'No, I don't suppose she is,' I said.

*

I took a carriage down to the Molhe. The *João Zarco* was still loading and I cadged a lift on one of the lighters. I found Fairbrother in rolled shirtsleeves and white flannels keeping watch over a gang of sailors as they brought his wine on board. He brushed a shank of hair from his eyes and gave me a sunny smile.

'Pinfold, old man. I was wondering when I'd catch up with you. I've been to your shop a few times but there's no one there except some fellow hiding in the rear. I've got something for you.'

'My money?'

'Absolutely.'

'Arthur Mainwaring is looking for you, too.'

Fairbrother looked briefly concerned, then smiled again. 'Can't think why. I paid him yesterday. Probably he wants to wish me bon voyage.'

'Are you leaving today?'

'Or tomorrow. You never can tell with the slapdash way these dagoes carry on.' He hesitated as though forgetting something and I caught a glimmer of the gaucheness that prevented one from truly liking him. He slapped his forehead with the palm of his hand. 'Lord save me, but I haven't offered you a drink. Come and have a Madeira Madman; I've been working on the recipe and it's bang-up spot-on now. Did I mention I've got a berth? These little tramps carry the odd passenger now and again.'

We went to a cabin in the forward section. It was a dingy hole with rust streaks trailing from the rivets down the white paintwork and a smell of mice and hot oil; and it surprised me because I'd put Fairbrother down as a fastidious man, though for no other reason than that it would have been of a piece with his diffidence. However, this morning he carried himself with a slight swagger, a whiff of the piratical Charlie.

I picked up a framed photograph.

'My fiancée,' he said.

It was of a vamp, shot in dramatic lighting to add an air of *femme fatale*, though she was most likely a young lady from Surbiton with a passion for tennis, in the flesh more like the attractive Miss Torbitt-Bayley. Fairbrother, however, swore that it was an exact likeness that 'got her to the tee'. I recalled that the late Robinson had a fiancée; so Pennyweight had told me. If I wrote to Lavinia and if she replied, perhaps afterwards I would write to the other woman to tell her – whatever I had to tell her.

'I suppose you've got a girl of your own back home,' Fairbrother said.

Yes, I thought bleakly, and I'll have yours, too, when once you've married her.

I said, 'I'll take a whisky-soda, if you don't mind. It's a little early in the day...'

He was fumbling clumsily with the bottles. Clumsiness was an aspect of his behaviour that made one always edgy in expectation that he would drop something

'Are you sure? I've been working on a lighter version of the Madeira Madman using sercial instead of malmsey. Now where's that piece of paper, the jolly old bill of exchange? Come on, I absolutely insist.' He mixed the drink, and while I sipped at it he fumbled among the documents in his brief case and produced a couple of sheets with a banker's letterhead, which as far as I could tell were a promise to pay me the sum agreed.

'Thanks,' I said, putting the sheets in my pocket.

'Can I top up your glass?'

'I'll be on my way,' I said, and I would have left the drink, but Fairbrother, with his poor sense of other people's need for distance, lowered over me until I'd finished.

*

I called on Senhor Agnello, though I'd no arrangement to meet Margaret and Sonny had said nothing to make me think she would be there.

'The weather ees hot, eh, Meestair Pinfold?' he said. He offered me a *poncha* and wouldn't take a refusal. My head was spinning with the heat and the Madeira Madman, and the ceiling fan wasn't working.

We settled on a dusty bench. The air was stiff as syrup and milky with French chalk and cigarette smoke. The pretty girl and her duenna had returned and the girl was dancing with Maria, clapping politely at the end of each record as she had learned from the suave Senhor Pinfold and the elegant Senhora Cardozo. Agnello dug me in the ribs.

'She ees beautiful, that one, *verdade*?

'Yes.'

'I much like to dance with 'er, but the ugly one will not permit. 'Er father, 'ee uses prostitutes, but 'ees daughter mus' be kept pure.'

Agnello's unshaven face was like that of 'characters' in the genre paintings my Uncle Percy collected, which, if they had any meaning at all, intimated a vague wisdom of a fleshy, earthly kind. His remark, too, hinted at a moral point, reminding me of my earlier conversation with Sonny and the more general, disquieting feeling that people were beginning to talk philosophy for my benefit. I wondered, with the refined indifference of the practised melancholic, if this perception were a prelude to madness. Agnello poured another shot of *poncha*.

'I 'ear you goin' back to England,' he said.

'Soon.'

He sighed. 'So no more dancin' with beautiful Senhora Cardozo?'

'No.'

'And Meestair Sonny, 'e go also, and she be left with no one, just all beautiful and lonely. Ah, well. Still, you remember me, eh? And bed in next room? Ha ha!'

I agreed I would remember him. The bed, too, and the floor filmed in French chalk traced with the kabbalah of dance, and the smell of rum, and the wiry hairs tangled in the sheets, and the scent of Coty. I no longer cared that Margaret wasn't here. And that was as well, because Johnny walked through the door.

In his pale suit and the dusty light he stood for a moment like the ghost of an entertainer, holding in one hand a straw hat and in the other a malacca cane and a pair of beige cotton gloves. I had no problem with the thought that he could do a soft shoe act or tap routine. Perhaps that was why I could never treat him completely seriously, though my reason told me that he was in all respects a very serious person.

'Michael!' he called out, raising an echo from the wooden floor and bare walls and stirring eddies in the bars of sunlight. The gramophone struck up another tango – *Lagrimas*, which Margaret and I had danced to at São Vicente. Senhor Agnello took hold of his bandoneon and began to squeeze out accompanying chords.

'Margaret isn't here,' I said.

'I know,' said Johnny. 'I dropped her at Reid's. She is taking coffee with Mr Sonny. You left so quickly this morning that we didn't have time to talk beyond our chat about the baby.'

'I didn't know we had anything to talk about. I went to see Fairbrother about payment for my wine. Has something happened? Has Pennyweight turned up?'

'No. Are you still concerned for him?'

'Not especially,' I said, which was true, though not because of indifference. I had an idea, possibly borne on the drift of my thoughts as I contemplated leaving Madeira and Margaret, that the universe would see the fat man all right. That he was a Holy Fool, and I'd never heard they got themselves killed.

I didn't ask how Johnny had found me. I hadn't said I'd be here: I'd come to Agnello's place only on the spur of the moment. Was he having me followed? Might I expect an encounter with a secret policeman named Robinson?

He said, 'I thought you'd like to be present while we question that fellow we caught. He may know where Bronstein has taken your friend.'

'Perhaps he knows why there's an angel up in the mountains.'

Johnny gave a thin smile. 'Now you are being flippant. Obviously you have recovered from your shock. Come on, old man, this may interest you.'

He waved a hand to conjure me out of my seat. He placed his straw hat on his head with a flick, patted it in place and gave his cane a spin. He looked around the room and observed, 'When you are gone home, Michael, I must find time to bring Margaret here myself. What do you think? I could learn to tango, yes?'

'I don't see why not,' I answered. He moved lightly, with a spring in him. He would dance very well, though with the Latin sinuosity the English despise. We crossed the room towards the door; and I noticed that Senhor Agnello had stopped playing the bandoneon and the pretty girl wasn't dancing but gripping Maria motionless in the middle of the floor, and her duenna was sitting solemnly. They were watching Johnny Cardozo and hanging onto his breezy words as if he were dispensing benedictions.

*

Once in the street, I asked, 'Where are we going?'

'To see our mutual friend,' Johnny said.

'Where are you holding him?'

'In a place I have,' he answered. I detected a mood on him, one that was oddly fey.

'The police station?'

'You forget that I am in the diplomatic service.'

Outside the Jesuit church in the main square, Johnny halted to give money to a beggar. He waited, until I, too, fished out a few coins. Then he smiled at me, his usual charming smile.

He said, 'You don't really know me, do you, Michael? You come into my life and my family and you dance with my wife, but you don't know me.' The beggar offered up a flower and Johnny took it and placed it in his buttonhole. He gave me a second flower.

'Who ever knows another person?' I said, thinking I could match anyone at this level of wisdom. I didn't imagine he was trying to bandy ideas. It was more that he was throwing out words like arrows to see which would strike home. I said, 'For instance, someone told me you were a colonel, but you never mentioned it.'

'A colonel in the Portuguese army? It is scarcely important, Michael: a "chocolate soldier".'

'Do you have any medals?'

'Don't be silly. Yes, I have some medals – for being Portuguese and a colonel, not for bravery.'

'Someone else suggested you were a secret policeman.'

'I am only a diplomat, Michael, with an emperor to take care of. Sometimes that involves difficult decisions and the use of severe methods. You killed people during the war. Did that make you a bad man? By the way, I hear you are a thief. You never told me so. Is it true?'

'Yes.'

'Ha ha! I am glad you admit it.' Johnny looked away and tilted his boater to keep the sun from his eyes. The square was aglitter with basalt and whitewash. Lawyers and clerks in stiff collars and cheap suits were going in and out of the Câmara Municipal. He said, 'You should wear a hat: a man with your skin, so pale like Margaret's. Do you want mine?' He removed it.

'I'm all right.'

Johnny flipped the hat between his hands and replaced it on his head.

He said, 'While we are at the business of truth-telling, did you kill Robinson? I could forgive you if you did.'

'Why?'

'I don't know. Friendship?'

'I didn't kill him. Did you?'

'Would you forgive me, if I were a murderer?'

'I don't know. Probably.'

'No, I didn't kill him,' said Johnny. I don't know that either of us believed the other.

We continued walking and crossed the main *ribeira* bisecting the town. Perhaps we were going to the police station after all. Meanwhile Johnny chatted about Margaret and the child they were both expecting, and perhaps – who knew? – I should be able to come back to the island to stand as godfather.

'What do you think, Michael?'

The child would bear my name, he insisted: the English name, not the Portuguese variant. It was a boy, naturally.

'When we return to the Embassy and he is a little older, I shall put him into a public school – Eton – Winchester. He will be a gentleman.'

I wanted to tell him that I was in love with his wife and that the child was mine. I would choose the school and there was damn-all chance that a Pinfold brat would turn out a gentleman.

In the Rua Santa Maria, where the street rises towards a church, a house stood behind a high wall, and in the garden an old jacaranda was casting its first lavender blossoms. Johnny had a key to the gate and let us in. The garden was overgrown with faded strelitzias and sprays of bougainvillea. Sunlight was splattered in patches among the foliage.

The door to the house was open. Johnny, whose manners never lost a touch of formality, stepped back to let me in to a shaded interior with the bare feel of a place that had been put up for rent and then forgotten because of sad associations. He called out a couple of names and one of the other doors opened and a man came out. Like the clerks at the Câmara he wore a suit and a stiff collar, but he had the stocky, sinewy build of a cane cutter or fisherman, though I was reminded of a small restaurant where the *patron* emerges from the back in his shirtsleeves to shake hands with a favoured but unexpected customer. He took Johnny's hat and cane, then didn't know what to do with them and fumbled over his apologies. I remember this – the embarrassment that was akin to shyness – for, as torturers go, I could have taken a liking to this one.

*

The old man named Andreas was lying on a palliasse. A second guard, dressed in the same seedily respectable manner as the first, was washing his face in a bowl of water. He grunted an acknowledgement. His sleeves, like a bank teller's, were fastened up with bands, though, now I thought of it, the arrangement would be equally convenient for protecting the cuffs while beating a prisoner. His shirt was covered by an apron and the apron was marked with blood spatters.

The old man was stripped to his shirt, and his thin legs, bony and blotched, were entwined. His scalp was covered in scabs where patches of his remaining hair had been torn away. His mutton-chop whiskers were singed: I could smell burned hair above the stink of tallow from the candle standing on the floor. The room was otherwise dark because of the shutters.

Johnny fanned himself with his cotton gloves. 'It is hot in here,' he said to me. 'By the way, on the subject of schools, do you have any opinion? Which one did you go to?'

'I went to several,' I said. 'This man has been tortured.'

'Yes,' Johnny agreed. When I didn't sit, he took a chair himself, still fanning with the gloves, and he looked from me to the old man and back again as if he could make no more of the situation than I could and everything was an accident.

Andreas sat up. His face showed no expression. He muttered a few words in Magyar.

'Does he speak English?' Johnny asked.

'You brought me here to ask that?'

'There are so few Magyar-speaking Portuguese – positively none, as far as I am aware.'

'He understands English,' I said.

'Good,' said Johnny. 'It would be needlessly cruel and a little ridiculous to torture a man who could not follow the questions.'

'You didn't need to bring me here to find that out.'

'That's true,' Johnny admitted.

We were silent for a while. Andreas mumbled. I thought he was praying, though I had no grounds for supposing so except the even tone of his voice and lack of interest in Johnny and me, and, perhaps, a suspicion I'd be praying in his situation. Johnny flapped his gloves, and a cockroach rattled along the length of a wall, scraping its wing case against the stonework.

'You are a brave man,' Johnny said. He reached over and began to waft cooler air in my direction. He meant me: that I was brave. 'Do you think you could withstand torture?'

'Who would want to torture me?' I asked.

'I'm speaking in the abstract.'

Andreas stopped his prayers. He leaned forward to snap off a hanging toenail. He stared at the blood flowing from the stump.

'Well – speaking in the abstract – no, I don't think I could stand being tortured. And you?'

'Frankly? No. I don't count myself a brave man.' Johnny glanced at me.

'Then that makes two of us.'

'We are alike, yes? By the way, do you know how much the fees are for Eton? Is it more expensive than Winchester?'

I didn't answer.

Johnny sighed. 'In the old days – the days of the Inquisition – it was the practice to show the instruments of torture to the accused before they were ever applied.'

'Is that so? Why?'

'Out of humanity. Most people would confess simply at the sight of the instruments.'

'I see. And what happened then?'

'They were forgiven, given a penance, and received back into the bosom of the Church. When one speaks of the horrors of the Inquisition, that is the part one tends to forget: that they loved the sinner and did not want to hurt him.'

'It's a comforting thought,' I said. I looked away to the old man and asked, 'Well, are you going to put any questions to him?'

I meant that Johnny might care to ask Andreas if he, too, was making love to his wife. He wasn't, but it is the questions put to the innocent that elicit the most interesting answers. The answers of the guilty are by definition predictable.

'Well?' I repeated.

Johnny snapped out of his reverie. 'No. Later perhaps, when you are gone. He won't tell us anything, but we shall torture him all the same because we have nothing better to do and he makes us angry. It is too depressing, eh, Michael?'

'I'd still like to know why you invited me here.'

'So that you can see what your friend does,' Johnny answered. He looked at me – I was about to write 'meaningfully', but the meaning escapes me. 'So that I can see myself through your eyes.' I recalled Margaret saying that he chose to make love under a mirror. I remembered also that he had taken me to lunch for the purpose of showing me Bronstein.

'So that I can believe that I am really doing this – I, who am not a bad person,' he said.

Abruptly he gave his man some orders and yielded his chair. The hat was delivered to him and he stared into it, then replaced it on his head. He said, 'This was not a good idea. Forgive me, Michael. I was trying to share some of the guilt for the things I have to do. Isn't that the purpose of confession? Ah, but I am not a religious man, and so I have to confess to you. Why is that?'

'Father Flaherty says I have the makings of a priest,' I told him for want of any better explanation.

'Is he right?'

I shook my head. If I conceded the point, I should become as barking mad as Robinson and have visions of angels. Instead it occurred to me to ask, 'Do you resent the Emperor?'

Johnny was puzzled. 'Why?'

'For keeping you here instead of in London. For making you do … whatever.'

He considered the point. 'Let me ask you a question instead. How do you feel about those generals who sent you to war?'

'I used to hate them for their stupidity. Now … it's pointless to think of them. They did their best according to their own lights.'

'They say the Emperor is very decent man.'

'So I understand.'

Johnny looked at me again as if he wanted me to pursue the subject, but I was making only small talk. And, since I was not to be tortured today, I wanted to get out.

In any case we were only discussing philosophy. Always the same banalities about which there is nothing useful to be said, which made me wonder why human beings discuss them. Yet we always do.

*

I left Johnny at the house in the Rua Santa Maria and we never spoke of the old Hungarian again, and I don't know for certain what became of him. I returned to the Rua do Conselheira Viera where I found Mrs Christie standing outside the shop and a crowd gathering.

'Mr Pinfold!' she exclaimed with the pleasure of someone bearing bad news.

'I'm surprised to see you again,' I said.

'Oh, it's nothing. I came only to pick up a souvenir or two because there's talk of the *Kildonan Castle* leaving, quite possibly tonight.' She placed a hand on my wrist and said confidingly. 'Before you go any further, I should tell you that there's a hanged man in your back room.'

CHAPTER NINETEEN

On my way back to the shop, I turned over the subject of Johnny's motives in showing me his prisoner. It is difficult to credit another's belief when one doesn't share it: difficult to accept fanaticism in pursuit of goals one finds absurd. I suspect that tragedy concerns itself with the affairs of kings because the aims of ordinary men are so modest that their frustration, viewed through the eyes of a detached onlooker, is merely comic.

Perhaps because I was grateful to have escaped, I began to see a comic side to the events at the house in the Rua Santa Maria. I suddenly had doubts about my assertion that the old Hungarian understood English. I'd only heard him give orders – 'Come – go – sit' – a command of a language that allows one to argue with waiters but nothing more. In which case he might die out of a misunderstanding as Johnny feared. Admittedly, this would be black comedy.

There may have been a tragedy, but, if so, it lay elsewhere. By his own account, Johnny Cardozo was a good man driven to evil deeds; and, whether or not one accepts the necessity or the morality, this seems to me to be tragic. Certainly I wasn't inclined to go behind Johnny's image of himself. I'd liked him from the first time we met and, being as susceptible to first impressions as the next man, I was as liable to explain away all contradictions in order to save that moment of innocence.

Concerning the body hanging in the back room, Mrs Christie said, 'It's your man. I'd made up my mind to buy another of the basket things containing those cakes – *bolos* do they call them? – that make them so suitable as a small present. Naturally he was nowhere in sight, and so I went looking and found him. I tested his pulse. He's quite dead, I assure you.'

I locked the door and pulled down the green roller blind. For a moment the shop seemed as dead as my relative: frozen in a glaucous light as if we had all drowned.

I said, 'You must be shocked. Can I offer you a drink?'

Mrs Christie answered in her brisk manner, 'No, really, that won't be necessary. I did hospital work during the war and I don't shock easily.' She urged me towards the back room, where my uncle-cousin-brother was hanging from a hook in the ceiling that had once served to hold an oil lamp. His tongue was swollen. In the normal way it would have been horrible except that it seemed to fit within his repertoire of sadness as an ironic commentary. Indeed there was something of the music hall about it, which made me speculate that my family's tendency to melancholia might be balanced by a macabre humour: a common characteristic of clowns.

'Do you have a knife?' I asked. 'I ought to cut him down.'

'You should have one somewhere,' Mrs Christie answered, 'for cutting twine and so forth.' She began to rummage in the drawers of the shop fittings until, as predicted, she found one, which she waved at me triumphantly. 'But do you think you really *should* cut him down? One would be disturbing the evidence.'

'What makes you think there's been a crime?'

'Well, one never knows, does one?' She smiled. 'Oh, do forgive me. You must be upset, and I'm treating this as if it's a tuppenny-ha'penny murder mystery in which the narrator stumbles over bodies as a matter of course and thinks nothing of it. You think it was suicide? That would be very bad if he was a Catholic – and so unfortunate for his family.'

I picked up a piece of paper from the floor. It was an invoice, on which Senhor Pereira had written in crayon one word, 'Sorry'. I'd never known him write in English and could imagine his struggling over this one word with more agony than he had felt in the matter of his death.

Mrs Christie said, 'That rather seems to settle it, doesn't it? Do you think there will be an inquest? Perhaps they don't go in for them here – I must ask the Consul. I do hope not, because I may be detained as a material witness. The *Kildonan Castle* is expected to leave at midnight and I absolutely must be on it.'

The day was dreaming through its siesta. A faint smell came from the corpse, which may have been usual as far as I knew. Hanging was a form of death of which the war had provided no experience. Mrs Christie ferreted in her bag for a flask of cologne and applied it to her neck and wrists.

'It's very hot,' she explained. 'Is it always like this?'

'It's milder as a rule – or so they tell me.'

She looked at me as if I were being a little stupid. 'You should be doing something – informing the authorities.'

Already a policeman had appeared at the door. Where he had come from and how the news had got to him were mysteries. Mrs Christie, concerned with practical aspects of her own affairs, said, 'Apparently the delay to the *Kildonan* was caused by sabotage. People have been arrested. Lascar seamen, I expect. Or Bolsheviks, who are up to every kind of wickedness.'

'I imagine you're right. Will you excuse me? There's someone at the door.' I let the policeman in and, squeezing beside him, a local pharmacist I knew by sight. They were gloomily respectful as though Senhor Pereira had been suffering from a long illness and his demise was anticipated at any moment. I led them in silence to the back room and showed the body. Only then did a sense of the enormity of the event strike me in a wave of guilt that I had been able to do nothing for my relative.

I blurted out, 'He's killed himself! You must see that!'

Perhaps because I spoke in English, or perhaps (and this is not wholly improbable on a small island) because they were aware of the Pinfold family's taste for self-immolation, my panicky excuse made no impression. They merely nodded without surprise so that one might have supposed that this was but one case in an epidemic of hangings.

'I must go,' said Mrs Christie.

No one was disposed to stop her. I felt I must make some farewell, and so said, 'I do hope you've enjoyed your stay here.'

'It's been very pleasant.'

'You found things to do?'

'Well, I had hoped to find material for a book.'

'A children's story?'

She was puzzled. 'Why on earth a children's story? No, I was hoping to make something of the Emperor Karl and the death of poor Mr Robinson.'

When my lack of interest became only too apparent, she said, 'Unfortunately nothing came to mind. In my books I can't be doing with an emperor who stays alive.'

*

'Well, he's strung himself up himself,' said Doctor Talbot, 'That's as plain as day.'

After a cursory glance at the body, he proposed we open a bottle of vermelho.

'Bless you, Michael,' he said. He gave my relative another lazy gaze and opined, 'People are extraordinarily good at it – hanging themselves. I sometimes wonder where they learn how to do it. I mean, it's not exactly something one picks up in books: you know? Not like mending a motor car. In fact people who haven't the foggiest about mending motor cars – or anything else for that matter – make a very neat job with a rope. It beats me where they get the knack. And it is a knack. It'd be very easy to end up with nothing more than an abrasion and a stiff neck.'

Senhor Pereira was lying on the large counter. His tongue had been reinserted in his mouth, and, save for the congested colour of his face, he looked as though he were asleep with his arms folded. His naturally grave manner and peculiar habits made this quite plausible.

'I suppose the black dog got him,' Doctor Talbot remarked. 'It tends to happen in the colonies – though Madeira isn't strictly a colony. I'm speaking of the British. The Portuguese are as merry as niggers: nothing seems to get 'em down. Except *fado*, that is. Have you ever listened to it? Miserable stuff, enough to make any man want to end it all. In my time I've buried a fair few of our fellow countrymen – oh, not because of *fado*. At least, not that I know of. Hanging is rather unusual. The men are normally content with a whisky bottle and a revolver, and the women poison themselves or jump off a cliff.'

I asked, 'Are you always called in on these cases? I thought you were retired.'

'I keep my hand in where the British are concerned. The natives don't like to get mixed up in our business. There was a scandal back in ninety-five. One of the local chaps diagnosed that a woman had topped herself with a dose of arsenic. He was quite right, of course, but there was her reputation to think of and an inheritance in the case – suspicions about the husband, that sort of thing. He got his wrist slapped, and since then we've been left to take care of our own. You'll have noticed that the bobby sloped off.'

He reached over to refill his glass. His rheumy eyes gave the wine a watery examination. 'This stuff is surprisingly passable. I hear you've got some bloody awful malmsey – not that I care – can't stand the stuff. I was told that young idiot Fairbrother bought it. Arthur Mainwaring is looking for him.'

'Senhor Pereira wasn't British,' I said.

'Not in the strict sense,' Doctor Talbot agreed.

'Is there another?'

The Doctor cleared his throat. 'Let's say that I knew your Uncle Gordon before he did a bunk to the Sudan. Mind you, I was only a young shaver fresh out of Barts.'

'He was Senhor Pereira's father?'

'Possibly.' Doctor Talbot answered. 'The by-blows of the Pinfold family are legend. Your great uncle shot himself over an affair. Gordon's penchant was for married women. He never married himself, but he couldn't keep his hands off 'em. There was some such story behind his sudden departure to join Kitchener.' He paused to give me a damp-eyed stare. 'I understand he isn't alone in his tastes turning in that direction.'

I let the last remark pass. I was more interested in the revelation concerning my late uncle. Until now I'd assumed my own affairs to be in some way the result of my childhood; but Doctor Talbot caused me to think of my father and raised a passing curiosity as to my various 'mothers' and whether his inclinations, too, had extended to married women. Would the case be any different if my own were the consequence of a family trait?

Doctor Talbot seemed ready to settle for the afternoon. He had quietly appropriated the bottle of vermelho. He glanced at Senhor Pereira, who was momentarily animated by a fly dancing about his lips. 'We'd better do something about that poor fellow before be starts to stink. Will you take care of the funeral? I can recommend da Silva. You'll find his place in the Largo do Comércio – you can pick up a decent pair of shoes in the boot market there, if you've a mind to. If you like, I'll look in on the Consul. He'll sort out the Quinta Vigia. By the way, do you have any problem with its being a suicide? We can call it an accident, if you like. I don't expect the Governor's people care one way or t'other. An accident would probably be the best story.'

'What do you normally do?'

'Oh, we plump for an accident, if we can. Suicide is always a problem for the burial – unhallowed ground – the corpse shoved under a crossroads at midnight if the priests have anything to do with it – no end of a fuss, and the relatives in a hell of a state. I hope your father isn't going to take on.'

'What makes you think he will?'

'The "Curse of the Pinfolds". The psychiatrists call it melancholia, but it's nothing more than an hereditary tendency to constipation, if you want my opinion, though I don't claim to be up-to-date. At all events his nerves are shot. How about you? Bowels all right? I can prescribe a laxative, though syrup of figs is as good as anything.'

'I'm fine, thanks.'

Disappointed, Doctor Talbot looked glumly at the bottle. His face twisted in a small agony and he sighed. 'No, better not. A fellow has to know his own measure, and mine is none too reliable where Madeira is concerned. Whisky, on the other hand…' He reached for his hat, a Panama that with age had acquired a tobacco-coloured patina. He rose and offered a hand. 'I'm reminded that I ought to look in on your father, but it's a damn nuisance trekking all the way up to Monte. Elsie does it.' (Only now did I learn that the formidable Mrs Talbot was called Elsie) 'Traipses to your place with pots of jam and Lord knows what to cheer your dad up. But that woman is an angel,' he added with an admiration coloured by disgust and alarm.

*

I closed the shop. I made a mental note to cancel the payments of rent. Let the landlord forfeit the lease; it made no odds. I called on Senhor da Silva at his establishment near the Bazar do Povo and explained my requirements for a funeral. He raised delicately the subject of payment in cash, his manner reminding me a little of Ronnie Fairbrother, though there was no physical resemblance, the undertaker being a small man whose face appeared darker by virtue of a glittering white collar and whose eyes hid behind an equally glittering pince-nez. His welcoming manner did not overcome my desire to be elsewhere.

'It is because of the economic depression,' he explained tactfully on the matter of payment.

The fact of suicide made no impression on him. It was the habit of exiles: a custom like suttee among Indian widows: barbaric but tolerated by the civilised Portuguese. And, if Senhor Pereira was not exactly an exile, still it was generally known that he was my relative. Only the Pinfolds, careless in spreading their seed, harboured doubts on the subject.

'*O Senhor* will take a drink with me?' asked my modest new friend.

'Why not?' I said, for the day was spoiled and a storm that had formed over the mountains was beginning to break.

*

My stay with Senhor da Silva lasted longer than I intended. I was unwise enough to tell him of my father's career in the music hall. He confessed in turn that he was esteemed a raconteur of comic monologues. He shut the shop in order to convince me at length. 'There will be no customers during the storm,' he said with the unsettling implication that corpses did not care to wander the streets in the rain but might reconsider if it were fine.

I stayed an hour until the weather settled to a steamy drizzle, then made my way unsteadily towards the station, intending to catch the train up to Monte. I was cutting through the Travessa do Punenta when a figure erupted furiously from a bar and gripped me in a bear hug.

'Got you, you bastard!' Van der Moewe snarled.

He threw me to the ground, then dragged me by the heels into an alleyway next to a potter's workshop, and set about belabouring me with his boots until I heard the clipped drawl of Doctor Crispin saying, 'There – there, Van, that's quite enough. I think Mr Pinfold understands our disapproval.' As I tried to rise, his toe shoved me down. 'Don't push your luck, laddie. I may not be as impetuous as Van, but I'm mighty put out all the same. You steal a hundred pounds from my cabin, cheat the pair of us at cards, and now it seems that the Company is going to let us go once we reach Cape Town. It's all quite enough to make one cross, don't you think?'

'It's your own damned fault,' I said.

'I think you'll find that, even if true, it won't serve as an excuse. There's nothing like being in the wrong to cause a fellow to become annoyed.'

'Go to hell.'

'Presently, no doubt. But at this exact moment, I'm wondering why I shouldn't give Van liberty to follow his instincts and smash your head in. Convince me.'

He allowed me to rise. I supported myself off the wall. My head was clear enough to recognise that both the others had been drinking. As on the occasion of our card game, alcohol made Van der Moewe irascible while affecting Crispin with a chilling, superficial charm. I picked up on their reckless air: I'd seen similar in the war when men, primed with rum, would laughingly face a machine gun. Horrors are committed in such a mood and the risk of being killed or caught makes no difference.

Crispin said pleasantly, 'Steady on, old man. You're still a little rocky on your pins. What d'you say that we all have a glass of something together, all pals sorting out our problems, eh?' He turned to his companion. 'You're not dealing with kaffirs now, Van. Mr Pinfold is a gentleman and open to a reasonable settlement of our complaints.

Aren't you, Michael?' He punched me in the abdomen as hard as any punch I've received. 'Oh yes!' He laughed. 'They don't come more reasonable.'

He gave a signal to Van and they frog-marched me out of the alley into a narrow street. Women in black dresses were gutting fish and scrawny cats and dogs kept a wary eye on each other like old enemies at a peace conference. Mid-way stood a bar with a table and a pair of wicker chairs in front. We ignored the table and pushed inside. A crowd of fishermen in nautical slops and tradesmen in aprons made way. A waiter asked what *Os Senhores* desired. We desired rum, a bottle and three glasses.

Crispin pinched my ear. 'Wakey wakey and pay attention, Michael. We'll sort out our business and get drunk, eh? All pals together.'

'Go to hell.'

'Ha ha! You're repeating yourself. Not the language of Shakespeare. D'you remember we had a conversation about Shakespeare? Someone was drowned in a butt of malmsey – was it your malmsey? – no, of course not. If anyone fell in your malmsey they'd die of poisoning not drowning, from what I hear.'

The rum came over. The South African splashed some into his glass, drank it and poured a round for the three of us.

'Thank you, Van,' said Crispin with ironic courtesy. He touched his glass to mine. 'To the future. Mine, as it happens, is a grisly one: the prospect of bunking with my friend here in a Capetown doss house until something turns up, then a post on a Shanghai tramp with a bunch of niggers. And all thanks to you, Michael. In the circumstances my patience is quite remarkable, don't you think?'

I said, 'You sabotaged the *Kildonan Castle*.'

'Congratulations. That happens, by the way, to be another ground of complaint.'

'How so?'

'We were promised five hundred pounds for the delay – not that it was all for us, you understand: I shouldn't like you to think we were greedy. However, we have received only two hundred – of which you took a half. I think we shall whistle for the rest, don't you?'

'Who promised the money?'

'A Hungarian of your acquaintance. He goes by the name of Count Bronstein. Don't disappoint me, Michael. Please don't pretend innocence. The last time I saw him, he seemed extremely interested in you. Any idea why?'

'No.'

'Ah well, I don't suppose it matters. It isn't for Van and me to meddle in your affairs – a lesson you could usefully learn. No, we only want money, old man. Not even revenge. At least, I don't. Van has a different opinion.'

Crispin splashed more rum into my glass. A pretty girl with swinging skirts walked past the open door. She carried a bundle of canes. Van's eyes rolled after her. 'She's barefoot,' he muttered. 'That's the ruin of a good woman.'

I said, 'I don't have any money. Perhaps a few pounds left from what I won.'

'Not good enough,' said Crispin. 'Perhaps we should all go up to Monte? Entertain your father and his darky?'

'Leave them out of it,' I said (there was something intrinsically predictable and pathetic about this dialogue). Then I recalled that I was carrying Fairbrother's bill of exchange: my ticket away from the island; from my father and Teddy; from the shades of Senhor Pereira and Pouco Pedro; and from Margaret and Angélica Soares whom I could never love as they deserved. 'Wait,' I said. 'I have something.'

'On you?'

'It's not cash – but as good as.' I reached in my pocket and produced the bill. Van grabbed it.

'What's this?'

'It's called a bill of exchange. I got it for some wine I sold. I think I can make it over to you by signing it. A bank will accept it.' Van seemed on the point of tearing the paper up. 'For God's sake!' I appealed to Crispin. 'That damn thing is worth money, I tell you.'

Crispin took the bill out of the South African's hands. He read it then held it to the light. I don't suppose he knew any more of bills of exchange than I did, but he had no reason to believe I was carrying around a forgery on the off-chance of meeting a pair of murderous drunks.

'It's like a cheque,' I said. 'All I have to do is endorse it on the back.' I had no idea if this were true. Rum and fear were bringing up bile in my throat. I urged, 'Look, you don't think I'd have accepted it if I didn't think it was good, do you? Look at the name at the top. It's as sound as the Bank of England!' My panic rising, I tried to force the issue. I grabbed a pencil from my pocket, seized the paper and scrawled my signature on the reverse. I offered it to Crispin. 'There. Are you going to take it or not?'

I didn't think he would. Like me he had the ingrained scepticism of the trickster. The ridiculous piece of paper hung between us, attracting the eyes only of the Portuguese. Crispin's were fixed on mine.

At last Van said, 'You've signed with a pencil.' At times the strangest people discover they are lawyers. 'I don't think you can sign with a pencil. It wouldn't be right.' He took the paper from me, and at the same time removed a pair of spectacles from the breast pocket of his shirt. He put them on and began to study the bill intently, judiciously even as though such things were a matter of daily familiarity. I could have blessed him.

Crispin, his eyes still clouded by greed and anger, remained silent.

Van removed the spectacles and folded them. 'A stamp,' he advised Crispin. 'It probably needs a stamp. Otherwise, in my opinion, it's all right.'

Distracted, Crispin seemed to lose his way. The South African's sudden shift had unbalanced whatever equilibrium had been established between them. I sensed the small, seismic movement, and, under other circumstances, I would have speculated as to the forces that matched this pair of madmen. But at this instant I felt only my life trembling on their decision and I didn't dare say a word in case it united them against me. At last, Crispin reached into a pocket. 'I have a pen,' he said and handed it to me. I wrote my name again.

'What about the stamp?' asked Van.

I said, 'You only need a stamp when you write a cheque, not when you endorse one.'

'Is that right?'

Crispin nodded.

I folded the bill of exchange slowly and neatly and asked politely which of them would take it. Again I saw the uncertainty before Crispin took it from me and placed it on the table.

'It's nice doing business with you, gentlemen,' I said. I stood slowly.

I quit the bar, leaving the two men silent over their rum and the scrap of paper. With it I left my future. The House of Pinfold was finally ruined.

CHAPTER TWENTY

On top of what I'd taken earlier, the rum Crispin forced on me meant I was fairly drunk; otherwise I doubt it would have occurred to me to clean up in Robinson's room.

The woman who guarded the stair made no difficulties about giving me the key. Perhaps all Englishmen looked alike and Robinson was no more than a hazy glamour who might be alive or dead, a matter about which I sometimes wondered. Most likely the rent was paid up. At all events, the room was unoccupied.

His clothes were still hanging behind the curtain, the shoes neatly aligned with toes pointing under the bed. Only a fine film of dust floating on the water in the jug indicated an absence. I poured the water into the basin, washed myself, then lay on the bed. My mind was filled with sickening thoughts at the loss of Fairbrother's money and the disaster to my prospects, but I dozed off for an hour to the sound of *fado* and mandolin from the restaurant below.

When I woke my head was clearer, though my bones ached from the drubbing Van der Moewe had given me. I took a drink from the water I'd washed in and left the room, intending to find transport home. The woman was at her station, suckling an infant. A piece of lace covered her breast.

Until now I'd thought her an old woman: indeed she wasn't young, perhaps forty; and this child was the last of a brood. I pass women of forty every day and think nothing of them, but she was looking at the child so tenderly, moving her lips to encourage its feeding, that I felt a shock. She was plain – ugly even: her face lined and bearing the trace of a moustache and her body thickened:

the underlying blueness of her breast visible at the edge of the lace. Yet she was beautiful: filled with the strange otherness of the women who haunt the rooms of Dutch paintings, women whose absorbing occupations may be interpreted as a quiet joke against men, always assuming we figure in their thoughts, which I rather doubt. This sense – that she was animating a scene at which I wasn't present – lasted only a moment because she noticed my shadow, cast a wary eye in my direction and took the child from her breast. But it encouraged me to say a few words more than a simple parting.

I asked, 'Did you know Senhor Robinson?'

She shook her head.

'Did you ever see him?'

She nodded.

'What was he like?'

She shrugged. A strange man enquiring about another strange man simply bored her. She gave me a meek smile to allay any hostility, then attended to the baby. It broke wind and she let out an exclamation of pleasure.

The baby was of the bonny, merry sort that make fools of strangers. Its fingers clasped and unclasped, waving at me. It gave me a windy smile then stuck its mouth to the teat again.

I wondered what Margaret's child would be like. I had been miserable and colicky. 'A Pinfold from the day of your first nappy,' my father had told me. 'I was the same by all accounts. Your Uncle Gordon, too. A foretaste of our ultimate fate, eh my boy?' he added.

But, I thought, it needn't be so. The child was also Margaret's, and there was a Margaret I did not see: the one partially revealed to old Sonny: luminous like the women of the Dutch Masters: like this woman on the stairs suckling her infant by candlelight: like the wives of other men: the women I saw in scenes at which I was not present.

I asked, 'Did Senhor Robinson have visitors?'

I held out my hand and the baby made a fist around my finger. No longer bored, the woman looked at me: the stranger in the soiled clothes, who had been in a fight and stank of rum: whose smile captured everything that was dangerous and deceitful about men.

'*Sim*,' she said cautiously.

'Did you see them? Or was it only one?'

'*Sim*.'

'You mean you saw them?'

'*Não*.'

'Heard them? I mean him – it was one person, yes?'

Yes it was one person she heard. Also Senhor Robinson, of course.

No, she did not see him because ... she glanced at the child.

They made a noise? Yes, a great deal of noise. Angry? Yes, angry. They frightened the baby.

'What language were they speaking?'

She could not say. English and German were the same to her. Magyar? Was there such a country? All of this happened a few days ago.

She hadn't seen Senhor Robinson since. Did *O Senhor* know what had become of him?

*

I found a *carro de bois*. The driver was drunk, the sled near broken, the bullocks half-starved.

'Forget him,' said the cheerful boy. 'I am your man. I will see you all right, *O Senhor*.'

'I don't want to travel with a drunk.'

'Ha ha! Don't worry. If he wakes up, I will beat him with my stick. We don't need him.' He patted the neck of a bullock. The beast turned to nuzzle his shoulder. 'My darlings listen to me, don't you? I am the Boss, eh?'

We settled on the fare. I mounted the sled, pushing the sleeping driver to one corner of the seat. The boy tapped the bullocks with his stick and gave an encouraging call. The animals responded stoically, heaving the sled across the cobblestones. Slowly we climbed the incline to Monte, gardens and terraces to either side, the paper flowers of bougainvillea dim like old bruises, and banana leaves fluttering in the night.

I was dropped in the square by the station. Mist had reduced the plane trees to shadows unlit by the white globules of the lamps. The holy fountain echoed with a plangent drip of water on stone. A faint scent of onion came from drifts of agapanthus among the laurels of the surrounding hillside.

I heaved my tired carcass up the narrow lanes, stirring the dogs to bark. The Quinta Pinfold was in darkness except for a glimmer of moonlight on the seaward side and a sparkle threading the line of the *levada*. I entered through the kitchen, where I found Teddy in a state of excitement. His shirt was clean, his hair was oiled and he smelled of bay rum and patchouli.

'Oh, Mister Michael!' he cried. 'How glad we are all being to see you!'

The boyishness that was always there behind his worried expression and slender frame bubbled forth.

'Steady on,' I said. 'How is my father?'

'No fear, isn't it! *Himself* is very joyous and civilized. *He* has changed clothes, too, and brushed hair, and is most pretty like me.'

He waited for my response. Apparently he had a surprise for me. Was it his birthday perhaps? (This was an open subject in my family: my father was never definite as to my birthday, claiming to have been away tending one of his Empires at the time; and he was vague, too, about his own.) As I tried to think of something encouraging to say, I became aware of how fond I was of Teddy: touched by his loyalty, sincerity, honesty and unfailing kindness. If he were, indeed, my brother I could not ask for a better one.

I helped myself to a glass of water from the hand-pump.

'You are teasing me,' Teddy complained but not seriously. 'You are not asking why there is so much merriment.'

'I'm sorry, Teddy. I'm tired.'

'You are smelly and disgusting,' he answered. 'But I do not mind.'

'Good point. All right, what is it?'

'We have a visitor!' He wagged his finger at me. 'No, no, I am not saying! A visitor – a very nice person – very lovely and with a beautiful stink! You must come with me, where your father is doing the needful, all gorgeous and entertaining.'

I'd given no thought to it, but I could hear the strum of a ukelele. As Teddy led me to the saloon, my father's voice came from the other side of the door, singing as if he were a young man at an Edwardian garden party with pretty girls to amuse.

'Dina from Deal,

Does she care how I feel?

Her wiles are alarming,

Her manner disarming,

She is wholly charming!

But not wholly real...'

Pushing open the door, I said, 'Hullo, Father.' He was dressed in a frogged jacket of crimson plush, and standing in a raffish pose with one leg on a chair, leaning on it as if in a serenade. His eyes, turned towards another person, bore an intensity of joy I didn't recognise. In a different way, it was a small epiphany such as I'd felt on seeing the woman with the baby: a sense of the intrusion of the sublime into the mundane. I couldn't remember when I had last seen him so happy – not even the night when we took Crispin for a hundred pounds.

'Michael, my own child!' he exclaimed. 'My pride, my joy, my lovesome boy! Do come in! We were just this moment speaking of you. What on earth do you mean by keeping me away from this most wonderful creature?'

'Hullo, Michael,' said Margaret with a smile.

*

They had been laughing. Margaret's face was faintly flushed. She was sitting forward in a chair, enthralled by my father's singing, and no doubt his jokes, too. A book of his old clippings was open on the lap of her ivory-coloured dress, and her arms, fair and downy, lay easy and relaxed across it. Her legs, tapered to fine ankles, were still folded at an angle as if they had only a moment before been curled cosily on the chair; and she had kicked off her shoes.

I said, 'I didn't see your car.' I reached for the cigarette box at my father's side.

'Is that any way to greet a lady?' he asked. The joy passed from his face.

Margaret said, 'You know how I feel about driving along these dreadful roads. I left it in the Largo da Fonte.'

I nodded. I even smiled. 'Well, I'm glad that you two have met.'

'And so am I,' my father answered. 'I have a bone to pick with you, laddie. You've been spreading calumnies that I'm a miserable old devil, who spends his days contemplating how to make away with himself. Tsk tsk! I've always regarded myself as charming and debonair.'

Margaret laughed. Teddy came in with drinks, bowing and grinning. My father told him to sit down and join us when he was finished. 'The boxwallah's whoreson is part of the family,' he explained to Margaret.

'Literally so?' I asked.

'It doesn't do to enquire,' said my father, then, turning his charm on Margaret, 'We old Anglo-Portuguese families are a little loose and forgetful. My own past is, shall we say...?'

'He used to be pals with emperors,' I interrupted.

Margaret threw me a sharp look then rallied. 'Have you met the Emperor Karl? He's almost your neighbour.'

'I saw him in England when he came over for the coronation,' my father answered in a tone that left open the possibility that they had had a beer together before pushing on to a club. 'Here in Monte, however, I rarely see anyone. My health doesn't allow it.'

When Teddy offered me a whisky, I refused. I asked for water. I could hear the resentment in my voice: feel it in my manner. But self-knowledge is so often a useless thing in the face of the passions that move us. Quite unreasonably, I treated Margaret's arrival as if it were a confrontation, and her evident good relations with my father as a reproach. Or perhaps it was that I had received an intimation that with others she could be happy. For her part she continued to smile, but I caught the hurt and quizzical glances and didn't know how to answer them.

'Speaking of emperors...' she began.

'Why are you here?' I asked.

'Oh ... well ... in a way we're talking about the same thing. Johnny isn't at home. There's ... I don't know ... some sort of brouhaha about the safety of the Emperor Karl. People – the Governor, I suppose – are frightened that an attempt may be made to assassinate him. Johnny's own people have a house in town...'

'I know it.'

'Johnny is staying there,' Margaret said. Then she stared at me, a naked stare that was pained and hostile and which, God knew, I deserved. 'I'm afraid – and alone,' she added bluntly.

'Well, this is all very jolly,' my father chipped in. 'Michael, I can see that you must be the star of your little social circle. You have quite a way with you.'

I softened a little. I asked Margaret, 'Would you like to dance? We haven't any records, but my father plays the piano.'

'The tango?'

'I don't think so. He might be able to manage a waltz.'

Already my father was at the piano and resuming his song.

'Delectable Dina,

Although you're a minor,

The thought of a fine or

The clink, makes me smile.

For, oh, what a waste!

That your love is so chaste.

Thank God I'm a swine or...'

'Father.'

'Yes, Michael?'

'A waltz, if you please.'

'Certainly,' he conceded primly and proceeded to knock out a tune from an operetta I didn't know. I held out my arms while Margaret unfolded herself from the chair and advanced uncertainly.

She said, 'Your face is bruised. You look a mess. Have you been in a fight?'

'I'm not as smart as Johnny, that's for certain.'

She shuddered. 'You haven't kissed me.'

I said, 'What have you told my father about us?'

'Nothing. I didn't consider it necessary. The situation is rather obvious, isn't it?'

'Is it?' I kissed her on the cheek. She rested her face on my shoulder.

We took a spin about the room. The Viennese waltz was too fast for the mood or my half-drunken condition, and I slowed it down so that we danced out of time as people do at the end of a wonderful evening when they are in love and the morning offers only the prospect of sad reality. That was how we had danced around the palm tree at São Vicente, when for a moment love had seemed perfect and possible. But tonight we were not in love and the evening was not wonderful.

Margaret asked, 'Why are you being cruel to me?'

I didn't bother to deny the accusation. In turn I asked, 'Does this mean that you've left Johnny?'

'I don't think you want me to.'

'I've asked you often enough.'

'Only because you're certain of the answer.'

'Don't you believe that I love you?'

'Oh yes. But it's sentimental, isn't it, to think that love solves everything? It isn't always practical or moral – it's just an emotion that people feel. I rather think that thwarted love must be experienced more intensely than love that's fulfilled. Perhaps we desire it because we know we're unworthy of anything better. Do you think you deserve me?'

'No.'

'That tells you a lot, doesn't it? I don't deserve you either.'

'Cynics would say we deserve each other.'

The music stopped.

We stepped outside into the mist-drenched garden. My father began vamping to another of his own compositions.

'Lizzie goes to St. Tropez,

Very bright and very gay...'

I offered Margaret a cigarette. I asked, 'Do you intend to stay the night?'

'If you want me to.'

Did I? When love fails, there is a desire to make the failure complete so that the grounds for pity may be more perfect. Sometimes we desire failure. It is success that overturns the world on its foundations. Perhaps I loved married women because disappointment, not fulfilment was the treasure to be won.

Not waiting for an answer Margaret said, 'Do you know that Ronnie Fairbrother has been arrested?'

'When? I saw him earlier today.' I wondered if she were joking. It was plausible. Fairbrother was someone about whom one made jokes: someone one might even hurt in a casual way, as one does those who are fat or ugly or otherwise out of the normal run.

'I don't know the details. Apparently Arthur Mainwaring swore out a warrant against him.'

'I knew Mainwaring had been looking for Ronnie.'

'Well, he found him. He says that Ronnie passed him a forged cheque … not a cheque…'

'A bill of exchange?'

'Does it matter? The point is that he's a cheat and a thief.' Margaret hesitated, then laughed, 'In fact he's like you, Michael!'

Yes, like me. I joined in the laughter. Partly it was at my own expense, but I had, too, the entertaining vision of Crispin and Van der Moewe presenting my own bill of exchange at the bank in the morning, and the reception that awaited them. As Father Flaherty might have remarked, God's footwork is cunning as He goes about His dance.

We went back inside. Teddy had curled up and was asleep on the rug. My father was watching him affectionately. He glanced up at me, frowned and said, 'I oughtn't to call him names, ought I? "Boxwallah's whoreson" – it isn't so very funny, is it?'

'No.'

'I don't know why I do it.'

I asked, 'Is he really my brother?'

My father was surprised. 'Teddy? Good Lord, no. I shouldn't care to say who he is. I inherited him when your Uncle Gordon cleared off to Africa. He left a note saying that Teddy was to be taken care of, and I've tried to look out for him in my fashion.'

'Then he's my cousin?'

'God alone knows. Does it matter?'

'I suppose not,' I said.

Teddy twitched in his sleep.

Just then came a noise from the direction of the kitchen. My father brightened. He said, 'Sometimes this place is like a ruddy railway station. I wonder who that is?' I said I would go and look, thinking it was most likely the rat who shared possession with us: the rat whom Teddy treated as a poor relation.

I got as far as the door when it opened of itself and a lumbering ginger-haired figure stumbled in.

Forcing a note of cheerfulness into his abashed voice, he announced, 'Here I am again! Always turning up like a bad Pennyweight, eh?'

CHAPTER TWENTY-ONE

'It's a bugger, being kidnapped,' said Pennyweight. With a heavy sigh he eased off his boots. His hairy suit, whatever its other limitations, had stood up well to the hardships of the last few days, giving him the air of a rough-coated dog with a taste for romping in mud. He stirred Teddy with the toe protruding from an unsavoury sock. 'Any chance of pouring Burra Sahib a peg of scotch, Teddy, old man?' To the rest of us he said, 'No, I wouldn't recommend being kidnapped.'

He appraised Margaret. I couldn't recall if they'd met: rather thought they hadn't. I said, 'May I introduce Mrs Cardozo?'

Pennyweight bowed gallantly. 'Charmed. We ran into each other at Captain Robinson's funeral.' Suddenly emotional, he added, 'It was pretty decent, the way people turned out. The Captain would have appreciated that.'

Margaret asked, 'Did you know him?'

Pennyweight's face assumed the stagey expression of an old soldier who had been through inexpressible horrors. 'David and Jonathan, as it says in the Good Book. We were like *that* –' he crossed his fingers. 'I was a captain, too – though it's a point I don't mention as a rule.' He looked around for Teddy who had gone to find a clean glass. 'I should have asked for some grub, too. My God, but it's good to be home!'

Watching him, I was reminded of another Biblical story: the Prodigal Son, whom I imagined recalling his sins in a similar shifty manner in front of reluctant relatives who had been chivvied by rabbis into doing the Right Thing. Pennyweight said, 'I suppose you want to know what happened and how I came to get away?' His face exhibited the remote hope that I might say I really didn't care. 'Yes – well – it's a rum tale. Very rum. Perhaps in the morning…'

'I'd rather like to hear it now,' I said. I took the glass of scotch from Teddy and handed it to the ginger man.

'Righty ho,' said Pennyweight. 'I just thought … the late hour … everyone tired and so forth. I mean, it isn't a tale of derring-do.'

'Even so.'

'Yes – all right, then. Teddy, is there any chance of food? Even a plate of *idlis* would be like nectar at the moment. And *sambhar* – I swear I'm getting a taste for it. Meals were a bit of catch-as-catch-can,' Pennyweight clarified. Then, seeing he couldn't avoid coming to the point he began.

'Don't expect me to be exact about times and places. I didn't have my watch and most of the time hadn't an earthly where we were.'

'I understand. Go on.'

'I suppose we should start with that island –'

'Porto Santo.'

'As you say. Bronstein had a steam launch moored just off the beach. He dragged me off in that direction during all the shooting. Not pleasant, I may tell you.'

'How many of you were there?'

'Three,' Pennyweight said firmly, as if this were the touchstone for the truth of the rest. 'Me, Bronstein, and some old fellow called Ferenc. Dunno what happened to the other one. Can't say if he's still alive.'

Neither could I. I had left him at the house in the Rua Santa Maria, to whatever kindness a troubled Johnny Cardozo might spare him.

'Anyway, off we sailed – no lights and the night as black as my hat – stomach decidedly queasy. Can't say where we were aiming for, except that it was Madeira, obviously. All I know is that it seemed to take for ever, and we fetched up as the sun was rising. Some place with cliffs and waterfalls, and bananas as thick as weeds. It could be anywhere, I suppose?'

I nodded, which seemed to encourage him.

'Well, we pushed off, once we'd got our wind. Bronstein was pretty clearly put out by the business on Porto Santo, but he's a tryer, I'll give that to him.' He paused. 'You do understand: I'd have got away earlier, but those two blighters, Bronstein and Ferenc, had guns and had shown themselves more than willing in that direction.

'Anyway, it seems they didn't have any hidey hole. Instead we went clambering up those damned mountains until we found a sort of shed with a cow tethered in it. A cow! And that's where we bunked for the day: yours truly bound hand and foot with a length of rope.'

'Did they hurt you?' Margaret asked.

Pennyweight shook his head. 'As Michael knows, they're fairly gentlemanly when it comes to that sort of thing. Old soldiers – I don't care what country they come from – they're usually pretty honourable types. Bronstein's as mad as a March hare, of course. Honourable all the same.'

'Come to the point,' I said. 'What did he want of you?'

'Dashed if I know,' Pennyweight said. 'All I got was more of the same old stuff. Questions about angels and Robinson. He gave me a long rigmarole about the glorious history of Hungary and the ancestry of the Habsburgs – about which I could have told him a thing or two. Oh, and he asked me if I was a Catholic.'

'Are you?'

'I reckon myself above such things,' Pennyweight answered smugly.

Teddy brought Pennyweight a plate of cold curried *espada* and a spoon. The fat man scoffed it, apparently glad of the diversion. He asked for a bottle of Bass and opened a packet of Gold Flake.

'You've changed your cigarettes,' I said.

Pennyweight stared at them. 'I ran out of *Players*. Bronstein gave me these.'

'How were you able to smoke them?'

'I don't know what you mean.'

'Your hands were tied. Isn't that what you said?'

'Not all the time, old man,' Pennyweight protested. 'You're becoming damned suspicious all of a sudden.'

'I'm sorry.'

'That's all right.'

'You'll understand that your turning up is a bit of a surprise.'

'Is it?' The question was sincere. Pennyweight's belief in life's uncanny patterns remained intact.

Margaret asked, 'Do tell us about your escape.' She was animated again, as she had been with my father: sensing something, perhaps the fat man's 'tremendousness'. I felt only another flash of mean-spirited resentment.

I interrupted, 'I'd like to know more about Bronstein's questions.'

'Angels and Robinson, old man. What else is there to tell?'

'I don't understand why Bronstein should keep repeating himself.'

'A blessed mystery,' Pennyweight replied.

Margaret took this as an opportunity to revert to the subject of the escape, but I talked over her question. 'That won't do. Bronstein decided on Porto Santo that you were the man for him – the man to carry out whatever it was that he'd engaged Robinson to do. Why should he keep going over the same old subject: the questions he was putting earlier when he wasn't certain of you? Why didn't he explain the job in hand?'

'Perhaps he still had his doubts?' Pennyweight offered.

I didn't believe him, but wasn't sure what he was hiding. It needn't be sinister; in fact, knowing Pennyweight, it possibly wasn't. He might have incurred some minor embarrassment – burst into tears under threats, perhaps – which loomed disproportionately in his mind. The Prodigal Son writhes in agony at the sight of the fatted calf, giving rise to suspicions of foul crimes, when the truth is that he has become vegetarian. Men have died from such absurd misunderstandings.

'I should still like to hear about your escape,' Margaret said. Pennyweight responded gamely.

'Nothing much to tell, really. I mean nothing heroic. I was left all tied up while Bronstein and his chum went about their business. They didn't make much of a job of the knots, and I managed to work myself free. As for the cowshed – well, it's hardly Wormwood Scrubs, is it? I was out of there in a jiffy.'

I said, 'They seem to have been remarkably careless.'

'Well, it wasn't as easy as all that,' Pennyweight answered. 'Perhaps I've given the wrong impression. I don't want to boast.'

'How did you get back here?'

'Walked.'

'You knew your way?'

'I steered by the moon and stars,' Pennyweight said. Recognising that this was vague, even for him, he elaborated briefly. 'It's a skill I picked up in the Flying Corps. Navigating, map-reading, that sort of thing. They said I could have made a go of it as a tracker. Had a knack for it.'

He left the room. When he returned, he was bearing his old bayonet. Noticing our curiosity he said, 'Sorry. You know, it's funny how, when one's in a difficult situation, the mind turns to odd things, and this one has been preying on me. Stuck there with Bronstein, I wondered what would happen to my kit, if I didn't come back. Most of it, I wouldn't give a damn about: but this old thing … well … It's all I brought back from the war. I didn't win any medals except those they gave to everybody, and the rest of my stuff got lost or stolen.'

'Did you..?' Margaret began.

'Use it?' Pennyweight became solemn. 'As a matter of fact I did. Killed a fellow. Didn't like it.'

I said, 'I thought you were an Engineer?'

'What? Oh, yes. But once in a way I'd find myself in the front line, supervising repairs to the wire or the trenches after the Hun had knocked them about a bit. I got caught there when they made one of those damn' trench raids. You remember those? They got on one's pip.'

Yes, I remembered. Bennett was killed and I won the Military Cross. Recalling the time now, it came to me that in those days I had given up stealing. I didn't know why.

'Anyway,' said Pennyweight, 'the beggars came over at night in the usual fashion, drunk as monkeys and laying about them every which way and devil help the poor chap who caught one. I don't remember much except that I stuck my bayonet into some great brute.' The recollection troubled him. 'I'm not proud of it. I've never held anything against the Germans – not the soldiers, at least. They were damn' fine men. But – I don't know how to put it – blood came into my eyes. I was in a perfect fury. I can get like that sometimes, if my nerves are on edge.' He looked to me for support. I felt again his strange appeal. Then, with a flash of the old Pennyweight, he remembered a scrap of useless learning. He said, 'The Vikings used to get that way. "Berserk" they used to call it. Yes – "berserk".' He hesitated. 'I don't know why I'm telling you this.'

The story had a dampening effect. Pennyweight said that he needed to see a man about a dog and sloped off to the latrine. My father had dozed off; Teddy was awake and

I asked him to fetch a shawl. The old fellow slept badly and I didn't want to disturb him.

Margaret said, 'I like your Mr Pennyweight.'

I stared at her. I wanted to say that he was an idiot, but the words wouldn't come. The fat man's good nature seemed to make any slander, no matter how truthful, somehow beside the point. I thought again of the tradition of Holy Fools. Though Pennyweight wasn't pious in the ordinary way (in fact it was difficult to classify his beliefs: sceptical at one moment and gullible the next), he had a queer aura of saintliness. If his revelations were ridiculous, there was a sanctity in his searchings.

I said, 'Everyone likes Pennyweight, but no one takes to Ronnie Fairbrother. Doesn't that strike you as odd? On the one hand a ginger-haired fat man with questionable habits, and on the other a perfectly personable looking fellow with polite manners. On the face of it, things are the wrong way round.'

'Yes, it is curious,' Margaret agreed. She studied me thoughtfully. 'It's a matter of chemistry, isn't it? I can't explain it. Some relationships work when they shouldn't and others don't work when they really ought to. I suppose someone very clever might analyse the thing and explain why it is as it is, but I suspect the explanation wouldn't be of much practical use. Explanations of human behaviour rarely are. No matter what we think we learn, we carry on in the same old way. I'm getting off the point, aren't I?'

I said, 'I'm a very funny man.' In some way I must have seen a connection with the last remark. It seemed to me that she had identified the flaw in matters between us. We were united by need and sundered by chemistry, and the conjunction makes for the bitterest of loves.

Margaret smiled. 'You've been keeping your light under a bushel. Or do you mean "funny-peculiar"?'

'I mean humorous. I tell jokes.'

'Tell me one.'

'I've forgotten them.'

'I see. I understood your family were all melancholics.'

'We are. Melancholics are often funny. Clowns are often depressed. My father used to be a Jewish comedian.'

'I didn't know he was Jewish.'

'He isn't. At least, I don't think so. Parentage is a questionable subject where the Pinfolds are concerned – apparently.'

My mothers used to laugh. Returning to our smoky room from an empty house at the latest Empire, filled on stout and cockles and supported by my father's comforting arm, they laughed uproariously as he did impersonations and recited comic songs while the wind blew and the rain fell on the grey roofs of whatever town we were in. He gave me one word of advice on the subject of women. 'Laughter – always keep 'em tickled, dear boy. The best looking young fellow is only an inch away from complete ridiculousness in the eyes of any sensible woman. My advice is to go with the grain of the creatures. Good looks fade, but a sense of humour wears well.'

Margaret asked, 'Have you made all your mistresses laugh?'

'Yes,' I said. 'All except you.'

*

I found myself awake in a room lit falteringly by a smoking oil lamp. My father was still asleep in his chair, now covered by a shawl. Teddy was curled up on the rug. Margaret, from sitting thoughtfully, had drifted off and was purring quietly. In repose her face was untroubled. Her hair, slightly disarrayed, fell in a soft tumble. She was, quite simply, lovely: beyond beauty even, which can be a hard, glittering thing. I knew then why Johnny Cardozo adored her, and why in the end she would be his and not mine. It was simply that Johnny made her laugh. I thought of the villa, where he sparkled for his guests and even those who rightly feared him were charmed by his light, debonair manner. The mystery of the upper rooms which I had never penetrated was innocent laughter.

Pennyweight returned from the latrine. He snorted, 'Pinfold, you're going to have to do something about Kensington Palace. I never smelled such a stench since the war ended. In fact that's what it reminds me of: rotting flesh. Has Teddy been slinging dead rats into the jolly old thunder box? Whew, what a pong!'

'Be quiet,' I said. I indicated the others.

'What? Oh! I wasn't thinking. Sorry, Pinfold.'

I examined my father and Teddy. Both were sound asleep. Margaret gave a faint moan. I turned on Pennyweight.

I said, 'There's a corpse buried in the garden.'

He blinked. 'Pardon? I didn't catch that. Did you say…?'

'There's a body in the garden. That's what you can smell.'

As I should have expected, Pennyweight wasn't surprised. He merely looked at me narrowly. He reached into his pocket for his packet of Gold Flake and offered me one. He asked, 'Is it anyone we know?'

I shook my head. 'You don't know him. His name is Doctor Soares. He was … he thought of himself as a writer.' He thought of himself as my friend. And was wrong in both cases.

'Ah.' Pennyweight considered the information. And, while he did so, I looked at him carefully, and saw for the first time that, behind the ginger moustache and superficial grossness, he had the makings of a handsome man; and understood, too, that, before the war and one trench raid or artillery barrage too many, he had probably been as sound as the next man and possessed of the ordinary blessings. The present Pennyweight, twisted by God knew what experience, was no more than a pantomime version of another reality: no more intrinsically absurd than any of us and equally capable of suffering. I didn't know how far he was aware of his fall from grace. He glanced at me and enquired, 'Murdered? This Soares fellow – was he murdered?'

'Not by me,' I said.

'Not your father, surely? And certainly not Teddy.'

'Bronstein killed him. Or possibly one of his men.'

'Good Lord. Why'd he do that?'

'I asked Pouco Pedro – people called him Pouco Pedro – I asked him to investigate the delays to the *Kildonan Castle*. I think Bronstein and his crew were planning to make their getaway on the ship after whatever it is they intend to do. They killed Pouco Pedro and sent his body to me as a warning not to enquire too closely or attempt to betray them. He might have killed me, but Bronstein still thought I was Robinson's pal and might be of use to him. He didn't know that you were Robinson's friend, not me.'

'Gosh,' said Pennyweight, not taking his eyes off mine.

'So –' I said '- you'll see that Bronstein is stuck here. I doubt he has any other escape route. Of course, he may be able to do what he came to do – and, knowing him, I think he'll try – but, afterwards, his position is hopeless. And so, if you understand me, is that of anyone who helps him. Quite hopeless. Johnny Cardozo will hunt Bronstein down – and I think he'll kill him.'

'Mayn't he get away on that launch of his?'

'The Canaries are nearly three hundred miles away: Morocco closer to four, possibly more.'

'I don't know much about launches. Bronstein's seemed a handy little craft,' Pennyweight speculated.

'It won't make it across open ocean. In any case Colonel Cardozo has probably found it by now.'

'"Colonel", you say?'

I nodded.

'Well, there's a pretty pickle,' Pennyweight said sombrely. 'For Bronstein, I mean.'

*

Pennyweight paced restlessly. He ignored suggestions he should go to bed. 'My nerves are shot, old man,' he said. 'I shouldn't sleep a wink.'

I was exhausted, but didn't want to disturb the others. Neither did I like the mood that was on the fat man: something of the unseen Pennyweight, the person he had once been. I could sense his reaching into unquiet memories as if they were the graves of ancestors interred alive for hideous crimes. I remembered his interest in geomancy – a belief that Cathar relics or Templar treasure could be conjured from maps by drawing patterns of lines between points of long-forgotten meaning – and thought that, if the past could be laid out in similar form, perhaps its hidden rhythms would grant a revelation.

As the oil lamp guttered, I refilled it. I shone it in turn on the faces of my father, Teddy and Margaret to be sure they still slept. Save for Pennyweight, in his persistent to-ing and fro-ing, there was silence. In my childhood, there were many watchful nights waiting for my father and my mothers to come home: not fretful nights but tense with expectation of a joke and a pat, a kiss and the gift of a toy or a portion of fried fish. Love was a present given by glamorous creatures to a good quiet boy. Love was unspeakably wonderful and no sooner gained than it must be won again on another night. Love was always the tremor of anticipation: the invisible laughter beyond the door at which I stared; my father's voice, so generous and unconstrained; the scent of my mother's perfume, telling me that she was there, almost within my reach.

Pennyweight halted.

'Damn,' he said. 'My shoelace is broken. That's bad luck, isn't it?'

'I don't think so,' I said.

He examined the lace anxiously. 'I'm sure it is. Seven years' bad luck – or maybe only three. Can you remember, Pinfold? Seven or three?'

'It isn't unlucky.'

'Are you certain?'

'You're thinking of breaking mirrors.'

He turned on me furiously. 'I hope you're bloody well right!'

'Don't worry,' I said. 'They'll be here soon.'

'"They"?' he snapped. 'What "they"? Who's going to be here soon? What do you know, Pinfold, that you haven't mentioned to me? Are you working some plot of your own?'

Pennyweight's goggle eyes fixed mine. His moustache, erratically clipped, drooped and he touched it with his fingers. He was – hilariously sad, I suppose.

He reached into his hairy suit and produced the inevitable Webley revolver, which I thought I'd glimpsed earlier. The threat was so wearisome and Pennyweight so ridiculous I felt like laughing. His hand shook and he looked badly in need of a drink. And I thought with indifference that I looked likely to die from idiocy, not malice.

In the silence I heard a motorcar engine from the direction of the lane. It was turned off and I counted the seconds to the opening of a door.

CHAPTER TWENTY-TWO

'Good evening, boys,' said Father Flaherty. 'Don't laugh, now, Michael, it isn't respectful to the cloth. And, Mr Pennyweight, will you please give me the gun? Before we know where we are you'll blow our bloody heads off, which would be a shame all round. Come now: the gun if you please.' He held out his hand, and the ginger man meekly handed him the weapon. The priest peered down the chambers and pocketed it. 'Well, isn't this fun?' he remarked.

He had appeared at the door in a straw hat and a dusty cassock, with a gun of his own stuck in the pocket. He brought with him a whiff of the night: jasmine and petrol fumes.

'I wasn't expecting you,' I said.

He said, 'No, I don't suppose you were. Is that Mrs Cardozo?' Margaret was stirring. My father, too. 'Hullo to you all. You must be Mr Pinfold Senior. Good evening, sir. Michael, will you pour me a drink? Irish preferably, but Scotch will do.'

Teddy woke up. He sprang to his feet, delighted at the sight of a priest. He hurried to get the whisky. Father Flaherty looked for a spare chair, and, finding one, sat down heavily. Despite his cheerful disposition, he looked tired and under strain. When Teddy brought the Scotch, he gave a polite thank-you and sipped it peaceably.

Pennyweight roused himself. He gave me a conspiratorial look – quite decently under the circumstances. He said, 'I've talked our business over with Pinfold, and he's with us a hundred per cent. Oh yes,' he went on, 'he's with us all right!'

Father Flaherty looked him up and down. 'Has anyone ever told you you're a bloody awful liar?' he said.

'Steady on, padre.'

'Tush, man, I'm not angry with you. I appreciate a fellow who takes care of his friends. "Greater love hath no man..." and so forth – the words escape me at present. But it's obvious to a babe that Michael hasn't a notion what you're blathering about. Tell me I'm mistaken, Michael.'

'You're not mistaken.'

'There. Didn't I always say you were honest at heart? You should seriously think about the priestly game. You have the makings of a fine Christian.'

'Like you?'

'Now that's unfair. As I recall, I told you I was a very accomplished sinner. I made no claims at all for my virtues.'

I nodded. He spoke no more than the truth. My surprise had something to do with a suspicion – some way short of a theological speculation – that sin and virtue were not antitheses, but emergent properties, each from the other, as close as Siamese twins. Not that it mattered except that my own too evident faults had always given me hope that they were testament to better qualities of which I was modestly ignorant.

Margaret looked in my direction. She was calm. Lack of nerve was never one of her faults. She asked, 'Do you know what this is about, Michael?'

'It has something to do with the Emperor,' I said.

'Karl?'

'And angels,' I added.

My father observed, 'I've run into several emperors in my time.' He was wide awake now and the affair seemed to have stimulated his sense of humour.

'And angels?'

'Not that I can think of off-hand. Though "angels" is what they call the financial backers in the theatrical business. I've met a few of those.'

'I don't think we're talking of theatre,' I said, though the explanation was as likely as any other. 'Are we talking of theatre?' I asked Flaherty.

'In a manner of speaking.'

'I think they intend to kill the Emperor Karl,' I said. And Pennyweight jumped to his feet with an appalled expression on his face.

'Good God, Pinfold! You don't really believe that, do you? The Emperor Karl is a descendant of Jesus Christ!'

I turned to his companion. 'Is he?'

'We are all children of the Lord.'

'That's a Jesuitical answer.'

'You forget that I'm a Jesuit.'

'One who's supposed to be travelling to South Africa as chaplain to the Bishop of Natal.'

'A lie, I'm afraid. Aren't I a terrible fellow?'

Apparently this exchange troubled Pennyweight. He asked, 'You aren't trying to kill the Emperor, are you?'

The priest said, 'Saving your presence, Mr Pennyweight, but we'd hardly need you, if assassination were what we had in mind. As for your question, Michael, don't worry. All will be revealed shortly.'

For a moment we fell silent until Teddy, kind to the last, said, 'I am apologizing, Father, most humbly. You are wanting food, isn't it?'

Flaherty beamed at him. 'Teddy – isn't that what they call you? – you're a good man. A little something would be much appreciated.'

'And another whisky,' I said.

'Tsk, Michael. You'll be after getting me drunk. A glass of water will do fine.'

'How did you get here?' I asked. 'I heard a car, but you don't drive – unless you lied about that, too.'

'No, I don't drive. But I have a friend. You'll meet him soon. He's about some other business.'

'Will I like him?'

'You've met him before.'

Teddy returned with another plate of fish curry. 'I am sorry, Father, but it is cold.'

'That's all right, my son.' The priest offered one of the guns back to Pennyweight. 'Just while I eat, mind you. And no killing anyone, if you value your soul.' He murmured a prayer over the food, then picked up a spoon. Before the first mouthful reached his lips, he halted and remarked, 'I can see you asking yourself, Michael, if what we are about is the Christian thing to do. And the answer is that I'm damned if I know. Religion is fine as to general principles, but leaves a man at sea when it comes to the details. There's no getting away from Free Will and moral choices.' He moved the spoon again. Hesitated again. 'I thought you might like to know that.'

Margaret snapped, 'You're full of platitudes, aren't you?' She rose and went to the table where Teddy had placed the whisky decanter. She poured herself a shot and drank it defiantly. Watching the gesture, I thought the priest was right and that, in a manner of speaking, we were indeed engaged in theatre: that substitute for ordinary action when the ordinary ceases to apply.

Flaherty put his spoon down. 'Would you believe the dreadful time I have getting fed in this job?' He turned to Margaret. 'Full of platitudes? So I am, Mrs Cardozo – so, indeed, I am. "Love thy neighbour as thyself". As wisdom goes, it isn't much when you come to think of it, is it? Most significant truths are platitudes.' He smiled. 'Ah, there I go again. I've often asked the Lord for more interesting work than mouthing pieties, but, for the most part, He doesn't listen. Flair is the thing. Any old rubbish will pass for profundity if you say it with style. The trick is in the doing, not the saying: and where the latter is simple, the former is damnably difficult. Now, will you let a poor priest get some food inside him?'

I reached for a cigarette and found I had none. Margaret offered me hers and, together, we lit them at the oil lamp. She asked me, 'Are they mad? If they don't intend to assassinate the Emperor, they must plan to escape with him.'

'I imagine so.'

'Then Johnny will catch them and kill them,' she said starkly.

'Do you hear that?' I said to Flaherty and Pennyweight. 'Colonel Cardozo is charged with taking care of Karl. He isn't going to be caught out. The Emperor is his ticket back to England.'

'I hear you, Michael.' The priest put down his plate and wiped his lips on the grimy sleeve of his cassock. 'The gun, please, Mr Pennyweight. Yes, I hear you. But, you see, Colonel Cardozo has his head facing backwards. He thinks – as you did yourself – that we're about to kill the poor man. The alternative hasn't crossed his mind because here the Emperor is, stuck on a rock in the middle of the Atlantic, and escape is simply impossible. There are only two boats capable of making the trip, the *Kildonan* and that freighter whose name I forget but which was to take Mr Fairbrother and his wine – your wine, Michael – and they are locked as tight as an Orangeman's arse. By the way, Michael, did you know that Mr Fairbrother has been arrested?'

'Yes.'

'What? Fairbrother?' exclaimed Pennyweight.

'Indeed,' said Flaherty. 'He's a crook, it seems. He bought wine in exchange for bad cheques, or something like that – I don't know how these things are done. I can't say I'm surprised. I never liked the fellow, though, I admit, the feeling was one of sheer prejudice on my part and highly uncharitable.'

'Fairbrother,' Pennyweight muttered. His disappointment was profound. In his simplicity, his capacity for faith, he alone had liked the man. Unfortunately, though his exotic theories might be maintained against all contrary evidence, people were less accommodating. Ideas in themselves were passive: people were active; and their behaviour could force the abandonment of even the most cherished notions of their character. Until they were dead, of course. Then one could think whatever one liked. What I did not see was the danger that lay in Pennyweight's faith in people. Of us all, he was the most tragic. And the funniest, too, it must be confessed.

I heard again the sound of a motor car drawing up. A second, I supposed, since I'd not heard the first one leave. My father must have caught the noise, for, before anyone arrived, he cried out, 'Come on in! It's Liberty Hall!'

Father Flaherty rose. He said, 'I caution you now to be careful. I'm an amenable fellow, but my friends are not so obliging and their nerves are not the best. Mr Pennyweight, please keep an eye on things. Michael, I know you don't like to be considered a hero, but I think you do yourself a disservice. I'd be grateful if you'd control your instincts in order to avoid accidents and for the sake of Mrs Cardozo.'

He opened the door to the next room, which was lit only by the lanterns carried by our visitors. I glimpsed Bronstein in his country wear and Alpine hat, an elderly man I took to be Ferenc, and a third figure in a pale grey military cape and képi. The last glanced in my direction, though without recognition or meaning. He was a man in his early thirties with indifferent looks and a moustache. I believed I had seen him once, working in the garden of the Quinta Gordon, but couldn't be certain because it was a face that would pass unregarded in a crowd. He turned away and gave a hearty sneeze. It seemed he had a very bad cold, or possibly the flu.

'I am pleased, at last, to meet your Imperial Majesty,' said Father Flaherty and closed the door.

*

Father Flaherty said, 'We'll wait a bit. The Emperor is feeling under the weather and all this dodging about in the dark has knocked it out of him. Teddy, if you have any brandy, will you take him some?'

'Me?' said an astonished Teddy. But he set about the task. 'It is greatly you are honouring me, Father, isn't it.'

The Emperor was still closeted with Bronstein and Ferenc in the next room. I asked Flaherty, 'Did Karl have much trouble getting away from the Quinta Gordon?'

'Not much.'

'Doesn't that puzzle you? Johnny Cardozo has been worried for days about your man's security. The place should have been guarded to the hilt.'

'You forget what I told you, Michael. The Colonel is facing the wrong way. His soldiers are looking for people breaking in, not for the Emperor breaking out.'

'How many soldiers were there?'

'I don't know.'

'If there weren't many, you should ask yourself why not.'

Flaherty studied me cautiously, then smiled and shook his head.

Margaret came to me and stood behind my chair, one hand lying on the backrest, with her finger tips stroking my hair. It was a gesture quite different in its easiness from the tension that usually marked her affection. I had seen people touch objects in the same way when they were bidding them farewell: a moment in which a value is found that has not been recognised before. There was no way of telling the meaning of this oddly tender action.

She said – speaking to Flaherty I think, 'Johnny will win out in the end. He always does. People underestimate him.'

The priest didn't answer. I could only guess at his moral commitment. He seemed indifferent to risk.

I asked, 'Did Bronstein kill Robinson?'

'He says not,' Flaherty answered.

'What about you?'

'Even you don't believe that, Michael.'

'I'm not a good judge of people. If I were, I'd be holding the gun.'

'Then what use is my telling you? No, I think we must accept poor Robinson's death as a mystery. Quite likely he was killed by some passing villain for money or jealousy or any of a thousand sad reasons. After all, what do we know of him? The error is to suppose that all things are connected – though Mr Pennyweight seems to hold the contrary view.'

The door opened and Bronstein beckoned Pennyweight. His smile, half anxious, half hopeful, was that of a man called to execution in only moderate expectation of an afterlife. 'I've never spoken to an emperor,' he said.

'Be polite and don't call him "Charlie",' said my father, who claimed some experience in the matter: who might be considered an emperor in his own small territory. His manner had become more lively and carefree as if the realisation of calamity had freed him from the burden of anticipation. He asked the priest, 'Do I understand it aright? You intend to put Karl back on the Austrian throne?'

'Only the Hungarian throne in the first instance.'

'Is that the policy of the Church?'

'So they tell me. But I'm just a clerical soldier. My superiors are perfectly capable of lying to me. Michael understands.'

I did understand. And felt sympathy, too, for the hoary old sinner. But I was tired of the war and its lamentations. Tired also of its lessons which were glibly formulated but never learned: the platitudes which apparently comprise wisdom and form the stock of every charlatan throughout the ages; and equally of every sage. It was not that these things were false but that they were useless in the face of the intractable nature of the human species: that they were the key to a door from which the lock had been removed to be replaced by iron bars of ignorance and selfishness. I did not want to know about the virtue of love: I wanted to know how to love: how to master and transcend my limitations by the active power of love: how to be someone who was worth loving. All theory, all learning collapsed before that matter of practice.

The night and the open doors had let in moths. They danced about the oil lamp; and, as our eyes followed them, conversation took on the remote quality of small talk at a cocktail party.

Father Flaherty, helping himself again to the whisky, said, 'Now that I come to think about it, is it not strange that I should be helping an emperor to regain his throne – me who's always been a republican?'

'I've always been an imperialist, myself,' said my father, though which of many empires he was referring to he didn't specify.

'I'm told that Karl is a very nice fellow – kind-hearted, decent and so on.'

'Would it make any difference if he weren't?' I asked.

'Let's say it helps that he's a good man.'

I should have preferred it if he were a monster. It would have simplified the question: on which side of the issue did I stand? The Emperor's restoration might indeed be a sound idea – in which case Bronstein, Flaherty and poor old Pennyweight were heroes – but for me it was a matter of saving my skin. I didn't know what Margaret thought, except that she was carrying our child. But there, of course, was the answer. Before that overwhelming fact she would not give a care for any other. Was she making some mean little calculation of her chances? Would she make some effort to charm Bronstein, who, I fancied, was susceptible? I shouldn't have blamed her in either case. On the contrary I would praise even a cynical commitment to life.

The door opened again. I caught sight of the Emperor sitting in a chair. He was leaning forward, clearly unwell, and his boyish face was pale in the light of the lantern at his feet. Ferenc was offering him a cordial of some kind to put him on his legs. I recalled that he had never expected the throne; had come to it by a chain of accidents: mysterious, tragic, absurd. Our families were not so different and our pretensions to imperial grandeur equally strange. Was he any more a descendant of Jesus than I was? Probably not, though it wasn't for me to say that Pennyweight was wrong. In one respect we were certainly different. He had a wife. Quite likely she loved him.

Count Bronstein came into the saloon, closing the door on his master. In one of the reversals of impression between meeting someone under unfortunate circumstances then again with time and opportunity to understand, I found myself liking him: admiring him at least. He was a man of principle, firm in his purpose and loyal to his duties. Dangerous, but without cruelty or malice.

Father Flaherty focussed a crafty Fenian eye on the Count. 'How is our boy?' he asked.

'He isn't well,' Bronstein said.

'But is he good for the journey?'

'He says so. He wants to try.'

The priest looked at Pennyweight. The fat man had been silent for a while. God knew what he was meditating on. As I've said, he had a sort of bravery but, like that of most men, it had to be brought to the pitch. In repose, the remnant of handsomeness was visible in his face. He smiled.

'Well?' said the priest. 'Are you game, Mr Pennyweight?'

Pennyweight nodded.

'Game for what?' I asked. Truthfully I should have known, for all the information was to hand; but my preconceptions concerning the fat man had distracted me. I directed my question at Bronstein. 'How the hell do you propose to get the Emperor off the island?'

'I should have thought the answer to that was obvious,' said my father: the old magician, who knew everything there was about distraction and illusion. 'They have an aeroplane. That must be the "angel" that everyone has been talking about.'

CHAPTER TWENTY-THREE

'Well, now you know,' said Pennyweight. His manner was cautious, perhaps with embarrassment at the deceit he'd practised, perhaps at the prospect of flying the Emperor, though, for all his genuine humility, I fancy he wasn't truly surprised at being called to a deed that might go down in history. He gave a low laugh. 'I'll tell you what: I didn't twig about the "angel". Rather a joke, that, eh? On the contrary, I was thinking there might be something to it. The End of the World has been on my mind lately.'

I asked, 'Do you mean that Robinson didn't tell you?'

'Not a word!' He sounded astonished. 'I spoke the truth about that. He wrote to me saying there was a job to be done and I'd be paid five hundred quid to do it. And that was all. Well … I mean to say: old Pennyweight was on his uppers, wasn't he?'

I remembered Johnny Cardozo had said that Robinson's passport bore no entry stamps. But, of course, it wouldn't have. He had flown over from Casablanca and landed at night. On the Paúl da Serra of all places. It was insane. Only one aircraft had ever flown to Madeira. It had happened the previous year and had been a seaplane; but I supposed such an aircraft would have been too visible on this occasion.

'Why land in the mountains?' I asked.

'Not as difficult as you might think,' Pennyweight said. He recognised my doubts and probably shared them because he added, 'Not for Robinson at least. The Captain was a wonderful flyer. I've been up there – we took some fuel for the flight – and there's a plateau. It goes on for miles.'

'The Paúl da Serra.'

'Whatever you say. Anyway, it's firm and flat as a pancake except for some rocks: pretty small ones at that. The only real hazard is the weather.'

Robinson had flown in mist and cloud, reading a map by a torch seen by the drunken shepherds. Had he really intended something so utterly mad?

'Of course,' Pennyweight explained, 'that wasn't the original idea. The plan was to land on the other place – Porto Santo? It's flat and dry and there's no cloud to speak of. But I fancy the Captain lost his way and was low on fuel. When he saw the mountains looming at him and a chance of putting his 'plane down on the plateau, I imagine he just took it.'

He took it, then got himself killed. And no one knew where his aircraft was except two ruffians who owned an illicit still and thought they had seen an angel. It was a perverse outcome calculated to appeal to Father Flaherty who believed in a God forever obscure and playful.

The priest said, 'Does that satisfy you for now, Michael? You can get more details as we're driving there.'

'Pennyweight is going to fly the Emperor?'

'Only as far as Morocco. There are people there who will take up the burden. For the moment what I want to hear is that, knowing now what it's all about, you're going to be a good man. It surely can't matter to you that Karl wants to return to the country of his ancestors?'

I said, 'I don't care one way or the other. But I'm not your problem. You're heading into a trap. Johnny Cardozo will have the roads barred and he'll kill you all unless you surrender.'

'You forget that we have Mrs Cardozo.'

'Johnny doesn't know that.' I wanted to convince him to leave Margaret behind. I said, 'Damn it, she's pregnant!'

Father Flaherty gave me a disappointed look. 'Then we shall have to have hope and faith, shan't we, Michael?' He turned to Margaret and spoke gently. 'The Lord asks some difficult things and isn't always very clear. I ask you to forgive a poor fool of a priest if I've got it wrong. You have my blessing on the infant. Do you happen to be a Catholic?'

Margaret nodded. She said, 'I converted when I married.'

'Then you might care to pray to the Holy Mother. I don't say it'll work: prayer isn't physics; but I don't see it'll do any harm. You will come with us, child? And behave yourself?'

Margaret nodded again. Her face had assumed an impassive expression: quite unreadable for me, who had in any case never been able to read her. I had a sense that, as earlier when she had stroked my hair, this was yet one more step in a process of detachment. By small nuances of gesture she was casting me off: or by small misunderstandings and misinterpretations I was casting her off – there is no privileged perspective from which the truth can be known: but, like passengers in adjacent trains, it is impossible to say who is moving. The metaphor of dance came to me then – comes to me now – but, conscious of the vast platitude of life, I didn't pursue it to its trite conclusion.

'Very well then, ladies and gentlemen, boys and girls – shall we all be going?' Father Flaherty energised himself with words. He turned to my father and the two amiable old villains eyed each other with respect not untinged with affection. The priest said, 'We'll be leaving you here. Now, I know you'll behave yourself.' My father raised a hand and drew the sign of the cross over the other man. Momentarily stunned, Flaherty laughed then turned to Teddy. 'And you, too, my boy. Stand up for yourself and don't let your father push you about.' Next he opened the door and said aloud to Bronstein and the Emperor, 'One way or another we'd best be going or give up the whole idea.'

'I shall go,' said the Emperor with painful dignity. They were the only words I heard him speak.

*

The two cars were parked in the lane. The hoods were soaked by mist. I hated to think how it would be in the mountains: a storm or torrential rain were both possible. The Emperor, shivering and swathed in his military cape, was helped into the front car. Bronstein took the driver's seat and old Ferenc sat next to his lord. Pennyweight, who had become sprightly, placed himself behind the wheel of the second car and beckoned us once I had got it started. Margaret sat next to him. I was behind her and Father Flaherty at my side.

We drove slowly through Monte past the silent villas and the square with its holy fountain and the terminal of the funicular railway. The mist raised scents of earth, of eucalyptus, agapanthus and mimosa. At the Monte Palace Hotel a ball was in progress. The weather had driven the guests indoors, but the empty gardens were strung with lamps and a dance band was playing 'Tea for Two'.

In Funchal the night was clear and the stars bright. The moon lay beyond the Ilhas Desertas, picking them out in silhouette against a purple horizon. The world seemed full of yellow dogs, snoozing in every corner under the jacarandas and kapoks. A tethered bullock sprawled in the roadway forcing us to edge around it. And Johnny Cardozo was absent, as was the *Kildonan Castle*.

We drove west to the muted putt-putt of our motors and the rustle of bananas by the roadside. We climbed the hills and descended the steep *ribeiras*. On the still sea beyond Câmara da Lobos fishing smacks were trawling by night. A cat glared from the window sill of a wayside cottage, yowled and scuttled away. At Ribeira Brava we halted.

The front car was overheating. So Father Flaherty informed us when he returned from investigating. Pennyweight went to lend a hand. We were by the small fort that guards the shore and the noise of the sea was very close.

'This is a lovely night to be held hostage,' Margaret said. She nestled against me. There was a faint chill. 'I shall tell our child about it.'

'And how will you explain my presence?'

'Children don't require complex explanations.'

'And adults don't understand them? I don't think you should tell the child about me. The omission would fit the traditions of my family.' To distract her I said, 'Do you realise that, once the Emperor has gone, Johnny will be free to return to England?'

Margaret said, 'Not if he escapes. Johnny will be in disgrace.'

'And if he dies?'

'That would depend on the circumstances. It would be easier to blame others.'

Bronstein was getting back into his vehicle. Pennyweight returned.

I said, 'I don't think the cars will make it up the gradient to Encumeada. And what are we going to do when we get to the Paúl da Serra? There's no road.' I glanced along the sheer-sided ravine behind the village. The top was lost in a layer of cloud. 'If we try to drive beyond Serra da Agua, there's every chance we'll come off at the bends. At Encumeada I doubt the visibility is above twenty feet. How on earth do you propose to take off?'

'We're going to lay up until dawn and take off once the sun's up. It should burn off the cloud.' Pennyweight spoke confidently; but he often did when at his most ridiculous. It was reality that humbled him.

I told him, 'You don't know Madeira. We're not talking about a ground mist. The mountains trap clouds.'

'I've seen days when they're clear as a bell,' Pennyweight retorted.

'And if it isn't like that tomorrow?'

The fat man looked hurt. He believed in Providence and, at the same time, feared that the unholy ju-ju of my unbelief might ruin the portents. He said, 'One of your problems, Pinfold – and the same goes for your father – is that you're too miserable by half. I don't know how you expect to achieve anything with an attitude like that.' He reinforced his point with a slight pugnacity in his posture, but it was the pugnacity of the defeated.

I said, 'You've never flown an aeroplane in your life, have you? You were never a captain in the Flying Corps. You were transferred from the Engineers to be Robinson's mechanic. That's why he invited you here.'

*

Once we were underway, Father Flaherty resumed his joviality. He said, 'Where now is your Colonel Cardozo?'

I said, 'That fact should worry you.'

Pennyweight was concentrating sullenly on his driving. I was prepared to believe he had made a study of flying, and in his mind that was probably the same as being a pilot.

Flaherty proposed, 'Would you like a nip?' He took a flask from his cassock. 'I took care to provide myself with a little something.'

I asked, 'Did you catch what I said to Pennyweight?'

'That he was never a pilot?' He unscrewed the flask, took a sip and sighed. 'I suspected as much. After all, Robinson was the pilot: why would he need a second man except as a mechanic?'

'Yet you're prepared to let him fly?'

'The Emperor knows and he's willing to take the risk.'

'And what about navigation?'

'All our friend has to do is head east by the sun. Africa is a big place. He's hardly likely to miss it. I tell you, Michael, the Emperor *knows*. That man has got the faith that moves mountains.'

'Perhaps he should be the priest.'

'I don't think so. A priest should always be riven by doubt. Humility in spiritual matters is a virtue. Now, will you have that nip?'

Then I asked the question that had puzzled me. 'Why did you all come to my house?'

Father Flaherty nodded. 'The Quinta Gordon was too closely watched. We could get Karl out of the place, but we could hardly all meet up there. Then again there was the chance of picking up a handy hostage in case of need – Colonel Cardozo having some regard for you, I'm told. And – who knows? – we might have made a convert to the cause: someone with a head on his shoulders and a good eye for a rifle? No, not likely, I'll admit.'

At Serra da Agua we halted by the broad dry bed of the river. I saw the cottage where the girl struck by smallpox lived. She was cured by belief in a false angel, but who was to say it wasn't a true miracle? If Father Flaherty was right, such irony was characteristic of his sly Divinity who taught by wit as much as wonders. On Bronstein's order we got out of the motor cars and clambered down the bank, disturbing the slumbering goats. A train of ponies was tethered among the willows, tended by two grinning rogues.

'Michael, I think you know my friends.' Father Flaherty shook hands with the two men and dispensed blessings. I smelled the stink of rum. They fell to their knees, drunk enough to be pious.

'Did they find the 'plane for you?'

'They're simple men for all their villainy. They believed in the angel and knew nothing of the aeroplane, but they gave me sufficient directions to enable me to find it myself. As you may have gathered, Bronstein tried earlier with them but he lacked the tact of a cunning old Jesuit. I told him he was wasting his time and he should leave the business to me. By the way, your assistance on my first visit was much appreciated.'

I ignored the priest's self-congratulation. I asked the men, 'Do you know of Colonel Cardozo? Has he been here?'

They pretended not to understand, but I saw fear in their eyes.

'We're walking into a trap,' I told Flaherty.

'So you said before. Sometimes we have to go forth blindly, trusting in the Lord – though that isn't a course I would recommend as a general principle, the Lord being what He is.' He looked at me with the gentleness that is supposed to be the face of wisdom. 'Peace now, Michael. You're right, of course. We're a pack of blithering idiots and like as not most of us will be killed. Bronstein knows it and Karl as well. Pennyweight should be safe because the Lord looks after His fools. But I admit that I worry for you and Mrs Cardozo. If you don't mind one of the platitudes that seem to annoy the lady so much, Death is really not such a bad thing, as I suspect you know well enough.'

'Dying can be a hard enough business,' I said.

'Now there you have me. It's hard indeed. I'm afraid that philosophy is always a little uncomfortable around the edges. Now, shall we go on to whatever it is that waits for us?'

Bronstein was strapping a bundle of rifles onto the lead pony. I counted four Enfields, old friends from the war. We were short one mount. Margaret hadn't been expected. With his old-fashioned courtliness Bronstein asked her with whom she would like to travel. She chose Mr Pinfold: her knight errant, her champion, her lover. I asked Pennyweight if he knew how to ride.

'I once had a go at a donkey on the sands. How difficult can it be, old man?' He was holding one of the lanterns and his face had a mysterious splendour.

'You're mad,' I said.

'Shouldn't be surprised if I were,' he answered.

'You're going to die.'

'That'd be a pity. But what's the alternative? Home in Blighty, selling pins from a tray, and the occasional night in the police cells?' Quite rationally he added, 'From where I'm standing, this is the sensible thing to do.'

'What will you do with the five hundred pounds?'

'Open a little garage. There's a future in motor cars.' He felt he could be patronising and jogged my elbow. 'Not like wine, eh, Pinfold? Ha ha!' His portly body shuddered with laughter and he turned his back on me as though I were the fool. With a struggle he mounted one of the ponies.

We got on the road again and made our way out of the village at walking pace into the thickening mist. I estimated the distance to Encumeada as less than five miles, but the way was steep and winding. We took breaks at half hour intervals for the sake of the animals. I had no exact sense of the time: two or three in the morning perhaps, and dawn several hours away.

At Encumeada we reached the watershed with ocean now to the north of us and the ground tumbling steeply in slopes of heather, laurel and *masaroco*. On the far shoreline was a single light, visible through a break in the cloud cover. Someone in the village of São Vicente was awake. A restless sleeper. A pair of furtive lovers. Margaret and I had been briefly happy there and danced the tango around a palm tree; and, for a space, I had thought that this was not a transient evening but that we had found ourselves authentically. Or perhaps I hadn't felt like that. It was difficult to be sure. Some moments become, in retrospect, private cenotaphs erected *in memoriam* to the casualties of Time: in themselves no more significant than the identity of the Unknown Soldier. Quite possibly this was one. Quite likely I have misdescribed it – misunderstood it entirely. I can't say what it meant to Margaret, for the meaning has become clear to me, and presumably to her too, only over the long years of our separation. As we turned west to follow the steep rise to Lombo do Mouro, the grip of her arms around me slackened, and she dozed to the rhythm of the pony.

At Lombo do Mouro we took a long halt while the exhausted animals recovered. I helped Margaret down and she gave me a dazed smile that was quite lovely, though it was meant for no one. Between intermittent gusts of wind came the trickle of water.

Father Flaherty offered whisky from his flask. 'Perhaps I was too pessimistic,' he said. 'I see no sign of Colonel Cardozo.'

'What is there to see?' I asked. We were in the cloud tops. A few stars were visible and mountains to the east, but below us the depths of the *ribeira* were hidden.

'It may be clear enough for Mr Pennyweight to take off. How are you, Mrs Cardozo? Bearing up?'

Margaret smiled. 'I shall have something to tell my child.'

'Ah yes, the child.'

He moved off to check on Pennyweight. The fat man had fallen from his pony like a sack and was squatting miserably on a rock. Bronstein and Ferenc were waiting on the Emperor.

'Karl doesn't look at all well,' Margaret remarked. She offered me a cigarette but the wind prevented my lighting it. 'I understand he wasn't brought up to be Emperor. One wonders why he bothers. Duty, I suppose? There must be something one can say about duty, but I can't think what it is. Isn't Father Flaherty the most sententious man you've ever met? He reminds me of those Victorian commonplace books with a Beautiful Thought printed on every page: lines from Tennyson and so forth. Or Oscar Wilde, who was very witty, but never said anything of significance when one studies the words carefully. I'm told the Empress Zita is beautiful and that she and Karl are in love.'

I took the fingers nervously spinning a cigarette and drew her to me. And I kissed her with puzzlement and passion, wondering as always what our kisses meant. She responded warmly, with the belly that held our child pressed against mine and her arms laid over my shoulders with the fingers loosely clasped across my spine. As lovers have always wished, I wanted the kiss to go on for ever; and, because it could not, I wanted to bring it to an end so that it would sooner become a memory. We pulled away and stared at each other, understanding nothing: though I may be partly wrong because I have always believed that Margaret understood more than I. Then I heard Bronstein call.

He was standing at the precipice where Lombo do Mouro looks down into the *ribeira*, scanning with binoculars through a break in the clouds. One by one we joined him and peered into the dizzying depths to where a chain of lights was visible on the road a little way below Encumeada. Johnny Cardozo's men were on our tail and, like as not, were up ahead of us too.

I found Pennyweight by my side. He said, 'Well this is a bit of a bugger and no mistake.' And then he laughed. 'Come on, old man! It's as good a time to die as any other.'

I turned on him angrily. 'Don't be a bloody fool!' But I couldn't sustain my anger. Pennyweight had become transfigured. He was serene. He had found that heaven where fatheads become wise men; and everything was clear to him.

I understood then what had happened to Robinson.

CHAPTER TWENTY-FOUR

Assuming Johnny's men to be on horseback, I calculated they were about an hour behind us. Dawn was perhaps also an hour away. If we wished to escape, we could push on across the moor and descend on the further side towards Porto Moniz or Ribeira da Janela; even Johnny couldn't have blocked all the routes. But, of course, escape was not an issue. Bronstein would carry out his mission like a good soldier and we would live or die as fortune favoured us.

He asked me, 'Mr Pinfold, you were an infantryman. What would you do?'

Left to himself, I thought, Mr Pinfold would run for it or surrender.

'There's a good field of fire from here over the path from Encumeada. But once we're on the moor, the ground is flat and we'll be outflanked.'

'So you recommend we stand and fight here? But the visibility is poor.'

There was nothing to be done about the visibility.

'The cloud may lift. In any case, one man can make a fighting retreat. With luck he'll gain us half an hour or an hour.' Since we were committed to the enterprise, I had in mind that, if we could delay Johnny's men, we might bring the thing off and still make an escape westward. I doubted that a few island gendarmes would have the skill or the stomach to make short work of even a single man holding a position in the mist and rocks of Lombo do Mouro. Provided, naturally, that it wasn't me who was left behind.

Bronstein nodded. He treated my answer with respect. Perhaps he believed in my loyalty. I can't say because my image of him remains imperfect: limited by my prejudices towards his role, so that he scarcely figures as an individual. He went off in search of Ferenc, who was watching the ponies, and came back with the old fellow dragging one of the Enfields. He set him to build a cairn of stones as cover at the vantage point commanding the path; then he ordered the rest of us to mount again. My last glimpse of Ferenc was of his Alpine hat resting on the rocks, and of a salute directed at his Emperor.

A thinning of the mist marked our arrival on the Paúl da Serra. 'I told you so,' said Pennyweight, and he began to take deep breaths in the same fraudulent way that he used to exercise. 'We'll get away and no problems, just you see.' Behind us the sky was brightening with false dawn. He jogged off, swaying and jolting to the front of the line, where Bronstein was scouting for the aeroplane.

It was difficult to imagine that he had murdered Robinson.

The path now was almost non-existent. The ground had levelled off except for occasional sandstone banks marked by low caves such as the one where the shepherds kept their still. We followed gaps in the swathes of bracken and heather and navigated by the rare pine trees that marked the plateau like sentinels. We had been underway some time when, to our rear, a shot sounded flat under a hollow sky. I counted the seconds and heard the rattle of returning fire; then a further shot, another reply, and silence. Ferenc's defence of Lombo do Mouro had lasted five minutes.

Margaret was mounted on the old man's animal. She rode alongside me and I missed the intimacy of her embrace. I felt another pang of our distancing and for a moment harboured the cruel thought that she felt nothing. She asked, 'How long do you think it will be before Johnny gets here?'

'An hour if his men are on ponies. Maybe half an hour if they have horses.' It was an accurate piece of information, brief and to the point; and only afterwards did it come to me that there was, as so often, another question which remained as always unanswered.

We caught up with Father Flaherty. He had halted, waiting for us. He said, 'Apparently it's my turn to hold the bridge against the Etruscan, Michael.' One of the Enfields was slung over his shoulder. His expression was tired and his wit faded. 'If I don't see you again, my blessing goes with you. And Mrs Cardozo, don't you go forgetting your duties as a good Catholic. Say a few rosaries for this wicked old rascal, who'll likely be in need of them. By the way, Michael, if you ever find your way to Flaherty's Bar in Dublin, will you tell my boy, Patrick, that I was thinking of him?' The old Fenian winked then trotted back down the path towards an outcrop of rock.

The mist thickened again. The bracken gave way to short turf scattered thinly with rocks. It occurred to me that Margaret and I could easily turn away and vanish into the cloud, but the thought passed in a feeling that I was somehow bound to this task and had better see it through. Margaret gave me a ghostly smile. The air was damp and she was shivering. I waited for more shots from the rear.

*

The mountains to the east masked the rising of the sun, but the day came on with a pearly light. I doubted the mist had lifted enough for take-off to be possible and I still wondered if Pennyweight would last the course. I thought of his courage as of the dogged sort. In a crisis I imagined him cowering in a foxhole. He was at the front with Bronstein. The Emperor, who seemed in a bad way, was slouched over the neck of his pony with his companion leading it by the reins.

Pennyweight fell back a little. I asked him, 'Is it far?'

He shook his head. His mood was grim and he was nibbling the ends of his moustache. Of a sudden he took out his false teeth and wiped them on a grubby handkerchief. He offered them to me like the relic of an obscure saint. He said, 'I don't like to get into a fight with my choppers in. Knew a fellow once, who choked on 'em. Could you look after these? We'll probably run into each other again, and, in any case, I'll have enough tin to buy a new pair – American ones: I hear they're good.'

I said, 'You can put them in your pocket.'

He stared at them. 'What? Oh – yes – you're right, of course. Don't know what I was thinking of.'

'Nerves,' I suggested.

'Yes – that's probably it.' He searched for something else to talk about. 'D'you think I'll get a medal out of this?'

'I should think so. Maybe even a title: Count Pennyweight – the Duke of Pennyweight. Emperors can do that.'

'Are you taking the mickey?'

'No.'

'No,' he repeated. 'Of course not. You're a chum.'

'Like Robinson,' I said, and he glanced at me sharply. He must have read my expression, for his own became more sombre.

'Ah,' he said. 'You know, don't you?'

'That you killed Robinson? Yes.'

'How did you find out?'

'Someone went to his room the night before he died, and there was an argument. I suppose Johnny Cardozo might have discovered Robinson's whereabouts – assuming he had any suspicions – but he would simply have arrested him. That leaves only Bronstein, the priest – and you. The others needed Robinson alive to fly the aeroplane. You see?'

'Gosh,' said Pennyweight quietly. 'That's awfully clever of you, Pinfold.' He looked at me at some length, then added, 'I'm glad it's out in the open. I shouldn't like your knowing and saying nothing, just thinking badly of me.'

'I wouldn't do that,' I said. I was sincere, though God knew why except that I had glimpsed, perhaps, the heart of the fat man's tremendousness: the spiritual secret he bore for those of us who were not wholly dead to feeling. It was simply this: that he existed as an object of compassion: that he had been placed on the earth by Flaherty's strange deity for no other purpose than to exhibit ignorance, absurdity and the hopeless search for the eternal verities. Whether this insight was true or false is by the way; for, like many others of the same character, the truths by which saints and charlatans make their names, it was untestable. What mattered – and it is of small enough consequence – was that at that moment I believed it; and I felt a lightness within me as if I'd heard a joke of infinite subtlety that could be studied in all its nuances during a lifetime. And it would always yield a smile.

Behind us the gunshots came again and in the same brief pattern.

'I suppose they got the padre,' Pennyweight said. 'I shall miss him. A rum cove, don't you think? All the same, I don't know that I approve of priests blazing away with rifles.' Ahead of us we heard the clip of Bronstein forcing on the pace. I looked for Margaret. She was slipping behind and looked dazed and tired.

The next moment she was gone.

*

We turned northward. The fall of hooves was muted by the turf. The light was increasing, but without any lifting of the cloud. Around us the world was white and I was soaked to the skin.

'D'you want to know how I came to kill Robinson?' Pennyweight asked.

'If you care to tell me,' I said. We waited for five minutes at the point of the turn, but Margaret didn't appear. The fat man seemed not to notice and I said nothing.

'I'd like to tell you. I don't mean to make excuses, but I'd like to tell someone – someone who'd understand.'

'All right, if you like,' I answered. I was debating whether to call her name. Would she hear? Would she come?

'Stop me if you don't want to hear any more,' Pennyweight said like the stranger on a train whose confessions will not be stopped until he has reached his station. He went on without pausing, 'It all began when I got drunk at Reid's with Ronnie Fairbrother. I shouldn't have, but I was put off my stride when Robinson didn't turn up to meet the boat. Then I mislaid that damned piece of paper with his address. And, by the time I found it again, I'd had another few and was in a bit of state.'

Stranded in Madeira with nothing to guide him but the Higher Wisdom, Pennyweight had sought help and found none.

'Anyway, in the end I did find it – the paper – and by showing it to a few people I got to Robinson's room, and he was there, and I thought to myself, "Thank God, my ship's come home", so to speak.'

'Except that he didn't want you,' I said.

'Are you a mind-reader, Pinfold?' Pennyweight asked, amazed. I shook my head: it would be too difficult to explain. Pennyweight pressed on with his tale of two men in a room, both of them shabby and one of them drunk like characters in a comedy that will soon turn to slapstick; for this was in many ways a funny story made funnier by the fat man's indignation and incomprehension. He said with tears, 'He took one look at me and said he didn't want to know me. He called me a buffoon. He said I'd been his third choice after two other fellows had turned him down. He said we'd never been chums. Never been chums!'

I think Pennyweight could have borne any insult except the last. With it he heard the shattering of his world; felt the snapping of the frail tie that gave him meaning among his fellow men; for, if he were not someone's 'chum', then who was he? What had he fought for?

'I went off in a huff.' He glanced at me to check that I'd taken in this display of moderation on his part. And, when I think of his agony, I have to admire him as I do so often. Anxious to bring his confession to an end, he pressed on. 'I had another few drinks and then found a park to sleep in. Then the following day, when I was still under the weather, I ran into Robinson in the street.'

'You quarrelled again?'

'No, not a word. Robinson cut me dead, and I wasn't one to force myself on him. But…'

'Yes?'

Pennyweight hesitated. He was confronted with the mystery within himself: a subject more difficult than that of Cathars and Templar treasure, but to which he had given less attention. He said, 'I don't know how to describe it. A sort of red mist came over me, the same as it did when I killed the German I told you about. I had my bayonet on me – I used to carry it everywhere, though I stopped after…. Anyway, I had it on me, and there was this red mist and Robinson was there, and…. There's nothing to say really except that I stabbed him and no one seemed to pay any attention. I don't suppose they care what foreigners do to themselves: what d'you think?'

'I'm sorry,' I said. I thought it unlikely no one had seen Pennyweight. In fact I remembered that I'd seen him there in the street on the occasion of Robinson's death and would have called out if Johnny hadn't distracted me. And Johnny knew – had always known – and had stored the knowledge to see what he could make of it.

'Sorry?' Pennyweight thought for a moment, and I thought he might become angry. I presumed he was so with himself and might be with me. But even now I can only touch the surface of the ginger man's character. His anger with Robinson had been exceptional: after all, one doesn't make 'chums' that way. He considered my response seriously, then answered, 'Sorry – yes – I don't suppose there's much more one can say.' He shook his head slowly and far too long so that I wondered if he was going to do something unpredictable: perform some terrible act of expiation. Then he recalled himself and said sadly. 'We *were* chums, you know: me and the Captain. He would never have denied it, if he'd been in his right mind – you do see that, don't you? But he wasn't; I can understand that now. He was still barmy: the same as he'd been when he got religion and saw angels. I should have remembered. I wouldn't have killed him if I'd twigged he was still quite barmy.'

*

Two sets of muffled hooves came stamping across the turf. I had time only to seize Pennyweight's rifle and work the bolt before a voice called out, 'Don't shoot, you damn fool, it's me!'

Father Flaherty, draped in his cassock like the ghost rider from a piece of poetry, came out of the mist and rain, bringing Margaret in his train.

'I wasn't expecting you,' I said.

'You don't sound glad to see me,' he answered.

'I thought you were dead.'

'Well, as you can see, I'm not. I decided I don't have the stuff of martyrs, and to pretend so would be terrible boastful in an old sinner. I fired a few shots to puzzle their poor brains, and then cleared off. I found Mrs Cardozo on my way here.'

I noticed then that he was holding the reins of Margaret's pony. She was looking not at me but rotating her face towards the sky, with the rain pouring down it and an expression of bemused indifference. I took off my coat and offered it to her; and then she seemed to see me, for she said in a flat voice, 'You left me.'

'I thought you'd gone to join Johnny.'

'Did I?' she answered as if she couldn't remember. 'I'm cold.'

'Take my coat.'

She took it and slowly put it on. Father Flaherty handed back the reins.

'We'd best be off,' he said. 'Colonel Cardozo is only ten minutes or so behind us.' He dug his heels into his pony's flanks and cantered out of sight. Pennyweight hesitated, then followed him. The mist closed in behind the pair, and Margaret and I were alone.

'You look done in,' I said. She didn't reply. I said, 'It seems our friends are finished with us. We have a choice. We can go with them or wait for Johnny.'

'What do you want to do?' she asked.

'Do you think Johnny will kill me?'

She shook her head. No, Johnny Cardozo wouldn't kill me. He had every reason to, but he wouldn't and I didn't know why unless it was for the same reason that I didn't hate him, though I was in love with his wife. We were bound in the complicity of trying to know Margaret.

Margaret said, 'He likes you.' I couldn't tell if she was crying. The rain was now falling harder and, caught in the white morning light, the whole sky seemed full of tears. She looked about her and smiled. 'Another of God's vulgar effects.' She even laughed and murmured, 'Listen to me – I'm talking like that bloody priest. Yes,' she said as tenderly as I have ever heard her speak, 'Johnny likes you. You've given him a child. He can't have children, and I wanted one so much. And I was unhappy, Michael. Do you understand, or is unhappiness so normal for you that the alternative is incomprehensible?' She paused, and there was tenderness in the pause too. The pony whiffled and she stooped to stroke its neck. I remember the gesture because it told me that nothing had been done cruelly but only apparently so. She said, 'So we stole a child from a thief.'

*

'I see that Mrs Cardozo isn't joining us,' said Father Flaherty. 'I thought she mightn't.'

The rain was blowing over, and the mist, no longer continuous, bowled across the high moor. The aeroplane, glistening with moisture, stood bright and silver in sunlight. The Emperor was already sitting in the rear of the two seats in the open cockpit, staring fixedly ahead of him. Pennyweight had put on a flying helmet and goggles, but was still wearing his hairy suit so that he looked like a member of those clown ensembles who specialize in motor cars that explode or fall apart at a touch. He was giving directions to Bronstein to remove the stones that blocked the wheels and spin the propeller while he fired the engine.

The priest studied him with the amused detachment he brought to everything. He observed, 'Don't you wish the fellow could at least dress like a hero? By the way, when this is over, I suggest we leave in the direction of Porto Moniz.'

'And then?'

'We lie our heads off, and, God willing, we'll be believed or no one will care either way. I may go on to Natal. The bishop there needs a chaplain, so they tell me.'

I heard a whinny close by but masked by one of the banks of mist.

Flaherty asked, 'Do you still have a rifle to hand? I think we'll be needing it. Try not to kill any of the poor devils.' He took his own from his shoulder and assumed a firing position among a patch of bracken. I joined him and we loosed off a couple of shots against an invisible target to put our opponents on their mettle.

The aeroplane began to roll forward.

*

Could Pennyweight fly? Thinking back, I suspect that he could after a fashion. He had an enormous capacity for study, and I imagine him pouring over books and training manuals in emulation of Robinson. It is difficult to say, for there can be several versions of what happened, depending upon the weight one attaches to the gunfire laid down by Johnny Cardozo's men, the rolling mists, the erratic winds, the stray rocks – and the fat man, of course. I like to think that he could have pulled it off, but this conclusion comes not from evidence but from my admiration for Pennyweight the Great, who overcame everything to take a shot at glory.

The 'plane bumped slowly over the grass, passing through shreds of mist like the flicker of a film. Once or twice the wheels seemed to leave the ground only to touch again. Then, at last, it rose twenty feet or so only to dip and finally to smash. It was all very slow – undramatic even, except that Flaherty and I were willing Pennyweight to succeed and, in that moment preceding the end, let out a cheer.

As to the fire, it may have started before the crash – the result of a shot fired by Johnny's men – or afterwards: a consequence of the impact. Accounts vary and no one can be trusted. Certainly not Johnny, who needed the Emperor to die, or, at least, was prepared to take the risk that he might, provided that he was clear of blame. Why else had he allowed the hopeless escape attempt to proceed so far?

The Emperor was thrown clear. Pennyweight wasn't. He was trapped in his seat as the fire caught hold and, if he was conscious, he must have died horribly.

I can't say definitely what happened to Count Bronstein. There were rumours that he was captured and that afterwards he died. I have often thought of the house in the Rua Santa Maria with its garden and its ancient jacaranda, blossoming purple in the spring. Through the windows one sees glum torturers at their labours. They believe in their cause, consider themselves good men, and love their wives.

Father Flaherty and I slipped away. We weren't followed.

TANGO IN MADEIRA

SCENE THREE

The garden as before. Ten minutes later. CHARLIE, ZOË, and ROBINSON are sitting at the table drinking tea. HERMANN is stalking up and down, brandishing the gun and occasionally pointing it at the others. CHARLIE and ZOË are relaxed; ROBINSON is nervous; HERMANN has an air of angry excitement.

ROBINSON: *[putting down his cup]* I needed that. Awfully decent of you.

CHARLIE: Don't mention it.

ROBINSON: I suppose you're going to kill me now?

CHARLIE: Would that be murder, assassination or execution? As you pointed out, there are different words to cover the subject.

ROBINSON: *[distressed]* I don't know. I suppose it depends on your point of view.

CHARLIE: Previously you seemed to be of the opinion that only one point of view counted – namely yours. Admittedly you did grant me a form of trial, but that was part of the comedy of English manners rather than an exercise in justice.

ROBINSON: Oh, God, I feel such a failure!

CHARLIE: *[sympathetically]* Bear up, there's a good fellow. I failed as King, but I didn't let it get me down. For that matter, I wasn't very good as a tyrant and warmonger. I suspect one needs a talent for these things.

ZOË: *[kindly]* May I ask a question? Did you fight in the War, Reginald?

ROBINSON: *[shuddering at the recollection]* Yes.

ZOË: Is that why you want to kill Charlie?

ROBINSON: Yes.

ZOË: I don't understand. Charlie didn't *cause* the War. He didn't *want* the War.

ROBINSON: *[In frustrated anger]* No one wanted the War! No one admits to causing it! I don't know whether this is true, but – don't you see? – *it doesn't matter.*

CHARLIE: No, I don't see.

ROBINSON: Forget who caused the War. The *risks* were borne by men like me: millions of us who were bayoneted, gassed, shot and blown to pieces. We didn't cause the War. We weren't even consulted. We went because our rulers told us that it was our duty and we believed them. But those rulers shared none of the risks! Now do you see? I wanted to kill you not because you started the War, but because justice required that you take the same share of the danger. It didn't matter that you were innocent. We were all innocent! But the rest of us paid the penalty, while you did not.

Everyone is sombre for a moment.

HERMANN: I shared the risks of war. I was a general of division.

CHARLIE: *[sarcastically]* Very risky. As I recall, you were based at Schornstein Castle. Dreadful plumbing, but I don't remember any fatalities.

HERMANN: At least I accept moral responsibility for what happened. The Hungonian cause was just. We owed it to our ancestors to hold to all our territory. And you took the coronation oath.

CHARLIE: That blasted oath again!

HERMANN: *[angrily]* Do you have no principles! – Sire?

CHARLIE: *[to ROBINSON]* Let me tell you about principles. I held to the principles of nationalism and democracy – no, you mustn't smile, it's true! I wanted to divide the Kingdom into national provinces and give each one of them its own parliament. Do you have the slightest notion of how difficult that is when nomads and barbarians have been charging all over the place for a thousand years? Let us take the Sklovenians to start with…

ROBINSON: *[correcting him]* Sklavonians – you said 'Sklovenians'.

CHARLIE: They're not the same people. The Sklavonians pronounce the letter 'O' as an 'A', while the Sklovenians pronounce the letter 'A' as an 'O' – or possibly it's the other way round: whatever the case, several wars have been fought over the difference. Now, where was I? Oh, yes! If one ignores several districts occupied by Hungonians, Boguslavians and Italians, Sklovenia is, as one would expect, inhabited by Sklovenians. *Except* that the capital, Pimp…

ROBINSON: Pimp?

CHARLIE: It means 'beautiful town'. May I go on? As I was saying, Pimp, the capital of Sklovenia, just happens to be a German city – save for those parts occupied by Hungonians, Boguslavians and Sklovenians. On the other hand, Sklavonia is quite different. Forgetting the bits where the Germans, the Italians and the Hungonians live, the place is Sklavonian through and through. *Except* that the capital, Tart…

ROBINSON: Tart?

CHARLIE: It means 'heavenly place'. Tart just happens to be a Czech city – always has been since Saint Wenceslas the Scourge of the Heathen drove out the original natives. *[He studies ROBINSON narrowly]* And so far we haven't discussed Boguslavia...

ROBINSON: *[hastily]* Before we do, what is the capital called?

CHARLIE: Bum – it means 'fragrant garden'.

ROBINSON: We can forget about Bum. I think I get the general picture.

CHARLIE: The only people in my wonderful kingdom who don't have a dispute with their neighbours over territory are the Jews and the Gypsies – and everyone hates them. Now, perhaps, you will understand why, in the event, my principles of nationalism and democracy counted for absolutely nothing.

HERMANN: *[to CHARLIE]* I could have told you as much. You should have forgotten all that nonsense and stuck to traditional rights and used force as necessary. The Crown of Hungonia...

CHARLIE: *[interrupting]* Hermann should have been born a Chinese. He believes in ancestor worship.

HERMANN: I believe in Christianity and Order! *[more calmly]* But that is all by the way. Lets get to the business in hand. We have to kill Robinson.

ZOË: You ought to call him Reginald.

HERMANN: We must kill *Reginald* because he is a danger to all of us.

CHARLIE, ZOË and HERMANN look at ROBINSON.

ROBINSON: *[frightened but brave]* Am I entitled to a last request?

CHARLIE: Oh, yes, of course. We have some cigarettes. Would you like a drink? There's a new cocktail, the 'Madeira Madman'; you might care to try one.

ROBINSON: I should prefer to dance – if that's all right with you – and with Zoë, of course. I can't do the tango very well, but … what is life for, if not for learning by experience?

CHARLIE: You want to dance with my wife?

HERMANN: That is against all protocol!

ZOË: *[fetchingly pleased]* Well, I'm rather flattered, and I don't mind in the least. I should be delighted to dance with you, Reginald.

CHARLIE: *[to ROBINSON]* From someone who not long ago was unwilling to pass comments on other men's wives, you've progressed pretty quickly.

ROBINSON: *[apologetically]* When one is about to die, one is forced into an urgent rethinking of one's opinions. *[earnestly]* The fact is that I've never been intensely in love – not even with my fiancée. Now – well, I suppose that this is as close I shall ever get.

CHARLIE: You're in love with my wife?

HERMANN: This is outrageous! You should be…

CHARLIE: He should be what? Do be quiet, Hermann. You can't threaten Reginald. We're about to shoot him. Things can scarcely get any worse.

ROBINSON: You're being very good about this … about my being in love with your wife. Not that I am actually in love in the strict sense…

ZOË: *[tenderly]* Don't spoil the effect, Reginald. I quite like the idea of your being in love with me – even if only a little bit.

CHARLIE: And don't worry about me. I'm perfectly content if another man is in love with my wife. After all, I wouldn't have married her if I hadn't thought that any man with a head on his shoulders ought to fall for her.

ZOË: Oh, Charlie! You do say the sweetest things!

HERMANN: *[still indignant]* You still ought to be jealous, Sire.

CHARLIE: Why?

HERMANN: It's a matter of principle. It's the done thing.

CHARLIE: Well, I disagree. I am perfectly happy if Reginald dances with Her Majesty, and my principle is to be happy.

HERMANN: No, Sire! Moral principles have nothing at all to do with human happiness. In fact I'd go so far as to say that the opposite is the case. I don't maintain that it's a rigid law, but show me a man in comfortable circumstances who is still miserable and I'll wager on his being a man of principle.

CHARLIE: *[to ROBINSON]* I don't know that I'd care to quarrel with Hermann. He may be quite right. Your principles seem to have made you frustrated, angry and thoroughly miserable. Not to mention the fact that you want to kill other people, which is about as principled as one can get. *[He sighs and puts a record to play.]* I think you should dance.

The record plays. It is the same tango as before. ROBINSON approaches ZOË shyly and formally. She accepts him with the same unfeigned delight with which she had earlier received her husband. ROBINSON begins a little clumsily. ZOË is indulgent and encourages him. Throughout what follows, CHARLIE is thoughtful and HERMANN mutely furious. By degrees ROBINSON finds the mood of the music and dances with passion, but he is more cautious of engaging his partner's eyes and this makes ZOË more assertive. In this version of the dance it is the man who is beaten: his control of his partner is challenged and her movements are mocking, wry, whimsical. At last ROBINSON responds to the thrill of his partner's independence. He seeks to reassert control, fails but is excited by his failure. At this point ZOË laughs, lightly and without malice. She falters to tease ROBINSON that he will succeed in holding her, pulls away, laughs again, and then allows him to grasp her so that the dance ends with a breathless reconciliation. As the music stops, each releases the other with a fond look as if they have been deliciously silly and are not a little in love.

HERMANN: *[disgusted]* That was the most squalid display I have ever seen.

CHARLIE: *[still thoughtful]* You were lovely, darling. And I compliment you, Reginald. You should give up pacifism and become a gigolo.

ROBINSON: *[shamefaced]* I'm sorry. I've behaved abominably.

CHARLIE: How so? *[ZOË sits herself on CHARLIE's lap. They kiss. CHARLIE strokes her face as though seeing something new in her. He turns again to ROBINSON.]* Why do you apologize for the most rational authentic emotion you have ever felt? You haven't apologized for wanting to kill me for the most specious and ill thought-out reasons.

ROBINSON: *[bridling]* I wanted to kill you in support of my principles.

CHARLIE: You have a very high opinion of your principles. Well, perhaps that's forgivable. But what is unforgivable is your arrogance in thinking your powers of knowledge and reason are enough to force your principles on to others: and still less forgivable, that you probably acquired them on the strength of what some idiot had to say on the subject. I have no intention of executing you on a point of principle. If I do kill you, it will be simply out of funk and cowardice – which I consider to be thoroughly reputable motives.

HERMANN: *[sharply]* That's because you have no principles.

CHARLIE: I deny that.

HERMANN: Name one.

CHARLIE: Spelling reform.

HERMANN: Ha!

CHARLIE: *[angrily]* Ha? You dare 'Ha!' me, General?

HERMANN: Ha! and double Ha! And … and *treble* Ha!

CHARLIE: *[rising to his feet furiously]* Treble Ha!?

ROBINSON: *[intervening before matters get out of hand]* I apologize for wanting to assassinate you.

CHARLIE: Not now, not now! THIS SCOUNDREL HAS INSULTED SPELLING REFORM!

CHARLIE lunges at HERMANN and tries to wrest the gun from him. They circle the table warily. ZOË starts the gramophone again and the two men make several circuits of the table to the accompaniment of the tango until, seeing their own ridiculousness, they stop; at which point ZOË halts the music.

ZOË: *[in a chiding tone]* Charlie, I understood you weren't going to kill anybody on account of spelling reform.

CHARLIE: *[shamefacedly]* But Zoë my love, this fellow is simply … *[He looks daggers at HERMANN]* … infuriating!

ZOË: Nevertheless, he's entitled to his own opinion on the subject.

CHARLIE calms down. ROBINSON is bemused. HERMANN composes himself and reassumes his stiff manner.

HERMANN: Sire, I wonder if I might be permitted to dance with Her Majesty?

CHARLIE: *[suspiciously]* Why?

HERMANN: *[sarcastically]* Since you appear to have introduced democracy into the matter, I thought I might be allowed to participate.

ZOË: I don't see the harm, dear.

Before CHARLIE can object, ZOË starts the music again. HERMANN tucks the gun into his belt and assumes a fierce dance posture. ZOË reluctantly allows him to hold her and the dance proceeds, watched by an angry CHARLIE and a still bemused ROBINSON. HERMANN's role throughout is aloof: an attitude of disdain with flickers of hatred. ZOË seeks to charm him, but her efforts at enticement are punctuated by moments of puzzlement when she withdraws and returns his scorn. This version of the dance is angry. There is passion enough and sensuality too, but little love. At the end ZOË tears herself away and flings herself on to CHARLIE's knee, where she buries her head, sobbing quietly into his shoulder. HERMANN looks triumphant. There is a moment of shocked silence before ROBINSON speaks.

ROBINSON: *[to CHARLIE, quietly and a little dismayed]* As I was saying, I'm sorry I wanted to kill you.

CHARLIE looks up from consoling ZOË.

CHARLIE: I'm grateful for that.

ROBINSON: Don't mention it. I've decided you're a good sort, after all.

CHARLIE: Thank you. You're a likeable fellow, too. On reflection, I don't think I want to kill you either.

ROBINSON: That's awfully decent of you.

HERMANN: *[to ROBINSON, confused and distressed]* How can you just make up your quarrel like that? He – *[indicating CHARLIE]* – has absolutely no principles, whether they concern his wife's honour or ... *spelling reform*!

CHARLIE: *[astonished]* Just a moment, Hermann: aren't you supposed to be on my side? You should be urging me to kill Reginald. He's opposed to everything you stand for. He's an internationalist vegetarian pacifist. He lives in Sevenoaks!

HERMANN: At least he believes in something! At least he feels there are things that are worth standing up for – even though I'd kill him rather than see him succeed. What do you have to offer except pragmatism, compromise and ... and ...

ZOË: And what?

HERMANN: *[with all the scorn of which he is capable]* Decency! *[to CHARLIE, sorrowfully to the point of tears]* Don't you understand, Sire? No progress has ever been made in human affairs by decent men. Everything worthwhile has been achieved by the obsessed, the deluded and the monstrous. Only their energy and commitment can overcome inertia. Only they have the vision that allows them to trample on the interest of others in the world as it is, or to compel the half-hearted to make the necessary sacrifice. Decent men are the enemies of the human race. Every step forward has been opposed by their kindness, by their regard for others, by the spirit of compromise: the hope that, somehow, humanity's salvation comes without a cost.

ZOË rises. She faces HERMANN with fearsome dignity.

ZOË: And what of your vision? You have one and Mr Robinson has another. Who is to say which of them is true? Perhaps neither of them is. Are the horrors and the sacrifices to be incurred in pursuit of a folly?

HERMANN: It doesn't matter. If the vision is false, History will in due course produce another prophet and another vision; and if this fails – if we human beings fail, Life will simply discard us and newer, higher forms of being will take our place. And so it will go on, century by century: an unending spiral of action and reaction rising towards perfection. Nothing succeeds like excess.

CHARLIE: Is that the only hope we have? If it is, then I don't want any part of it.

HERMANN: *[respectfully]* Alas, Sire, it is. *[He looks to ROBINSON, who finds himself nodding unwillingly]* You see? Even though we are at opposite poles, Mr Robinson agrees.

HERMANN takes the gun from his belt and points it at CHARLIE. ROBINSON makes a dash to stop him, but is easily brushed aside, falls to the ground and slowly raises himself.

HERMANN: *[to ROBINSON, his tone superior but not unsympathetic]* That's the decency inside you. You must learn to overcome it. You should have shot the King straight off, without leaving space for argument or doubt. In my opinion you would have been in the wrong, but your mistake would have been glorious.

HERMANN focuses on CHARLIE again, who stops any effort by ZOË to shield him.

CHARLIE: *[gently]* I'm not being brave, dear. But it seems there's no stopping these fellows. I wonder if I'll be considered a martyr to spelling reform? I should hate that. In any case, I'm an optimist. Hermann won't really...

HERMANN fires.

CHARLIE: *[covering his chest where the bullet has struck him. To ZOE:]* Don't let anyone say I've died for a good cause. All I wanted was to be happy with you and the children, and that's no one else's business at all. Play the music again. I do so love a tango...

He rises from the chair, then falls in silence. HERMANN stands gravely with his hands to his side. ROBINSON, on his feet, is paralysed. ZOË rushes to the body and nurses the head in her lap.

ZOË: *[slowly, as if the whole business is incomprehensible]* You've killed the King.

HERMANN: Truly, ma'am, I'm sorry. Believe me: as a human being I loved him: he was as fine and good-hearted a man as ever lived. But nothing much was to be expected of someone whose notion of happiness was to dance with his wife.

ROBINSON goes to the table, winds the gramophone slowly as the others watch him, and starts the music again.

CURTAIN

REUTERS

FUNCHAL – 2ND APRIL 1922 – EXILED AUSTRIAN EMPEROR DIED YESTERDAY OF PNEUMONIA – BURIAL AT MONTE, MADEIRA.

SACRED TO THE MEMORY

Of

FLIGHT LIEUTENANT MICHAEL JOHN CARDEW

1922 – 1943

Only Son of Colonel "Johnny" and Mrs Margaret Cardew

"Inherit the Kingdom prepared for you" – Matthew 25:34

TO MR GEORGE BERNARD SHAW

Madeira

17th May 1924

Dear Mr Shaw,

This is perhaps the most difficult letter I have had cause to write, but I feel it necessary in order to close a chapter in my life of which I have many reasons to feel ashamed. I ask, too, for forgiveness, confident that you will find it in your generous heart to grant it.

During the War I lost my fiancé. So, indeed, did many other young women who found themselves in their hundreds of thousands condemned to a loveless and childless existence. I ask you simply to accept how unsupportably painful such a condition must be, and yet it is one which they face bravely and without complaint.

I, however, in a fit of what now appears to me to be insanity, hit upon the scheme of asking the foremost playwright of the age to father my child: as if you would feel either a duty or an inclination to do so. I wrote to you a number of intemperate letters, for which I am deeply sorry, and then, at the height of my distress, presented myself at your door screaming the insults of a madwoman. For I was mad.

In course I recovered. I reconciled myself to shame at my conduct towards you and to acceptance of my unmarried, childless state with all its bitterness. I believed it would last for ever.

However, I have married. There are, indeed, happy endings. I was blessed to meet a man who had known my fiancé during the War: who had been with him at his death and was able to give me the sweet assurance that it was painless. I cannot tell you how much this has meant to me.

I have a child – as merry as a monkey! We have called him Reginald, after my fiancé and Michael, after my husband and I thank God every day.

My husband makes me laugh and we often go dancing; and these are blessings after so much misery. He also tells me that you and he have a slight acquaintance, and he sends you his best wishes. He says that you once passed a holiday here in Madeira and that you both shared a partner in the tango.

Yours sincerely

Elizabeth Pinfold

AFTERWORD

Karl von Habsburg was the last emperor of Austria-Hungary. He was intelligent and idealistic but came to the throne by accident in 1916 after the assassination of the previous heir. He tried to end the First World War and convert his empire into a commonwealth of democratic national states and failed on both counts. At the Peace he was banished from his homeland. He made two attempts to recover the Hungarian throne but was betrayed on both occasions by those who owed him everything. Exiled to Madeira, he was abandoned and neglected. Still in his early thirties, he died unexpectedly on 1 April 1922. His tragedy is almost forgotten.

Agatha Christie called briefly at Madeira on board the *Kildonan Castle* in 1923 as a member of a mission to promote the British Empire Exhibition.

George Bernard Shaw passed a holiday on the island in the winter of 1924-25, staying at Reid's Palace Hotel. The experience gave him background for his play *You Never Can Tell*. During his stay, he learned to tango.

In my depiction of Madeira I have taken many liberties, but its beauty remains genuine. The attitude of the English characters towards Portuguese people reflects their time and class. The people of Madeira are charming and helpful.

Notes for Readers

Having read Tango In Madeira, you may want to think about and discuss the following points. I didn't write the book programmatically, and most of the questions came to me from a re-reading. I suspect writers often wonder what it is they've written.

1. The novel is factually inaccurate in placing George Bernard Shaw, the Emperor Karl and Agatha Christie in Madeira at the same date. Is this anachronism of any significance? In what sense is this an historical novel?

2. Is the Narrator, Michael Pinfold a good or bad man? What do you make of his moral position? Is Margaret's conduct towards him, in taking his child, justified?

3. Does the insertion of the correspondence and the play work or get in the way of the story?

4. What is the point of the play? Does it complement the themes of the main narrative?

5. Is this a serious or a comic novel – or both? Does it matter?

6. The book is in part a homage to Graham Greene, in particular to The Comedians. Is this evident and does it contribute anything?

7. The Narrator, Pennyweight and Father Flaherty have different religious perspectives. How would you characterise them and do you identify with any of them?

8. Empires, angels, Robinsons and tango – I've used these motifs as extended metaphors. What do they stand for? Do they enrich the book or simply get in the way of the story?

Connect with Jim Williams and Marble City Publishing

http://www.jimwilliamsbooks.com/

http://www.marblecitypublishing.com

Join Marble City's list for updates on new releases by Jim Williams:

http://eepurl.com/vek5L

Follow on Twitter:

http://twitter.com/MarbleCityPub

Printed in Great Britain
by Amazon

82363287R00222